Praise for *The Heaven of Animals*

An Amazon 2014 "Best Book of the Year"
One of *The Millions'* "Most Anticipated" Books of 2014
A *Washington Post* "Out Now" Pick

"A wise debut collection . . . Poissant's characters are often a mess—belligerent, impulsive, smart in all the wrong ways—but he manages their lives with precision, intelligence, and clarity. . . . Beautiful [stories], with a rogue touch."

—Rebecca Lee, *The New York Times Book Review*

"*The Heaven of Animals* targets the tough and tender dynamics that make and break families."

—*Elle*

"[This] collection is some ⋯ ⋯ead Book")

"*The Heaven of Animals* n⋯ ⋯aders of two stylistically disparate story collections—⋯ard Ford's *A Multitude of Sins* and Amy Hempel's *The Dog of the Marriage*—which are surely not bad company to keep."

—Tod Goldberg, *Los Angeles Review of Books*

"Masterful . . . Poissant's gift of fiction writing [is] a great big gift. So big that it stretches the short story form a bit; he turns typical short story writing pitfalls into strengths. . . . You can move among William Faulkner, Harry Crews, and Flannery O'Connor to find the muscle that is in ['Lizard Man'] (and many of the others here), and among Eudora Welty, Lee Smith, and Jill McCorkle for the tenderness. . . . A great strength of this collection: Poissant shows us how much alike we all are—as fathers, mothers, friends, children, liars, and lovers—no matter our pedigree. . . . Poissant can do the seemingly impossible. . . . I hear a novel is on the way. Look out."

—Clyde Edgerton, *Garden & Gun*

"It's rare to come across an author who consistently writes perfect stories, nailing each one like the Beatles did with every song. It's almost an impossible feat, and only a handful seem to be able to do it. Names that come to mind are Junot Díaz, Don DeLillo, Alice Munro, T. C. Boyle, and David Gates—I refer to such writers as Story Masters. And now I might have to add David James Poissant to this elite group, because every single story in *The Heaven of Animals* is fucking incredible."

—*Tweed's*

"No small feat. . . . The much-anthologized Poissant justifies his status as a favorite of the literary quarterlies with this debut collection of unsparing yet warmly empathetic stories. . . . Poissant holds out hope that the simple human ability to move on can at least partially heal many wounds [and] finds beauty in our imperfect strivings toward love and connection. Rueful and kind, akin to both Anton Chekhov and Raymond Carver in humane spirit and technical mastery."

—*Kirkus Reviews* (starred review)

"A deeply evocative masterpiece. . . . A roller-coaster of an emotional ride. . . . Of the short story authors I've read, I've always considered Raymond Carver the king. I think I may have just found the heir to that throne."

—*Florida Book Review*

"Poissant demonstrates that mankind, especially American males, may not be so separate from the animal kingdom after all. . . . [*The Heaven of Animals'*] real subject is all too human."

—*Atlanta Journal-Constitution*

"[A] collection of vicious and heartbreaking vignettes."

—*Orlando Sentinel*

"An engaging, well-crafted collection. . . . The author's deep caring for his characters surfaces in his compassionate attempts to unpack the perplexities of the human condition. Poissant's . . . tight storytelling will appeal to fans of Raymond Carver, Richard Ford, and George Saunders."

—*Booklist*

"Excellent. . . . We care about and sympathize with Poissant's characters, even the most conflicted and difficult ones. . . . The brief and beautiful moments of human connection shine through in every story."

—*Library Journal* (starred review)

"Entertaining . . . Standouts include 'Lizard Man' and the pitch-perfect 'Last of the Great Land Mammals.'"

—*Publishers Weekly*

"A real achievement . . . This is Poissant's first book, and if Brock Clarke predicts (in blurb form) that Poissant will become 'his generation's Richard Ford,' who am I to argue?"

—*Electric Literature*

"Great fun to read. . . . Unlikable characters demand attention and hold it wildly from page to page, bringing unexpected beauty to a world that is often wicked. . . . By book's end you know you've spent your time valuably, and in the hands of a deft and skillful writer."

—*The Rumpus*

"Told in honest and inventive prose, *The Heaven of Animals* is not afraid of the beautiful but painful complications of the heart."

—*Interview* magazine

"Full of stories that linger long after you have closed the book and turned off the light."

—*One Story*

"*The Heaven of Animals* promises us a book teeming with wildlife, with metaphysical questions, with people yearning for answers, and the stories deliver. . . . In one breath [Poissant] can both make us laugh and raise what Faulkner called 'the old verities and truths of the heart.'"

—*Tin House*

"Poissant's debut story collection is as taut and emotional as they come. . . . Readers will want to take their time and savor each story—with a box of tissues nearby."

—*Bloggers Recommend*

"Poissant has a way of using premises that . . . sneak up on you, knock you over the head, and steal your heart."

—Tayari Jones

"*The Heaven of Animals* is an extraordinary debut from Florida author David James Poissant—a Venn diagram of the miraculous and the absurd. Like Flannery O'Connor's, Poissant's stories are marked by violence, humor, and grace; like Saunders, Poissant can spoon-bend reality; like Carver and Díaz, he writes scenes soaked in kerosene and seconds from combustion. In these pages you'll find charming reprobates and self-deluded hustlers, young lovers, alligators and dead dogs, fathers and sons, all the warped love of family, the batshit hilarity of the South, and the 'geometry of loss.'"

—Karen Russell, Pulitzer Prize finalist and author of *Swamplandia!*

"Wow. David James Poissant has written a fantastic, beguiling book. Often offbeat and always enthralling, *The Heaven of Animals* seduces the reader, again and again, with our weird, urgent attempts to understand each other. These stories lure the loners and romantics out of America's backwaters, then march them into the moonlight to break your heart."

—Claire Vaye Watkins, author of *Battleborn*

"Wild as two men wrestling an alligator, tender as a father stretching out on the floor next to his sleeping son, the stories in *The Heaven of Animals* will make you stop and wonder. David James Poissant digs deep until he reaches the heart of each tale, unearthing unexpected connections with his vivid and graceful prose. These men and women, parents and children, all stand at the precipice of loss, and in their final moments, reach out for each other."

—Hannah Tinti, author of *The Good Thief*

"It's not often you read stories with this much range, precision, power, and emotional depth in a first collection. It's not like a 'first collection' at all, in fact. This is beautiful, exciting, accomplished work. David James Poissant is one of the best-of-the-best new writers out there, and I have no doubt there's a lot more to come."

—Brad Watson, award-winning author of *The Heaven of Mercury* and *Aliens in the Prime of Their Lives*

"A character in 'Lizard Man' has tattoos that, if you look closely, secretly hold another image in the design. David James Poissant's writing has that same effect, the initial and wonderful strangeness giving way, slowly but surely, to something deeper, something difficult, something beautiful. Poissant is a writer who knows us with such clarity that we wonder how he found his way so easily into our hearts and souls."

—Kevin Wilson, *New York Times* bestselling author of *The Family Fang* and *Tunneling to the Center of the Earth*

"David James Poissant is one of our finest young writers, with a taut and subtle prose style, a deep knowledge of craft, and a heart so vast it encompasses whole worlds. I read his fiction and became a lifelong fan; I promise that you will too."

—Lauren Groff, author of *Arcadia*, *The Monsters of Templeton*, and *Delicate Edible Birds*

"There is much to admire in David James Poissant's excellent debut story collection. His men and women are never mere caricatures. They are flawed but fully human and their stories are compelling and true to life's complexities. There is a refreshing lack of glibness in his work; he is a serious writer and these are serious stories."

—Ron Rash, *New York Times* bestselling author of *Serena* and *Nothing Gold Can Stay*

"Poissant is a first-rate storyteller who has an appreciation for the absurd turns of events that press down into all we try to keep buried until we have no choice but to face the people we are when we're alone in the dark."

—Lee Martin, Pulitzer Prize finalist and author of *Break the Skin* and *The Bright Forever*

"Throw in an alligator in a kiddie pool and, dear reader, you've got one hell of a story. Poissant is an extraordinary talent."

—Laura van den Berg, author of *The Isle of Youth*

"David James Poissant will end up being his generation's Richard Ford: his fiction is full of big ideas, of startling insights into how we live now; and his writing is so smart, so sensitive and self-deprecating and full of empathy. He is one of our very best young writers. I know, know that we will be talking about him for years and years to come."

—Brock Clarke, author of *Exley, An Arsonist's Guide to Writers' Homes in New England*, and *The Ordinary White Boy*

The Heaven *of* Animals

STORIES

David James Poissant

Simon & Schuster Paperbacks

NEW YORK   LONDON   TORONTO
SYDNEY   NEW DELHI

Simon & Schuster Paperbacks
A Division of Simon & Schuster, Inc.
1230 Avenue of the Americas
New York, NY 10020

First Simon & Schuster trade paperback edition March 2015

Information about previous publication of the stories is on page 260.

SIMON & SCHUSTER PAPERBACKS and colophon
are registered trademarks of Simon & Schuster, Inc.

For information about special discounts for bulk purchases, please contact
Simon & Schuster Special Sales at 1-866-506-1949
or business@simonandschuster.com.

The Simon & Schuster Speakers Bureau can bring authors to your
live event. For more information or to book an event contact the
Simon & Schuster Speakers Bureau at 1-866-248-3049
or visit our website at www.simonspeakers.com.

Designed by Paul Dippolito
Jacket design by Roberto de Vicq de Cumptich

Manufactured in the United States of America

1   3   5   7   9   10   8   6   4   2

The Library of Congress has cataloged the hardcover edition as follows:
Poissant, David James.
[Short stories. Selections]
Heaven of Animals : Stories / David James Poissant.—First Simon & Schuster
hardcover edition.
pages cm
I. Title.
PS3616.O5467A6 2014
811'.6—dc23
2013037118

ISBN 978-1-4767-2996-1
ISBN 978-1-4767-2997-8 (pbk)
ISBN 978-1-4767-2998-5 (ebook)

for Marla
always

Contents

Contents

The Heaven
of Animals

Lizard Man

I rattle into the driveway around sunup and Cam's on my front stoop with his boy, Bobby. Cam stands. He's a huge man, thick and muscled from a decade of work in construction. Sleeves of green dragons run armpit to wrist. He claims there's a pair of naked ladies tattooed into all those scales if you look close enough.

When Crystal left him, Cam got the boy, which tells you what kind of mother Crystal was. Cam's my last friend. He's a saint when he's sober, and he hasn't touched liquor in ten years.

He puts a hand on the boy's shoulder, but Bobby spins from his grip and charges. He meets me at the truck, grabs my leg, and hugs it with his whole body. I head toward Cam. Bobby bounces and laughs with every step.

We shake hands, but Cam's expression is no-nonsense.

"Graveyard again?" he says. My apron, rolled into a tan tube, hangs from my front pocket, and I reek of kitchen grease.

"Yeah," I say. I haven't told Cam how I lost my temper and yelled at a customer, how apparently some people don't know what *over easy* means, how my agreement to work the ten-to-six shift is the only thing keeping my electricity on and the water running.

"Bobby," Cam says, "go play for a minute, okay?"

Bobby lets go of my leg and stares at his father, skeptical.

"Don't make me tell you twice," Cam says.

The boy runs to my mailbox, drops to the lawn, cross-legged, and scowls.

"Keep going," Cam says, and slowly, deliberately, Bobby stands and sulks toward their house.

"What is it?" I say. "What's wrong?"

Cam shakes his head. "Red's dead," he says.

Red is Cam's dad. "Bastard used to beat the fuck out of me," Cam said one night back when we both drank too much and swapped sad stories. When he turned eighteen, Cam enlisted and left for the first Gulf War. The last time he saw his father, the man was staggering, drunk, across the lawn. "Go then!" he screamed. "Go die for your fucking country!" Bobby never knew he had a grandfather.

I don't know whether Cam is upset or relieved, and I don't know what to say. Cam must see this because he says: "It's okay. I'm okay."

"How'd it happen?" I ask.

"He was drinking," Cam says. "Bartender said one minute Red was laughing, the next his face was on the bar. When they went to shake him awake, he was dead."

"Wow." It's a stupid thing to say, but I've been up all night. My hand still grips an invisible steel spatula. I can feel lard under my nails.

"I need a favor," Cam says.

"Anything," I say. When I was in jail, it was Cam who bailed me out. When my wife and son moved to Baton Rouge, it was Cam who knocked down my door, kicked my ass, threw the contents of my liquor cabinet onto the front lawn, set it on fire, and got me a job at his friend's diner.

"I need a ride to Red's house," Cam says.

"Okay," I say. Cam hasn't had a car for years. Half the people on our block can't afford storm shutters, let alone cars, but it's St. Petersburg, a pedestrian city, and downtown's only a five-minute walk.

"Well, don't say okay yet," Cam says. "It's in Lee."

"Lee, Florida?"

Cam nods. Lee is four hours north, one of the last towns you pass on I-75 before you hit Georgia.

"No problem," I say, "as long as I'm back before ten tonight."

"Another graveyard?" Cam asks.

I nod.

"Okay," he says. "Let's go."

◆　　◆　　◆

Last year, I threw my son through the family room window. I don't remember how it happened, not exactly. I remember stepping into the room. I remember seeing Jack, his mouth pressed to the mouth of the other boy, his hands moving fast in the boy's lap. Then I stood over him in the garden. Lynn ran from the house, screaming. She saw Jack and hit me in the face. She battered my shoulders and my chest. Above us, through the window frame, the other boy stood, staring, shaking, hugging himself with his thin arms. Jack lay on the ground. He didn't move except for the rise and fall of his chest. The window had broken cleanly and there was no blood, just shards of glass scattered over flowers, but one of Jack's arms was bent behind his head, as though he'd gone to sleep that way, an elbow for a pillow.

"Call 911," Lynn yelled to the boy above.

"No," I said. Whatever else I didn't know in that time and that place, I knew we could never afford an ambulance ride. "I'll take him."

"No!" Lynn cried. "You'll kill him!"

"I'm not going to kill him," I said. "Come here." I gestured to the boy. He shook his head and stepped back.

"Please," I said.

Tentatively, the boy stepped over the sill's jagged edge. He planted his feet on the brick ledge of the front wall, then dropped the few feet to the ground. Glass crunched beneath his sneakers.

"Grab his ankles," I said. I hooked my hands under Jack's armpits, and we lifted him. One arm trailed the ground as we walked him to the car. Lynn opened the hatchback. We laid Jack in the back and covered him with a blanket. It seemed like the right thing, what you see on TV.

A few neighbors had come outside to watch. We ignored them.

"I'll need you with me," I said to the boy. "When we're done, I'll take you home." The boy was wringing the hem of his shirt in both hands. His eyes brimmed with tears. "I won't hurt you, if that's what you think."

We set off for the hospital, Lynn following in my pickup. The boy sat beside me in the passenger seat, his body pressed to the door, the seatbelt strap clenched in one hand at his waist. With each bump in the road, he turned to look at Jack.

"What's your name?" I asked.

"Alan," he said.

"How old are you, Alan?"

"Seventeen."

"Seventeen. Seventeen. And have you ever been with a woman, Alan?"

Alan looked at me. His face drained of color. His hand tightened on the seatbelt.

"It's a simple question, Alan. I'm asking you: Have you been with a woman?"

"No," Alan said. "No, sir."

"Then how do you know you're gay?"

In back, Jack stirred. He moaned, then grew silent. Alan watched him.

"Look at me, Alan," I said. "I asked you a question. If you've never been with a woman, then how do you know you're gay?"

"I don't know," Alan said.

"You mean, you don't know that you're gay, or you don't know how you know?"

"I don't know how I know," Alan said. "I just do."

We passed the bakery, the Laundromat, the supermarket, and entered the city limits. In the distance, the silhouette of the helicopter on the hospital's roof. Behind us, the steady pursuit of the pickup truck.

"And your parents, do they know about this?" I asked.

"Yes," Alan said.

"And do they approve?"

"Not really."

"No. I bet they don't, Alan. I'll bet they do not."

I glanced in the rearview mirror. Jack hadn't opened his eyes, but he had a hand to his temple. The other hand, the one attached to the broken arm, lay at his side. The fingers moved, but without purpose, hand spasming from fist to open palm.

"I just have one more question for you, Alan," I said.

Alan looked like he might be sick. He watched the road unfurl before us. He was afraid of me, afraid to look at Jack.

"What right do you have teaching my son to be gay?"

"I didn't!" Alan said. "I'm not!"

"You're not? Then what do you call that? Back there? That business on the couch?"

"Mr. Lawson," Alan said, and, here, the tone of his voice changed, and I felt as though I were speaking to another man. "With all due respect, sir, Jack came on to me."

"Jack is not gay," I said.

"He is. I know it. Jack knows it. Your *wife* knows it. I don't know how you couldn't know it. I don't see how you've missed the signals."

I tried to imagine what signals, but I couldn't. I couldn't recall a thing that would have signaled that I'd wind up here, delivering my son to the hospital with a concussion and a broken arm. What signal might have foretold that, following this day, after two months in a motel and two months in prison, my wife of twenty years would divorce me because, as she put it, I was *full of hate*?

I pulled up to the emergency room's entryway, and Alan helped me pull Jack from the car. A nurse with a wheelchair ran out to meet us. We settled Jack into the chair, and she wheeled him away.

I pulled the car into a parking spot and walked back to the entrance. Alan stood on the curb where I'd left him.

"Where's Lynn?" I said.

"Inside," Alan said. "Jack's awake."

"All right, I'm going in. I suggest you get out of here."

"But, you said you'd drive me home."

"Sorry," I said. "I changed my mind."

Alan stared at me, dumbfounded. His hands groped the air.

"Hey," I said, "I got a signal for you." I gave him a hitchhiker's thumbs-up and cast it over my shoulder as I entered the hospital.

⋄　⋄　⋄

I wake, and Cam's making his way down back roads, their surfaces cratered with potholes.

"Rise and shine," he says, "and welcome to Lee."

It's nearly noon. The sun is bright and the cab is hot. I wipe gunk from my eyes and drool from the corner of my mouth. Cam watches the road with one eye and studies directions he's scrawled in black ink on the back of a cereal box. He's never seen the house where his father spent his last years.

We turn onto a dirt road. The truck lurches into and then out of an enormous, waterlogged hole. Pines line the road. Their needles shiver as we go by. We pass turn after turn, but only half of the roads are marked. Every few miles, we pass a driveway, the house deep in trees and out of sight. It's a haunted place, and I'm already ready to leave.

Cam says, "I don't know where the fuck we are."

We drive some more. I think about Bobby home alone, how Cam gave him six VHS tapes. "By the time you watch all of these," he said, "I'll be back." Then he put in the first movie, something Disney, and we left.

"He'll be fine," Cam said. "He'll never even know we're gone."

"We could bring him with us," I said, but Cam refused.

"There's no telling what we'll find there," he said.

Ahead, a child stands by the side of the road. Cam slows the truck to a halt and rolls down the window. The girl steps forward. She looks over her shoulder, then back at us. She's barefoot and her face is smeared with dirt. She wears a brown dress and a green bow in her hair. A string is looped around her wrist, and from the end of the string floats a blue balloon.

"Hi there," Cam says. He leans out the window, hand extended, but the child doesn't take it. Instead, she stares at his arms, the coiled dragons. She steps back.

"You're scaring her," I say.

Cam frowns at me, but he returns his head to the cab and his hand to the wheel. He gives the girl his warmest smile.

"Do you know where we could find Cherry Road?" he says.

"Sure," the girl says.

She pumps her arm, and the balloon bobs in response.

"It's that way," she says, pointing in the direction from which we've come.

"About how far?" Cam asks.

"Not the next road, but the next. It's a dead end. There's just the one house." Her wrist flails, and the balloon thunks her fist.

Cam checks the cereal box. "That's the one," he says.

"Oh," the girl says, and for a moment she is silent. "You're going to visit the Lizard Man. I seen him. I seen him once."

Cam looks at me. I shrug. We look at the girl.

"Well, thank you," Cam says. The girl gives the balloon a good shake. Cam turns the truck around, and the girl waves goodbye.

"Cute kid," I say.

We turn onto Cherry.

"Creepy little fucker," Cam says.

◆   ◆   ◆

The house is hidden in pines and the yard is overgrown with knee-high weeds. Tire tracks mark where the driveway used to be. Plastic flamingos dot the yard, their curved beaks peeking out of the weeds, wire legs rusted, bodies bleached a light pink.

The roof of the house is littered with pine needles and piles of shingles where someone abandoned a roofing project. The porch has buckled and the siding is rotten, the planks loose. I press a fingernail to the soft wood and it slides in.

Our mission is unclear. There's no body to ID or papers to sign. There's nothing to inherit, and there will be no funeral. But I know why we're here. This is how Cam will say goodbye.

The front door is locked but gives with two kicks. "Right here," Cam says. He taps the wood a foot above the lock before slamming the heel of his boot through the door.

Inside, the house waits for its owner's return. The hallway light is on. The A/C unit shakes in the window over the kitchen sink. Tan wallpaper curls away from the cabinets like birch bark, exposing thin ribbons of yellow glue on the walls.

We hear voices. Cam puts a hand to my chest and a finger to his lips. He brings a hand to his waist and feels for a gun that isn't there. Neither of us moves for a full minute, then Cam laughs.

"Fuck!" he says. "That's a TV." He hoots. He runs a hand through his hair. "About scared the shit out of me."

We move to the main room. It, too, is in disarray, the lampshades thick with dust, a coffee table awash in a sea of newspapers and unopened mail. There is an old and scary-looking couch, its arms held to its sides with duct tape. A spring pokes through the cushion, ripe with tetanus.

The exception here is the television. It is beautiful. It is six feet of wide-screen glory. "Look at that picture," I say, and Cam and I step back to take it in. The TV's tuned to the Military Channel, some cable extravagance. B-24 bombers streak the sky in black and white, propellers the size of my head. On top of the set sits a bottle of Windex and a filthy washcloth along with several many-buttoned remotes. Cam grabs one, fondles it, holds down a button, and the sound swells. The drone of plane engines and firefight tears through the room from one speaker to another. I jump. Cam grins.

"We're taking it," he says. "We are so taking this shit."

He pushes another button, and the picture blips to a single point of white at the center of the screen. The point fades and dies.

"No!" Cam says. "No!"

"What did you do?" I say.

"I don't know. I don't know!"

Cam shakes the remote, picks up another, punches more buttons, picks up a third, presses its buttons. The television hums, and the picture shimmers back to life.

"Ahhh," Cam says. We sit, careful to avoid the spring. While we watch, the beaches at Normandy are stormed, two bombs are dropped, and the war is won. We're halfway into Vietnam when Cam says, "I'm going to check out his room." It's not an invitation.

Cam's gone for half an hour. When he returns, he looks terrible. The color is gone from his face and his eyes are red-rimmed. He carries a shoebox under one arm. I don't ask, and he doesn't offer.

"Let's load up the set and get out of here," he says. "I'll pull the truck around."

I hear a glass door slide open, then shut, behind me. I hear something like a scream. Then the door slides open again. I turn around to see Cam. If he looked bad before, now he looks downright awful.

"What is it?" I say.

"Big," Cam says. "In the backyard."

"What? What's big in the backyard?"

"Big. Fucking. Alligator."

◆　　◆　　◆

It *is* a big fucking alligator. I've seen alligators before, in movies, at zoos, but never this big and never so close. We stare at him. We don't know it's a *him*, but we decide it's a *him*. He is big. It's insane.

It's also the saddest fucking thing I've ever seen. In the backyard is a makeshift cage, an oval of chain-link with a chicken-wire roof. Inside, the alligator straddles an old kiddie pool. The pool's cracked plastic lip strains with the alligator's weight. His middle fills the pool, belly sunk in a few inches of syrupy brown water, his legs hanging out. His tail, the span of a man, curls against a length of chain-link.

When he sees us, the alligator hisses, and his front feet paddle the air. His jaws open to yellow teeth and a throat the color of a turkey skin pulled inside out. Everywhere there are flies and gnats. They fly into his open mouth and land on his teeth. Others swarm open sores along his back.

"What's he doing here?" Cam asks.

"Red was the Lizard Man," I say. "Apparently."

We stare at the alligator. The alligator stares back. I consider the cage and wonder whether he can turn around.

"He looks bored," Cam says. And it's true. The alligator looks bored, and sick. The jaws close, and his open eyes are the only thing reminding me he's alive.

"We can't leave him here," Cam says.

"We should call someone," I say. But who would we call? The authorities? Animal control?

"We can't," Cam says. "They'll kill him."

Cam is right. I've seen it before, on the news. Some jackass raises a gator. The gator gets loose. It's been hand-fed and knows no fear of man. The segments always end the same way: *Sadly, the alligator had to be destroyed.*

"I don't see that we have a choice," I say.

"We have the pickup," Cam says.

My mouth says no, but my eyes must say yes, because before I know what's happening, we're in the front yard examining the bed of the truck, Cam measuring the length with his open arms.

"This won't work," I say. Cam ignores me. He pulls a blue tarp from the backseat and unrolls it on the ground beside the truck.

"He'll never fit," I say.

"He'll fit. It'll be close, but he'll fit."

"Cam," I say. "Wait. Stop." Cam leans against the truck. He looks right at me. "Say we get the alligator out of the cage and into the truck. Say we manage to do this and keep all of our fingers.

Where do we take him? I mean, what the hell, Cam? What the hell do you do with twelve feet of living, breathing alligator? And what about the TV? I thought you wanted to take the TV."

"Shit," he says. "I forgot about the TV."

We stare at the truck. I look up. The sky has turned from bright to light blue and the sun has disappeared behind a scatter of clouds. On the ground, one corner of the tarp flaps in the breeze, winking its gold eyelet.

Cam bows his head, as if in mourning. "Maybe if we stand the set up on its end."

"Cam," I say. "We can take the alligator or we can take the television, but we can't take both."

◆　　◆　　◆

Electric-taping the snout, Cam decides, will be the hard part.

"All of it's the hard part," I say, but Cam's not listening.

He finds a T-bone in Red's refrigerator. It's spoiled, but the alligator doesn't seem to mind. Cam sets the steak near the cage, and the alligator waddles out of the pool. He presses his nostrils to the fence. The thick musk of alligator and reek of rotten meat turn my stomach, and I retch.

"You puke, I kick your ass," Cam says.

We've raided Red's garage for supplies. At our feet are bolt cutters, a roll of electric tape, a spool of twine, bungee cords, a dozen two-by-fours, my tarp, and, for no reason I'm immediately able to ascertain, a chainsaw.

"Protection," Cam says, nudging the old Sears model with his toe. The chain is rusted and hangs loose from the blade. I imagine Cam starting the chainsaw, the chain snapping, flying, landing far away in the tall grass. I try to picture the struggle between man and beast, Cam pinned under five hundred pounds of alligator, Cam's head in the gator's mouth, Cam dragged in circles around the yard, a tangle of limbs and wails. Throughout each scenario, the chainsaw offers little assistance.

Cam's hands are sheathed in oven mitts, a compromise he accepted grudgingly when the boxing gloves he found, while offering superior protection, failed to provide him the ability to grip, pick up, or hold.

"This is stupid," I say. "Are we really doing this?"

"We're doing this," Cam says. He swats a fly from his face with one oven-mitted hand.

There is a clatter of chain-link. We turn to see the alligator nudging the fence with his snout. He snorts, eyes the T-bone, opens and shuts his mouth. He really is surprisingly large.

Cam's parked the pickup in the backyard. He pulls off his oven mitts, lowers the gate, exposing the wide, bare bed of the truck, and we set to work angling the two-by-fours from gate to grass. We press the planks together, and Cam cinches them tight with the bungee cords. The boards are long, ten or twelve feet, so physics is on our side. We should be able to drag him up the incline.

We return our attention to the alligator, who is sort of throwing himself against the fence, except that there is nowhere to back up to, no way to build momentum. Above his head, at knee level, is a hand-sized wire door held shut by a combination lock. With each lunge, the lock jumps, then clatters against the door. With each charge, I jump too.

"He can't break out," Cam says. He picks up the bolt cutters.

"You don't know that," I say.

"If he could, don't you think he'd have done it by now?" Cam positions the bolt cutters on the loop of lock, bows his legs, and squats. He squeezes, and his face reddens. He grunts, there's a snap, and the lock falls away, followed by a flash of movement. Cam howls and falls. The alligator's open jaws stretch halfway through the hole. All I see is teeth.

"Motherfucker!" Cam yells.

"You okay?" I say.

Cam holds up his hands, wiggles ten fingers.

"Okay," Cam says. "Okay." He picks up the T-bone and throws

it at the alligator. The steak lands on his snout, hangs there, then slides off.

"He's not a dog," I say. "This isn't catch."

Cam pulls on the oven mitts and slowly reaches for the meat resting in the grass just a few feet beneath all those teeth. Suddenly, the pen looks less sturdy, less like a thing the alligator could never escape.

The cage shakes, but this time it's the wind, which has really picked up. I wonder whether it's storming in St. Petersburg. Cam should be at home with Bobby, and I almost say as much. But his eyes are wild. He's dead set on doing this.

Cam says, "I'm going to put the steak into his mouth, and, when I do, I want you to tape the jaws shut."

"No way," I say. "No way am I putting my hand in range of that thing."

And then this happens: My son walks out of my memory and into my thoughts, his arm hanging loose at the elbow. The nurse asks what happened, and he looks up, ready to lie for me. There is something beautiful in the pause between this question and the one to come. Then there's the officer's hand on my shoulder, the "Would you mind stepping out with me, please?" Oh, I've heard it a hundred times. It never leaves me. It is a whisper. It is a prison sentence.

I want to put the elbow back into the socket myself. I want to turn back time. I want Jack at five or ten. I want him curled in my lap like a dog. I want him writing on the walls with an orange crayon and blaming the angels that live in the attic. I want him before his voice plummeted two octaves, before he learned to stand with a hand on one hip, before he grew confused. I want my boy back.

"Come on!" Cam shouts. "Don't puss out on me now. As soon as he bites down, just wrap the tape around it."

"Give me your oven mitts," I say.

"No!"

"Give me the mitts and I'll do it."

"But you won't be able to handle the tape."

"Trust me," I say. "I'll find a way."

We do it. Cam waves the cut of meat at the snout until it smacks teeth. The jaws grab. There's an unnatural crunch as the *T* in the T-bone becomes two *I*s and then a pile of periods. I drape a length of tape over the snout, fasten the ends beneath the jaws, then run my gloved hands up both strands of tape, sealing them. Then I start wrapping like crazy. I wind the roll of tape around and around the jaws. The tape unspools, circling, a flat, black worm. When I step back, the alligator's jaws are shut and my hands shake.

"I can't believe it," Cam says. "I can't believe you actually did that shit."

◆   ◆   ◆

The alligator's one heavy son of a bitch. We hold him in a kind of headlock. Our arms cradle his neck and front legs. Our fingers grip his scaly hide. We sidestep toward the pickup, the alligator's tail tracing a path through the grass. His back feet scramble and claw at the ground, but he doesn't writhe or thrash. He is not a healthy alligator. I stop.

"C'mon," Cam says. "Almost there."

"What are we doing?" I say.

"We're putting an alligator into your truck," he says. "C'mon."

"But look at him," I say. Cam takes in the alligator's wide, green head, his upturned nostrils and Ping-Pong-ball eyes. He looks up.

"No," I say. "Really look."

"What?" Cam's impatient. He shifts his weight, gets a better grip on the gator. "I don't know what you want me to see."

"He's not even fighting us. He's too sick. Even if we set him free, how do we know he'll make it?"

"We don't."

"No, we don't. We don't know where he came from. We don't know where to take him. And what if Red raised him? How will he survive in the wild? How will he learn to hunt and catch fish and stuff?"

Cam shrugs, shakes his head.

"So, why?" I ask. "Why are we doing this?"

Cam locks eyes with me. After a minute, I look away. My arms are weak with the weight of alligator. My legs quiver. We shuffle forward.

◆   ◆   ◆

I didn't give Jack the chance to lie. I admitted guilt to second-degree battery and kept everyone out of court. I got four months and served two, plus fines, plus community service. Had that been the end of it, I'd have gotten off easy. Instead, I lost my family.

The last time I saw Jack, he stood beside his mother's car showing Alan his new driver's license. They leaned like girls against the hood but laughed like men at something on the license: a typo. *Weight: 1500*. I watched them from the doorway. Jack kept his distance, flinched if I came close.

Alan had helped me load the furniture. With each piece, I thought of Jack's body. How it hung between us that afternoon, how it swayed, how much like a game wherein you and a friend grab another boy by ankles and wrists and throw him off a dock and into a lake.

Everything Jack and Lynn owned we'd packed into a U-Haul. I wasn't meant to know where they were going. I wasn't meant to see them again, but I'd found maps and directions in a pile of Lynn's things and written down the address of their new place in Baton Rouge. I could forgive Lynn not wanting to see me, but taking my son away was a thing I could not abide.

I decided I would go there one day, a day that seems more distant with each passing afternoon. And what would Jack do when he opened the door? In my dreams, it was always Jack who opened the door. I would spread my arms in invitation. I would say what I had not said.

But, that afternoon, it was Alan who sent Jack to me. Lynn waited in the U-Haul, ready to go. Alan gestured in my direction. He and Jack argued in hushed voices. And finally, remarkably, Jack moved toward me. I did not leave the doorway, and Jack stopped just short of the stoop.

What can I tell you about my son? He had been a beautiful boy, and, standing before me, I saw that he had become something different: a man I did not understand. His T-shirt was too tight for him, and the hem rode just above his navel. A trail of brown hair led from there and disappeared behind a silver belt buckle. His fingernails were painted black. The cast had come off, and his right arm was a nest of curly, dark hair.

I wanted to say, *I want to understand you.*

I wanted to say, *I will do whatever it takes to earn your trust.*

I wanted to say, *I love you,* but I had never said it, not to Jack—yes, I am one of those men—and I could not bear the thought of speaking these words to my son for the first time and not hearing them spoken in return.

Instead, I said nothing.

Jack held out his hand, and we shook like strangers.

I still feel it, the infinity of Jack's handshake: the nod of pressed palms, flesh of my flesh.

◆   ◆   ◆

The rain arrives in sheets and the windshield wipers can hardly keep up. I drive. Cam sits beside me. He's placed the shoebox on the seat between us. His arm rests protectively against the lid. The alligator slides around with the two-by-fours in the back. We fastened the tarp over the bed of the truck to conceal our cargo, but we didn't pull it tight. Now, the tarp sags with water, threatening to smother the animal underneath.

Cam flips on the radio, and we catch snippets of the weather before the speakers turn to static.

"*. . . upgraded to a tropical storm . . . usually signals the forma-*

tion of a hurricane . . . storm will pick up speed as it makes its way across the gulf . . . expected to come ashore as far north as the panhandle . . . far south as St. Petersburg . . ."

Cam turns the radio off. We watch rain pelt the windshield, the black flash of wipers pushing water.

I don't ask whether Bobby is afraid of storms. As a boy, I'd been frightened, but not Jack. During storms, Jack had stood at the window and watched as branches skittered down the street and power lines unraveled onto sidewalks. He smiled and stared until Lynn pulled him away from the glass and we moved to the bathroom with our blankets and flashlights. It was only then, huddled in the dark, that Jack sometimes cried.

"We should go back," I say. "The power could be out."

"Bobby's a tough kid," Cam says. "He'll be fine."

"Cam," I say.

"In case you've forgotten," he says, "there's a fucking alligator in the back of your truck."

I say nothing. Whatever happens is Cam's responsibility. *This,* I tell myself, *is not your fault.*

Thunder shakes the truck. Not far ahead, a cell tower ignites with lightning. A shower of sparks waterfalls onto the highway. Cars and trucks are dusted with fire. Everyone drives on.

I don't know where we're headed, but Cam says we're close.

Cam, I think, *after this, I owe you nothing. Once this is over, we're even.*

"If it's work you're worried about," Cam says, "I'll talk to Mickey. I'll tell him about Red. He'll understand if you're a little late."

"It's not Mickey I'm worried about," I say. I don't say, *Mickey can kiss my ass.* I don't say, *You and Mickey can go to hell.*

"Look," Cam says, "I know why you're pulling the graveyard shift. Mickey told me about the customer you yelled at. But this is different. This he'll understand."

I recognize the ache at the back of my throat immediately. The second I'm alone, it will take a miracle to keep a bottle out of my hand.

"Take this exit," Cam says. "At the bottom, turn right."

I guide the truck down the ramp toward Grove Street. The water in back sloshes forward and unfloods the tarp. Alligator feet scratch for purchase on the truck bed's corrugated plastic lining.

"Where are you taking us?" I ask.

"Havenbrook," he says. I wait for Cam to say he's kidding. But Cam isn't kidding.

◆   ◆   ◆

The largest of the lakes cradles the seventeenth green. Cam's seen gators there before, big bastards who come onshore to sun themselves and scare off golfers. I've never golfed in my life, and neither has he, but Cam led the team that patched the clubhouse roof after last year's hurricane. He remembers the five-digit code, and it still works. The security gate slides open, and we head down the paved drive reserved for maintenance.

No one's on the course. Fallen limbs litter the greens. An abandoned white cart lies turned on its side where the golf cart path rounds the fifteenth hole.

Lightning streaks the sky. The rain has turned the windshield to water, and sudden gusts of wind jostle the truck from every direction. I fight the wheel to stay on the asphalt. Even Cam is wide-eyed, his fingers buried in the seat cushions. The shoebox bounces between us.

We reach the lake, but the shore is half a football field away. The green is soggy, thick with water, and already the lake is flooding its banks. The first tire that leaves the road, I know, will sink into the mud, and we'll never get the truck out.

"I can't drive out there," I tell Cam. I have to yell over the wind and rain, the deafening thunder. It's like the world is pulling apart. "This is the closest I can get us."

Cam says something I can't hear, then he's out of the truck, the door slamming behind him. I jump out, and the wet cold slaps me. Within seconds, I'm drenched, my clothes heavy. All I hear is the wind. I move as if underwater.

As soon as Cam gets the tarp off, the storm catches it, and it billows into the sky like a flaming blue parachute, up into the trees overhead. It tangles itself into the branches, and then there is only the *smack smack* of the tarp's uncaught corners pummeled by gusts.

Cam screams at me. His teeth flash in bursts of lightning, but his words are choked by wind. I tap my ear, and he nods. He motions toward the alligator. We approach it slowly. I expect the animal to charge, but he lies motionless. I check the jaws. They're still wrapped. This, I realize, will be our last challenge. If he gets away from us before we remove the tape, he's doomed.

I'm wondering which of us will climb into the bed of the truck when the gator starts scuttling forward. We leap out of the way as hundreds of pounds of reptile spill from the truck and onto the green. The gate cracks under the weight and swings loose like a trapdoor in midair, hinges busted. Then the alligator is free on the grass. We don't move, and neither does he.

Cam approaches me. He makes a megaphone of his cupped hands and mouth and leans in close to my ear. His hot breath on my face is startling in all that fierce cold and rain.

"I think he's stunned," Cam yells. "We've got to get the tape off, now."

I nod. I'm exhausted and anxious, and I know there's no way we'll be able to lug the alligator to the water's edge. I wonder whether he'll make it, if he'll find his way to the water, or if the fall from the truck was the final blow, if tomorrow the groundskeepers will find a gator carcass fifty yards from the lake. It would make the *St. Petersburg Times* front page. A giant alligator killed in the hurricane. Officials would be baffled.

"I want you to straddle his neck," Cam yells. "Keep his head pressed to the ground. I'll try to get the tape off."

"No," I say. I point to my chest. I circle my hand through the air, pantomiming the unraveling. Cam looks surprised, but he nods.

Cam brings his hands to my face again and yells his hot words into my ear. "On my signal," he says, but I push him away.

I don't wait for a signal. Before I know it, I'm on the ground, my side hugging mud, and I'm digging my nails into the tape. My eye is inches from the alligator's eye. He blinks without blinking, a thin, clear membrane sliding over his eyeball, back to front. It is a thing to see. It is a knowing wink. I see this and I feel safe.

The tape is harder to unwrap than it was to wrap. The rain has made it soft, the glue gooey. Every few turns, I lose my grip. Finally, I let the tape coil around my hand like a snake. It unwinds and soon my fist is a ball of dark, sticky fruit. The last of the tape pulls clean from the snout, and I roll away from the alligator. I stand, and Cam pulls me back. He holds me up. The alligator flexes his jaws. His mouth opens wide, then slams shut. And then he's off, zigzagging toward the water.

He is swift and strong, and I'm glad it is cold and raining so Cam can't see the tears streaking my cheeks and won't know that my shivering is from sobbing. Cam lets go of me and I think I will fall, but instead I am running. Running! And I'm laughing and hollering and leaping. I'm pumping my fist into the air. I'm screaming, "Go! Go!" And, just before the alligator reaches the water, I lunge and my fingertips trace the last ridges and scales of tail whipping their way ahead of me. The sky is alive with lightning, and I see the hulking body, so awkward and graceless on land, slide into the water as it was meant to do. That great body cuts the water, fast and sleek, and the alligator dives out of sight, at home in the world where he belongs, safe in the warm quiet of mud and fish and unseen things that thrive in deep, green darkness.

•   •   •

Cam and I don't say much on the ride home. The rain has slowed to an even, steady downpour. The truck's cab has grown cold.

Cam holds his hands close to the vents to catch whatever weak streams of heat trickle out. We have done a good thing, Cam says, and I agree, but, I worry, at what cost? We listen to the radio, but the storm has headed north. The reporters have moved on to new cities: Clearwater, Homosassa, Ocala.

"There was this one time," Cam says at last. "About five years back. I spoke to Red."

This is news to me. This, I know, is no small revelation.

"I called him," Cam says. "I called him up, and I said, 'Dad? I just want you to know that you have a grandson and that his name is Robert and that I think he should know his grandfather.' And you know what that prick did? He hung up. The only thing Red said to me in twenty years was 'Hello' when he picked up the phone."

"I'm sorry," I say.

"If he'd even once told me he was sorry, I'd have forgiven him anything. I'd have forgiven him my own murder. He was my father. I would have forgiven everything."

He rubs his hands together in that vigorous way of trying to get warm.

"Do you know why I got all these fucking tattoos?" he says. "To hide the fucking scars from the night Red cut me with a fillet knife, and I'd have forgiven that if he'd just said something, anything, when he answered the phone."

Cam doesn't shake or sob or bang a fist on the dashboard, but, when I look away, I catch his reflection in the window, a knuckle in each eye socket, and I'm suddenly sorry for my impatience, the grudge I've carried all afternoon.

"But you tried," I say. "At least you won't spend your life wondering."

We sit in silence for a while. The rain on the roof beats a cadence into the cab, and it soothes me.

"You know, I served with gay guys in the Gulf," Cam says, and I almost drive the truck off the road. A tire slips over the lip of asphalt, and my side mirror nearly catches a guardrail before I bring the truck back to the center of the lane.

"Jesus!" Cam says. "I'm just saying, they were okay guys, and if Jack's gay it's not the end of the world."

"Jack's confused," I say. "He isn't gay."

"Well, either he is or he isn't, and what you think or want or say won't change it."

"Cam," I say, "all due respect. This doesn't concern you."

"I know," Cam says. He sits up straighter in his seat, grips the door handle as we pull onto our block. "I'm just saying, it isn't too late."

We pull into the driveway. Cam jumps out of the truck before it's in park. The yard is a mess of fallen limbs and garbage. Two shutters have been torn from the front of the house. The mailbox is on its side. Otherwise, everything looks all right. I glance down the street and see that my house is still standing.

When I turn back to Cam's house, what I see breaks my heart in ten places. I see Cam running across the lawn. I see Bobby, his hands pressed to the big bay window. His face is puffy and red. Cam disappears into the house, and then he is there with the boy, he is there on his knees, and he pulls Bobby to him. He mouths the words "I'm sorry, I'm sorry," over and over, and Bobby collapses into him, buries his head in Cam's chest, and my friend wraps his son in dragons.

I watch them. They stay like that for minutes, framed by window and house and the darkening sky. I watch, and then I open the shoebox and look inside.

I don't know what I was expecting, but it wasn't this. What I find are letters, over a hundred of them. About a letter a month for roughly ten years, all of them unopened. Each has been dated and stamped RETURN TO SENDER, the last one sent back just a week ago. Each is marked by the same shaky handwriting. Each is addressed to a single recipient, Mr. Cameron Starnes, from a single sender: Red.

And I know then that there was no phone call, no forgiveness on Cam's part, that Cam never came close until the monster was safely out of reach.

I stare at the letters, and I know who it is Cam wants to keep me from becoming.

I pull out of the driveway. I stop to right Cam's mailbox, then I tuck the shoebox safely inside. I follow the street to the end of the block. At the stop sign, I pause. I don't know whether to turn right or left. Finally, I head for the interstate. There's a spare uniform at the diner, clean and dry, and, if I hurry, I won't be late for work.

But I'm not going to work.

It's a ten-hour drive to Baton Rouge, but I will make it in eight. I will make it before morning. I will drive north, following the storm. I will drive through the wind and the rain. I will drive all night.

Amputee

The first time Brig saw her, he was sure she was Kate. She had Kate's dark hair, Kate's eyes, Kate's taut swimmer's build. She was not Kate. Kate was long gone. Were Kate here, she wouldn't look like this girl, or Brig didn't think she would. Three years change a person, and who, at thirty, could still pull off twenty? Brig couldn't. His hair was the giveaway, sideburns silvered, the gray spreading like racing stripes over his ears. He needed to dye it. He needed glasses. He needed to lose the gut that had lassoed his middle. Would Kate know him now if she saw him? Would he know her?

The girl who looked like Kate but was not Kate sat on a curb, her back to a lamppost, hair gauzy beneath the bulb. She wore denim shorts and a red sweatshirt, the pullover kind with the kangaroo pouch in front. There was no moon, but lamps lined the sidewalks and lit up the U of the apartment complex. A pool glowed blue at the horseshoe's center. It was late, the parking lot crowded with cars.

He'd been out twice that night, but this was his first time seeing the girl. What he'd hoped to see was the cat, to find it before something else did. The Sonoran Desert was rough on wayward pets. Rattlesnakes and hawks, a scorpion, even a pack of wild pigs—any of these could do Boots in. He'd been careful, so careful, and then the cat was an orange streak out the open door.

And what to tell the neighbor he hardly knew? Soon as she asked him to watch Boots for the week, Brig should have said he was no cat sitter. But he'd been distracted. A troubling phone call had just come, then the knock on the door, and Brig had said, "Fine, fine." Because who wasn't up for the easy work of walking next door once a day? Who couldn't clean a litter box or operate a can opener and remember to keep a door closed?

When she got back, he wouldn't be able to face her. She was too kind and too old. She spoke of the cat the way you speak of a friend. No, the cat had to be found, or else Brig had to move.

The girl on the sidewalk was smoking a cigarette, and Brig found himself drawn to the ember end. It had been almost a decade since his last smoke. A few months into their marriage, Kate had put her foot down on cigarettes, even the ones after sex. But Kate was gone, the voice in his head a reflex, a false alarm that curbed bad habits through force of memory alone.

"Bum a cigarette?" he said.

The girl rose. She let go a puff of smoke, and Brig tasted a familiar, candied mustiness. She pulled a pack from her front pocket, shook a cigarette from the pack, and passed it.

She said, "In movies, this is how the rape-part starts."

Brig stepped back. He threw his hands up.

"It's okay," she said. "You look safe. More sloppy than rapey."

Brig considered his khakis' frayed cuffs, the white T-shirt and its constellation of mustard stains. The girl was right to be wary. Before leaving Atlanta, a cursory search of Tucson had turned up the fact that the city was, among other things, one of the country's most dangerous, right up there with Baltimore, Memphis, and D.C. Rape and gangs, methamphetamines. Border violence— those who wanted in and those who meant, by any means, to keep them out. Corpses were fished routinely from the cactuses. The week before, the body of a child had been found, his chest a crater. Brig learned these things from a buddy at work whose Border Patrol brother regaled him with stories.

Tucson, he'd further learned, was America's third hottest city. A *dry heat,* people said who'd never been, though, at 115 degrees, what difference did it make whether you boiled or baked? First summer in Arizona, his Georgia driver's license, left in the glove box overnight, had turned wavy, illegible. Another day, a McDonald's cup fused to the car's cup holder.

"Brig," he said.

He held out his hand. Instead of shaking, the girl held out a lighter, which he took.

"Brig," she said. "Like the ship."

"Like the ship." He got that a lot.

What he got less, and what was true, was Brig short for Brigham. His parents were Mormon, devout and unrelenting. He'd been baptized at eight, made a deacon at twelve. By fourteen, he'd begun to question everything. He missed meetings, spoke his mind, and left the church before becoming an elder. He hadn't needed to throw out his LDS friends with his faith, but he had. He'd gone to college, met Kate, married young, then paid the price for marrying young. He still talked to his parents, who tolerated his calls but seldom called him. He hadn't seen them since the divorce.

Brig lit the cigarette and inhaled.

The world slipped. It was like that sound effect, the noise a record player makes in the movies when someone's said the wrong thing and the crowd goes quiet.

He coughed. He sat.

"It's weed," she said.

He nodded, and she sat beside him.

He coughed some more. He couldn't remember how long it had been—since before Kate, surely—but he remembered well enough to know this made a joke of what had passed for pot in college. This stuff packed a punch.

Nearby, something moved—an amber flash. He jumped up but stopped short at the bumper of the closest car. A sandwich wrapper winked in the lamplight, all foil and orange paper.

He turned. The girl was watching him.

"You haven't seen a cat, have you?" he said.

"I haven't seen a cat," she said. "Dog, either. There was this guinea pig. Irascible fellow. Didn't care for him."

"I'm joking," she said when Brig said nothing, and it was like she'd thrown a cup of cool water in his face.

Her name was Liliana. Friends called her Lily, and he could too. She was a junior.

"High school?" Brig was floored. The girl looked twenty-two, twenty easy.

"Seventeen," she said. She should have been at prom *as we speak*, but bad grades had gotten her grounded.

"Prom's overrated," he said.

"You're just saying that," she said.

But he wasn't. He meant it, and he said it again, meaning it even more. His own prom date, Heather Something, had been a bore. Half the night, she'd stood in one corner with her gossipy girlfriends. She'd only dance slow songs. And, after all of it—the limo, the dinner, the corsage, and the tux—she pushed his hand away when he tried to anything but kiss her.

"You're what?" Lily said. "Twenty-five?"

He was five past that, but he liked her thinking he was young. "Twenty-four," he said.

What did he do, she asked, and he admitted that he repped for a drug company.

"Mostly, I try to convince doctors that our allergy medication beats the competitors'."

"Does it?"

"Nope."

He sucked at sales, and his boss hated him for it. Doctors wouldn't see him or take his freebies. Receptionists, eyeing the drug-stuffed suitcase, pulled their blinds at his approach. His territory extended from Phoenix to Tucson, as far east as Benson, as far west as the state line. His returns were among the company's lowest, his take among the lowest too. Most months, he didn't even commission out. But he didn't care. The job got him out of his apartment, out seeing the Arizona he'd come to see: deserts and canyons, boulders balanced on boulders like in the Road Runner and Coyote cartoons. Even, once, a real roadrunner, its legs a whirling, oval blur.

Brig pulled on the cigarette and held the smoke in. He hadn't lost the hang of it.

"Married?" Lily asked.

He shook his head. He did not say *divorced,* then wondered why he hadn't. That fact was one he kept only from women on first dates. But this girl was half his age, or nearly. He wasn't up to what it looked like. He didn't think he was. Then, thinking it, he wondered if that *was* what he was up to. Was that even legal? Seventeen? He knew eighteen was fine—or, not *fine* but *legal,* or whatever. But what about girls who *looked* twenty? Wasn't there a clause or something, some new law?

Since Kate, he'd had three dates in three years, and he was starting to think there was something wrong with him. Getting out more, he might have met more women. But he was always on the road, in faraway towns and hotels, and, when he wasn't, he liked his apartment: the familiar couch, the friendly TV, PBS with its informative documentaries that made him feel dumb for all he didn't know, then smart, later, when he could rattle off a dozen facts concerning the masonry of sixteenth-century European castles or the characteristics of Asian versus African elephants.

Lily's nose was small, a pistachio, and now she wriggled it, bunny-like. She dropped her spent joint, crushed it with her heel, and quickly, one-handedly, lit another. He couldn't figure it. The cigarettes weren't hand-rolled. They were manufactured, filtered, stamped with a name he didn't know. But there was definitely pot in there. Had she tapped the tobacco out of each cigarette and snuck the pot in? That seemed like more work than it was worth.

A car appeared in the parking lot, taking a corner too fast. He hid the joint behind his back. The car pulled past, and he took another hit.

"Here you are," Lily said, "past midnight, alone in a darkened parking lot with a seventeen-year-old girl, and it's the pot you're worried about?" She watched him. Her nose did the wriggle-thing again. The bulb flickered overhead. "You're a funny guy."

Brig's cigarette was down to the filter, and he let it drop to the blacktop.

"I want to show you something," Lily said. She flicked her joint across the parking lot. It sailed, a meteor, and touched down on the hood of a car, where it smoldered and rolled.

"That's my car," Brig said.

The girl got to her feet, apologizing.

"Kidding," he said.

She watched him a minute.

"You're all right," she said.

She watched him a minute more, then she said, "Come on."

She took his hand and her touch was electric. He couldn't remember, just then, the last time he'd felt another person's touch. His head buzzed. His lungs were two balloons lifting into night. And then she was pulling him across the lot, down the sidewalk, past lampposts, to the pool.

◆   ◆   ◆

The last time he'd seen Kate, he'd been behind the steering wheel of a U-Haul truck into which he'd loaded what was left of his possessions. The things they'd shared—the house, the furniture, the car—all of it was Kate's or in Kate's name. She'd been the breadwinner, director of a home for the elderly and infirm. Daily, she put her little stamp of humanity on the world, and the work made her happy. She'd been patient, waiting for Brig to find *fulfillment*—her word—in work of his own. But Brig didn't find work fulfilling. Work was work. What Brig found fulfilling was a Whopper, a six-pack, and HBO, the well-acted shows that were almost-but-not-quite pornography. You couldn't watch porn and still feel good about yourself, but HBO walked the tightrope, and, afterward, you felt sophisticated, horny without feeling guilty.

He'd tried, on multiple occasions, to explain this to Kate. "That's not happiness," Kate would say. "That's depression." And Brig would shrug and pull another Dorito from the bag. He liked the napalm glaze the chips left on his fingers, liked sucking them clean when the last chip was gone.

In five years, he'd cycled through half a dozen jobs, but nothing stuck. Some he lost and some he quit.

"Say you could be anything?" Kate asked.

"Astronaut," he said, because it was like saying *movie star*, like saying *President of the United States*, a job he definitely wouldn't want. Even astronaut—he didn't think he'd care for it, the zero gravity and food in tubes, the sleeping-standing-up.

"I give up," Kate said.

He thought she meant her role as his career counselor, but she meant the marriage, meant him. "You're too unhappy," she said.

Brig argued that he'd never been happy, at least not as long as she'd known him, and Kate admitted she knew this, she'd known, but that he used to be better at faking it. "I liked it better when you would pretend."

"What?" he said. "So I can't be myself?"

"Honestly, Brig, what does that even mean?"

He didn't know. He only knew what he'd thought, which was that Kate could be happy enough for the both of them. But a couple couldn't keep on like that, one person content, the other whatever he was. There was balance to account for, harmony. Without it, they were just two people sharing the same cutlery.

The morning he left Atlanta, the sun beat down on the roof of the cab and hot air came in through the open window. The truck had A/C, but no radio, and it was going to be a long drive west. Kate stood in the driveway, frowning at him. But, then, she'd been frowning at him for years. Perhaps he'd given in too easily. Could her declaration have been an experiment, a test to see what he was willing to fight for, and what he wasn't? Perhaps if he said *no*, got his act together, refused to leave . . .

But, then, he was already in the truck, belongings boxed, emergency brake disengaged. The thought of undoing, after all of this—it seemed like so much work.

Kate reached a hand into the cab. She squeezed his shoulder the way you would an aging aunt's. She asked *where to,* and he told her. He had some experience in pharmaceuticals, and, because Arizona was where old people went to die, he figured he'd find work fast. He had three thousand dollars—a gift from Kate—to live on until then. He'd seen pictures, the city ringed by mountains, monsoons in summer and the blooms they left in their wake. Saguaros huddled like hat racks on the ridges. The desert was not the moonscape people thought it was. It was brown, but it was also sage and green, sand busy with the footprints of animals. And he would see it all. He would see and he would sell, and he would do his best to put Kate out of his mind.

If this was a test, he thought, then let it be hers. Let him back down the driveway. Let him call *her* bluff.

But all that happened was that Brig drove away. In the rearview, Kate waved, then turned, her back to him before he'd made the first bend in the road.

◆   ◆   ◆

A chain-link fence circled the pool. Lily produced a key from her front pocket, fitted it, and the gate swung wide.

"Travis has a crush on me," she said. Travis was their unit's maintenance man. Blue-jeaned and droopy, Travis could often be seen skimming the pool or sawing the dead limbs from tall palms. Too early Sunday mornings, he pushed a mower down a Mohawk of grass five feet from Brig's door.

Brig imagined Lily flirting, then following the man to his shadowy utility shed. He reminded himself that Travis was twice her age. But, then, so was he.

Picturing Lily wasn't hard: her on top, surprising Brig with her sexual prowess. He could see her completely comfortable at the breakfast table, sun coming up, her confession that she hadn't been grounded for grades, but for sneaking out nights.

Brig was considering all of this, what he might want and what that made him, when, quietly, and without warning, Lily took off her arm.

There was a snap, followed by a little click, and the limb unhinged at the shoulder. *Click,* just like that. The arm slipped through the red skin of her sleeve and out the hole where the hand had been.

"If it bothers you," she said, "I can put it back. I just can't get it wet."

Brig shut his eyes. The pot had been good, but not that good. He opened his eyes.

Her sleeve hung empty at her side. In her right hand she held her left. The arm dangled, a parenthesis unyoked from the pair. Its color matched the shade of her face exactly.

"Catch," she said, and then the arm was airborne and coming at him. He braced for something solid, but what he caught was light as a baseball bat. It was one piece, bent slightly at the elbow. From a distance, the hand had looked real. As he held it, though, the fingers revealed themselves to be plastic—sculpted, lined and veined to look real as anything in one of those creepy museums stuffed with wax celebrities. A pair of buckled straps hung loose from the arm's shoulder end.

"Starter arm," Lily said. "The good one bends, and I can pick stuff up with it, but people see the pinchers and they freak."

Brig wondered—he couldn't help it—whether the arm made her more likely to be the girl who put out, or whether it made her less. He wondered where this left him. He wondered what he wanted, whether he wanted her still, whether he wanted her *more.* His parents would say damnation awaited anyone who messed around before marriage, would say that their son, divorced at twenty-seven, could never have sex again without rolling the dice on his soul. Mormons didn't teach hell, not exactly, but that hadn't kept Brig's father from threatening it. Brig didn't believe in hell, and he was scared of hell. He was scared of a hell in which he didn't believe.

He held the arm in both hands and watched the wind unsmooth the surface of the pool.

"Yep," Lily said. "You're one of those."

"One of what?"

"The don't-lookers," she said. "There're those who look and those who don't. And then there're those who look too much. Like: *Look, I'm so comfortable, I can stare right at it.* That kind of looking."

Brig looked. He forced his gaze on the sleeve where the arm had been.

"I'll tell you when it's been too much," Lily said.

She smiled and pulled off her sweatshirt. Pool shadow slithered over her abdomen. A gecko rode her hip, red and orange. A blue bra pushed up her breasts and partly hid what looked like a holster. Her shoulder, where the arm went in, dissolved into a knob of flesh like the licked end of an ice cream cone.

She slid the holster out from beneath the bra, draped it over a deck chair, and then she made her way to him. She reached, and, for a moment, both of their hands were on the arm. A current ran the arm's length, electric longing down his body and back up. He let go. She propped the prosthesis in a chair. She undid her shorts and let them drop to the pool deck, then stepped out of them.

Even in the looking away, Brig couldn't help noticing the shaved legs, the blue panties and black curl beneath. His eyes wound up back on the shoulder, that trinity of collarbone and neck and the gradual slope into nothing.

"Here's the short version," she said. "My parents are missionaries. They brought me with them to Brazil. We were hiking, I fell, and a fer-de-lance went up my sleeve. It's a snake, a viper. The doctor said I was lucky to lose just my arm. This was three years back."

"God," he said. "Your parents must feel terrible."

"Not really. Dad says all things work together for the good of the Kingdom."

If there was a kingdom, Brig had been left out of it. He wanted to say as much, to tell her that this kingdom business was what you said when you didn't want your daughter blaming you for Brazil, except, here she stood, one-arm-happy, and Brig had the strongest sensation that it wasn't his place to say.

Instead, he said: "And you're sure of that? That all things work together for good?"

"I'm sure of one thing," she said. "At meets, this arm wins me sympathy points, big-time." She turned the shoulder toward him, and the end, that ice cream cone end, wiggled just like the tip of her nose. Then she moved past him, around the pool to the diving board, and he understood what she'd wanted him to see. Not her nakedness, not the arm, but this.

The diving board had three steps. She climbed them, then walked the board's length. The end sagged. She bounced, and the board's lip broke the surface. The tap sent rings shivering over the water.

"I'm more of a platform diver," she said. "Plus, a springboard should be a meter up. This one's a foot, maybe, so don't hold that against me."

She backed up, then charged forward. She leapt. She bounced. She flew.

Her body, in air, was a ball, and the ball made one, two revolutions. Then the ball unfurled and Lily's body snapped straight. She hit the water like a wand—hand, head, torso to legs, toes last. Where two hands might have met overhead, there was only the one, sure and unwavering as the blade of a knife. She cut the water clean, splash so small it was almost no splash at all.

It happened very quickly, so that Brig hardly had time to register it before she was climbing the pool ladder and standing before him. Her hair hung tangled and dripping, nipples dark beneath the bra. Brig stepped back and fell into a chair. He reclined like the chair was one he'd meant to lower himself into, and Lily looked away laughing.

She moved to the board and dove again. This time, the air seemed to cradle her before it let her go. Her body folded, a toe touch, then unfolded in time to hit the water clean.

She dove and dove, and his gaze returned, again and again, to the arm—to the space in air where an arm belonged. The diving, which might have drawn attention away from the arm, instead emphasized it. He wondered whether she knew this, or, knowing it, whether she cared. He felt weirdly and suddenly protective of her, like the arm-void was sacred, her body a saint's, the poolside his station. He was a guard in a Roman cathedral. He glanced around, but around him were only bug noises and night. Through drawn blinds leaked the light of a single, flickering TV, but no tourists came to see. They were alone.

Lily climbed the ladder for the last time, moved to him, and took his hand. The air was warm, her body cold. She pulled him out of the chair and close. He was ready for the kiss, but there was no kiss, only tumbling and a sky spun like a turntable.

They hit the water together, and Lily came up laughing. He'd gotten a mouthful. He spit. He cursed. His head buzzed and he tasted chlorine. He gripped the wall, shaking.

She swam at him, and he shrugged from her touch. He spit again.

"I could have broken my neck," he said.

Lily backed away. She treaded water at the pool's center, a graceful, wing-broke ballet.

"I don't really think you could have broken your neck."

Brig clung to the wall. He couldn't catch his breath. Finally, he just said it.

"You can't what?" she said.

"Swim," he said. "I never learned how to swim."

"Oh," she said. "Oh! Let me help you."

She swam at him, and he held up one hand, then quickly returned that hand to the wall.

"I'm okay. Just give me a minute."

"If I'd known," she said.

"I know," he said. "People throw people into pools. This isn't the first time. I'll live."

Lily moved to the shallow end. She lifted herself onto the pool's concrete lip and crossed her legs.

"At meets, we throw the coach in when we win," she said.

Coach. He laughed. He was stupid. Stupid and old. He considered the current, the prosthesis between them. Had he really thought this girl, this beautiful girl with Kate's face—her emerald eyes and button nose—could feel what he felt at her touch? She didn't belong here with him in a pool. She belonged at prom with a boy her age, some kid who'd take whatever she gave him with grateful admiration.

Then again, high schoolers were high schoolers, adults minus the manners, and so maybe no one had asked her. Maybe she'd asked and more than one boy had said no, which would be too bad. This girl was funny, uninhibited, smart.

Kate had been smart. Smarter than him. Smart enough to know when to get out. He didn't feel ill will toward her as much as he missed her. She'd been more than someone to come home to. She'd been, what? A friend? How was it a friend felt more intimate than a fuck? Not that Kate couldn't fuck. They'd been fine in that department, right up to the end.

Had it really been three years?

He peeled off his shirt and heaved it at the deck chairs. It landed with a *thwap* not far from Lily's arm. He pulled off his shoes and set them on the deck. He balled his socks and dropped them, soggy, into the foot holes.

"I'm thirty," he said.

"I'm sorry?"

"I'm not twenty-whatever-I-said. I'm thirty. Next month, I'll be thirty-one." He kept one hand on the wall, but turned, as if for her to take in the chest hair, the flabby pectorals and rotund gut.

"I know," she said. "I mean, I didn't *know* know. I just knew no way were you twenty-four. But you were trying so hard. It was, I don't know, cute."

"Don't do that," he said.

"Endearing, then."

"Don't feel sorry for me."

She uncrossed her legs, then crossed them again. She was small, but her thighs were massive, muscled as an animal's. He began working his way down the wall, hand over hand. The water was warm as the air.

"I don't feel sorry for you," she said. "I'm impressed. You told me something true. Took you a while, but you did. You know how often that happens? To me? At swim meets? At school?"

"How do people speak to you?" He imagined the name calling. *Captain Hook,* he was thinking. Or, who was the other one, the guy with scissors for fingers?

"That's just it," she said. "No one talks to me. Or they talk, but they're only saying what they think they're supposed to. Like, last week, this lady comes up to me after a meet and tells me I'm *brave*. I wanted to punch her in the face. But I didn't punch her in the face. You know what I did? I said *thank you*. So, I guess I have a problem with the truth too."

She wrapped her arm around her middle and looked away. The bug sounds had coalesced into a pulsing, rhythmic thing, a super-cricket amplified a few thousand times.

"What I mean is, I know all about people feeling sorry. I know how it feels, and it sucks. I try not to feel sorry for anyone, and I *definitely* don't feel sorry for you. Even if you're old."

"Thanks."

"And can't swim."

Brig laughed. "You're a trip, you know that?"

It was what his dad would have said. When Brig, as a child,

did something goofy or precocious or unexpectedly kind, his father would run a hand over his hair—not ruffling it, just a stroke, crown to eyebrows, like petting a dog. "You're a trip," he'd say.

The last time he'd seen his father, the man had come to watch him pack.

"I won't help," he said.

"I'm not asking you to," Brig said.

"You're making a mistake," he said, and, when Kate walked into the room, he added, "both of you. You're both making a big, giant mistake."

But Brig had heard that before. Leaving the church had been a *big, giant mistake,* along with marrying Kate, a Methodist. Not having kids right away had been a big, giant mistake, then not having kids at all. His father hadn't been quick to pronounce Brig's whole life a big, giant mistake, but maybe, if he did, he'd be right. Thirty years down, who knew how many to go, and still Brig had no partner, no profession, no place to call home.

Fuck, but he had to quit this line of thinking. The only thing worse than having someone feel sorry for you was feeling sorry for yourself—not exactly a profound sentiment, but sometimes the truth wasn't.

Brig's toes scraped the bottom, and then he was standing. He let go and waded to where Lily sat on the wall. He didn't want to try lifting himself out, flopping like a doomed fish in front of her, so he used the stairs. He joined her on deck, feet in the water. He ignored the wet press of his khakis, boxers blue beneath. He gave Lily space, a few arm lengths between them.

Lily was watching the water. "Tell me something else that's true," she said.

"I'm divorced," he said. It shot out, a spring-loaded snake from one of those trick cans labeled NUTS.

"How long?"

"Years."

"What happened?"

"I forgot how to be happy," he said. But that wasn't quite it. With Kate, he'd only forgotten how to fake it.

As for happiness, true happiness, *unadulterated* happiness—he tried thinking back to when he'd last been happy, but all he came up with was his father's hand on his head. The world had been so orderly then. Heaven and hell and a surefire way to trade one for the other. He'd had all the answers, the keys to kingdom—kingdoms, three of them. Outer Darkness yawned at his heels, but he'd never tip back, not unless he rejected what he knew. And then he rejected what he knew. Better never to have known than to know and let go—that was unpardonable. That was the unforgivable sin.

He'd tried to find his way back, but if belief is an uphill battle, believing again is a war, musket fire and bayonets grooved for blood.

What did Brig believe now, poolside in wet pants on a night with no moon? He believed whatever he felt. Moment to moment, he was sure he could walk this girl to his room just as he was sure that he couldn't. Was sure he would find the runaway cat, and sure the cat was dead already. Sure that, one day, phone in his fist, Kate's voice would bloom, a rhododendron in his ear, and sure, so sure, that she was gone for good.

"You still love her?"

Brig breathed in, breathed out. "I think answering that question would require another joint."

Lily laughed.

"Your turn," he said.

"You want me to say what you've already guessed?"

"No date?"

"No date."

"Sucks," he said.

"Yup," she said.

They were quiet awhile. A light came on in one window then went out again.

"Tell me something else," he said.

She kicked her feet underwater, and the surface mushroomed in little burbs.

"One time," she said, "changing classes, it unsnapped, just . . . fell off. Swim team's one thing, but *school*? It was like I'd rolled a grenade down the hall. One girl screamed so loud, I swear the lockers shook. Everyone got out of the way. Then everyone tried not to look, they just . . . walked around it, like one of those yellow signs custodians put up when the floors are wet."

"That's terrible," he said.

When she met his eyes, her look was suspicious, unbelieving.

"And I'm sure you would have picked it up."

"I caught it, didn't I? I didn't drop it."

"That's true," she said.

Her feet left the water and her knees met her chin.

"We're bringing each other down," she said.

"Sorry."

"Don't be sorry. Let's just bring each other up."

She stood. Inside of a minute, she'd refastened her arm and pulled on her clothes. She wrung water from his shirt and held it out.

She said, "Are you going to show me your place, or what?"

◆   ◆   ◆

The apartment was small, four hundred square feet, give or take, outfitted with the essentials and little else. The main room was a coffee table, a couch, and a plastic crate overturned with a TV on top. The carpet was worn without being stained. The only thing segregating this room from the next was the kitchen's linoleum and the narrow, transitional strip of aluminum tacked between. If Lily expected a bachelor pad, posters on the wall and nudie mags in a stack, she'd be disappointed. His was a den of divorce. Half the time on the road, he didn't require much, and, perpetually broke, he couldn't have stocked up on much if he did.

"Cozy," Lily said. Then: "It's nice." She ran her hand down

one bare wall, beige. All of the walls were that innocuous shade of Band-Aid that put Brig in mind of hospitals or synagogues.

"Can I get you anything to drink?" he said.

"Let's do shots," she said.

Air blew cold through the ceiling vents, and Brig moved to his room. He changed into dry clothes, then reappeared with shorts and a shirt for her.

"You've done shots before?" he asked.

Lily rolled her eyes and took the clothes from his hands.

When she emerged from the bathroom, her hair was combed. It hung, a wet veil, like black drapes around her face. He'd picked his smallest shirt, an old *X-Men* tee from high school that he'd never summoned the heart to throw out. It was a medium, and still it hung nearly to her knees, sleeves at her elbows. Wolverine leapt from the center, claws out. The fake arm gleamed, a tan, creamy plastic in the lamplight. Behind Lily, through the open door, a bra and panties hung from the shower rod, shorts and sweatshirt balled on the floor.

He thought to retrieve his own clothes, tossed, water soaking into his bedroom carpet, but there was some momentum to be accounted for, and he didn't want to lose it.

"Tequila okay?"

"Great," she said, which was good. It was all he had, tequila and PBRs, a case in the fridge and two more in the closet.

He searched the cabinets for a shot glass. He thought he'd had one once, but there was no telling. Finally, he pulled down a pair of mugs. One was yellow, a smiley face on its side. The other, white with brown stenciling along the lip, was an old Waffle House coffee cup, something a friend had stolen for him as a joke. Somewhere was the complete place setting: dish, cup, and saucer, fork and knife. He filled the mugs a quarter full with tequila and walked them along with a saltshaker to the coffee table. He returned to the kitchen and opened the fridge. On a shelf between an expired half gallon of skim and something in Tupperware leaned a lime of questionable integrity, rind chalky and soft. He cut it up anyway, then carried a pair of wedges to the couch.

Lily was seated, and he sat beside her. *Pharmaceutical Representative*, the industry's trade journal, lay in her lap, pages open to a Samsonite ad.

"Which one do you have?" she asked.

"Those are three-hundred-dollar bags," he said. "Mine's over there."

In the corner stood his suitcase, black and tan, his only piece from a matching set. The suitcase had a retractable handle and two wheels but lacked the lightweight frame people had these days, the four wheels that swiveled and turned on a dime. The set had been a present from Kate's parents, a wedding gift as practical as they were. They'd tried saving the marriage, her parents, offering to pay for fertility treatments or pay off debts, anything they thought might be wrong. When the dilemma proved ineffable, they offered money for a marriage counselor. But Kate's mind was made up. Brig wondered whether her parents knew the way it had gone down, or whether they blamed him, whether they assumed he'd left their little girl. He wanted them to have the whole story. He didn't know why, but he wanted that.

Lily tossed *Pharm Rep* onto the coffee table and held out her hand. He tapped salt onto her skin, then tapped some onto his own.

"You first," she said, which should have been his first clue. He licked the salt, took the shot, bit the lime. The liquor was cheap. It scalded his throat going down, then churned, syrupy and lava-hot, in his gut. He handed Lily the smiley face mug.

"Count me down?" she said, and Brig did.

On three, Lily licked her hand and downed the tequila, but she didn't make it to the lime. She was coughing too hard, flapping her hand in front of her face, eyes watering.

"Oh my God," she said. "Oh my God."

"The lime gets the taste out of your mouth," he said, but she waved him off.

"I thought it would taste like a margarita."

She wiped her mouth with the back of her hand. She rubbed her shoulder. He wondered whether the arm ever itched or burned. One late-night documentary had taught him about amputees and the phantom limb pains they sometimes got.

"You know how I promised to tell you if you were staring?" Lily said.

He nodded.

"You're staring."

He apologized. He took the mug from her hand and finished the shot. More throat scouring, more burn.

Lily said nothing. Her unused lime segment sat on the table, and she touched it with one finger. It rocked back and forth, a little green boat.

"What are we doing here?" he said.

"How do you mean?" She scooted closer so that their legs touched, and Brig stood.

"Enough," he said. "This is getting weird. Can I just come right out and say that this is getting weird?"

"This got weird an hour ago," she said.

"And whose fault is that? Who took off her clothes? Who got me high?"

Lily laughed. She stood and Wolverine stood with her.

"I'm five foot four with one arm. You really think I could get you to do anything you didn't want to?"

She moved to him, pressed the full length of herself against him, hard, and put her lips to his neck. She didn't kiss him, just let her lips lie there, soft, warm worms on his skin. Then she pulled away and pulled his hand with her to the bedroom.

◆   ◆   ◆

A year, he'd waited for Kate's call.

"Call me when you get there," she'd said. "Just so I know you're safe."

He'd waited a month, then called. He got the machine with his voice still on it, and he left a message. Maybe he'd waited too long. Maybe, waiting, he'd hurt her feelings. But he'd been afraid to call without good news. Because, if he called with good news—proof he could get a job, hold it down, contribute to society and all that—maybe he could make her see he'd change, that, short of being the kind of happy she wanted him to be, he could at least be useful.

He left her his new number and the address to his apartment. He told her what he'd been up to, told her work was good—a lie—and the city was safe—another lie. He told her how, just that morning, a quail had crossed the parking lot, identical brood trailing her like the miniature middles of a Russian nesting doll. Kate loved nesting dolls, had kept a dozen on the mantel in their home. He talked until he heard a beep, then called back and picked up where he'd left off. He told her everything he could think to say except that he missed her, which he did, terribly.

"Call me," he said at the end.

He waited another month, then, worried she'd missed the first messages, called again. This time, the voice on the machine was hers. She was going by her maiden name, and the new outgoing message was no-nonsense. *Leave your name and number, and I'll call you back,* it said like a reprimand.

He gave her his information again, then he gave her more news. He'd gotten a raise, he said—big lie. There was a chance he might be transferred to Atlanta—big, giant lie. He said he missed her, that he should have told her that the last time he called. Anyway, he wanted her to know just how much he missed her, how he didn't care for this arrangement, how, before a year was up and the divorce became final, they might consider other options available to them. Could she call him? Please? And soon?

A year went by.

He called, left his message at the beep. If he could just have a minute of her time. All he really wanted was to say that he was sorry. He was so sorry, and, even if what they'd shared wasn't happiness, exactly, then at least it was something familiar and good, certainly better than what he had now, which was nothing. Maybe, if it wasn't too much to ask, maybe she would take him back and everything could return to the way it had been. *Better* than the way it had been. He would try harder, no matter what trying harder meant. He would work. He would take her places. He would listen when she talked. He really would try this time, if only she'd give him the chance. If it wasn't too much to ask.

The next week, the papers arrived.

He didn't sign them. By now, he knew enough to know it was over. He only wanted to talk to her. He thought, if he held back on the signing, she'd be forced to call, but the only calls that came were from her lawyer, then his.

He signed.

"Now leave her alone," his lawyer said. "Don't call. Don't write. Don't give her reason to request a restraining order."

This seemed, to Brig, excessive. Had he missed something? Was this necessary? Restraint? Restraint from what? Brig had never raised a hand to her. He'd never raised his *voice*. He'd seldom raised his ass from the couch, and *that* had been the problem. But he'd outgrown that. A year in the desert, and he was a new man. He hoped he was.

He hoped that this, all of this—the threat of restraint, Kate's refusal to take his calls—was, in fact, proof of her affection, proof that maybe she cared *too* much, found the pain too acute to keep him in her life. And, if it was easier to cut him out of her life altogether, that didn't mean she didn't still love him. He believed this. He had to. This abiding belief kept him off the couch.

Still, he wanted—needed—to hear Kate's voice one more time. But, when he called, the number had been disconnected.

Two more years, and word came from his parents that Kate was engaged. The guy was a big-shot lawyer. The announcement had filled a quarter page of *The Atlanta Journal-Constitution*.

"I'm sorry," his mother said, but the conversation was cut short by a knock on the door. The woman in the next apartment wanted to know if Brig might be able to watch her cat.

◆   ◆   ◆

They sat on the bed, then lay down. There was one pillow, and Brig let Lily have it. She stretched out on her back and studied the ceiling. He lay on his side and studied her. Her real arm was closest to him, and he wondered whether she'd picked her place on the bed on purpose, whether she lay on her back to shield the prosthesis from view.

"Why *Brig*?" she asked.

"Family name," he said.

"As in, a family of shipbuilders?"

"Brig's short for Brigham, as in Brigham Young, as in Mormon. And, before you ask, my dad had one wife. Like most Mormons. Just one. That fucking TV show's got everyone confused."

"I love that show," Lily said, and, when Brig gave her the eyebrow, she shrugged and said, "I'm kidding. I don't watch TV."

He shook his head. "Who *are* you?"

"Just a girl," she sang, "just an ordinary girl." She laughed at the ceiling.

He wanted to tell her to knock it off. He wanted to say: *For one second, be serious*. But he also wanted to be inside of her. Or, he thought he did. Was he scared? He guessed he was. It wasn't that it had been so long, though it had been. And it wasn't that she was so young, though she was. It was something to do with the fact that the only woman he'd been with was Kate. The measuring stick of his love life came down to Kate, and sleeping with Lily meant doubling that count. Maybe he should have started sleeping with women right after the divorce, but that wasn't the way he'd been raised. No matter that he no longer *believed* in the way he'd been raised — some things you couldn't shake. And say he did it? Say he slept with Lily?

How many women would he have to sleep with before each time didn't feel like it meant so damned much?

"You want to know who I am?" she asked.

He did.

"I started out a gymnast, and now I'm a diver. I'm an A student. I like birds, and I've kept the ticket stub to every movie I've ever seen: a hundred and forty-two—a hundred and thirty if you don't count the ones I saw more than once. My parents are Baptist. They voted for Bush. *Twice*. They try to get everyone to convert. But, wherever they go, Brazil or Belize or wherever, they bring food, books and maps, crayons for the kids, so that's cool. Sometimes people go along with it just for the food at the end. You can tell."

Brig's parents had been strict, but not mission-oriented. Either you were Mormon or you weren't, and God have mercy on those who were not—that was their position.

"My parents actually worry about them," she said, "about the ones who play along, then go back to worshiping the river gods, or whatever. One time I said, 'So what?' I meant it as in 'At least you're helping them out.' But my parents don't think that way. They don't care about saving lives. They care about saving souls. I got a month in my room for that one."

"They lock you in your room?"

"Not literally. I just mean they grounded me for a month. No phone, no friends."

She pushed her hair out of her face, let her hand fall on his leg and rest there.

"But you know what that's like," she said. "You must."

He couldn't deny it. On the more absurd end of the spectrum, he'd once been grounded two weeks for trying Coke at a friend's party.

"You've done coke?" Her eyes widened at the ceiling. She looked so impressed, he almost let it go, but he couldn't.

"Coca-Cola," Brig said. "Soda."

"Mormons don't drink soda?"

"Or coffee, or tea. Tequila's right out."

Lily laughed. "Holy shit." Her hand moved up his thigh.

"And your tattoo?" he asked.

"They've never seen it," she said.

"How is that possible?"

"Speedo covers it. Plus, we don't show much skin in my family."

Brig's either. His parents had been big on modesty, pants for Dad and high necklines for Mom. First time he'd brought Kate home, she'd worn a blouse that made good use of her cleavage. They'd said nothing, his folks, but he'd sensed the disapproval in their thin smiles.

"Your parents," he said, "if they knew you were here?"

"Oh, they'd shoot you," she said. "I mean *Thou shalt not kill*, sure, but let's be honest. They'd shoot you dead."

"And what about you?" he said.

"What about me?"

"You buy into it, all the God stuff?"

Lily seemed to think on this. Her hand worked its way up his leg until her fingers found the drawstring of his shorts.

"I do," she said. "Not the way my parents do, but I do. It all just seems too big for there not to be one."

She pulled, and the bow he'd tied came undone at his waist.

"I mean, just because my parents have this kind of messed-up take on it doesn't mean there can't be a God. And just because I do stupid stuff doesn't mean I don't want someone up there watching me do it."

Her knuckles were at his navel, the back of her hand turning slow circles into his abdomen.

"It's just, the arm," he said. He was feeling dizzy, euphoric. He felt the way you felt coming in out of a cold rain, waiting for the shower to warm. "If it were me . . ."

"It's not you," she said. There was a line, and he'd put one foot over it.

"Besides," she said, "you've got your own shit to worry about. Don't bring me into your shit."

"You don't know anything about my shit," he said, and the warmth was suddenly gone, the warmth and the hand, the slow circles setting his skin aflame. She turned onto her side. She faced him, now, watched him with the same intensity she'd been giving the ceiling.

"You're angry," she said. "You still love her, and you're mad at God."

He shook his head. "I've been mad at God a long time. Kate couldn't change that. She thought she could, but she couldn't."

He reached for her hand, but her arm was beneath her. If he wanted a hand now, it would have to be plastic.

"Anyway, I'm done with God."

Lily smiled. "But what if it's not God you're mad at?" she said. "What if the thing you're mad at is this idea of God, this really bad idea you got from other people. What if God exists? What if God is love? Aren't you going to feel stupid later?"

"I don't believe in afterlives," he said. He wanted to, but getting rid of hell had meant jettisoning heaven. He'd practiced the rhetorical backflips of one without the other, but what was grace without justice? Halos begged firebrands, fangs wings.

Better the ground. Better the great, white blank.

"You believe in heaven?" he said.

Lily turned onto her back, and again her hand was at his waist. "I have to," she said.

She slipped her hand down his pants, took hold, let go.

"You have protection?" she said.

♦   ♦   ♦

In the bathroom, he braced himself against the sink. His head spun, and he wondered whether he was coming down with something, whether the tequila might come back up. He shut his eyes and opened them. He splashed water on his face. The comb she'd used sat on the countertop, and he pulled a black hair from it. He took hold of each end and stretched the hair to its full length, two, maybe two and a half feet. He thought of flossing with it, then dropped the hair into the sink. He turned on the faucet, and the hair curled in the water, then slipped down the drain. With Kate, he'd been forever snaking the bathroom sink, pulling fat, globby hunks of hair like drowned mice from the drains, the smell so bad he often gagged. And it occurred to him that, since Kate, he hadn't needed a snake. Three years, and not once had his drain clogged.

He opened the medicine cabinet and pulled down the condoms. He'd bought the box before his last date, but she hadn't hinted, and he doubted he would have gone through with it even if she had. He pulled one end of the accordion from the box and tore along the perforated line. He had to check the expiration date. They were good for another month. He weighed the packet in his hand, then dropped it back into the box and returned the box to the cabinet. The cabinet rattled when it closed.

He lowered the toilet's lid and sat. Lily's underwear hung overhead, dripping, and he pulled the bra down. The cups were small: 32B. Each cup was the size and shape of the paper masks he used to wear to mow the lawn. He fitted one to his face and breathed in. The cup smelled like chlorine and something else, something floral and inviting. He dropped the bra. Her towel hung from the bar on the wall, and he stood and pressed his whole head into it. He moaned. The tears came and the towel ate them.

He went back to the room. She'd gotten under the covers, hair on the pillow like a nest for her head. On the floor, crumpled beside the bed, were the clothes he'd given her. She'd pulled the top sheet to her neck, but just on one side, toga-style. One arm rested above the covers, muscled, welcoming, lightly haired. The prosthesis was hidden from view. She'd seemed so comfortable with him, with her nakedness, right up to the moment they'd climbed into bed.

He stood at the footboard. A foot stuck out from the covers, toes curled, nails unpainted, perfect as pearls.

He touched the smallest toe, then brought his hand to the back of his neck.

What was she doing here? How had he let it get this far?

"Don't hate me," he said.

The girl's face scrunched up.

"I want you to promise me something," he said.

"Okay."

"Promise me you won't do this again."

She sat up, and the covers fell to her waist. The gecko seemed to have grown, seemed to be scaling her pale hip. The prosthesis hung at her side. Stretch marks radiated from her nipples like the wavy rays of a child's hand-drawn sun. "From coming in too fast," Kate had explained. She'd had them too.

"I'm not a child," Lily said.

He wanted to say he was no less a child than her. He wanted to say that adults were just kids who'd made up their minds. Instead, he said, "I know that."

"You aren't protecting me from anything," she said. "This isn't my first time."

"I didn't think it was," he said. But he had wondered. He'd taken her for Lolita, then the arm was in the air, and, catching it, he hadn't known what to think. Perhaps he'd flattered himself thinking she might want him for her first.

"You should go," he said.

"Jesus," she said. She threw the covers back, and the fullness of her nudity shocked him anew. Her body was a coil, muscled, marble-smooth.

"You . . . you look just like her," he said.

Lily was quiet a minute. She looked down, taking in the length of herself, then met his eyes.

"That must be fucked up for you," she said.

Brig looked away. He moved to the bedroom window, put his fingers between two miniblinds, and scissored them open. The lot was lamplit. He hoped, any second, to see Boots cross the long shadows of parked cars. He hoped against the double pendulum of head and tail, orange between coyote teeth. But no cat appeared, in or out of jaws.

He wasn't sure how long he watched, but, when he turned, Lily stood in the bedroom doorway, her shorts and sweatshirt back on, undergarments balled wet in her hand.

"I guess I'll be going," she said.

"I'm sorry," he said.

"Hey," she said. "It happens. I hear it happens a lot to older guys."

And he was glad to have the teasing back.

"I hope you find your cat," she said.

He told her he did too. "Those cigarettes," he said.

"One for the road?" she said.

"If that's okay."

She pulled the pack from her pocket and shook one out. This time, he studied the pack, caught the logo and the name. She dropped the cigarette into his open palm. Her fingertips grazed his skin, but the current was gone, burnt out or too diffuse to feel, like in high school physics, the experiment they'd done with electricity. They'd stood in a circle, those brave enough to take part, and all held hands. The first loop, the current passing through them, he felt the pulse. The charge weakened, circling, until six, seven revolutions later, he felt nothing at all.

He slipped the joint into his pocket. "I'm sorry," he said again. "I never meant to—"

"Sleep with me?"

"Change my mind. I never meant to change my mind."

"That's all right," she said. "Next time you want to sniff a girl's panties, though, there's *got* to be an easier way than all this."

He was disgusted with himself. He wondered how she could

have seen into the bathroom, but then she was laughing, saying, "I'm kidding. Jesus. Lighten up."

And then she was at the door, then opening it, then crouching, making kissing noises into the night. He saw the red of her sweatshirt, the alligator's ridge of her backbone cutting the shirt in two. And then he saw the cat in her arms.

"She came back!" Lily said. The cat purred and rubbed its muzzle across her middle. Briefly, the head tucked itself into the pocket of her shirt, then pulled back out, shaking, like a dog shaking off water. Lily laughed, and Brig didn't have the heart to tell her, first, that the missing cat was not his own, and, second, that this was not the missing cat. This cat, a tom, belonged to the Indian couple upstairs. They let the cat out nights to fight and fuck, and it never surprised Brig to see him wandering the complex, a slash down the calico bridge of his nose or one eye oozing, swollen shut.

The cat hissed when Brig took it.

"Can I see you again?" he said.

"What for?" Lily said.

And Brig saw he didn't have the answer to that question.

"Maybe I'll catch one of your swim meets sometime," he said.

"Maybe," she said.

They nodded the way people do when they agree to something both know will never happen and, in agreeing, know the other knows.

The cat writhed in Brig's arms, and he lowered it to the floor. It moved through the room, sniffing, then rubbed its side along one coffee table leg.

"I hope you find a way to be happy," Lily said and, before he could say anything, kissed him on the mouth—once, twice, three closemouthed kisses in quick succession—and then she was out the door.

He waited for what felt like long enough, then opened the door and threw the cat out.

Then he moved to his suitcase, pulled his laptop from the front flap, sat on the floor, and flipped the laptop open. He pulled the joint from his pocket. It wasn't hand-rolled, but neither was it manufacturer-perfect. It was closer to the prerolled cones a friend of his used to pack tobacco into, but it was stamped with a logo Brig had seen somewhere before.

He searched the name on the cigarette's side, and things made sense quickly: five medical marijuana dispensaries in a ten-mile radius, and laws loose enough he didn't doubt a minor could stock up even without her parents' help.

He didn't know her last name, but searching "Liliana Tucson swimmer arm" pulled up the *Tucson Weekly*, the human interest story, and the truth.

A snake had seemed a far-fetched way to lose an arm, and he wondered whether the cancer had reached her other bones. He wondered at the rest of what she'd told him, how much was true. Her parents *were* missionaries, that much the article confirmed. In one picture, Lily stood beside them on the front lawn of a small, brick house. He knew it immediately for one of the ranches in the development down the road. But the neighborhood was huge, houses identical. He could wander the cul-de-sacs and cursive streets nightly and not be sure which house was hers.

And say he could be sure? Finding her, what would he do? Shake her hand? Say *Sorry for your cancer*? Meet her folks?

He read "High School High Dive" twice, looking for the words *remission* and *cancer-free* and, not finding them, knew what not finding them meant.

There was another paper, an announcement that needed reading. He could almost see Kate's face, serene, cheek pressed to the lawyer's. Or maybe they were smiling, gazing into one another's eyes. He considered pulling the page up. But he hadn't looked yet, and he wouldn't. He didn't want to see the picture. He didn't want to know the guy's name, didn't want to know which church, how soon, what day.

He shut the laptop. He stood and returned the computer to

his bag. He searched the kitchen drawers until he found a box of matches, then stepped outside.

◆   ◆   ◆

The night was insects, and Brig cut right through the middle of the roar. The joint was really working on him, so that the cicadas' rhythmic pulse swelled in his head to the shape and size of a heart monitor. He'd never seen one, a heart monitor, except in bad movies, the kind with the green line and sonar beep that meant the coma patient's heart was still beating. Stumbling, calling for Boots, Brig waited for the line to fall flat, bugs cut off in a sudden, strangling hush, like birthday candles blown the fuck out.

He was high.

And Boots was gone. Or hiding. Or in the belly of some other animal already.

"She's an indoor cat," the woman had said. Pampered, spayed, declawed, the cat had never set so much as one paw out-of-doors. "She's my little sweetie." The woman ruffled the cat's mane with one liver-spotted, skeletal hand. A diamond ring collared her fourth finger, and Brig wondered how long she'd been widowed.

He wondered now how long she'd had the cat. Divorced, he'd considered a dog for companionship, but work made it impossible. Had Boots perhaps been a dead man's replacement? Had Brig lost more than a cat? Had he lost a husband substitute?

The joint burned his fingertips, and he dropped it, stomped it out. He sat and put his head in his hands. He stood. The palm trees spun. He made one more trip around the apartment complex and wound up back at the lamppost where he'd first found Lily. He touched the pole. He shook it, but it was too deep in the ground to move. He looked up. Bugs crowded the light, dive-bombing and circling. A black-shelled beetle head-butted the bulb a half dozen times before hitting the sidewalk. Caught on its back, the beetle squirmed, wings folding and unfolding beneath it, legs pedaling air.

He watched the beetle a long time. He hated bugs, the grotes-query of mandible and eye, antennae twitching, the threat, always, of flight.

Come on, he thought. *Come on*. But the beetle couldn't get itself turned over. Brig couldn't leave it, couldn't touch it either. Grass grew from a crack in the sidewalk, and he plucked a blade. He tried to flip the beetle over with the blade of grass, but the insect was too heavy. He was pushing it across the concrete. He stopped. He worried he'd hurt it, worried he'd torn up the beetle's wings. Then the legs, searching, hooked the grass, and the beetle turned itself over. For a moment, it rested, then its back unbolted like the doors of a DeLorean, wings flickered, and the beetle lifted off.

Brig had no idea what time it was. It was still night, no warmth, no sunrise softening the sky. Tomorrow, he had a meeting in Tempe that he'd skip. He'd skip the whole week, maybe. Maybe take a month off. He could make it a month on credit cards, but this would cost him. In the long run, he'd pay twice as much.

Or not. Every few weeks, in the mail, he got an offer, another card with zero interest on balance transfers for twelve or eighteen months. He knew a guy who'd open an account, move his debt, then, a year later, move what he owed again. It was a migration that had been going on a decade, and, in this way, he'd stayed out of debt. Brig could do this, and he wondered why he hadn't, why he let his several thousand dollars fester on a three-year-old Visa and an even older MasterCard, both with shitty interest rates. Filling out an application would take ten minutes. Instead, each month, he wrote two more checks.

His own laziness impressed him—triumphant laziness, laziness in the face of clear, available solutions.

He pulled his key ring from his pocket and found the neighbor's key. He crossed the parking lot, stopped at her door, and let himself in.

Same floor plan, the apartment was a mirror image of his own.

The furnishings, however, were exquisite, walls crowded with dressers, bookcases, a desk of dark, carved wood. It was an apartment trying to hold everything once held by a house. Inside, the smell was cat and potpourri. A low table stood beside the door. A lamp stood on the table, and he pulled the chain.

On the kitchen counter, by the sink, six cat food cans were stacked like hockey pucks. A page of handwritten instructions was weighted down by a manual can opener with rubber grips. He'd never bothered to read the instructions, and now he moved the opener aside to take a look. Printed at the top of the page were three phone numbers. There was the number of the cat's veterinarian, the number of an emergency vet, and the number where the woman was staying. The first instruction began: *Boots is an inside cat*. Brig read that and couldn't read the rest.

He unstacked the cans and made a pyramid. He turned the cans so the cat on each label faced him, then spun the cans so the cat faced away. He'd hold on to them a few more days, in case Boots came back, but, on the last day, he'd open each can, switch on the disposal, and dump the food. He'd tell her the cat had *just* run off. That seemed kinder, unless he was only telling himself this because it was easier.

The only other option was to call. He could beg her forgiveness, ask advice. And, who knew? Maybe this had happened before. Maybe she knew a place the cat might hide. But, looking around the apartment, at the careful placement of furniture in each room, he knew this cat had never gotten out before, knew this just as he knew he couldn't make the call.

He hadn't meant to fuck up, hadn't meant to make another big, giant mistake. It seemed unfair—brutally, relentlessly unfair—that certain big, giant mistakes weren't made so much as begun with smaller, simpler ones: a wrong turn, a pan left too long on the stove, an open door.

Brig opened cabinets until he found a glass. He filled the glass with water and drank. There was dish soap on the countertop, and he washed the glass, then returned it to the cabinet where he'd found it.

The woman's kitchen and main room were divided by the same thin, silver strip that divided his own, and he stepped over it. He crossed the room, then sat with his back to the door. He reached up, pulled the lamp chain, and the room went dark.

He closed his eyes. He would wait out the night. Eyes shut, he'd listen for a scratch at the door, and he would not sleep. He'd wait through the silence, listen past the silence, until his head hurt from all the listening.

If you hoped hard enough, you could wish a thing into existence. He'd believed that, once. He wanted to believe it again. Eyes closed, hoping—it was as close as he could get to prayer.

100% Cotton

The night is cold. The buildings are tall. The sky, except where it's starlit, is black. Black like black checker pieces or what's left of wood after the fire.

Also, I should mention that there's a large gun pointed at my face.

And because there's a large gun pointed at my face, things speed up the way they do in nature films, how a seed sprouts, turns to stalk, and takes leaves in ten seconds.

Things here are speeding up just that way. Stars pinwheel beyond the buildings. The moon rises, sets, rises again. And then things slow way, way down.

"If you don't want to be caught dead in that shirt," he says, "you'd best take it off."

The guy with the gun's not fucking around. I don't know anything about guns, but this is a big one. It looks like the kind that holds a lot of bullets, the kind that leaves your corpse unrecognizable when the cops come, which is okay because there's no one to miss me, no one left on this spinning planet to faint when the coroner lifts the sheet from my bullet-riddled face.

The gun's pointed at me because the guy asked for my wallet and I said no.

"No," I said, and he said, "How'd you like to die?" and I said, "Well, I wouldn't want to be caught dead in this shirt."

Which isn't exactly true. If I hadn't wanted to be caught dead in this shirt, I wouldn't have worn it. It seemed fitting for the occasion. The shirt's black with a skull-and-crossbones emblem on the pocket, what you see printed on bottles, the kind with caps to keep out babies and old people.

Maybe the skull and crossbones wasn't an inspired choice, but fuck you. Pick out your own death-shirt.

The guy with the gun didn't like my tone. He said, "I don't like your tone."

He didn't get my smugness, that it was on purpose, so I said it again, the thing about not wanting to be caught dead in this shirt, which is when he told me to take it off. Which pretty much brings you up to speed.

I pull the shirt over my head. I kneel and fold the shirt on the sidewalk, a rectangle, department-store-perfect. Work five years at the Gap, and you get really good at folding clothes.

"You've never been held up," the gunman says.

I could tell him the truth, that it's my third time this week, that for months I've watched the local news in order to pinpoint the Atlanta intersection most likely to get me offed. That I picked *this* street in *this* neighborhood and wander it nightly. That I've been roughed up, cursed, and mugged. I've lost two wallets, a watch, my phone, but not one guy would pull the trigger, because it turns out what they want, really, isn't blood—it's money.

Noncompliance, I decided, was my best option.

Last night, I sang, did a little dance. "My milk shake brings all the boys to the yard!" I belted it, gyrated my hips, but that only freaked the guy out. He didn't even stick around for the cash.

This guy, though. This guy looks like he wouldn't mind firing a round through your forehead if only you found the right words to provoke him.

"Wallet," he says. "Now."

I'm on my knees, the shirt the only thing between me and his feet. We're in the dark where he grabbed me, but there's enough moonlight to light up the skull, which isn't the same material as the rest of the shirt, but something firmer, rubbery, like a kid's iron-on jersey decal.

I point at the shirt. "One hundred percent cotton," I sign. English is my first language. My second's American Sign Language.

The guy looks around. He's getting antsy.

This is how my father died.

My father was born deaf and he taught me his language, though it wasn't his language, not for years. In this country's history, there was a time when sign language wasn't allowed, when the deaf were taught to speak in tongues, to mouth sounds they couldn't hear leave their lips, as though all of America was afraid of hands, of what the deaf might do with a language all their own.

My father found happiness with a deaf woman who taught him to speak with his body. She stuck around just long enough to give him a son. He never remarried. He died last year when a man asked for his wallet. Dad kept walking, and the man shot him.

"Couldn't your father read lips?" people ask, as though the answer to this question determines whose fault it is he's dead.

A wind kicks up. Shirtless, my skin prickles. The sidewalk hurts my knees.

"Count of five," the guy says. "Five."

At the Gap, I read tags until I came to know a material at the touch of a sleeve. Even cotton-polyester blends I can guess, give or take ten percent on the ratio.

My T-shirt between us looks lonely, and I wonder if my father fell like that, whether he folded or crumpled like a dropped shirt.

"Machine wash warm, with like colors," I sign.

"Four," the guy says.

I don't know whether my father misunderstood his killer, whether he saw the gun, whether he walked on knowing what came next.

"Gentle cycle," I sign.

"Keep it up," the guy says. His thumb jumps. Something clicks at his end of the gun. He steps toward me, and he's almost on the shirt. His boots are black lace-ups.

It won't be long now.

"Three."

You want to know why I want to die, but what answer could I give good enough for you, you who want to *live*?

Putting a thing like that into words, it's like trying to explain what stands between people, what keeps us from communicating — I mean really *communicating* — with each other.

We move through the days with our hands at our sides, and I believe that whatever holds us back, whatever keeps people at bay, maybe it's the same thing that left my mother tethered at the neck by an orange extension cord to our attic's rafters.

Maybe it's what sings in my ear to follow her.

She wasn't afraid to do to herself what I'm asking someone to do for me.

"Tumble dry low," I sign.

If I fall forward, my head will catch the shirt like a pillow. I'm ready.

"Two."

We talk in our sleep, and so do the deaf. Nights I snuck into my father's room, his hands worked over his chest, signing. It was the language of dreams, incomprehensible, but it was gorgeous. His hands rose and fell like birds with his breathing.

"One."

Except sometimes, sometimes, meaning crept in. A transmission. My father, who spent his life missing my mom, that sign: index fingers beckoning, then hands pulling air in the direction of the heart.

I close my eyes, and it's there, the gun muzzle, ice between my eyes.

I want to cry out. I hold my breath.

I wait.

I wait.

You want to know what my father was saying, and I'll tell you. It's what I shout once the gunman's given up, returned his weapon to his jacket pocket. It's what I call after his heels slapping the sidewalk.

It's my voice to the gunman and my father's hands to my mother in the night, calling: "Come back. Come back. Come back."

The End of Aaron

Aaron calls to say we're running out of time, and I know that we're going to have to do it all over again, the collecting, the hiding, the waiting to come out of the dark.

"Grace," he says. "Where are you? Where are you right now?"

He's got that warble in his voice, like he's just swallowed a kazoo, that and the tone that means business, like in movies when the screen splits and we see the people on both ends of the line, the air traffic controller telling the twelve-year-old girl how to land the plane, or the hero asking the chief which color wire to cut.

"Publix," I say. "I'm at Publix."

"Perfect," Aaron says. "I want you to get ten—twenty—gallons of water, eight rolls of duct tape, five pounds of jerky, and a pear."

He still calls it *duck* tape, like the bird. Last time I corrected him, he didn't talk to me for two days, so I let it go.

"Why the pear?" I ask.

"I like pears," Aaron says, and it's like he's saying: *Just because the world's ending, I can't get a pear, goddammit?*

Except that, for Aaron, the world is *always* ending. It's the third time this year, and it's only July. I'm thinking last night's fireworks set him off, but there has to be more to it. Probably he's off his meds. Aaron loses it, and, nine times out of ten, it means he's gone off his meds.

Used to be, he'd warn me. "I'm just going to try," he'd say. "Just for a week or two."

When I stopped supporting these experiments, he stopped telling me. Now, I have to guess, which isn't hard given the things that come out of his mouth. The trick is figuring out how long he's been off.

First day, he'll feel nothing. By the end of the first week, he tends to claim a clarity and empathy he hasn't felt in years. "I want to fuck the world!" he'll say, pulling me onto the bed.

Then, week two will hit, and like clockwork, or something more precise and calculating than clockwork, Aaron will start in on that year's fear.

It wasn't always the end of the world. For a while, Aaron was afraid to leave the house. Those weeks were okay. We'd lie in bed, snuggle, watch TV. One time, we watched *Labyrinth* three times in a row. By the third viewing, Aaron was sobbing. I shook the pills into his palm, and he drank them down.

Then there was the year of the bees. Bumblebee or butterfly, it didn't matter. Aaron would see a bug and freak out. When he was a child, a bee sting put him in the hospital for two days. Now, everywhere he goes, there's an EpiPen in his pocket. Aaron gets stung, he has less than a minute to plunge the needle into his leg before his throat swells shut. It's a fear I respect, a fear that makes sense when you're all the time only seconds away from death.

He's only been stung the one time, but twice he's put himself back in the hospital. "I really thought there was a bee," he'll say, EpiPen empty in its little tan tube.

This year, though, it's the apocalypse that's got Aaron in hand-cuffs. Not the Rapture or any trumped-up Mayan shit, but what Aaron calls *the real deal*. He doesn't know how the world will end, only that it will be bad. He doesn't know when, only that it will be soon.

"Won't be long now," he'll say, canning fruit or sharpening the blade of a knife. "Won't be long at all."

I blame his parents. Not for the depression—I mean, maybe that's their fault. Maybe there's something fucked in their genes that got more fucked up when his dad fucked his mom. I don't know. I don't know how DNA works. I only know that his folks bought into the whole Y2K thing, and Aaron's never been the same since.

Imagine it: You're eight years old, all of your friends are partying with their families or up late with other friends at New Year's Eve sleepovers, and, instead of watching the ball drop with your parents, you're huddled in the basement watching your mom cry. The basement is stocked with two years' worth of water, batteries, and green beans. Upstairs, a TV's been left on, and Dick Clark counts down. Downstairs, you shut your eyes and wait for the end of the world.

You could say Aaron's been waiting ever since. I should know. I've known Aaron most of his life. In kindergarten he pulled my pigtails, and by high school I was letting him pull down my pants. Neither of us were college material, so, after graduation, he got a job at Arby's and I got a job down the street at Payless shoes. Sometimes our lunch hours overlap, and we meet at McDonald's. He smells like old beef and I smell like feet, and we eat our McNuggets and pretend that we're better than this. Truth is, we're twenty and we live with our parents, but that's okay because we have each other, and I've come to believe that each other is enough.

Most nights I spend at Aaron's. His parents call me the daughter they never had, which is sweet but also kind of fucked up since they must know by now what I do in bed with their son.

At Publix, I get everything off of Aaron's list that will fit in the cart. I have a card from my parents to cover food, and, so long as I keep it under two hundred a month, Dad won't yell. Most meals, I pay for myself so I can stock up on weeks Aaron goes a little crazy. His therapist calls this enabling. I call it love. She says I'm a problem, and I, for one, have agreed to disagree.

At home, I pop the trunk. It's got a dozen gallons in it, and I grab the first two. I start up the front steps and almost kick over the jar. This I'm used to. Every few months, we find one, a mason jar fat with amber, lid collared by a yellow bow—a sort of thank-you for ignoring the bees.

A while back, the woman next door set up a hive. Generally, the bees stay on her side of the fence, though, from Aaron's backyard, you can watch them rise, a fog of tiny helicopters circling the house. Aaron's mom called the county, but it turns out there's no law against keeping bees.

She petitioned the homeowners association to dub the neighborhood bee-free, but the beekeeper threatened litigation, claiming it was because she was black.

"I don't care what *color* the woman is," Aaron's mom said. "I don't want those things stinging my son."

In the end, the HOA let the lady keep her bees provided no one got stung, and, in two years, no one has. The women settled their differences, and now we get honey.

Aaron meets me at the door.

"Sweet!" he says. He pulls the jar from my hand, leaving me to juggle the gallons.

"There's more in the trunk," I say.

"Those can wait," Aaron says. "Get the pear."

I go back to the car, get the pear, and find Aaron in the basement. This is where he lives. The place is spotless, the way it gets his first week off meds. First he cleans everything, then he lets everything go to shit. The clothes he has on are the clothes he wore yesterday, and I wonder how long it's been since he slept.

"Come on, come on," Aaron says.

The basement is two rooms. One's a bedroom. The other's been converted to a living-room-slash-kitchen. It's all belowground, setup intended for the Y2K end that never came.

Aaron's on the bed, honey jar open between his knees. He balances a plate on top of the jar, and I drop the pear onto it. Aaron likes knives, keeps knives all over the house, and now he pulls one from his pocket, a Swiss Army deal, and unfolds a long blade from the handle. He splits the pear, picks the seeds from the middle, and hands me the plate. Then I watch as he lowers the blade past the open mouth and deep into the jar's gold, glorious middle.

The knife rises, and it's gilded, honey-sheathed. I lift the plate and wait for the drizzle.

Listen: If your honey comes in a bear-shaped bottle, you've never had honey, and if you haven't had honey, you haven't lived. Real honey, honey fresh from the comb, is sweet, yes, but it also tastes like clover and sage, like cinnamon and lemon trees. I can't explain it except to say that, before you die, you owe it to yourself to take a taste.

We eat the pear and make love, and, when we're done, I run back to the car and unload the gallons, the rolls of tape, the jerky in its fat, five-pound bag.

I make half a dozen trips up and down the stairs, carrying water, and Aaron stocks the gallons in his pantry. What he's got is an old wardrobe, converted, crowded with shelves. Together, we cut a hole in the drywall just big enough to tuck the wardrobe in. You can hardly tell it's not a real pantry.

When Aaron gets scared, we stock up. When he comes out of it, we eat whatever we stocked up on.

I come down the stairs with the last gallon, and Aaron is crying.

"There's no room," he cries. The pantry is packed. "There's no more room!" He screams it, then sobs.

I touch his shoulder and he turns, wild-eyed, like a dog touched at the food bowl.

I hold up the last gallon. "We can slide it under the bed," I say. "We can put it anywhere." I should know better. There's no use reasoning with Aaron when he gets this way, and, today, for whatever reason, he's decided the only food and water we can keep is what fits on the shelves.

"Take it away," he says. "Give it to Mom and Dad. They're going to need it."

Early on in his delusions, this was a sticking point for us.

"People will want in," Aaron will say, "but you've got to be ready. You have to be prepared to tell them no."

"Even our parents?" I'll ask.

And Aaron, without a trace of sympathy, will say, "Even them."

"Okay," I'll say.

It bothers me, I'll admit, imagining my mother and father wandering the bomb-scarred wasteland, scavenging for food while Aaron and I get fat on beef jerky and canned corn. But, then, the end isn't coming, and so my agreeing with Aaron isn't the biggest of concessions. Compromising your ethics is one thing. Compromising your hypothetical ethics is another. And so I say, "Okay."

That *okay*, it's like *enabling*—another word that, in my mouth, means *love*.

I love Aaron. *How*, you're wondering. *How could she love a man who yells, who cries, who makes her carry jugs of water up and down the stairs?* But you're only seeing Aaron unwell. Aaron at his best is better than you or me, better than anyone I've ever known. He's gentle. He's kind. But those are just words. Here's a story:

I'm twelve. The girls at school have boobs, and I don't, not yet, and one day this girl, Mandy Templeton, she empties her carton of milk onto my tray and floods my lunch. "What're you gonna do," she says, "cry about it?" And then she calls me Baby-tits. "Baby-tits, Baby-tits," she sings.

We're at that age where, at lunch, boys sit with boys and girls sit with girls, but Aaron hears this and stands and walks over. He taps Mandy Templeton on the shoulder, and, when she turns, he punches her, hard as he can, right in the mouth. She hits the ground, screaming, spitting blood.

And even though she's a girl and Aaron's a boy and the rules of chivalry sort of demand things like this not be done, because Aaron's so small, always getting picked on and never—I mean *never*—standing up for himself, and because Mandy's known by students and teachers alike for being a bitch, Aaron gets ten days expulsion, and that's it.

Mandy's teeth never looked right afterward, and no one ever messed with Aaron again.

Here's another story:

Junior year, Aaron takes me to prom. We dance. We kiss. That's all we've ever done. The dance is over, and, instead of driving me home, Aaron surprises me with a hotel room.

We undress and get into bed. We touch each other. Then, just as he's about to put it in, I say, "Wait. I can't. I'm not ready." And, Aaron, he smiles. He strokes my cheek. He says, "Sure, Grace, okay," and takes me home. No fight, no fuss, not one word meant to make me feel bad.

I was so grateful I couldn't get out of the car.

"I'm sorry," I said.

"Don't be sorry," he said.

And then I gave him a hand job. Right there in his parents' driveway, I gave him probably the best hand job ever given in the history of the world.

The next month, there was nothing we hadn't done.

Point is, high school guys don't work that way, but Aaron's always worked that way. And if the trade-off is that, a few weeks a year, he goes cuckoo, then that's a trade-off I'm willing to take.

Aaron's therapist calls him a *wounded bird,* but, I ask you, who wouldn't care for a wounded bird? What kind of person sees a bird with a broken wing, cat on the horizon, and walks on by?

And so I buy the water. I tape the windows. I hunker down with Aaron, and, when I can, I get him to take his medication, knowing that, in a few days, it will kick back in and the man I love will come bubbling up from the ocean floor. He'll break the surface. Exhausted, he'll rest his head on my shoulder and say that I deserve better, and I'll tell him to shut up, and I'll rub his back and he'll sleep and I'll watch.

I carry the extra gallon upstairs. It's Thursday, our shared day off, but Aaron's parents are at work. I wonder whether they've noticed the change. Most episodes, they don't. When it comes to Aaron's parents and Aaron's illness, check the sand. That's where you'll find their heads.

I head back downstairs, and Aaron's still trying to make room for the jug. Finally, he gives up. He pulls the honey jar down from the high shelf, uncaps it, and sticks a finger in. He puts the finger into his mouth. He does this a few more times. He doesn't offer me any, and I don't ask. Off his meds, Aaron can be thoughtless, but I try not to make him feel bad. Guilt's not a motivator when he's like this. Guilt only makes things worse.

He fastens the lid and returns the jar to its place on the shelf. He lies down on the bed, and I lie next to him. The sheets are musty, unwashed.

"It's going to be tonight," he says. He shudders. There's a pillow under his head, and he pulls it up and over his face.

"How do you know?" I say. I may as well be asking a toddler how the spaghetti sauce got all over the walls, but I have to try.

"I can feel it," Aaron says, voice thin through the pillow. "It's here."

"How does it happen?" I say.

Aaron is quiet so long, I nudge him just to make sure he hasn't smothered himself. When he jumps, I realize I've woken him. He throws the pillow across the room. It hits the TV and falls to the floor.

Aaron pulls the remote from his pocket and turns the TV on. According to the news, there's been a strike in Pakistan. Something to do with American missiles. Something to do with the threat of nuclear armament. The anchors theorize. *Which countries have the bomb? Which don't? Tune in at ten to find out*—that sort of thing. It's nothing you don't see every few days, but it's all the evidence Aaron needs.

"If there's a detonation, even a hundred miles away, the fallout alone will keep us underground for ten years," Aaron says.

That's a lot of bottled water, I want to say. Instead, I tell him that it's all right, that no bombs are falling, that I'm here.

I don't know where Aaron gets his information. Maybe he makes stuff up. Maybe he's trying to scare me, or maybe he believes what he says. Some of it he gets online. I know from his laptop's browser history, which is war and death and almost never porn.

"I love you," I say.

Aaron changes the channel. More Middle East, more death.

The pill bottle is on the dresser by the bed. I uncap it. The next part, I have to be careful.

"How about some medicine, sweetie," I say, and Aaron knocks the bottle from my hand.

I'm on my hands and knees, picking up the little white pills, when Aaron says the country's started testing new poisons on its own people. "They drive them out to New Mexico and gas them," he says.

"I'm sure that's not true," I say.

The first pill's the hardest, but it's only the beginning. They're antipsychotics, not miracle drugs, and sometimes it's a week before they kick in. Even if I can get this one into him, I have a long road ahead of me.

"It's totally true," Aaron says. "I saw footage."

I let it go. I pick up the last pill.

"I'll make it worth your while," I say.

I stand and pull off my shirt.

"We just did that," he says, and I point out that we didn't do *everything*.

Aaron pops the pill, and I go down on him.

Do I feel bad? Bad for using my wiles to get a pill into Aaron's gut? I do not.

He groans. He's just been inside me, and I don't even want to think about what I'm tasting, and, before I know it, it's over.

There's no basement bathroom, so I brush my teeth over the kitchen sink. When I move back to the bed, Aaron's asleep.

◆　　◆　　◆

It's almost midnight when he wakes. I'm watching a TV movie, and Aaron puts his hand between my legs.

"Not now, sweetie," I say. I'm tired. I'm worried. I turn the TV off.

"For me?" he says.

I tell him to take another pill and we'll talk. He takes the pill and pulls down his pants.

"Not until you wash it," I say.

He sighs and moves to the kitchen. I laugh, watching him from the bed, his little butt flexing as he stands on tiptoes, trying to get himself stretched out over the sink. He gives up, goes upstairs, and, when he comes back down, he's already hard.

I'm in no mood, but a deal's a deal.

I get to work, he comes, I clean up, then I roll onto my side.

"I love you," he says, and I hear him move to the pantry, hear the honey jar lid come unscrewed followed by a quiet, occasional slurping.

"Wake me up for the end of the world," I say, and Aaron says, "Don't worry, I will," no trace of irony, sarcasm, any of it.

He'll laugh when I tell him. When he's well, we'll have dinner someplace nice. We'll celebrate another episode overcome. I'll repeat the things he said, and he'll shake his head, embarrassed, but also amazed.

"I don't know," he'll say. "I don't know what gets into me." And he'll reach across the table and take my hand and squeeze.

The TV comes on and Aaron turns the volume down low. I feel a hand on the back of my head, and I hope it's not the one covered in honey. He smooths my hair, and I think how this is maybe going to be an easy one. In March, Aaron and I spent an afternoon under the bed. In May, he stayed in the basement, lights off, for a week. I'd leave for work and come home to cups brimming with piss. At the end of the week, it took a day's worth of laxatives to empty him out.

In the morning, I'll call Arby's. Aaron's boss knows the drill and, to date, has been surprisingly accommodating. Aaron has five days paid vacation left for the year, but I'm hoping to get him back to work in a day, hoping one of these years, by the end of the year, Aaron will have some days left and we'll go somewhere the way people go places when they're young and in love.

"Aaron," I say. "I need you to take your medicine."

"I will," he says, but his hand stops smoothing my hair.

"Promise," I say. "Promise me that in twelve hours you'll take another pill."

"I promise," he says.

Here's what I know: I know that, one of these times, it's not going to be so easy. One of these days, no matter what I do, I won't be able to get Aaron back on his meds. What I don't know is what comes next. This is *my* fear, the fear of the unknown.

And, in this way, maybe Aaron and I aren't so different—two people afraid of things beyond our control. Except that, in the end, I have a pretty good idea whose nightmare is destined to come true.

The mercury's rising, ice caps flattening into the sea. We've got dams collapsing and power plants blowing sky-high, plus enough bombs to make the earth's surface match the surface of the moon.

The end of the world? It could happen. No one's denying that.

But it's the end of Aaron that scares me.

◆　◆　◆

I wake. I turn to put my arm around Aaron, but all I get is pillow. The TV's off, the room dark. It's still dark outside. I check under the bed. I check the cabinet below the kitchen sink. I check upstairs, then I go back to bed.

But I can't sleep. Aaron doesn't leave the basement, not when he's like this. This is new, and new is scary, and, after a few minutes, I rise and turn on the lights. I move to his side of the bed. There's a sock on his dresser, weirdly out of place. Beneath the sock, I find the pills, chalky, deformed, and I wonder how long each stayed tucked under his tongue before I looked away. This worries me, but not as much as what I see next, which is the honey jar empty, licked clean.

I tell myself no way could he be where I think he is, but, nights like this, I know better than to underestimate Aaron, and I don't even bother to tie my shoes.

I'm up the stairs in seconds, out the door and running through the yard in a T-shirt and panties. My laces strike my ankles like the tongues of snakes. There's a half-moon, and it slicks the driveway in a wet, ivory shine. The garage door is up and the lawnmower's been pulled out. Gardening tools scatter the driveway like a tornado came and hit just the garage. I run faster, into the neighbor's yard.

I've never seen her backyard, only the bees that rise from it. The perimeter is a fence of wood planks too high to climb, but an open gate tells me which way Aaron went. I pass through the gate and a floodlight flicks on.

And there, in the lamplight, is Aaron. And there is the hive. It's just a white box, a white, wooden box half a coffin in length.

I don't see any bees.

No, what I see is Aaron with a rake in his hands. He's standing as far back from the box as he can, reaching with the rake in what I can only guess is an attempt to pry open the lid. The rake quivers in his hands and the wide metal fan combs the hive.

Also, he's got an EpiPen in each leg. They bob from his thighs like banderillas from the back of a bull.

I don't know what a jarful of honey and two shots of adrenaline do to a man, but Aaron doesn't look good. He shakes, almost convulsing, back heaving with every breath.

I could call 911. I could run back to the house and pick up the phone, but by then it would be too late.

"Aaron," I say, and he jumps.

"Stay back!" he says. "It's not safe!" He turns, and his face glistens, soaked, like ten years' worth of tears just poured out of his eyes.

I'm a few yards away, and I take a step closer. I don't want to scare him. I don't want him making any sudden moves.

"I wanted to surprise you," he says.

"I'm surprised," I say. "Please, sweetie. Come back to bed."

"I'm not tired," he says.

His arms tremble and the rake scrapes the box. From some-where, a bee rises and swims, lazy, in the air around us.

"Aaron," I say. "I want you to put the rake down. Now."

Perhaps they're sleeping, I think. Perhaps, at night, the bees go to bed and don't fly and don't sting. God, I want to believe it.

I take another step forward, and Aaron shrieks.

"Stop!" he says.

I hold up my hands like a bank teller on the wrong end of a gun.

"I just want to help you, Aaron," I say.

Somewhere in the beekeeper's house, a light comes on.

"I ate all the honey," he says, fresh tears fattening his cheeks.

"I don't care about that."

"No," he says. "It's not fair. You didn't get any."

"I did," I say. "Remember the pear? I had some. I'm fine. The rest was for you." I take another step. "I don't even like honey all that much."

The rake slaps the hive and rattles the lid.

"Don't *lie* to me. You love honey. I know it."

A bee lands on the rake, then lifts back into the sky. Another circles Aaron's head.

I take another step. I'm close. If I lunged, I could grab the rake, but I don't know about Aaron. He's little, and I'm thinking I could take him down, but I worry what it will mean if I'm wrong.

A window opens above us and a head pokes out.

"You kids crazy?" the woman calls. "Get away from there! Get away from there right now!"

A hum has started up in the box, and that can't be good. It sounds the way a button sounds when it's come loose from your shirt in the dryer, only multiplied by, like, a thousand.

"Call 911!" I yell, and the window slams shut.

"Aaron," I say. "Aaron, I want you to put the rake down and come inside."

He's looking right at me, but it's like he can't hear me, can't hear past the grim determination to do the thing he set out to do.

He looks at the hive, and a bee lands on his shoulder.

My own tears are coming now. I'm no crier, but I can't help it. Because it's my fault. Because I shouldn't have slept except when he slept. Because, finding him missing, I can't believe I went back to bed. *Those five minutes,* I think. In those five minutes, I might have found him, stopped him before he left the garage.

"Once the bombs fall, there won't be any honey," Aaron says, his voice garbled and faraway-seeming. There are bees in his hair, bees covering the lid of the box, a patina of bees with fat abdomens and bright wings. Their wings shine like diamonds in the security lights, and I give up the hope that Aaron hasn't been stung.

When we were kids, our moms took us to play at a park with monkey bars and swings and a slide. On one side of the playground, a red pipe rose like a snorkel from the earth. It connected belowground to another pipe that rose from the other end of the park. Each pipe was fitted with a megaphone the shape and size of a showerhead and perforated by the same tiny, black holes. I'd stand at one end and Aaron would stand at the other, and, across the playground, we would throw our voices at each other. Our words came out cavernous, like shouts from behind closed doors. We giggled. We practiced cursing. We told dirty jokes. And, one day, Aaron said, "I love you." I laughed, and Aaron said, "I do, Grace. I love you." We were ten years old, and we've said it ever since.

"It's for you," he says now, and his voice arrives like an echo, like it used to when he told me he loved me before either of us knew what loving the other meant or what it would mean.

The first sting is in my side. I see the bee caught in my shirt. It wriggles, trying to get free.

"All of the honey," he says. "For you."

I leap. I knock Aaron to the ground and pry the rake from his hands. I fling it like a javelin across the yard, far from the hive, and I sit on Aaron's chest, hands pinning his wrists to the lawn.

A door opens, and a storm trooper steps out. Or that's what

she looks like, our neighbor dressed in white, some kind of bee-keeper's suit and what looks like a watering can at her side.

Her face is hidden behind something like a mask made for fencing, but, when she speaks, her words pierce the mask, clear and unfiltered.

"I don't know what you kids are up to," she says, "but, for the love of God, please don't move."

They say that, with enough adrenaline, you can do anything. You hear stories of men wrestling torn arms back from alligators and mothers lifting cars off their kids. I'm on top of Aaron, but I see too late that the weight of my body is nothing compared to what courses through his veins, and I see that I've failed him again.

"Please," I say, and then I'm in the air. I'm flying. I'm falling. I'm tumbling, and I hit something, hard. The hive comes apart, the buzz turns to roar, and the moon, like magic, goes out of the sky.

I hear grunting and turn to see Aaron dragging himself toward me on his elbows. He's like a soldier passing beneath barbed wire. The woman in the bee suit stands over him, pumping a thin fog from her can into the air.

I feel a sting, then another. My legs are lightning, and, soon, I can't even look at Aaron, who's no longer crawling, but rolling, a man on fire.

I look up, into the night, into the heart of the pulsing, vibrating ceiling above.

And then the swarm descends, looking, for all the world, like the end of the world.

Refund

The evening began in argument. Luke's first-grade teacher had called a parent-teacher conference, and Joy and I were expected that night at school. This was not the standard midyear check-in. For months, we'd been getting notes. Luke wasn't finishing his schoolwork. Luke didn't play well with others. Luke wasn't paying attention in class.

Dinner was over, the table cleared of everything but a cup, a fork, and my son's plate. On the plate sat a sad mound of boiled-to-death broccoli.

"No cookies," Joy said. "No dessert until dinner's done."

Luke had never been big on vegetables. Even as a baby, he'd spit out anything green.

"Broccoli's good for you," my wife said.

"Not like this," Luke said. "Boiled vegetables have no nutritional value. That's what turns the water green, the vitamins and minerals. What's left is fiber. And fiber just makes you poop."

My son, six years old.

Joy sighed and shot me a glance. "C'mon, Sam, back me up on this."

In the pantry, the Oreos waited, their torn cellophane and the stale ones I always skipped on my way down the row to the cookies that still snapped when halved. I said nothing. A limp stalk hung from Luke's fork, wet and terrible, and all I could think was how I hadn't eaten mine.

Luke didn't whimper. He didn't whine or cry. He was a quiet kid. If he had complaints, he kept them mostly to himself. His fork rose, pushed the pale, little tree past his lips and into his mouth. He chewed, eyes closed, hating it.

"Let the kid have an Oreo," I said.

Joy's look let me know that, once again, I'd fucked up. We were supposed to be a team, to put up a unified front. But we both knew who was Abbott in this marriage and who was Costello, who looked like the idiot and who called the shots. And, even if I got the boy's laughs, it was Joy who got the last good-night kiss, the first hug home from school.

Luke shoveled what was left on his plate into his mouth, chewed, and chased the broccoli down with milk from a coffee cup, the blue one with the steam engine circling the side.

"Very good," Joy said. She pulled the Oreos from the pantry. Our rule was two, but, because he'd been such a good boy, Joy gave him three. Luke beamed and squeezed her arm. That *I* had been his Oreo advocate had, it seemed, slipped his mind.

Joy was always doing this, stealing the moment. Just that morning, I'd surprised the family with breakfast, only for Joy—Luke stumbling, sleepy, into the kitchen—to cry, "Look, honey, pancakes. We made you pancakes!"

There was no *we* about it as Luke pushed his face into Joy's hip, hugged her leg. Then she got to sit with him, butter his cakes, and ladle warm syrup to his liking while I was stuck, sweating, behind the griddle. My fear was that she would leave me, and, that morning, it was as if I was out of the picture already, pushed past the mat, past the frame.

Luke was now on Oreo number three.

A man shouldn't marry someone smarter than him. He does, and he'll spend the rest of his life feeling like something less than a man. Joy was smart. She'd gone to college, graduated debt-free on her parents' dime. I'd done college too, but Joy was crazy-smart. And, any argument she couldn't win with logic, she'd win by riling me up.

"I'm going for a walk," I said.

"Hmmm?" Joy said, ignoring me and . . . something else. Was she? She was! Slipping Luke Oreo number four. Motherfucker!

"I said I'm taking a walk."

"In this weather?" Joy said.

I slipped on my jacket, my hat and shoes.

"Well, hurry," she said. "We have to meet Luke's teacher in an hour."

⁂

Walking the neighborhood's what I did when I was angry, when I was tired but couldn't sleep, when I was bored. But mostly when I was angry.

And so I walked. In rain, I walked. In rain and tornadoes. In ice storms. Around me, the houses of River Run Heights huddled for warmth, rooftops licked by moonlight. Icicles hung from rain gutters and made mouths of windowsills. Driveways glowed gray beneath streetlights.

Across the street from the neighborhood stood the school. Tall and boxy, it rose into the stratosphere. Who'd ever heard of a four-story elementary school? But Atlanta land was at a premium. Desperate architects were reaching new heights of creativity and whimsy.

That week, we were in the grip of an ice storm, the city's first in two decades, and so the windows of River Run Elementary hovered in suspended animation, frosted, opaque. Standing on my front lawn, I watched the school awhile, my breath coming out in clouds, then I turned and made my way, cautiously, down the driveway to the sidewalk and into the neighborhood.

We belonged to the neighborhood and we did not. The land behind us had been bought up once we moved in. The developer offered good money for our lot, twice what the house was worth, but Joy and I were newly married and very much in love. Which isn't to say that we finished each other's sentences. It is to say that we didn't need words, as though whole conversations were exchanged—whole worlds erected and razed—with a smile, a wink, a nod. The implications, of our first home wrecking-balled into oblivion, we found unsavory and metaphorically problematic. That was then. Now, I'd have traded the house for the cash were it not for the school, a good one, the kind of school Joy wanted for our son.

So, we'd stayed and were accepted, reluctantly, into the development. Our neighbors didn't hate us, though most kept their distance. We were enemies of symmetry. We'd thrown off the development's feng shui, imperiling property values. In the end, we scored free lawn service, plus access to tennis and two pools. In exchange, a concrete marker the size of a compact car was lowered by crane onto our lawn. In imitation marble, it read: RIVER RUN HEIGHTS. And, below this: A KEN BUTLER PROPERTY.

I circled back, down side streets and past houses with turrets, until I came to a small, white house leaning into the wind. The house was not like the others. It was old and without brick, and it was ours. With its mossy shingles and peeling paint, our house failed to advertise River Run Heights' grandeur, just as the neighborhood failed to live up to its namesake: Amid the property lines and cul-de-sacs of the developer's wet dream, there was not now—nor had there ever been—a river. Instead, there was a dry creek bed that, come spring, trickled runoff approximating, in both color and odor, the pleasures of raw sewage.

Inside, my family waited for me.

All I had to do was open the door. Then we'd bundle our boy in his warmest coat. I'd sling his train bag over my shoulder, we'd each take a hand, and, with Luke between us, Joy and I would cross the street. We'd take small steps.

◆　◆　◆

The elementary school was well-lit and clinically clean. We followed our son up three flights of stairs, Luke bounding the whole way, Joy and I pausing at each landing to catch our breath. The stairwell smelled like paint and character education. Each wall was plastered with artwork, the deformed dogs and amputated cats of childhood rendered in finger paints. Everywhere were smiling suns and happy rabbits. On a wall left over from November, Native Americans and Pilgrims enjoyed a smallpox-free feast.

Miss Morrell met us at the door. She was a stern-looking woman, tall, in her thirties, with dark eyes and dark hair that hung to her shoulders. Her bangs had been cut to fall in a sharp line across her forehead. The line seemed to balance on her eyebrows. She led us to her desk. A pair of chairs faced the desk, and we filled them. Joy emptied Luke's train set onto the floor. He sat and began fitting track together.

"Well," Miss Morrell said, "you must be very proud."

Joy and I looked at each other. Then Joy nodded, though neither of us knew why she was nodding.

"You got my memo, yes? The yellow sheet in Luke's Friday folder?" Miss Morrell drew in an exaggerated breath. "Okay," she said. "The reason you're here is that we would like to enroll Luke in River Run Elementary's Gifted and Talented Program. It's not curriculum replacement, but it *is* enrichment, enrichment that we believe Luke needs."

There was a long pause before Joy asked, "So, he's not in trouble?"

Miss Morrell returned our look of confusion with one of pity. I recognized the expression. It was the one Joy gave the Kroger bag boy, Down Syndrome Doug, whenever he bagged meat with bleach or lowered a melon onto our bread.

"You may have noticed that Luke isn't like other boys his age," Miss Morrell said.

Joy nodded, and I knew that, later that night, I would get the I-told-you-so talk of the century. From infancy, Joy had speculated that Luke was unique. I figured he was but hadn't wanted to give Joy the satisfaction of knowing he'd gotten more of her genes than my own. Now, she had the confirmation she needed.

"The first graders take IQ tests," Miss Morrell continued. "Luke's score is several standard deviations above the mean. He fell into the hundredth percentile."

"That's wonderful," Joy said.

"It's beyond wonderful," Miss Morrell said. "I'm not saying he's bright. I'm saying that your son is effectively smarter than ninety-nine percent of his first-grade peers. Nationwide." She leaned back in her chair and crossed her arms, as though to let that sink in.

"Well, so is everyone in this room," I said. I reached down and ran a hand through Luke's hair. He was intent on his trains. He didn't look up.

Miss Morrell leaned forward. She uncrossed her arms, grabbed the lip of the desk, and squeezed her knuckles pink.

"Mr. Davis," she said.

"Call me Sam," I said.

"Sam," she said, "I don't doubt you're smarter than a first grader. But I will tell you that if Luke's development is allowed to proceed uninterrupted, if his intellect is properly nourished, then his mind will surpass everyone's in this room. And I don't mean by a little." She let go of the desk. She leaned back, looked at us like we were a couple of assholes.

I knew what she was thinking. Here was the mother who sold makeup and the father who got by in telemarketing. Like our house, we didn't look like much. And here she was thinking of the apple, how it sometimes falls far from the tree. Except that, like I said, we weren't idiots, Joy especially, just underachievers, people who'd settled into the steady income of easy, after-college jobs, then, getting older, let our chances at better work pass us by. I won't defend our choices, but I won't apologize either.

On the floor, Luke had assembled his wooden set into a circle. One train waited on the tracks while he added an engine and caboose to another. The assembly was taking longer than usual, maybe because he'd been listening, maybe because he was wallowing in his puffy winter coat. Sitting there, fitting together toy trains, he didn't look all that special.

"You have to understand," Miss Morrell said. "Most parents

would kill for a kid like yours. Parents *beg* me to place their children in the gifted program. I've turned away bribes."

Joy and I knew these parents. At fund-raisers and picnics, on skate nights, conversation invariably turned to the kids: which children were walking by one, potty-trained by two, reading by four. When Luke was reading at three, I wanted to be thrilled the way Joy was, but what I wanted, really, was for my boy to be normal, to be like me.

"I've always known Luke was special," Joy said.

Miss Morrell nodded. She'd found her ally. Already I could see her joining Joy in the fight, and I hated this woman for it. I hated the way she looked at me. I hated her hair, those bangs like a black gash opening up her pale forehead. But mostly I hated how she talked like Luke wasn't in the room.

I turned to the window. From the fourth floor, the view of midtown was striking: River Run Heights's cluster of homes and the tall buildings beyond, the city blued by night. All the world was ice. I imagined Miss Morrell pushed out the window and flailing the way villains do when they fall from high buildings in bad movies.

"We owe it to Luke to see that his potential is reached," Miss Morrell said. She spoke slowly, succinctly, eyes and bangs blazing. "We'll do everything we can for him at school, but you two . . ." She paused, watched me, resumed. "You need to create an environment in the home that fosters learning."

"What does that mean?" I said. I knew, but I was tired of playing along.

"It means," Miss Morrell said, "that you do whatever it takes."

On the floor, Luke brought two trains together in a head-on collision. He pulled an engineer from the cab of one and pantomimed a spine-crushing dive to the tracks below.

"I'm on fire!" he yelled. "Help! The pain! The pain!"

The other engineer joined him, screaming, "Stop, drop, and roll! For the love of God, man, stop, drop, and roll!"

The plastic men were spun up and down the tracks. They muttered in fiery agony.

"Look, Joy," I said. "Our boy's a genius."

*   *   *

I made my money on the phone. At work, I was given products to sell and the telephone numbers of those to whom I should try to sell them. A bad job for someone with my disposition. People swore at me. Most hung up within seconds. The danger of such work is that you get used to this. You start thinking everyone on earth's awful when only *most* everyone is.

Joy worked part-time at Lenox, Atlanta's fanciest mall. Her job was selling cosmetics to average-looking women who left her counter looking like supermodels. "This lip liner," she would say, "will change your life." She talked and women listened. Her targets were the sad, the disenchanted, those desperate to believe in the restorative power of an eyebrow pencil. These women surrendered startling sums of money, unaware that, at home, they'd never be able to duplicate what Joy had done.

"They don't know it's not the makeup," Joy said. "It's me, these hands."

For years, she'd tried to persuade me to sit for her.

"Men's makeup," she said the last time. "It's never really taken off, but you'd be amazed. You can't even tell. No one would know you're wearing it." With men, she explained, it wasn't about accenting. It was about concealing. "Just imagine," she said. "Blemishes. Broken capillaries. The creases at the corners of your eyes. All of it: gone."

"Never going to happen," I said. "No guy wants that."

"I could make you look twenty again." She studied my face, sighed. "Twenty-five."

In the end, the work I did and the work Joy did wasn't so different. We caught customers unaware, at the dinner table or walking through the mall, then we pressed our merchandise upon them.

Difference was, Joy was good at what she did. That, and her clients loved her.

She'd finish, turn the mirror, and they'd sigh. And she'd buy into it, sure she was destined for something better than the mall and the life she had. Some nights, she'd come home talking about how if she'd only gone to grad school, if she'd only started showing her art young, as though she'd picked up a paintbrush in ten years. In the garage, her canvases leaned in a dusty stack.

"Go back to school, then," I'd say, knowing she wouldn't.

Joy was talented and she was smart, but she was also afraid the way we're all afraid. What happened if she put herself out there, studied, painted, cast a line and nobody bit? And so she'd settled. She'd settled on me.

◆   ◆   ◆

The next night, Joy got home late laden with yellow bags. Each bag sported a blue label that read BABY GALILEO. Joy dropped the bags and joined me at the kitchen table.

"I stopped at the education supply store," she said. "It's where teachers shop. Miss Morrell recommended it."

"Okay," I said. I stared at the bags. There were six of them, each overflowing. "But what's all this?"

"Well, I've been thinking about Luke's learning environment and how we can foster it." She pulled items from the bags. Picture books, workbooks, thick tomes on parenting: *Your Special Child* and *Pick My Brain*. I picked up *Pick My Brain*. On the cover, a well-adjusted-looking boy, hair stiff with hairspray, overalls starched, sat in a chair and puzzled over a Rubik's Cube. He wore sensible shoes and an expression that said: *This is all well and good, but my real passion is long division.*

I flipped to the author's bio.

"MD and PhD," Joy said quickly.

"Then we're in good hands," I said.

The corner was torn from the dust jacket, the place where, in small black print, the price would have appeared. I set the book on the table. I reached into a bag and pulled out a shrink-wrapped bundle of CDs.

"Music," Joy said. "Classical. For the synapses."

"Synapses?"

"They're stems, like these little hairy carrots in the brain. If they don't connect, Luke won't be able to learn a foreign language. The lady at the store explained it." In case I still had doubts, she added, "It's scientific."

"That may be," I said, "but we have libraries. We have the Internet."

I moved to the floor. Spilling the contents from the remaining bags, I was surrounded by shiny, pricey merchandise: Maps (geographic and constellation) slipped from their long plastic cylinders. DVD cases advertised happy children. A small, heavy box marketed itself as the first safe, child-friendly chemistry set. NO ACID, NO GLASS, the box bragged in splashy red letters.

"Christ, Joy," I said.

"I knew you'd do this." Already Joy was standing. "I knew you'd take one look and make me the bad guy. Well, excuse me. Excuse me for caring."

"That's not fair," I said.

Joy ripped into a green box. "I want what's best for our son."

"This is our entire holiday budget." I lifted a bag and shook it. "Right here. You think, Christmas morning, Luke wants to unwrap Mozart?"

Joy dropped the box. It hit the table, and beads spilled out, hundreds of them. They dropped to the floor and scattered like insects, small and scared and black.

Joy's thumb traced the hem of her shirtsleeve. "He might like Mozart," she said.

"Oh, bullshit."

"You've never appreciated how smart he is."

"That's not true. I just want the kid to have fun, to get a few toys at Christmas."

"We can still get him toys," Joy said, but, when she nudged a Baby Galileo bag with her toe, I saw she knew that we couldn't. She looked up and admired the ceiling, a practiced move for keeping tears from spilling over.

"It's okay," I said. "We can return these and use the money to buy normal toys."

"That's what you'd like?"

"That's what I'd like."

"For Luke to be normal?" she said.

"Luke is *six*," I said. "I don't care how smart they are, when it comes to Christmas, kids who are six want baseballs, they want bicycles, not"—I pulled a box from a bag, held it up—"not '*Kiddie Accountant: The fast-paced coin-counting game that's fun for the whole family!*'"

"We can't deny Luke the mental stimulation he craves."

"Craves?" I said. "Where's craves? I see a kid who enjoys a steady diet of Play-Doh and crayon wax, but I don't see craves."

"I won't let you hold him back." Joy took a deep breath, exhaled, sat. She put a hand on my knee, and a shiver ran down my spine. It was the most intimate moment we'd shared in weeks.

"Haven't you noticed that Luke has no friends? None. He's not like other kids. He needs to be challenged."

"Great," I said, "then we'll get him friends, gifted friends, and they can all play abacus together."

"I'm serious."

"So am I. I'll find the kid friends. When I'm finished, he'll have so many friends it'll be a fucking sitcom."

"I'm done," Joy said.

She stood and left the room. I heard her move through the bedroom we hadn't shared in months to the bathroom that, out of convenience, we shared still, heard her shower, flush the toilet, brush her teeth.

I rose and made the rounds, extinguishing lights and locking doors. Then I returned to the kitchen. On my hands and knees, though, picking up beads, I couldn't stop thinking about Luke's synapses.

For the first time, I was worried about the welfare of my son's hairy carrots.

•   •   •

I was determined to find children like Luke, and, in the end, the neighbors did the work for me. Not forty-eight hours had passed before the phone rang.

It was Devon Tweed, the Englishman who lived four doors down. "The house with the purple wreath hanging from the portico."

"Yes," I said. I did not say that I had no idea what a *portico* was.

As it turned out, there was already a group dedicated to the gifted youth of River Run Heights. The children numbered five and gathered on Friday evenings. While the kids played, the adults enjoyed card games and wine.

"We meet fortnightly," Devon said.

I rolled my eyes, but, for Luke's sake, I would make a good impression. Still, something troubled me.

"How did you hear?" I asked. "About Luke."

Devon let loose a throaty laugh.

"This Friday," he said. "It's the last gathering before the holidays. Do come."

I waited for him to say "Ta-ta" or "Cheerio." Instead, I got only the click of a cradled receiver. It was a sound I was used to.

Joy was beside herself. "What do we wear?" she said.

"Clothes, I imagine. Unless they're beyond all that. Clothes," I said, trying on my best Devon Tweed, "clothes are the coverings of peasants and vagabonds."

Joy shook her head. "Don't mess this up for Luke."

"Skulduggery," I said.

"I'm not kidding," she said. "I'll leave you."

Those words, she'd glared them and stomped them and slung them with the slam of a shut door, but she'd never spoken them out loud.

"Don't threaten me," I said.

"It's not a threat," Joy said. "I'm serious as fuck."

"You can't take my son from me."

"Don't mess this up," she said, "and I won't."

I walked. Oh, that night, how I walked.

◆　◆　◆

When I got back, Luke was in bed reading from a picture book called *If It Runs on Rails*. According to Joy's parenting books, obsession was a common trait among the gifted. *Obsession* was not the word the books used, but obsession is what it amounted to, the tendency of the gifted to cling to things, to identify themselves as experts in a chosen field. Among the young, common interests included dinosaurs, horses, and space exploration. Luke's thing was trains. He couldn't get enough of them.

I came in, and he sat up, his locomotive comforter bunching at his waist. He wore a Thomas the Tank Engine shirt.

"Dad," he said, "I bet you can't guess the top speed of Japan's fastest bullet train."

"Bet I can't," I said.

"Come on," Luke said. "*Try.*"

"Hundred miles an hour."

"Ha! Try twice that."

I sat on the bed. Luke pulled the comforter aside and scuttled into my lap. "Look," he said. He held out the book, and I took it. In the picture, a train traversed the Asian countryside. Trees traced the track. Mountains rose, majestic, in the distance. The train was a blue-gray blur. I admired the picture for what seemed an appropriate amount of time, then put the book down.

"Listen," I said, "I have good news. You know how Miss Morrell said you get to be in a special class?"

Luke nodded.

"Well, you get to be in a special club too."

"A club?" Luke said. He frowned and his brow furrowed. He had remarkably bushy eyebrows for a child. It was the single feature we shared, the thing picked out by anyone who saw a picture of me as a kid.

"A special club," I said. "With special kids like you. Kids from the neighborhood."

"Will Marcy Jenkins be there?" Luke said.

"I don't know," I said.

"Because she kicks me," Luke said. "On the bus." He lifted the cuff of one pajama leg to show me his shin, the two green-brown bruises there.

"Maybe she likes you," I said. But the bruises, they looked fierce.

"No," Luke said. "I know what you're talking about, but not Marcy. Marcy pretty much hates my guts. She calls me Butt-Face."

Bitch, I thought. I pictured a girl run over, pigtails flattened, face black with the latticework of fat school bus tires.

I rubbed my son's legs. "I'm sorry," I said. "I'm sure she won't be there. This is a club for good kids, like you. So, what do you think? Want to give it a shot?"

Luke thought it over. A night-light the shape of a steam engine dusted his face gold. He left my lap and crawled back under the covers.

"Okay," he said. "I'll give it a shot."

"That's my boy," I said. I stood, then bent and kissed his forehead. "Good night."

"Oyasumi nasai," Luke said.

"What?" I said.

"That's how they say *good night* in Japan."

I moved to the doorway. I watched Luke for a minute, and, watching him, I saw him for the first time not as a father does but as another first grader might. He was puny, and his brown hair, cut in the shape of a bowl, stuck up in back. His front teeth betrayed a gap that would one day need braces. And his glasses, resting in their plastic case on his bedside table, were too big for his face.

"Luke," I said. "The kids at school, do many of them pick on you?"

Luke studied the wall. He seemed to consider the question, then he turned his head, looked me in the eye, and said, "Yeah."

Before then, I hadn't recognized it, the power of a single word to make you suddenly, unaccountably sad.

"Everything's going to get better," I said. "No more bullies from here on out, I promise."

I was a liar. I was a man spinning promises from sadness, the kinds of promises life's least likely to let you keep.

◆   ◆   ◆

A week before Christmas found us shivering on the front stoop of the Tweeds' massive brick house, Joy and me, Luke between. The purple wreath hung, as promised, from the ledge above the front door.

"You know," I said, running my hand along the ledge, "in England, they call this the *portico*."

Luke and Joy stared at me. Through the O in the wreath and a window in the door, I saw a fireplace and a fire and a number of people milling about, dressed up, drinks in hand. Joy licked her palm and smoothed Luke's hair, running her thumb along the part. She wore her best coat and a dress she'd sworn wasn't new but which I'd never seen before. I'd agreed to a blazer but drawn the line at a tie. Ties were for weddings or when someone died. Even at work I didn't wear one.

Before I could knock, the door opened to a tiled foyer and a wide staircase and a girl. Judging by the look on Luke's face, I knew exactly which girl this was.

Marcy Jenkins was not cute with blond pigtails. Marcy Jenkins was wide of body and forehead, a young linebacker in training. Her lips were puffy. Her eyes bulged. The gap between her teeth was more spacious than my son's.

I'd kept the secret of Marcy to myself. I'd told myself I didn't want my wife to worry. But, Joy at my side, unalarmed and smiling at the bulldog-faced child, I knew the truth: Luke had given something to me and *only* me. And I didn't want to share.

Marcy smiled, performed a weird little curtsy, and said, "Hello, Luke."

Luke said nothing. He grabbed my pant leg.

"Won't you come in?" she said.

We stepped inside.

"You must be Samuel." Devon Tweed stepped into the foyer, extending his hand.

"Sam," I said. Devon took my hand and crushed it between his two, pumping with zeal. He let go, helped Joy with her coat. His eyes lingered on her chest.

"The children are on the second floor," he said.

And then Marcy was up the staircase, not waiting for Luke.

Wide-eyed, my son stood at the bottom of the stairs. I crouched and pulled him toward me.

Joy gave me a look. "He's fine," she said, then, turning to Luke: "Go upstairs, honey."

Slowly, pitifully, Luke mounted the staircase. At the top, his fingers gripped the banister. He watched us.

"It'll be okay," I said. I hoped it would be okay, wanted it to be.

Devon Tweed ushered us into the living room, where glasses were fitted into our hands, wine poured. Neighbors we'd never met gathered round, smiling, expectant. I'd imagined Joy at my side, us against them. But, soon, she was drifting, talking, as though we weren't together, were, instead, two people who'd happened to arrive at the same time.

"Thanks for having us," I said at last, and the crowd nodded, a sea of khaki and Christmas-themed sweater vests. All of the holiday icons were in attendance: Frosty, bisected by buttons, top hat in hand; Rudolph, nose like an angry red pimple; and jolly Santa Claus, squat in his sleigh, a cadre of tired-looking reindeer braced to do his bidding.

"We were so pleased to hear about Luke," said a tall woman with stringy red hair. "I've been telling Frank," she said, elbowing a man, presumably Frank, in the side, "that you live in the little house behind the River Run sign. But he didn't believe me!"

She laughed and another woman laughed, and Frank looked into his drink. Everyone seemed to search everyone else for the proper reaction. Then Joy smiled, raised her glass, and laughed, and everyone chuckled, smiled, exhaled. I chewed the inside of my cheek. I was already ready to leave. I wondered about these people, whether I'd ever interrupted their dinners, whether any had hung up on me.

The couples proceeded to introduce themselves. There were the Tweeds, Devon and Marie, and their dear friends the Martins, Judith and the aforementioned Frank. There were the Rays, Al and Debra, college professors both, and the Porters, Ted and Sue, the couple closest in age to Joy and myself. He was an electrical engineer. She was a *baby engineer*. She practically squealed this, patting her waist for a few laughs.

Then there were the Jenkinses, Tag and Meredith. Like the offspring they'd spawned, they were large people. Big-hipped and pendulous of breast, Meredith Jenkins had half a sofa to herself. Her husband stood behind her. His hands draped her shoulders like steaks.

"Our Marcy simply adores your boy," Meredith said. "She's been looking forward to this all week."

"That's wonderful," Joy said.

Yelps and footfalls echoed from upstairs.

"They have so much energy at this age," Tag said, clapping a hand to his wife's back.

"I know," Joy said. "Luke wakes up and hits the ground running. How he does it, I'll never know."

Her words were stilted, not her own, like she was choosing each one with care.

"He looks like you, you know," Devon said. "Luke has your eyes." Joy's wineglass was half full, but he topped it off. He smiled at her.

Joy smiled back. "That's a lovely Picasso," she said, pointing to a print on the wall. *Lovely*, a word I'd never heard pass her lips. *These people aren't us*, I wanted to say, but Joy needed this, their validation, that and whatever she thought they could do for Luke.

"Oh, thank you," Marie Tweed said. "Devon picked that up in Florence, was it?"

"Paris," Devon said, and Marie said, "Of course."

"You like art?" Devon asked.

Joy sipped her wine. "I'm a painter," she said.

I laughed. This got everyone's attention, which, once I had, I didn't know what to do with. Had Joy said, "You know, I do a little painting," or, "I used to paint," I would have smiled, nodded, let it go. But I'd lost it. I had no patience left for Joy and her art degree or the Gentleman Tweed and his wandering eyes, no patience left for the promise I'd made not to mess tonight up. I shrugged off my blazer.

"Joy sells makeup," I said.

"Of course," Meredith said. "I *knew* I recognized you. Lenox, right? I bought blush from you once. Only, when I got home, the color was all wrong."

"Too funny," Marie said, but you could tell she didn't think it was. Her party was in danger, the mood souring.

Joy didn't find it funny either. Across the room, she shot hot, eat-shit daggers at me from her eyes.

The upstairs, I noticed, had grown suspiciously quiet.

"Well," Devon said, turning to Joy, "I think I speak for all of us when I say that we'd love to see your work sometime." He offered more wine, but Joy's glass remained impossibly full. She was being extra-careful. Two drinks, and she got giggly. I drained my glass, moved between my wife and Devon. I pulled the wine from the man's hand, filled my glass, then handed back the empty bottle.

A door opened, and from the kitchen emerged a woman I hadn't seen. She was dressed in gray, not quite a uniform, but not normal clothes either. She whispered into Marie Tweed's ear.

"Oh," Marie said. "The children's dinner is ready. Darling, can you call them?"

Devon moved to the bottom of the stairs and called up for the kids.

We all listened, heard quiet, then a laugh.

"I'll check on them," Devon said.

"Let me," I said, and, before anyone could argue, I started up the stairs, legs wobbly with wine.

At the landing, Luke's T-shirt and red caboose sweater lay tangled. I followed a hallway toward the sound of laughter and found Luke's pants folded neatly on the floor. At the end of the hall, I opened a door to the Tweeds' bedroom. The room was enormous. A wide canopy bed stood against one wall. Along other walls towered mahogany dressers and a chest of drawers. This wasn't the IKEA assemble-yourself set that Joy and I had saved up for or even something more expensive, say Ethan Allen. The furniture looked one-of-a-kind, probably imported from France along with the Picasso print.

I heard whispers. There were two doors. The first opened to a walk-in closet and a row of suit coats arranged by shade. Racks of many-colored sweaters scaled the walls. Leather shoes lined the floor.

The second door opened to the master bathroom, its marble floor and claw-foot tub, and to Luke. He stood on the lid of the toilet seat, arms at his sides. He was in his underwear. A thick coat of red lipstick streaked his face. Two crimson ovals encircled his nipples. Ribbons of toilet paper ringed his chest and circled his legs. The gifted and talented children of River Run Heights crowded around him, hushed now that I'd entered the room.

Luke saw me and he did not cry. Except for Marcy, the children looked terrified. Marcy met my eyes, then held my gaze with steely determination. The others ran from the room. Luke didn't move. Marcy stood her ground.

I knelt, grabbed the girl, and pulled her to me. I held her by the arms and squeezed too hard. I pictured welts rising to the skin's surface, bruises taking shape before morning.

She was a child and it was unforgivable, and I didn't care.

Marcy's eyes widened. She looked down.

"Look at me," I said, and she did. "Get. My. Son's. Clothes." I let go. "Now!"

She didn't run. With whatever remained of her dignity, Marcy left the room at an ordinary pace. She appeared a minute later with Luke's clothes, set them at my feet, turned, and walked away without a word. I shut the bathroom door, then turned to face my son.

He'd begun to shiver. A strip of toilet paper, torn, fluttered from the elastic waistband of his underwear.

"You said she wouldn't be here," he said.

"I'm so sorry," I said.

"When I asked, you didn't really know if she'd be here. You shouldn't have said when you didn't know."

I nodded. "You're right."

He held out his hands, and I took him into my arms. I pulled the toilet paper from him. I wetted a washcloth with warm water and wiped the lipstick from his mouth. It was only when I dabbed at the red circles on his chest that Luke began to cry.

It took a long time. When I was done, Luke's face and chest were raw, smeared pink, and the washcloth was ruined. I dropped it into a ceramic trashcan. Luke covered his face and cried, quietly, into his hands. The lipstick lay on the floor, its tip ground into the tile like an accusation. I threw the lipstick away and rubbed the tile with a tissue until it came clean. Marie Tweed's makeup case stood open, and I shut it. The toilet paper was bundled and flushed, the roll returned to its tube on the wall. I tried to make it like we were never there.

Luke stopped crying and I helped him dress. He held the sleeves of his shirt while I fitted his sweater over his head. He sat very still while I tied his shoes. Then he took my hand and we made our way downstairs and out the front door.

We were two houses down when Joy caught up to us on the sidewalk.

"What's going on?" she said.

I looked at Luke. His expression was not unlike Marcy's moments before I'd come to my senses and relaxed my grip on her arms. He let go of my hand.

"Luke was ready to go," I said. "That's all."

Joy studied us, then squatted so that she and Luke were eye-to-eye. "Honey?" she said.

Luke was mute. She ran two fingers over the boy's brow. He flinched, took my hand again. Joy stood. She watched me for a long time, recording the moment for later when she'd say, *I could have used your help back there, you know?*

I knew then that she'd made up her mind, made it up even before buying the dress she now smoothed against her hips. I knew then I'd sent my son upstairs for nothing.

"Fine," she said. "I'm going back for our coats. And to tell the Tweeds that we had a nice time. And to apologize." She turned and marched up the sidewalk. Every few steps, she paused, then shuffled over a patch of ice.

Luke still held my hand. Wordlessly, we turned and walked home.

◆   ◆   ◆

That evening, getting ready for sleep, Joy let me have it. I sat on the edge of the bathtub. Joy stood at the sink, face pasty with cold cream, a towel curled on her head like a shell.

"We'll be lucky if those people ever ask us back, the way you two took off," she said. "I was *mortified*."

"Is this about you or Luke?" It had been a long day. I wanted the fight over, even if that meant making Joy cry to end it.

"I mean it," she said. "I refuse to let you screw up our son. You think you know what's best for him, but you don't. You don't listen to the experts, and you certainly don't listen to me. You haven't cracked one book I bought."

Untrue. One, I'd read cover to cover, but I let it go. I'd lost interest in defending myself.

"You said you'd take those books back," I said.

"No," Joy said. "*You* said I'd take those books back. I agreed to no such thing."

I couldn't shake it, the thought of Luke perched on the toilet, his nipples, the lipstick. All of it my fault.

Joy pulled a pair of tweezers from a drawer. Staring into the mirror above the sink, she brought the tweezers to her face and pulled a single, creamy hair from the center of her chin.

She watched my reflection in the mirror.

"One thing," she said. "I asked you for one thing, and not even for me. For Luke!"

They say a relationship is over when one person walks out. Maybe not the first time, but well before the last. You interrupt fights with a door in the face, with keys in the ignition or a walk around the block, and you call it blowing off steam. And, though you don't know it yet, you're walking out on more than the moment. You're walking out on your marriage.

This was what I was thinking as I stood and moved to the door. Months, I'd walked out on our arguments. Months, I'd imagined the man Joy saw in me, a noble man working hard not to lose his temper, when all she'd seen was her husband hurrying away.

I turned and walked to her.

"Okay," I said. "Do me."

Joy staggered like I'd sunk my fist into her stomach.

"You have got to be kidding," she said.

"I'm not asking you to sleep with me." I uncoiled the bath towel from her head, folded it, and dropped it into the laundry hamper. I opened the linen closet and pulled down the purple polyester satchel of men's makeup. Joy watched me with something like wonder. I sat on the lip of the tub, cradling the bag in my lap.

"Last chance," I said.

Silent, Joy brought a hand towel to her face, wiped away the cold cream, then knelt on the shaggy mat at the foot of our bath. She pulled a box from the purple bag. Across the front of the box was stenciled "Jeffers: Men's Line," in blue curlicue.

"Close your eyes," Joy said, and I did. "Don't open till I say *when*."

I felt her hands on my face, the first dab of cream on my cheeks.

"Will we make it through Christmas?" I asked.

"Don't talk," she said. "You'll mess me up."

She ran a comb through my eyebrows, pulled with her thumbs at the corners of my eyes.

"Will we make it through Christmas?" I asked again.

Something cool swabbed my forehead. My chest tightened with anticipation.

"Okay," Joy said. "Christmas."

If we could do that, then what kept us from continuing? If we could only make it to New Year's, to Valentine's Day, St. Patrick's. Holidays like stepping-stones, and who was to say we couldn't cross the river that way, or keep going, until—

"Keep them closed," Joy said.

Her hand was on my chin, polishing, kneading, and I could smell the night's wine on her breath.

For a while, I felt Joy's hands on my face, and then I didn't.

Then there was the telltale click of her tools on the counter, the shuffle of slippers out the door.

I wondered whether I'd open my eyes to a clown face or maybe a woman's, whether she'd made me up like one of the guys from Kiss. A good joke. I might even have laughed.

The bathroom lights, after I'd had my eyes closed so long, were headachy and bright. The boxes and products, little brushes and cotton balls, cluttered the countertop. Beige smears stained the sink's silver faucet and knobs. Tissues littered the floor like scabs.

Finally, I faced the mirror.

From the look of things, she'd used only powders and creams. There was no lipstick or eyeliner, no whiskers or rosy cheeks. The consummate artist had done the good job she'd always promised to do. Anyone who knew me maybe could have told, but I understood now what she'd meant. I didn't look like a man wearing makeup. I looked young, like a younger, healthier version of myself. A version of myself from better times.

And I wondered whether it was this, seeing me this way again, that had sent Joy from the room, sent her out before I'd opened my eyes.

◆   ◆   ◆

Luke's room was warm, but cool at the window, where the frost crept in and grew veins in the glass. I stood at the window and took in the view of where, so many nights, I'd walked. In one direction, streetlights followed the sidewalks, lawns tucked into their curbs like blue blankets. In the other direction ran the main road and the power lines that hummed in their jackets of ice. Then there was our house, our small house, caked in crystal and caught between, old and ready to fall over. Soon, I imagined, we'd sell and the neighborhood would gobble it up, our house knocked down and a new one put up in its place, a house that matched the rest.

Luke rolled toward me. The train night-light illuminated his face. His eyelids fluttered in sleep, and I knelt beside the bed.

Right then, the thought came that I could scoop him up, could be out the door and in the car in seconds. We wouldn't need clothes or toothbrushes or food. We'd just drive. Or, better yet, we could hop a train. We'd be stowaways. Together, we'd trade Atlanta for Wyoming. Or Montana. Somewhere wild. Somewhere no one would find us.

"Luke," I said. He stirred. I cupped a hand over my mouth. I wanted so badly to believe that I was as much his world as he was mine.

He slept. He slept.

Tomorrow, I would collect all of the Baby Galileo products and dump them into the trunk of my car. I would drive to the store, pile everything beside the register, and demand a refund. I didn't care about store policy. I didn't care about receipts or time limits or torn packaging. I would make the return. I would get our money back. And then I would go to the toy store and buy everything with a train on it that I could find.

The bed was too narrow for both of us, so I stretched out on the floor, close as I could. I felt the cold at my back, the cold coming through the wall, but I knew that under the covers my boy was warm. With the sunrise, he'd see me, or else his hand might slip over the side of the bed and touch my hair. He'd find me in the morning, was how I imagined it, find me there, his father, awake and waiting for him.

Knockout

It did not end in one of the usual ways. It did not disintegrate or implode or go up in flames. Max and Allison Bloom's marriage ended in a five-round fight in a ring on their front lawn.

All morning the vans came and men got out, and by night a ring was erected. All day we spotted flyers: on telephone poles, on windshields, plastered to the windows of the Piggly Wiggly. The flyers advertised the match and the boxers: Max "The Adulterer" Bloom and Allison "Soon to Be Smith" Bloom, a husband-wife lineup. NOT TO BE MISSED! the flyers screamed in red letters.

And miss it we did not. That evening, we took our seats hesitantly, lined the sidewalk and spilled into the street. The neighborhood buzzed with gossip and talk of what this might do to property values. Bets were made on the fight. Money changed hands. Neighbors, who had not seen each other in months, clasped hands, patted backs, and turned to watch a couple beat each other up.

Max and Allison faked and jabbed, bobbed and weaved. For a moment, we wondered if this was all in fun, a show, something to bring us together. Then glove hit skin. The first uppercut Allison took made us flinch, but it was she, after all, and not Max who had boxed in college, and so we resigned ourselves to the sight of a man hitting a woman. And Allison got in her share of shots. Jumping around the ring, she let us know whose idea this had been.

By the end of round three, Max's front tooth was loose and his nose was a cherry tomato. And before round five, before the final blows that sent them both to the mat, gasping, those of us close enough, those of us with ringside seats, heard the whispered pleas to the trainers in their corners: Max saying "I don't want this. This isn't what I want," and Allison, red gloves gripping her knees, hair slick with sweat, both eyes purpled and swollen shut, Allison saying only "Cut me."

Last of the Great
Land Mammals

She's still waiting when Arnie pulls up in the truck, tires spraying gravel. A curve of jaw, the weekend beard, shows through the window tint. He has on flannel, a checkerboard of red and blue.

She stands and turns. The stump she'd been seated on is smooth, rings blurred by a century of sittings. The sides sag, soft and damp. A spine of yellow mushrooms climbs the trunk like Frisbees someone's hammered into wood. There's grit under her nails from where, the last hour, she's worried the bark.

She knows Arnie's behind her before she feels his hands on her waist, before she bends into the abbreviated hug. It's enough, for now, and they separate.

"Maddy's soccer game," he says. "Sorry."

"It's all right," she says.

She's learned to wait, sometimes for hours. It used to upset her, but it doesn't upset her anymore. He always shows up. The waiting, that's just part of it.

He's married, and she's waiting for him not to be. He'll never not be. She knows this and she doesn't. She knows it and at the same time thinks: *Someday*.

In a heartbeat. That's what she told him. In a heartbeat, she'd leave the man she married.

But Arnie won't leave his daughter, his wife, his house or his yard, his money, his dogs. Far as she can tell, everything is as he likes it—his cake, her too.

So where does *she* fit in? What is she to him?

She is cuff links. She's a pocket watch. A thing slipped on for special occasions.

♦   ♦   ♦

Linda looks good. Tight jeans and a shirt he can see her nipples through. And—these are new—boots. They're leather, the sides fringe-lined. The toes are something. Each comes to the kind of point you could chop wood with.

Her lips are red, her face done up, but, the look she gives him, it's like she hasn't decided if she's happy he's here. Some days, he knows there'll be trouble. Days with no makeup. Days a comb hasn't touched her hair. Those days, they'll talk, she'll cry, and he'll leave feeling bad. Days like that, they might not even fuck, which is kind of the whole point.

Those days make him miss the way things started, before sex was a given, when this, all of it, was startling and new, like when he was a boy and he first watched the hand reach in, in *Indiana Jones*—how the hand left the man's chest, the heart and the fist around it, pulsing.

Those first times together: the shock of the body, white, shadowy beneath the sheets. The weight of pearls on the tongue. How she didn't feel like any girl he'd been with. How, now, she feels nothing like his wife.

The sex is great, don't get him wrong, but *this*. In some ways, it's his favorite part, the meeting place, the place they go *before*. Any place will do—bus station, museum, shopping mall. His favorites, though, are places with animals. The zoo, the game ranch, the aquarium in Newport with its loggerheads and moray eels, the tube that steers you through the tank of sharks.

Tentacles, fur, these put him in the mood. Four legs: *Good.* He can't explain it, would never tell her. But, then, you could fill a book with things he's not telling people these days.

Their rule: Each month, somewhere new. And there are only so many animal hot spots in Ohio. Even considering the tristate, it's like a riddle: How close to Cincinnati can you stay before you run out of menageries?

This one, the state park in Kentucky, came like providence. Maddy's birthday party, a sleepover, and one of her friends brought along a stuffed buffalo. He'd been, like, "Hey, that's some buffalo," and the child said, "Bison," and he said, "Nice bison, then." She let him examine the tag, which read BIG BONE LICK. A joke, he thought, porn-perfect. But then he was online, looking it up, and there it was: Big Bone Lick State Park. Which was when he learned that *lick* wasn't just something you did with your tongue. It could also mean *salt spring or exposed mineral deposit, the kind frequented by animals*. In this case, *lick* translated to *basin full of bones*. Here was a place the last of the great North American land mammals had come, ten thousand years ago, to lick their last. Here they had come to taste some salt, slip into a tar pit, and die.

"Romantic," Linda had said. Her voice on the phone always sounded pinched and distant.

"And, get this," he said. "*Bison*. They have a *herd* of *bison*!"

"Aren't they mean?" she said, and he said, "No, no. You're thinking bulls. Bison are gentle giants. They're like manatees, but on land."

"Manatees," she said.

"Equivalently," he said.

He promised to take her wherever she wanted afterward, which, he knew, meant somewhere fancy.

Now, the two of them beside his truck and her in these boots, her saying nothing, he's not sure what kind of day it will be. And this, the not being sure, it's enough to make him want to hop back in the truck. Because he can't stand the thought of it, another sobbing, face-in-the-pillow day—and, lately, there have been more and more—another round of *If you love me, leave her*.

But, then, he hasn't given Linda a chance. He owes her that much.

"Nice boots," he says.

Linda looks down. "No place like home," she says. She gives the heels a click.

He waits. What she says next could make or break the day.

And, then, she is smiling, she's moving, she's saying, "Come on," working those boots across the gravel lot, walking like she knows where she's going.

◆   ◆   ◆

She *hates* the expression. How come no "kissing sisters"? Why no "fucking uncles"?

They can't be the only ones. But, if it's so widespread, so common there's a name for it, how come she's never met anyone like them?

◆   ◆   ◆

What he calls *fucking*, she calls *making love*. And where they fuck/make love depends on who picks.

He likes motels, stucco-walled and neon-bright. Places they bolt the TVs to bureaus and telephones to tables. Places they don't bother asking, "Smoking or non?" Places that make you pay cash up-front.

It's not that he can't afford nice things, far from it. It's the *chaos* of a place he loves, the mismatched furniture and threadbare sheets, the coffeemaker someone's used and not cleaned out, the *art*—if that's the word for it—all those seagulls and beachscapes in cheap pastels. A place like that, he can *relax*, because in no way does it remind him of home—home's white walls and careful rooms and the maid keeping everything clean, clean, clean.

His favorite motel room, the one about which Linda said, "Never again," boasted a watercolor of a blue heron. The usual, except that someone had pried the frame loose and returned the picture, corners curling, to the wall. The hook poked through the canvas like some profane, silver tail sprung from the heron's head.

That room had a sink that ran hot water but not cold. The water came in staccato bursts, rousing from Linda the kind of profanity that he thought might liven things up in bed. They tried it, but, really, it wasn't Linda's style, and the dirty talk left them feeling even weirder than usual.

Linda likes nice places. She likes resorts, bed-and-breakfasts, places where the rates aren't tacked to billboards that overhang the highway. Linda likes wherever there's wallpaper or white china or rugs so plush the fibers reach between your toes to tickle the tops of your feet.

Her favorite's a golf resort and spa they frequent in Indiana, the one by the riverboat casino. Neither of them golfs or gambles, nor have they seen the inside of the spa. They stay in, mostly, watch TV, order room service, drink wine, and do what they came to do.

The suites come with bathrobes, his and hers. Soon as they arrive, she puts hers on. She takes it off for sex, sometimes not even then. He never changes into his. Before they go, she returns hers to the closet. The robe hangs next to his, and always she seems sad to leave them there, suspended, their middles cinched by belts.

◆   ◆   ◆

Today, they begin with the museum, one room and a winding hallway that details the park's two-century history. Before it was a park, she reads, Big Bone Lick was a dig site. Before that, it was a stop on Lewis and Clark's cross-country expedition. Mostly, the museum is dusty skulls in glass cases. The bones are mammoth and mastodon and giant sloth. The cases gleam, bright with track lighting, greasy with fingerprints, and she can't help thinking what Windex and paper towels could do for the place.

She stops before one of the displays. A bone, coffee-brown and long as a broom handle, fills the case. She thinks of Charlie on Halloween night, bounding across the kitchen, singing the song he'd brought home from school: "The thigh bone's connected to the *hip* bone . . ."

Arnie leans in. "Big bone," he says, his voice a cartoon cave-man's. He steps closer, their shoulders touching, then she feels it, her neck, his tongue. "Big bone *lick*."

She moves out of reach, looks to be sure no one's seen.

"Christ," she says, and Arnie laughs, like it's a game.

The corridor dead-ends in a gift shop, T-shirts and park para-phernalia mostly. A wire carousel of postcards creaks at her touch. A shelf of shot glasses announce: LICK THIS! She wonders how long the park resisted before getting in on the joke.

Arnie moves to a bin of stuffed animals and pulls out a bison, brown with gray horns. He carries it to the register, where a woman waits in a green state park shirt. Glasses hang from her neck on a cord of tanned leather. She buffs her fingernails with an emery board.

"These," he says. He holds up the bison. "Where can I find them?"

The woman is older, tired-looking. She gives Arnie a look that seems to say she'd be polite if only they paid her more. She gestures toward the gift shop bin, then returns her attention to her nails.

"No," he says. "The real ones. You know, the kind that snort and eat grass?" He gallops the stuffed animal over the countertop, a bison pantomime.

The woman sighs. She lays down her file, blows on the nails of her right hand, then pulls a paper map from a rack beside the register. She unfolds the map, points, refolds the map, slides it to-ward—but not quite to—Arnie, then picks up her file and begins work on the left hand.

Arnie leaves the bison on the counter. He turns, and now he's moving toward Linda, grinning, goofy-looking in his enthusiasm.

"Oh give me a home . . ." he sings, and the excitement must be contagious, because, suddenly, she feels it too, a thrill, and, forgiving his carelessness—because, really, what are the chances that, way out here, they'll see someone they know?—she lets him take her hand.

◆   ◆   ◆

Practice.

That's what he called it the first time. Because what else *can* you call it when you're horny and fourteen and trying to get your cousin to kiss you? Linda was fourteen too, both of them too old never to have been kissed.

"It's not like it counts," he said. "You still get to have your first kiss. It's just practice so that, when the first kiss comes, you don't mess it up."

Linda's expression advertised her skepticism.

They'd spent the afternoon at the public pool and now lounged in damp swimsuits in front of the television, their skin pimply with air-conditioning. As kids, they'd run through the sprinklers with their shirts off while, on the back porch, their fathers sipped scotch. But those days were over. Her parents weren't home, and he hadn't seen Linda shirtless in a decade. The summer had filled in the blank of her bathing suit, and, just to catch a glimpse, just to kiss her, the idea was almost more than he could bear.

On TV, an earthquake shook an elevator still, and Zack delivered Mr. Belding's baby. The theme music kicked on, and the credits scrolled.

"Never mind," Arnie said. "I was only kidding anyway."

Except that, right then, Linda scooted across the carpet. She was close to him, then closer. Their knees touched.

"Just practice?" she said.

He nodded.

"Promise?" she said.

He couldn't speak, could barely catch his breath as her eyes closed, her face scrunched, and her head neared his. He shut his eyes.

The first kiss was quick, was hardly a kiss at all. Their eyes opened, shut. They tried again.

◆   ◆   ◆

Get-togethers make her edgy. Those dinners or afternoons when it's the six of them, Arnie and his wife, she and Frank, the children.

Charlie and Maddy kicking each other under the kitchen table, and all she can think is that it starts with kicks, then it's mouths, fingers, and tongues.

It's not that she doesn't like his wife. There's nothing *wrong* with Anne except that she's married to Arnie. Apart from that, Anne's kind. She's generous. She makes good pies.

And Frank and Arnie get along fine. They like the same movies, same sports teams, same beer. Standing in the garage, they'll smoke cigars and contemplate for hours the finer points of Ping-Pong or the intricacies of a table saw.

Watching them together, she can't understand it.

"Frank's a good guy," Arnie will say. "What's not to like?"

"But doesn't it drive you crazy?" she'll say. "Seeing him? Knowing, when you're not with me, he *is*?"

She wants this to drive him crazy, wants to know that, when they're apart, Arnie's at least *occasionally* overcome with grief. She wants the thought of Frank, of her—of Frank on top of her—to make Arnie want to strangle the man.

But Arnie only shrugs. "I like knowing you're with him," he'll say. "You're safe with him. You could do a lot worse."

She wants to shake him. It's been twenty years. They've been seeing each other in secret longer than they haven't. Except, she had her chance. After his father died and before he married Anne, Arnie extended the invitation.

"Let's just come out with it," he said. "Come out, and fuck what people think."

She'd offered all the old arguments: Their mothers would disown them. Their friends would freak out. And their jobs, who knew?

Arnie was patient. "Cousin-fucking," he said, "is not grounds for termination."

"No," she said.

"Please," he said.

In the end, it was Linda who said, "Never," and Arnie who moved on.

Her predicament now is like when Charlie was younger, when they'd play Candy Land or Life. Her son would roll the dice and land on a square that sent him back. "Do-over!" he'd scream. "I want a do-over!" When she didn't let him roll again, he'd scream and scream. Sometimes he'd holler until his throw-up choked him and he ran, crying, from the room.

Yes, that was what she needed now, a do-over, the chance to prove Arnie right, to prove they should have been together all along.

But there'd been a chance, and she couldn't imagine the day when there would be another.

◆   ◆   ◆

The trail winds through the woods, and he's walking fast because he can't wait to see the bison. He's trying to remember whether he's seen one before, seen one anywhere besides in a book or on TV. He doesn't think he has.

"Picture it," he says. "These things side by side with mammoths, with saber-toothed tigers, and they're what's left."

He's decided there must be something special about the bison to have cheated history and made it out alive.

At fifteen, he watched his father use a tire iron to turn his mother's face into something from a horror movie. She lived, made her son swear he'd never become that man, and he hasn't. He's become something else—adulterer, cousin fucker—but his father? No. He's never hit his wife or wanted to.

It's in him, though, whatever made Dad do it. He feels it, the pull toward recklessness, toward *wild*.

Sometimes he just wants to *he doesn't even know what*.

His father's dead. Pulled over for a DUI, he unloaded a revolver into the policeman's chest. When the other officers arrived, they found him handcuffed to the car. "I done it," he said. "I done it myself, so there." This didn't keep the cops from pummeling his father in the name of their fallen friend, a beating that led to hemorrhaging, then death, a beating that a woman with a camcorder got on tape, start to finish. The lawsuit that tape triggered left Arnie with a cool two million.

He loves the money, though, secretly, he'd trade it all to have been there, to have said, "Hand me a baton," to have shaken the other men's bloody hands clean at the end.

His father is dead. Not so the mighty bison.

Survival.

"An animal like that has dignity," he says.

He throws a hand up to the woods around him, as though, any second now, a bison might come lumbering through the trees.

"An animal like that demands respect!"

And he sees she's no longer at his side. Linda's seated on the footpath ten yards back, her hands at her ankle.

"These boots," she says.

He kneels before her and takes her feet into his lap.

"My little Cinderella," he says. He pulls off one boot, then the other.

Her feet are swollen, red.

"Boots like these," he says, "you have to break them in."

He lifts one foot and rubs the heel between his palms. The toes curl like shrimp. He wants to fit the foot into his mouth.

He says, "I wonder if their hooves ever hurt."

"What?"

"The bison," he says. "Their hooves."

She groans. "You and your fucking bisons."

"The plural of bison," he says, "is bison."

It could end any number of ways.

They could be caught. Unlikely, but it could happen. The thing about sleeping with your cousin is that you'd have to try hard to get caught. People see you in public, they think: *How nice that family gets along so well.*

There's pregnancy to consider—that accidental henchman. Linda's not the type to get rid of it, so they'd be stuck with who knows what. Some three-eyed monster. Some tangle of however many limbs.

But Linda's on the pill. She doesn't want another kid, not his and not Frank's. If she wanted to trap him, that's not how she'd do it.

How *would* she do it? An announcement, maybe. Linda, at dinner, standing before his wife and daughter, her husband and son, saying, "Since we were fourteen, Arnie and I have been in love," after which Frank would punch him in the nose, the kids would cry, and Anne would leave him.

And he can't have that. He loves Linda, but he loves Anne too. And he loves Maddy most of all. Seeing her today, working the ball up and down the field, blasting it from grass to sky, past the goalie's gloves and into the net, he knows he couldn't stand it, a divorce, anything that meant weeks off and on.

No, the way things are, it will have to do. There was a time. Now, though, once, twice a month with Linda—it's enough.

Her feet are hot in his hands. He's rubbing, rubbing.

"Carry me," she says, and he does. He expects the weight he feels at parades or amusement parks, Maddy on his back. But Linda's heavier, too heavy. Before long, his knees hurt.

They follow a trail of yellow, bison-shaped markers. Sunlight struggles through the canopy and the day grows sticky. Still, he presses on, past pines that threaten to swallow the path, branches closing in on either side, a labyrinth of needle-thickened limbs.

◆   ◆   ◆

Through the trees, she sees the bison, sees them even before Arnie steps into the clearing. No other visitors have braved the heat or the hike, and they're alone. A chain-link fence cuts the clearing in half. It rises nine, ten feet high. From the fence hang signs. They read: NO TRESPASSING and KEEP OUT. The animals can be aggressive, the signs warn.

Beyond the fence, the bison loom like cows on steroids. She

counts twelve. The largest has horns like cornucopias. The rest have less dramatic horns. Even the little calf who weaves among the bent necks, among the mouths that graze like the mouths of cattle, has horns. The calf butts a bison across its flank. The larger animal flicks its tail.

Their hair is brown and black, matted and patchy, and she wonders how they can stand the heat. Not far from the bison is a gleaming, silver trough, but the water seems a small consolation. She imagines the animals shaved, like dogs in summer, and wonders how much of their bulk is muscle, how much hair.

Arnie moves toward the fence. She's still on his back. Her feet throb. She carries her boots under one arm.

The boots were a gift, sweet and stupid, from Frank. She only wore them so that, when Arnie asked, she could say, "Birthday present," and he'd feel bad. But Arnie never asked, just as he never remembers her birthday. A week has passed, a week without a gift, a card, a message on her phone.

Arnie stops before a brown and yellow state park placard. The placard is titled ADAM'S HAREM. It seems the bison, all but one, are female, and they all belong to Adam. He is the herd's "alpha male."

"Now, that's what I'm talking about," Arnie says. He says it singsongy, joking. He laughs. Her body lifts as he leans forward, snorts and stamps a foot.

"Put me down," she says before adding, "please."

She's thirty-four years old. In fifty, sixty years, she'll be dead, and everything reminds her of this fact but him. With Arnie, she imagines she might live forever.

And what would it look like, to be with him at last?

It would look like Christmas morning:

Arnie curls beside her before the fire. His huge, brick house—now theirs—yawns around them. The hearth is lined with four cocoa-stained mugs. The floor is carpeted in torn wrapping and tissue paper. Outside, Charlie fits a carrot into a snowman's face while Maddy buttons his chest with charcoal briquettes.

And where have the spouses gone? What's become of Frank and Anne?

She doesn't like to think it, but maybe they're dead. A messy business, but over with so quickly. The kind of cancer that ravages the body and you're gone almost before you know you're sick.

Or else they've moved away, left her and Arnie with the children and run off to Mexico together. Even now, they're drinking daiquiris. No hard feelings.

And the children? The children are happy. They're well-adjusted. They never miss their other parents, never miss the way things used to be.

Arnie pulls her to his chest. His body keeps her warm. They watch the fire and wait for the New Year.

That's the dream.

Then, there's how it *would* be, and she's not so naive she doesn't know the difference.

Arnie would lose the house, that's a given. He'd lose half of everything, and so would she. The spouses would be bitter. The family friends would side with Frank and with Anne.

At best, they'd share custody. And what if Arnie only got Maddy two weekends a month? Already, she can picture Anne, vindictive. She'd show up late with Maddy Friday nights, arrive early on Sundays with someplace to be, Arnie fighting Anne for every hour.

It's her he'd blame, not Anne. "Your fault, Linda," he'd say. "Your fault my girl's good as gone."

In bed, Arnie's body would grow familiar as Frank's, and what then? What becomes of clandestine sex translated to the everyday?

In the end, resentment. And would Arnie take his father's lead? Would he drink or disappear days at a time? Would he raise a tire iron to her face?

The bison hide their faces in the grass. They eat and eat.

Arnie shrugs her from his shoulders the way one does a coat.

Her feet touch the ground, and now she's shaking because, oh God, all this time, and what has she been waiting for?

She sits. Her breath catches with the pain of pulling on the boots. And Arnie above, watching her with wonder, saying, "What is it? What on earth?"

If she could put it into words, she'd tell him that their two-decade experiment has reached an end. He'd ask: *Why now?* And she'd have to shake her head, unsure, understanding only that what's come before is gone and what she wants can't be. The future, the past—both are impossible.

Arnie seems to sense it, the approach of something that will arrive irrevocable. He seems to want to keep her from saying it.

"I'll take you anywhere," he says. "That place you like, the place with the robes."

For a moment, it's almost enough. She pictures herself in bed, Arnie beside her. She's in her robe, and he's in his. It's enough to make her take his hand, to let him lift her to her feet. But, with his touch, the moment is gone.

She doesn't cry. She doesn't collapse into his arms.

He'd called the bison *gentle,* and she wonders whether he believes this or whether it's the kind of thing he knows she likes to hear.

But they aren't gentle. All the signs say so.

She climbs the fence, and before he can follow she's across the field. The bison quit their grazing. Their heads lift. The calf tucks itself between two members of the herd.

She picks a bison and moves to it. She doesn't know whether age determines size in bison, but, if it does, she guesses this one's a scraggly teenager. Its head rears back. A blue tag marked "11" hugs one horn.

She's close, now, and Arnie's calling her name, yelling in a way that lets her know he knows just what kind of violence these animals are capable of.

She lays a hand on the bison's coat, and a shiver ripples its side. One eye, wet and wide, bobs in its socket. The nose, snot-slick, expels air with a tremendous snort.

Arnie rattles the fence, begging her back, and the other bison break away, bodies curving, tails twitching. They move across the field with a sound like a dozen bowling balls launched down a dozen lanes, the balls rolling and rolling, picking up speed and no pins in sight.

But her bison doesn't budge. It snorts and snorts. The eye rolls, hypnotized.

Arnie is climbing the fence, so she climbs too, and it's just like childhood, like summer camp, when she and a friend left their cabin in the night and rode the camp horses bareback. The bison's pelt twists in her hands, and she's up and over and aloft, the animal warm and trembling beneath her.

And now Arnie is over the fence, and now he is waving, sprinting, screaming her name, his face otherworldly, his voice a siren, and she's never seen him move so fast, and she is not afraid.

She kicks. She kicks again. She kicks once more, and, at last, the great beast charges. It ignores Arnie, moves right past him. It moves away from the fence, away from the other bison, in the direction of the open, uncomprehending field.

And, for a few glorious moments, just like that, she rides.

What the Wolf Wants

So, it's the middle of the night and there's this wolf at my window. He stands like a man on his back legs. His hindquarters bulge, all muscly and stuff. He's so silver he'd almost be blue in the moonlight, were there moonlight. But this is the suburbs, so, instead, he's almost blue in the lamplight, the streetlights, back porch security lights, light from the flicker of across-the-street TVs, the radiant glow spilling out of downtown. A lot of artificial illumination round these parts, is what I'm getting at.

Delusions aren't new to me. This last year, I haven't been getting much sleep. But, the longer I stare at the wolf, the more I realize he's no delusion—this one's *real*.

He's not a werewolf, not exactly. There's nothing mannish about him. No human hands or face. No pants. His balls hang immodestly between his knees. They swing in the breeze like something, like balls.

I shouldn't open the window, but I do, and he climbs in. I'm in just boxers, but his balls are out, plus, he's a wolf, so what does he care? I slide my feet into moccasins. They're my favorite, a gift from Tyler, leather with fur lining.

The wolf follows me to the kitchen, seats himself in my Rooms-to-Go Dynasty Collection dining room chair at my Rooms-to-Go Dynasty Collection dining room table. I want to put down a towel, something to get those balls off the chair's imitation maple laminate surface, but the look on the wolf's face tells me I'd best keep my hands away from his testicles.

"Coffee?" I say.

The wolf nods and does that thing dogs do, that bob of head, curl of lip, that almost-smile. His teeth *gleam*.

Wolves like instant. I learned this somewhere, Wikipedia, I think. I'd been out of instant since the eighties, but just last week stocked up on Starbucks, their new line, VIA. They won't call it instant, but instant's what it is.

I pour the coffee into a shallow bowl for him to lap from. I set the bowl on the table before the wolf. He blows on it to cool it down. He does this, and I think of my mother, how she taught us, me and my brother, to cool soup by blowing on it. It never worked, just like kissed cuts never hurt less. The first sip still scalded, but we pretended—me, Tyler, Mom. We drank our soup, pretending we could taste it, pretending our mouths weren't on fire.

The wolf does not pretend. The first sip burns. He lifts his head and howls. It's so loud, I cover my ears. He growls, and for the first time I wonder about the welfare of a man with a wolf in his house. My body parts, I like all of them.

The wolf watches me.

A toe's not the end of the world, I think. *I could lose a toe.* I bend to unslipper one foot.

"Yes," the wolf says. Here, I should be surprised, should be, like, "Oh, oh my God, it's a talking wolf, ahhhhh!"

But I'm not surprised, not really. Because why else *would* he be here, if not to talk, if not to ask a question or offer me wolfly counsel?

Except that it's not advice he's here to give, there's something he wants. And it's not a question he wants answered, or a piece of me to eat, it's my *slippers.*

"Moccasins," I say.

"Whatever," the wolf says. "Those are what I want."

"Anything else," I say. I'm hoping he'll take the chair. *Take the chair and your ball sweat with you,* I want to say but don't.

Let's be adult about this, I think. *Here you were, ready to give up a toe, and all he asks is one worldly possession, a souvenir from his big trip out of the woods.*

I consider furniture, clothing, maybe a nice household appliance. Something he can show off to all of his wolf friends and be, like, "See, I went *inside*, man. I went into the box with the roof!"

"Consider the Whirlpool," I say. Only two years old, the dishwasher's good, the kind you can load without washing things first. "Seriously," I say. "I tried it. Just like in the commercial. A whole cake went in there, and, when it was done? The dishes: *spotless*."

The wolf shakes his head.

I proffer an Emerson brand microwave, a Lands' End thermal fleece, a 2009 Storybook Mountain Vineyards Zinfandel, my favorite. "Fifty dollars, retail," I say. "Excellent vintage."

But the wolf, he needs none of these. Food he eats raw. Fur keeps him warm. And wine, well. Wolves, he informs me, drink white.

"The moccasins," he says. "Really, they're all I want."

I ask why. The wolf shrugs.

"It's rough out there," he says. "You ever had a pine needle jammed in your pads? Ever cross a snow-covered field in bare feet?"

I admit that, no, I have not.

"Try it," he says. "Try it, and, trust me, you'll be begging for moccasins."

I sigh. "Okay," I say.

I slip off the first moccasin, then the second. The stitching is yellow. It rises like Morse code through the leather. The fur lining is soft, white.

"Real rabbit," I say, and the wolf gives me a look like, *There's nothing that* you *can teach* me *about rabbit.*

I hand the moccasins over, and the wolf stands and steps into them. They're too big, but he tugs on the laces until they bunch up around his paws like tennis balls, the kind that Tyler fastened to the feet of his walker after he lost the first leg.

"They're all I have left of him," I say.

The wolf closes his eyes and lowers his muzzle, somber-like, an expression that says, *I'm real sorry* and *I'm still taking them* at the same time.

His tail wags.

"Gotta go," he says, and, before I can say goodbye, he's out the front door and down the driveway, running fast in moccasined feet.

I shouldn't have said what I said to my brother that Christmas: "Slippers? What the hell am I supposed to do with *slippers*?"

He'd just returned from Alaska, where I guess buying local was the thing to do.

"I like them," my mother said. She held out her matching pair. A tongue of tissue paper hung from one of the holes where the feet go in.

"I buy you a thousand-dollar Cuisinart espresso machine, the Tastemaker's Model, with dual espresso dispensers and an advanced steaming action wand, and all I get is a couple of lousy *slippers*?"

"They're moccasins," Tyler said. "Hand-stitched."

"They smell like dead animal," I said.

Tyler shook his head. His hair had just grown in. He'd lose it again before summer. From the casket, he'd look back at us without eyebrows.

"I don't know what to say," he said. "I'm sorry."

I stuffed the moccasins back into the box.

I was a bad person then. Maybe I still am. It's been a year, but it takes longer than that. I think maybe it takes a while to redeem yourself in the eyes of the dead.

I go back to my room. The window's still open from where the wolf came in, and I close it. Outside, more light's coming on, real light, the sun's pink peeking through the black.

I move to the phone by my bed. I call my mother.

Her voice, when she picks up, is soft, cottony. I picture her in her bed, alone in her big house on the other side of the country. The red Renaissance quilt I got her two birthdays back comes up to her chin, and there's fright in her eyes.

"Mom," I say. "There's a wolf at my window."

"Yes," she says. "There's one at mine too. I'm just now looking at him."

The Geometry of Despair

I. Venn Diagram

Every Wednesday, after dinner, we drive to the nondenominational church across town. Here, for an hour, a dozen of us sit in a circle of aluminum chairs in a small, well-lit room telling our same sad stories. Sometimes there's coffee. Sometimes there's chocolate cake. Usually, there's a tissue box that orbits the empty center of our circle like a misshapen moon.

Each week, Pam, our counselor, reminds us that it isn't a competition, that the goal of group therapy is not to outdo each other or to rank our circumstances. Misery, she assures us, cannot be measured. But our greatest comfort is in the comparing. Validation awaits those who tell the best stories. And, since talk won't bring back the dead, we make do with our little game of grief. What it comes down to is the following equation: If a train leaves Chicago at sixty miles an hour and another train leaves Atlanta at eighty miles an hour, when they both collide in Kentucky and everybody's babies die, who is the saddest?

There's Lydia, who had an abortion in order to finish college, then wanted the baby back after graduation. Then there are Lucy and Beth, with their multiple miscarriages. We pretend to feel sorry for them, but, really, they never had children they loved and lost. Then there's Dot and Drew, whose son was decapitated when he tried to drive home after too many tallboys. Granted, a tragedy, but at least they had him for eighteen years. And, hey, if they'd been better parents, who knows?

One week, a weepy, red-faced woman stops by. She introduces herself as Jenna, then tells us her story, and, for a moment, we have a winner. Her three-month-old died without explanation, and it wasn't until a year later, after interrogation by two cops and a coroner, that the husband admitted to shaking the baby. In this way, three became two, then one. Still, my wife says, it's not the same. Jenna has someone she can be mad at. Jenna has somebody to blame.

What happened to us, Lisa says, in poker terms, is like being dealt three of a kind. You go all-in and show your hand only to see that, really, all you have is a pair, and the whole time you're wondering how you ever mistook that three for an eight.

With SIDS, despair isn't tied to regret or what-ifs or whose fault. With sudden infant death syndrome, the only thing you want to know—after you wake with the shock that you slept through the night, after you sit up and stare and consider the silence, the stillness of the cradle, after you swallow your paranoia and go to the baby, only to feel the warm rush of panic again flooding your chest, after the touching, the holding, the shouting, the running, the phoning, the signing, right here, on the dotted line—after all of it, the only thing you want to know is *why?*

It's the question we ask each Wednesday, a question for which there is no answer. So, why do any of us return, week after week? Because, at the conclusion of every session, there remains a single, blessed assurance. In the end, all satisfaction lies in the certainty of this, our shared secret: that each of us knows we have it the worst.

•   •   •

The divorce rate for couples who lose infant children is almost ninety percent. Most couples split up inside of a year. Our own one-year mark a week away, I've decided that Lisa and I are no exception. It's not that we've stopped loving each other exactly, only that every time I look into my wife's eyes, all I see is my little girl. Lisa is holding out for a miracle, the thing that will bring us together, unite us in our sorrow. But the only miracle here is that we've lasted as long as we have.

Lying in bed, one tired Wednesday night after group, we consider what would happen if I left. This isn't the first time the subject's come up. It's not meant as a threat. I just want Lisa to be ready when I go.

Lisa hasn't bothered to wash her face, and her eyes are still bloodshot, her eye sockets mascara-stained. In the lamplight she looks like a sleepy raccoon.

"Where would you go?" she asks. She takes my hand, wants me to see she's taking this seriously, but she's exhausted, drained by the meeting. This, of course, is why I waited until now. Because I can't face Lisa when she cries. Because on any given Wednesday night, with no emotion left, we can talk about separation like two strangers discussing the weather.

"I'm not sure yet," I say.

"You don't have to leave," she says.

"Actually, I kind of think I do." I rub the back of Lisa's hand with my thumb. "I mean, we tried. We gave it our best shot. It's just too much. All of it."

And this is how we've come to speak of our dead child, as though saying her name will summon what happened back into being. Say *June* and someone might say *Jinx*.

"We can make this work," Lisa says.

I don't say, *We're doomed.*

I don't say, *What happened, it's going to haunt us as long as we're together.*

"Maybe," I say, "but not like this."

"If we just keep going to group," Lisa says, and I wonder if she believes this. She lets go of my hand, pulls the covers up to her neck. Beside me, she seems small, a frightened animal.

"I'm not talking divorce here," I say. "What do they call it? A trial separation."

"Right. Because those always have such happy endings."

"I just think we need some time apart."

"You. You need time apart. Not me. You don't know what I need."

That shuts us both up. When I speak again, I choose my words with care. "Lisa," I say, "I need this. I need space, some time to figure things out. Solve for x, you know? I want you to be okay with this." But I think we both know the truth. When I leave, it will be the end.

Lisa sits up. She puts one hand on her pillow, as though any second she might bring it down over my face. "Listen to you. Do you even hear yourself speak? I'm not a variable, Richard. You can't just take me out of your little equation and expect it to balance on both sides."

I don't want to cry, but suddenly I do.

"Lose me, and you wind up with less than you had."

"Lisa," I say, "please."

"No. Enough. You want to leave? Leave." There are tears in her voice, but she doesn't cry. She fluffs her pillow a few times, dramatically, violently, then pushes it against the headboard and lies down.

"You can't escape what's happened by leaving this house," she says, rolling onto her side. "The only thing you escape if you leave is me."

◆   ◆   ◆

The first thing they do when you lose a newborn is pump you full of drugs so you don't kill yourself. Lisa took the antidepressants, but I refused. I had my reasons. I wanted it to hurt, was certain I deserved the pain.

Have you ever been to a baby's funeral? There's an absurdity to the pageantry: the miniature casket, the floral arrangements done up in pastels. I don't remember anything the minister said. I only remember I couldn't breathe. Lisa sat on my right, my mother on my left. Each of them leaned in. By the end of the service, my shoulders were wet and my hands ached.

After, friends and relatives followed us home. "You shouldn't be alone right now," they said. Lisa nodded. She wore a smile I'd never seen before and haven't seen since. She was determined to do whatever everyone thought was best.

Something about death makes people bring food. In North Georgia, people still operate under the pretext of "southern hospitality." Neighbors whose names I'd never learned came bearing balls of aluminum foil.

"You'll never finish all this by yourselves," everyone said. Our guests set up card tables and folding chairs around the house. Our kitchen counter was transformed into a buffet. Soon, everyone was helping themselves to turkey and ham, noodle salad, little sandwiches cut into triangles.

The air was full of the aroma of rolls being warmed under the broiler when Lisa and I began to fight. I wanted to be left alone. Lisa said she liked the company. The argument escalated quickly, our voices competing with the din of the crowded living room. I yelled something. Lisa screamed something back. Then ours were the only voices left. People drew near, surrounded us. Sentiments were whispered. Hands patted my shoulders, rubbed my back. I felt like a bird with a broken wing, the neighborhood cats closing in.

"Please," I said. "She just died. Please leave us alone."

"Oh, and now you care," Lisa said. "Now, when you didn't even want her."

At that, everyone took a collective step back.

"It's your fault!" Lisa said. Her body shook. "You didn't want her, and she died!"

Lisa collapsed into me, pressed her face to my chest, heaving. A second later, I heard the words, processed the meaning of what she had said. And, in that moment, I hated my wife. Her very touch repulsed me.

I pushed her. I meant only to separate our bodies, to get away, but there was a miscalculation of force. Lisa fell backward onto a table. A tray of carrot sticks hit the floor.

That could have been the end right there, except that it wasn't.

The next day we went on as though nothing had happened. I started taking the pills I'd been given, ignoring the recommended dosage.

* * *

It's true, though, what Lisa said. The pregnancy was not what people call *planned*, and I hadn't wanted the baby, not at first. It's not as if I told her, spoke the words aloud: *I don't want this baby*. But Lisa knew. She knew the moment she told me she was pregnant.

I was teaching when the news came. Lisa had thrown up that morning, called a sub, and gone back to bed.

The high school is where we met, where I'd been teaching math to teenagers for ten years. Lisa was right out of college, the hot, new biology teacher all the boys, and some of the girls, had a crush on. The decade's difference in our age went unnoticed by both of us. We kept the relationship a secret as long as we could. Public school gossip, after all, is seldom kind. The smaller the town, the worse it is, and this is a small town. Of course, when Miss Adams returned one fall and told everyone to start calling her Mrs. Starling, it wasn't long before people put two and two together.

The voice coming through the intercom ordered me to the front office. I had a call waiting on line one.

When Lisa told me, I dropped the phone. We'd only been married a year, and we'd been careful. I put a hand on the office copy machine to keep from falling over. My thumb caught the keypad, and then the copier was humming and whirring. White paper streamed into a tray on the floor. I watched the paper coming out, sheet after sheet. I fully expected a baby to tumble from the mouth of the machine, down the chute, and into the gray basket.

I bent over, grabbed the phone, brought the receiver to my ear.

"Well," Lisa said, "aren't you excited?"

They were there, all the words I knew I should say, the words one uses for such an occasion, but none found their way to my tongue.

"Fine," Lisa said. "I'll see you when you get home."

So, I feigned joy, went through the motions as I thought a better man might. I painted the spare bedroom blue, then, after the second ultrasound, repainted it pink. I helped Lisa's friends at school throw a shower. But, in time, real pleasure crept in. Action blossomed into belief, and belief turned to love, a love for what grew inside Lisa, love even before the baby came. I bought the baby book, the one Lisa still looks at every day, the first month the only section filled in.

Our daughter was born in June, and we named her just that: *June*.

It was only after June died in July that the subject of my initial reluctance resurfaced. Lisa has not mentioned it since the day of the funeral, but it's stayed with us, a green cloud hanging low in the house. When we fight, I feel her holding back, and with each argument I have waited—am waiting still—for her to throw the accusation back in my face, as though death is a thing I wished upon our daughter.

♦   ♦

I decide to postpone the separation, again, this time with the stipulation that I no longer have to attend group. Lisa can go, but I've had enough.

After all, I'm hardly a model candidate for group therapy, especially group therapy with a spiritual component. Me, I'm a believer in the concrete. Give me statistics. Give me data. Give me a line, fat and sturdy, working its way across a grid.

I believe in a calculable world, even when the math doesn't quite make sense. Take Lisa and me, for example. We, x, may be expressed as follows: $x = [3 - 1]$ but $[1 + 1 \neq 2]$.

Lisa and I used to be a lot alike. My world was made up of numbers, hers of biological processes. She saw everything through a scientific lens. Her outlook changed, though, after June died. When Lisa couldn't pin the blame on me, she turned to God. Suddenly, meaning attached itself, leechlike, to every facet of her life. Everything that happened happened for a reason.

Soon, she was reading the Bible every day and memorizing scripture. *God's will* became a favorite catchphrase. Sunday mornings now find me home alone.

*   *   *

Lisa agrees to my terms. I can stop going to group. She also says I owe her an apology, so the Friday following our fight in bed we drive an hour south to Atlanta to the opening of a new film at the Fernbank Science Center. We sit in the theater's front row. Lisa's just nuts for nature documentaries. This one's called *The Amazing Journey* and chronicles an annual herd migration across the Serengeti Plain. The film pretty much follows the standard African migration documentary format: Gazelle and zebra and water buffalo travel hundreds of miles, terrorized by lions and cheetahs, fording crocodile-infested waters, all so they can make it to a lush basin somewhere in Kenya. In the basin, the grass is long and green. Plant life of all kinds abounds, and there is fresh water enough for every animal. It is like a kind of heaven. Then all the animals fuck and go home.

Only, here's the thing. As it turns out, they don't all go home. Every so often, a particularly astute zebra or savvy antelope will say to itself, "Hey, why not stay here?" These few remain in the basin, where they live rich, long lives free of hardship.

"So, what I want to know," I say, my arm around Lisa, as the lights come up and the credits scroll, "is why don't more stay? Why would any of them leave the basin?"

"Simple," my biologist wife says. "The habitat could never sustain that degree of life. The basin only thrives as long as the resources aren't used up."

I nod. I watch the muscles in her neck move as she speaks.

"From an evolutionary perspective," Lisa continues, "the animals are drawn away so that they don't destroy what they have."

"And what about the ones that do stay?"

"Well," Lisa says, "I guess they just managed to outsmart evolution."

●   ●   ●

After the funeral, Lisa and I worked at being miserable, as though happiness might disrespect the dead.

One night, coming home late from school, I found Lisa on the sofa watching a sitcom. I sat down, and she moved close, rested her head on my shoulder, an intimacy I hadn't known in weeks. Something funny happened on the show, and, without warning, Lisa let out a laugh. The sound emerged sharp and loud and strangled at the end. She put a hand over her mouth. We watched the rest of the show refusing to laugh, Lisa keeping a hand near her face just in case.

It was six months before we made love. It wasn't planned, couldn't have been. To speak of sex would have made it impossible. Instead, having gone to bed early, unable to sleep, we held each other. I kissed Lisa on the forehead. Her body tensed, and I apologized. "No," she said, taking my face in her hands. She kissed me hard on the lips, grabbed me, tore at my T-shirt. It was over in minutes.

"That was nice," she said.

"Yes," I said. I was bewildered, but Lisa seemed happy. That was what mattered.

A minute later, from the bathroom, over the hum of the fan, the gush of the faucet, through the closed door, I could hear Lisa sobbing.

●   ●   ●

"Did you enjoy the movie?" I ask once we're in bed. When it's quiet, we think about June. Most nights, we fight to fill up the silence. Tonight, though, we have something to talk about.

"It was good, but hardly groundbreaking," Lisa says.

"Oh," I say. "I beg your pardon."

"No. It was fine. I only mean that the filmmakers made no new discoveries."

"Such as?"

"Well," she says, "take, for example, a documentary I saw last week. It had to do with the Nile and the animals that live there. Mostly, it was about hippopotamuses and crocodiles, how they share the river."

"They live together?"

"Sure," Lisa says. "It's the Nile. For the most part, it's no problem. Typically, the crocodiles leave the hippos alone. Nothing can take down a full-grown hippo. But, sometimes, if a group of crocs is hungry enough, they'll attack one of the younger hippos."

I try to picture it, a crocodile wrestling a hippopotamus, the splashing, the waves, the water's red surface.

"But, here's the good part," Lisa says. She smiles. "What really got me was this footage they shot of a hippopotamus funeral."

"A funeral?"

"Well, sort of. Something that had never been caught on tape. See, this baby hippo had been mauled by crocodiles. It managed to pull itself onto a sandbar in the middle of the river. Then the other hippos surrounded the calf until the crocodiles swam away. Once it died, the hippos licked the baby."

"What do you mean 'licked the baby'?"

"I don't know how else to explain it," Lisa says. "The hippos made a circle around the dead baby and licked it. And they actually have these very long tongues. They must have licked every square inch of it, then they all lay down and rested their heads on the body. After a while, they stood up, walked back into the water, and swam away."

"That's wild," I say. "So, why do they do it?"

"Who knows? It's an entirely unexplored phenomenon. At the very least, it proves these particular animals have learned to mourn."

For a moment, neither of us speaks. We contemplate the complexity of nature, the mystery, the beauty of love manifested among hippos.

"That's fucked up," I say. Lisa frowns. I have miscalculated. "I mean, it's weird, that's all. Sad hippos." But it's too late. The magic was gone the second I opened my mouth.

"It's not weird," she says. "It's beautiful. How can you not see that?"

"Lisa, I didn't see the show."

"But the idea! These animals, they lost one of their own, and they came together to grieve. Can't you see the beauty in that?"

"Honey, we're talking hippos here. They don't *feel* anything. You taught me that, about animals and emotion, how they don't experience loss like we do."

"You're right," Lisa says. "They don't. And you know what else they don't do? They don't abandon their mates. And, get this, more than anything, instinctually, they know enough to care for their young."

And there it is.

I pull the chain on the bedside lamp. Lisa begins to cry. I move to the edge of the bed and squeeze my pillow to my ear to muffle the sound. But, when I close my eyes, I picture the hippos. I fall to sleep, and they follow me into my dreams, chasing me with their big, pink tongues. I spend my night on the banks of the Nile, running from them, and the next morning I wake, shower, and eat breakfast, all the time unable to think of anything else.

◆   ◆   ◆

I was the one who discovered June. It's why I don't sleep well, why morning sends me looking for the cradle that's no longer there.

At first, Lisa wouldn't let me disassemble the cradle. For weeks, it held only a pillow, a pacifier, and a yellow stuffed duck. One Sunday while she was at church, I took the thing apart, packed the pieces into a box, labeled the cardboard with black Magic Marker, and carried the box to the attic. When Lisa got home, I was in bed.

The morning had taken everything out of me. Lisa stepped into the bedroom, stopped, and for the longest time stood very still.

"What's wrong?" I asked, knowing full well the thing she was missing.

"Nothing," she said, everything easier this way, everything unspoken.

◆　　◆　　◆

Wednesday night hurls us back into argument. Lisa comes in from gardening, one of her hobbies. Her hands are stained with Georgia red clay, but otherwise she's clean.

"I'm going to shower," she says.

"What for?" I ask.

"Group. We have to leave in less than an hour."

"We? What's this *we*? We had an agreement, remember?"

We pull into the parking lot five minutes late. Lisa, who despises tardiness from both her students and herself, hurries toward the church doors.

I linger by the car. "I'll be there in a minute," I call across the lot. I look up and the sky is a disappointment. From our yard, just outside of town, the night is black and the stars are bright. Here, though, electric light bounces off of everything, light commingling with light, the stars obscured by a hazy luminescence.

It will be my last night with Lisa. By morning, I decide, I will be gone.

◆　　◆　　◆

Pam opens with the usual prayer, the one that concludes with our standard chant: "Lord, grant us peace. Let us rejoice in your glory. And give us strength, that we may rejoice in our suffering, for we know that suffering produces perseverance, perseverance character, and character the hope that springs eternal. Amen." I mouth the words but refuse to speak them.

Pam asks who would like to share, and, immediately, Lisa raises her hand. I know that she is going to tell everyone about the hippos, and then she does. By the end of the story, everyone is crying, even the men. Everyone but me.

Lisa shoots me a look that says, *I told you so*. But she doesn't stop there. Next, she relates the hippos to her own grief, and someone goes for another box of tissues. Finally, she reminds the group that tomorrow marks the one-year anniversary of June's death.

Before I know what I'm doing, I stand. My chair tips, falls to the floor behind me.

"They're just hippos!" I bellow.

I have everyone's attention, and I'm seething, an animal myself, trapped in the circle. No one says a word.

"Don't you get it?" I say. "You keep searching for reasons and meaning and signs, but there is no meaning. None of it means anything! Our kids are dead. We're not special. We just got fucked by chance, by bad luck. Everyone in this room just has really, really shitty luck."

Lisa looks pale, horrified.

"Why can't we get past this? I just want this to be over already."

Pam approaches me. "Richard," she says, "it's never over. We just keep going, and this is how. This is how we continue." She places a hand on my shoulder. "You're angry, but I promise you, it gets easier."

I can't explain what happens next, but here it is: I am laughing.

"Remember," Pam says, "God will not give you more than you can bear."

I laugh so hard I fall forward. My knees hit the floor, and I sit.

"Let's pray over him," Pam says, and then I'm surrounded. My laughter is like a drawn-out roar. People speak, but the words don't reach me.

It's when I start feeling the hands all over me that everything stops seeming so funny. They come from every direction, patting me, stroking me, holding me. A hand touches my face, and I know without looking that it is Lisa's. I miss most of what's said. The words are all tangled up. But the feeling of hands on my body stays with me, even after the hands are gone, after I've left the church. Even in bed, the feeling remains: the heat, the press of palms on my skin.

I fall right to sleep. It's not the same sleep as the last few hundred nights. Nodding off, I feel something holding me down, heavy as light, silent as summer rain. It's like leaving purgatory at last. It's like, at last, being dead.

◆   ◆   ◆

In the morning, I wake and look at the clock. It's nearly nine, impossible to make my escape now without causing a scene. I head downstairs, drawn by the smell of coffee. I pause on the bottom step, thinking about whether or not I should leave Lisa. But I cannot make up my mind.

Lisa stands at the window in the kitchen. She wears her bathrobe, a mug of coffee in one hand, the curve of her neck cradled in the other.

I go to the window. As I expected, there are deer on the lawn.

Our property is situated on an acre in the country, woods on one side, road on the other, our house and the lawn and Lisa's flower gardens in between. I'd always taken a kind of maniacal delight in lawn care: the geometry of mowing, the chemistry of fertilizers. For years, the deer came, drawn by the lush, green fescue. After June died, though, I let the grass go to shit. Now the lawn is pocked with brown spots and weedy throughout. Except for Lisa's well-groomed gardens, the yard is an embarrassment. Still, the deer come, two or three at a time, at daybreak or dusk. They eat around the dead places.

This morning, there are four of them, and it's nice. I can't remember the last time we stood at the window and watched the deer. It was before June died, I'm sure of that.

"Coffee?" Lisa says.

"Yes, please," I say.

She moves to the cupboard, the stove, and returns with a second cup. I reach out, and the mug is hot in my hand. I twist the mug around, hold it by the handle. Outside, the deer approach the house. Soon, they are close, closer than I've ever seen them come. Is the grass near the house that much better than the grass at the end of the yard?

"They must be hungry," Lisa says.

"Yes," I say.

"Richard?"

But the deer are advancing, and all of a sudden they're in Lisa's garden. One paws a tentative hoof at the mesh encircling a flowerbed, then stretches its neck over the wire and nibbles at the head of a pansy.

Lisa throws open the window and leans out of the house. "Hey!" she screams. "Hey! Shoo! Get out of here! Out! Out!"

The deer lift their heads and their ears flick forward. For a moment they look like lawn ornaments, deer statues. Then, they explode, deer in every direction. They run to the edge of our yard and into the thicket. Lisa falls away from the window and slips to the floor. Sitting with her back to the wall, she looks up at me and her face is wet. I feel like I'm meeting her eyes for the first time since the funeral, and I am scared and ashamed and full of hope.

"Lisa, I don't want to go." I say it and, suddenly, it's true. Because it would be the easiest thing in the world to walk out that door, but, in the end, it doesn't matter who's suffered most or what's been said.

There's a graphic organizer in mathematics called the Venn diagram. It's two circles, a pair of rings run together, and the place they intersect is called the union. For the last year, Lisa and I have traveled in circles, both charting our own paths around what's happened, each of us pursuing an unending course. And only now have we met in the middle, in the quiet overlap, the space between.

I kneel beside Lisa and help her up. Holding each other, we

stand very still and look out the window. We stand and we wait for what feels like days.

Stay, she will say. I imagine it, try to summon the words into being.

And, when the invitation comes, it is as if there was never the need for a choice.

"Stay," she says, and I do.

The Geometry of Despair

II. Wake the Baby

Lisa sleeping. Lisa turning in sleep, moonlight sliding cheek to chin. She kicks. She wakes, watches me.

At last, she says, "Another one."

"Which one?" I say.

"The one where she's five," Lisa says. "She was five and we called her Junie." She uncovers herself and stands. "Would we ever have called her Junie?"

Lisa moves to the bedroom door.

"Please don't," I say.

"I won't wake him," she says.

In a minute, in the other room, Michael is crying.

◆　　◆　　◆

The next morning it is Sunday and we take Michael to the park. We sit on a bench and watch the big kids climb the jungle gym. Lisa holds Michael in her lap. He laughs and points when birds fly overhead.

"Let him crawl," I say.

Lisa ruffles the grass with the toe of her sneaker. "It's dirty," she says. "There're bugs."

"It's nature," I say. This is not really true. The park is a twenty-acre rectangle of green at the city's center. Stand anywhere in the park and you still hear cars whiz by. But there's a playground, a walking trail, a duck pond. It's the best you're going to get downtown.

"Do you want to see the ducks?" I say.

Michael gurgles. He's not quite a year old, and he's not walking just yet, another thing Lisa worries about, though the pediatrician assures us that he's fine, he's healthy, that all is well.

"Let's go see the ducks," I say.

Lisa holds Michael close as we walk the pond's perimeter. We find another bench and sit. Some of the ducks paddle our way, and this really gets Michael going. He reaches. He waves. He shrieks.

"You like the duckies?" I say.

"Gaaaauuuuu!" Michael says.

There's no fishing allowed, but an older man in overalls stands with a bucket and rod on the other side of the pond. He tips his hat, and I half-wave.

The diaper bag is in the car, so I look through Lisa's purse.

"Anything to eat?" I say.

"Animal crackers," Lisa says. "But those are Michael's."

"Not for me. For the ducks."

"Oh, don't do it," she says. "You know how much I hate that."

"But he loves it," I say. "Don't you?" I say to Michael. "Don't you love when Daddy feeds the duckies?"

I find the crackers, pull out a lion, and snap off its head.

The head in the water excites the birds. Soon, there are a dozen of them: a mallard with its scaly green cap, a couple of drab brown ducks, a white swan with a tumorous orange knob sprouting from its beak. There's a cluster of sleek, black and tan Canada geese, all honking, their heads bobbing on question-mark necks.

I fling crackers, and Michael squeals. I've done this before, but, this time, something is different. The birds are louder, closer, like they've been promised food all day and I've just now shown up without enough to go around. They're frenzied.

I take a step back. They hurry forward on their little yellow dragon feet, wings flapping, beaks shish-kebabbing the air.

"Gaaaaaaa!" Michael screams.

"Honey?" Lisa says.

I'm out of crackers, but the ducks, the geese, they keep coming.

"Richard!" Lisa yells.

She stands, and, as she stands, the white goose charges, hissing. It plunges its orange bill into Lisa's leg. Lisa doesn't make a sound.

I reach for Lisa's purse. The goose pecks her again. I swing the purse and miss. I swing again and the purse connects solidly with the bird's back. The goose squawks, flaps its wings, and turns toward the pond. The other birds follow. It's only once they're all in the water that I see what I've done.

Lisa's bag, unzipped, sits at my feet. Everything that was in it has flown out. The birds swim through the bobbing flotsam: lipstick, sunglasses, pens.

I turn to see Lisa. There is a bright red mark where beak broke flesh, a trickle of blood shin to shoe. But it is the rest of her I watch with something like reverence. She holds Michael high, overhead. One hand cradles his neck, his soft skull, the other his crotch. She holds him, and her eyes don't leave him, and I know that her legs could be sawed off and still she would not let go.

•   •   •

Back home, Lisa stands at the sink wringing water out of anything from which water can be wrung. A compact mirror and reading glasses are still somewhere at the bottom of the pond. A row of wet one-dollar bills wallpapers the kitchen counter.

"How can I help?" I say. I put a hand on Lisa's waist.

"Don't touch me," she says. A bandage conceals the gash on her leg. There's a red dot at the center of the bandage where the blood has seeped through.

"Let me do this."

"Richard," she says.

At the bottom of the sink, a tampon has bloomed with pond water and burst from its plastic tube. Beneath it is Lisa's wallet. Tucked inside, no doubt, are pictures of June. Not big pictures. Not even good pictures. Little Olan Mills two-inch-by-three-inch cheapies, of which there are another dozen in a dresser drawer. Already, though, I can foresee the day when Lisa will hold this against me, the destruction of these pictures from her wallet, these photographs from June's last afternoon.

"I'm sorry," I say.

Lisa says nothing.

"The ducks were just hungry," I say. "Michael's fine. He was never in danger. I wouldn't have let it get to that point."

"*You* wouldn't," Lisa says. "Say it again."

"Lisa."

"No, say it. I want to hear you say it."

"All right, fine. I *wouldn't*. I wouldn't have let it get to that point."

"Good," Lisa says. "Now say it to my leg."

◆   ◆   ◆

Once Michael's down for the night, I join Lisa in bed. She hasn't said more than ten words to me all evening.

"It was an accident," I say. "You can't make me feel like this is my fault."

"I'm not making you," she says. "If you feel that way, maybe there's a reason."

"Jesus," I say. "Goodnight."

A minute later, Lisa is crying. *Don't touch me*, she'd said, and I don't.

But then she turns to me, and I can't help wrapping my arms around her.

"I can't sleep," she says.

"You just lay down," I say.

"No. I mean, I can't. I can't do it. I can't stand them anymore."

"The dreams will go away."

"In three years they haven't gone away."

We lie like that for a while, Lisa's body against mine, her head in the hollow of my shoulder and chin. Her breathing settles. Her heartbeat slows.

"Richard?" she says. "Would you have called her Junie?"

"I would have called her whatever you liked best," I say.

Soon, she is sleeping. I'm almost asleep when Lisa snaps awake and jumps up.

"No," I say.

"I just want to check," she says.

"He's fine. You'll wake him."

"I'll stand at the door."

"You say that. And then you're just at the crib. And then you're just feeling for breath. And then you're just checking for fever. And then and then and then, and he never sleeps. He's a baby. You have to let him sleep."

"Richard, move."

But I don't leave the doorway.

"Richard," Lisa says, "I swear to God."

She reaches for the doorknob. I hold it tight in my hand.

"Let me see my baby!"

She slaps my hand. I hold tight. And then she is kicking me, screaming, yelling, "Move!" But I'm twice her size. I will not be moved. I sink to the floor. I feel her kicks in my stomach, my ribs, my groin. I cover my face with my hands.

She doesn't stop until Michael's crying can be heard from the other room. She backs away from me then. She sits on the edge of the bed, breathing heavy.

I hurt all over.

She says, "If you do that again, I'll leave you."

But we both know I won't have to.

Because now, somehow, we are even.

How to Help Your Husband Die

The morning your husband, the chef, stays in bed, bleary-eyed, sweating, and says for the past six months he's been coughing up blood, turn hysterical. Demand he drive you both to the emergency room at once.

Ask why he didn't see a doctor six months ago. Ask why he's such a *man* when it comes to his health. Ask what he thought would happen if he kept smoking. Explain how much better it would be, should this turn out to be something serious, had you both caught it at its outset. If you scold and scold, when the bad news comes, it won't be your fault. When the bad news comes, you can say, *I told you so.*

When the bad news comes, cry and regret what you meant to say. He will not cry. He will not say anything at all. You will ride home in silence. Tell him not to worry, that it could be a thousand things, that the hospital only said *possibly*, that no good doctor diagnoses something like *that* on a first visit. At home, when you think of the way you spoke to him that morning, run to the toilet and throw up. When he asks what made you sick, blame the week-old pizza you reheated for lunch. Blame your time of the month. Blame anything but him.

Order more tests: MRIs, CAT scans, lung scans, X-rays, blood tests. Schedule appointments, consultations, what the cheery receptionists call *visits*. Plan to get second opinions, thirds, however many it takes to find a doctor who will say, *This is not what it looks like.*

Accompany him to every appointment. When he tells you how much it embarrasses him, stop crying in front of the doctors. Stop crying before he asks you to stop coming along.

Learn tricks to keep yourself from crying. When a doctor talks, cross your arms. Rub your thumb along the smooth crease at the inner hinge of your elbow. Imagine the skin is an eyeball, your eyeball, and you are massaging back the tears. When the doctor leaves the room, press your thumbs to your eyes and suck in air. Before your husband can ask, say, *I'm okay.*

✦   ✦   ✦

Wait. By the time this is all over, you will know patience in a whole new way. Wait for the nurses. Wait for the doctors. Wait for his name to be called, the last name always mispronounced. Keep track of time. On average, find you spend five to six hours a week sitting in rooms waiting for people to see you. Compare this to the thirty minutes a week you spend in the company of the person who earned the framed piece of paper hanging at a five-degree angle on the wall.

Wait. When he gets bored, entertain him. Play Twenty Questions. Play I Spy. Keep him from playing with the plastic models of organs on physicians' desks.

Learn new ways to wait. Bring books. Bring bills. Bring board games. In waiting rooms and offices, play cards. Hearts, Spades, Crazy Eights. Quit Slapjack after you miss the pile and leave a bruise on his hand that lingers for weeks.

✦   ✦   ✦

After a month of meetings, catalog the manifold possibilities, the differing opinions of the two dozen doctors you've met. You will think, *Perhaps it's the diabetes.* No matter what the doctors say, decide that it is only the diabetes, just as it has always been the diabetes whenever he's been sick, that he will be fine. Tell yourself that you are tired of doctors, that tomorrow's X-rays will be the last. Smile when you imagine the wait is almost over.

Hold the thin transparency in your hands. Run a fingertip over the two gray pork chops, the pockets of light in each lung. The doctor will insist that the masses are not benign. Just shake your head and say *well*.

The doctor will tell your husband that he has several options, but only one, really, if he wants to live. Listen and smile as you would at a man telling a joke that's not funny, a joke secretly meant to hurt your feelings. Smile the way you do at a person you wish would just, for God's sake, please stop talking.

Discuss the odds of survival as though they are not odds but suggestions should one choose to die.

What the doctor won't tell you is that, in tandem, the two diseases will tear your husband apart. That so many of the medicines needed to treat his diabetes will interfere with the chemotherapy and radiation, with the antibiotics for the pneumonia that will fill up his lungs. That he will be sicker than he has ever been. That, in the end, it will be the cure that kills him.

But you will glimpse this. Will, somehow, in the flicker of an instant, see what lies ahead. Will know it as surely as you have always understood that it is cancer and that your husband won't see another summer. And, quick as it comes, put away this little revelation, tuck it beneath the blanket of your brain, and ask the man in the white coat what comes next.

◆   ◆   ◆

He will begin treatments in a week. You both hate attention, pity, curiosity masquerading as concern. You've never liked flowers or casseroles, never cared for sympathy cards printed in pastels with loopy script and passages from Proverbs. Make a pact to tell no one. Immediately, tell your sister. He will tell his brother. You will both wish your parents were still alive.

Remind him, as the doctors have, that it's not too late to quit smoking. Watch him laugh, slide another cigarette from the pack, and step outside. Stand at the back door while he smokes. Glare at him with your arms crossed. When he smiles and waves, stamp a foot, turn, and walk away.

Find new ways, each day, to express your displeasure with his habit. Refuse to wash his clothes with yours. Though it has never been a problem before, tell him they smell, that his smoky shirts stink up your clothes. Leave clippings under his pillow, magazine articles on the dangers of cigarettes. Fold them into pants pockets and ball them up in his socks. Stop after he comes to you with a stack of crumpled papers, saying, *Darling, I know. I could do the PSAs is how much I know.*

Beg him to quit his job. He will say he's not giving up that easy. Yes, he knows your health insurance could cover him. Yes, he knows he needs rest, that the kitchen of a four-star restaurant is no place for a chemo patient. No, he won't quit his job.

Quit your job. You never liked it anyway. Who grows up saying, *I want to be a dental hygienist?* Kids want to be artists, veterinarians, firefighters.

When it hits you that you may not, now, have children, fast as you can, put the thought out of your head. If you consider this for too long, it might come true.

•   •   •

When you find you have too much time on your hands, decide to learn everything there is to know about cancer. Decide you want to know exactly how your husband is going to die. The moment you do, believe that you can save him.

Study the disease. Go to the public library. Read every book they own on cancer. File for interlibrary loans until the research librarians know you by name. Give up and drive across town to the college campus.

See the university library for the first time. Strain your neck searching the dome, the dark sky, constellations painted on in white lines, as though all of your answers are there in that dome, those lines, in the silver of fake stars. Once you've stared long enough, check your watch and get to work.

Search for the card catalog. Ask a lean boy in a black shirt and glasses—the one who hasn't shaved in a few days but doesn't seem to be trying to grow a beard either—to point you in the direction of the card catalog. Watch him raise a single eyebrow over one wire-rimmed lens. *Yes,* he will seem to say, *you have a lot of learning to do.*

Learn the Dewey decimal system. Learn to use microfiche. Learn to search the library database online. Watch your productivity soar.

Visit the university library every other day. Throw yourself at books, magazines, scholarly journals. If you learn enough about the cancer, you can conquer it. If you search long enough—comb every essay, read every study, explore each article—you will find a treatment. If he dies, it will be your fault, the cure right under your nose if only you'd picked up last winter's copy of *Acupuncture in Medicine,* circulation 4,000.

Spend fifty dollars a week in dimes. Learn that, once the light on the photocopier blinks red to yellow, you can lift the lid to turn a page, even while the machine is still whirring and clicking, still rocking on its stumpy steel feet. This will save you valuable seconds per copy. Press page after page to the platen glass. Watch the paper leave the photocopier's side like ticker tape.

Take breaks to rest your brain. Run your fingers through the water fountain's stream. Massage your temples. Trade the silence of the library for the silence of the library restrooms. For weeks, think of the library as one big bathroom. Before you leave each evening, wash your hands.

◆   ◆   ◆

Become a regular at the library. Make this your day job, five days a week. Bring the librarians coffee from Starbucks. Learn the major of each student worker. After a month, you will never pay late fees again.

To battle fatigue, work harder. Don't stop. Read five hundred pages a day. Read everything. Read the notes on the type at the back of each book. Learn to spot different fonts. Decide you like Garamond best and look for volumes with this typeface. Value their opinions more highly than books printed in lesser fonts. Don't consider this behavior unusual until you mention it to your sister and take her stunned silence for good sense.

Stay at the library all day, every day. Don't leave until your fingertips are gray with ink, until your tailbone aches from the curve of the library's stylishly modern chairs, until the letters of words run together, taunting you in a jumble of tiny black serifs. When you can't take any more, are ready to give up, you will know guilt.

◆   ◆   ◆

Don't mention his meals, the salty meat, the too-sweet desserts.

Sure enough, one evening, he'll return from work, sit at the kitchen table, and, for a long time, watch the wall. Join him. Touch his shoulder. Ask what's wrong, and he'll say only, "I can't *taste* anything."

◆   ◆   ◆

Give up. Sit in your favorite chair at home and watch daytime TV. Watch all of the hospital soap operas and wish it were that easy: the lifesaving operation, the miracle cure. Let your thoughts drift back to cancer. Dream of lung transplants.

Recall a piece in *The New York Times*, the cancer-ridden chimps tested at Johns Hopkins and the experimental drug that saved their lives. Try to remember why a drug getting such extraordinary results was not approved for public use, what side effects rendered it too risky. Wonder whether the drug will be sold soon. Know that it will be ten, twenty years.

Wonder whether the drug is for sale on the black market. Commit yourself to several Internet searches. When nothing legitimate turns up, launch your keyboard across the room. On a piece of white stationery, scribble FUCK THE FDA in angry black ink. Tape the paper to the wall above your computer.

After a few days of this, go back to the library.

·   ·   ·

By winter, you will know more than the doctors. Surprise the physicians with your repertoire of medical terminology. Throw around cancer jargon, the consecrated slang of the disease. Recommend treatments. Exude condescension before the doctors get the chance. Inquire in regard to the latest studies. Question their methods.

Grow irritated when a doctor hasn't heard of a specific drug or experiment or clinic in Southeast Asia. When the doctor apologizes, blow a short burst of air up into your bangs and look out the nearest window just to let him know you can't be fooled.

·   ·   ·

When your husband comes home from the restaurant one night and falls to the floor, understand it's time for him to stay home. Forget the library. Help him forget his work. Concentrate on chemotherapy. Concentrate on radiation. Concentrate on making it through each day.

Notice the hair in the bathroom. Strands in the sink and shower, tangles in drains. Dark hairs on white tile. Piles collected in corners as though swept there. When you find clumps in the bed, collect the hair. Save it in a Ziploc bag like a child's first haircut keepsake. When he finds the bag and yells at you, throw it out.

Once he's lost the last of his hair, tell him that he is beautiful. When you want to hear him laugh, stroke the dome of his head and purr like a kitten.

Discover that you both love to sing. At night, in bed, sing old standards, improvising your own lyrics. On Christmas Eve, when he sings *Chestnuts roasting on a funeral pyre,* follow it up with *Gangrene nipping at your toes.* He will laugh and laugh. Wait until he's asleep to sob.

Try church. Have him recall his altar boy boyhood. Let him teach you the Doxology, the Lord's Prayer. Learn how to take communion. When the priest places the wafer on your tongue and says, "This is His body, broken for you," think, *This is his body.* Spend the rest of the day whispering it to yourself: *This is his body. This is his body.*

⁕ ⁕ ⁕

There are certain things you should know.

There will be things you can't make better. Don't try to hold his hand when he coughs. Don't try to trade *Seinfeld* reruns for hours of meaningful this-is-your-life conversation. (He'll want nothing to do with such talk.) Don't attempt to help him upstairs if he nods off watching the news, even when you think he'd sleep better in bed.

Be reminded that chemotherapy can cause sterility. Accept that he will never give you children. Wonder why you don't have children already. Wonder why it is that you never want a thing until it's no longer inevitable.

Know that no matter how many laps you walk to raise money for research, no matter how many free T-shirts you earn, in spite of remissions, life's short revisions, your husband is still going to die.

⁕ ⁕ ⁕

The night his blood sugar level drops, when he has the first seizure, call 911. Ride in the ambulance with a paramedic who will try to make conversation. Her words will sound like a song sung through a tunnel a mile away. Ask her to stop talking. Ask her again. When you realize you're screaming, bury your face in your husband's shirt and cry.

Once he comes out of insulin shock, sit beside him on the thin hospital mattress. Watch him sleep. Stay awake, all night, running your hand down his arm, shoulder to elbow, elbow to wrist. Realize you spent so much time studying the disease that you forgot to prepare for what comes next.

Study the room and find you don't know the name of a single piece of medical equipment or what each instrument does, aside from the IV bag and the heart monitor. Or, you will think you know which screen belongs to the heart monitor—the life of the man you love graphed in electric green—but there will be so many screens, your husband hardwired to a dozen machines.

Try to get comfortable in the recliner by the hospital bed. Tell yourself that you could sleep if only you knew the name of the mechanism hanging over his head, the black accordion pumping up and down in the glass tube, collapsing in on itself like a Slinky, then stretching, exposing its ribs as it inflates.

◆   ◆   ◆

From this point forward, spend your days in the hospital room, for this is where he is meant to spend the rest of his life. Learn to tell when he wants to talk about this and when he doesn't, regardless of the words that come out of his mouth.

Buy a potted plant, something beautiful but easy to care for. Place the plant on a table by the window, where it will get plenty of light. Water it every day. Tell yourself that as long as the plant lives, he will live. On his worst days, imagine the plant as his lifeline. *The plant is alive. He cannot die.*

Get used to seeing blood drawn from his body. Eventually, he won't notice the needles. At night, trace the veins of his arms. Rub the purple circles left by needles jabbed too hard. Hold your breath and kiss each bruise.

Give him cigarettes. The first time he asks, spend a day rationalizing doctors' orders. Once you accept the pointlessness of this, once you see that cigarettes are just another kind of morphine, that the end is *here*, that the only thing left to sacrifice is suffering, you'll give him whatever he wants.

Be brave. Outside the hospital, on the sidewalk, hold him up while he smokes. When he says something like *There go seven more minutes,* try to laugh. Walk him back to bed, wheeling the IV stand the whole way.

On an evening when he is awake and alert, in a good mood, when the doctors have gone for the night and the visitors, like so many spectators, have filed out of the room, pull back the covers and touch him. Caress him. Take him into your mouth. Don't stop when he cries out. Don't finish him off, the way you always have, with your hands. Don't stop until it's over, until the warm rush fills your mouth and his feet rattle the rail at the end of the bed. Don't make him have to say thank you.

❖   ❖   ❖

While he's still lucid, write the will. Forgive yourself for not doing this sooner. Write the will quickly, then put it away in the safety deposit box at the bank with the marriage license and birth certificates. Marvel at how these three—birth, death, and the union that came between—fit into an inch-deep metal drawer.

At the hospital, bring him books. Bring him every book he never finished, every book he always wanted to read. Read them to him, as many as you can. Don't talk doctors or painkillers or funeral arrangements. Don't make him leaf through brochures to pick out a casket, flowers, the perfect burial plot.

There is no last lesson, no big picture, no final words, so waste less time on what's real. Read to him and let his mind wander. Let him fall in and out of sleep. Read even when you know he's not listening.

❖   ❖   ❖

When the very end is in sight, tell him you're leaving. You're leaving and you're taking him with you. Clean him and dress him and pull out his IV. Let the fluid flow from the tube to the floor. Unplug the heart monitor, and pull the black pads from his chest, from the crop-circle whorls they've made in his chest hair.

When he protests, you must not give in. He will thank you

later, no matter what he says now. He'll worry about expenses, about insurance coverage. He'll worry about *being a burden*. Tell him he's too young for that. Tell him the word *burden* doesn't mean what it did when your ailing mother said it because he *means* it, and because he never could be. When all else fails, tell him to shut up because you're not spending another night in the hospital.

When you lift him, his lightness will make you dizzy. He will feel like a child in your arms. Help him into a wheelchair, then make a break for it. Wheel him out a side door, and, when you hear a woman's voice, don't look back. Drive home and pull all the phones off of their hooks.

◆   ◆   ◆

Put him to bed in his *real* bed. Lie down beside him for the first time in months. Understand that things will move quickly now, without fluids and pills, monitors and morphine, electrodes and tubes. Wipe his forehead and neck as he sweats. Bring him more covers when he grows cold.

While he sleeps, listen to him breathe. Watch the covers rise and fall. Lie awake counting breaths, timing the space between, considering their distance. As the breaths grow farther apart, try to formulate an equation to see whether, at this rate, he'll make it until morning. Wonder, in the silence of daybreak, whether each breath you just heard was the last. Do this, and you will know despair. You will know helplessness.

Fall asleep with the sunrise, weak, feeling alone.

◆   ◆   ◆

Wake to his smile beside you, and see he's been watching you sleep. He'll be too tired to talk. Don't try to fill up the silence with words.

Help him out of bed with quick, simple commands. *Lift your head. Help me with your feet. Hold my shoulder.* Otherwise, keep quiet. Nothing you say can make this sacred. Everything you want to tell him before he dies is only for you, so pray it to yourself tonight when he's gone.

Take him to the beach. Take him because it is beautiful. Take him because you can. Take him midmorning, bundled in blankets, because it's spring and still cool before noon. Sit on the shore and trace your initials together in the sand like high school lovers. Play tic-tac-toe and let him win. Hold him as he coughs and coughs and coughs. He will rattle like a skeleton in your arms. Dig a trough in the sand for him to spit into. Scatter sand over the yellow-brown bile when the hole is full.

Sit like tourists watching the water and you'll wonder why you never did this. Fifteen miles from the ocean, and in ten years you never came here together, not once. Consider this, but don't dwell on it.

When your husband turns, gives you his confession, when he tells you every terrible thing he's done, every way he's wronged you, no matter how it hurts, don't make him beg your forgiveness. Tell him you love him, that nothing else matters. Do this because you've reached the end together, because why make it harder? Because maybe love is more than fidelity. Because maybe a broken promise can still be kept.

Love him, this man who now begs you to find someone else and soon, who wants nothing for you but happiness.

The whole round world will funnel into nothingness, and you will see the truth in his eyes: that life, that *living,* is more than what's come before. That all you have is this moment, this sun and this sand, these seagulls overhead and white clouds and blue sky, and don't look away or he'll disappear. The world is here only as long as you look for it, only as long as you keep your eyes open. Keep your eyes on him and he'll never leave you, will stay if you can just keep from blinking.

And your eyes will ache, they'll burn from holding them open for so long, and when you blink, like that, he'll be gone.

Me and James Dean

Jill's had James Dean since college, a gift from her parents before they died—car crash—which makes him extra-special to her, a last link to her ancestry or something. For Jill's sake, Dean and I maintain an amicable enough relationship, though there's been tension from the start, each of us sure Jill belongs to him.

The courtship was rocky, Jill waiting for Dean to warm to me. Our lovemaking was interrupted more than once by barking and a paw on my pillow. Five years after our wedding, he still jumps in bed between us, growling if I turn in my sleep. More than once, I've had nightmares of waking unmanned.

◆　　◆　　◆

Tonight, after Dean's been let into the bedroom, he nuzzles Jill's crotch and glares at me in a way that says: *I smell where you've been, buddy.*

Jill says, "Do you think we're meant to be?"

"What do you mean?" I ask, thinking, *Here we go again.*

"I mean," she says, "what if, in the end, your husband and your soul mate and the person you're supposed to be with—what if they all turn out to be different people?"

"Are you seeing Roger again?" I ask.

"No, sweetie, I told you. That's over."

"Are you sure?"

"Sure I'm sure," she says, rolling onto her side. She switches off her bedside lamp and pretends to fall asleep. I reach out, and Dean moves to shield her from my touch. He gives her elbow a lick, then looks me in the eye. He will not sleep until I do.

"Jill," I say. Jill offers only a quiet grunt. Dean moves to cushion the small of her back.

Clearly, she's still seeing Roger.

◆　◆　◆

This morning, I roll over Dean in the driveway. Just crush him. An honest mistake—not cold-blooded murder, just bad driving. Backing up without checking the mirrors, the kind of thing that lands a neighbor's toddler in the ICU and you on the evening news.

A simple case of wrong place, wrong time. That, and we had a deal, and Dean broke the deal.

It's my responsibility to walk Dean in the mornings. My *only* (Jill's word) responsibility when it comes to *her* (my word) dog. Dean, an old beagle with a nose like a coke fiend's, takes his time making his way around the block, stopping every few feet to sniff another dog's piss, to piss on another dog's piss, or to lick the place on his body where the piss comes out. Not a morning person, I never particularly wanted to get up early to walk Dean. The deal, then, was this: I get up and let Dean out. He has free rein in the neighborhood, leash laws be damned. In return, he comes home before I leave for work.

Both parties have found the arrangement appealing: I get to sleep in. Dean gets to take his time, pissing all over whatever he likes. For years we've operated like this, under the guise of what-Jill-doesn't-know-won't-hurt-her.

Usually, Dean scratches at the back door just as I'm buttering a bagel or pouring milk over a bowl of raisin bran. But, this morning, Dean doesn't come back. Not after I've finished breakfast and washed my plate. Not once I've made a second pot of coffee for when Jill wakes up. Not even after I stand at the open door, briefcase in hand, and quietly call for him.

I go to the garage, get in my Jeep. I've never had to look for Dean before. I think of Mr. Lancaster, imagine the man chasing Dean out of his vegetable garden, pitchfork in hand. Or, perhaps

Dean's made it under Ms. Mead's fence, at last having his way with the hot little Papillon who wags her ass at us whenever we walk by. I even envision Dean dead, the target of some gang initiation whereby one must off a dog in order to get his first bandanna and biker jacket.

What I don't picture is Dean hit by a car, not until the moment I feel the thud, hear the crunch, the unmistakable sound of beagle bones snapping under fifty-thousand-mile Michelin tread.

• •   • •

I don't have much experience with death. There were Jill's parents. There was a great-aunt whose name escapes me. There was my middle school guinea pig. Something was wrong with him, and his ass exploded. Really, he started shitting his intestines. It wasn't pretty. But that was a guinea pig, a rodent. People don't cry over dead rodents.

This is nothing like that. Dean appears unhurt. Only a thin string of red runs from his open mouth. He pants. I place my hand on his side. He doesn't yelp, just closes his eyes. His rib cage feels like a bag of potato chips.

This dog, I think, *will never make it. This is a doomed dog.*

At this moment, I can do many things. I can tell Jill, or not. I could say Dean ran away, got out the door while I fiddled with his leash and collar. But, then, what to do with the body? A neighbor's trashcan seems risky. There are woods nearby, but boys play there. I could drive out to the country, dig a little hole.

Except there's more to consider than just disposal. I can't bury Dean while he's still breathing. I mean, I could, but I can't. I'm not that man.

How long does it take a dog to die?

I consider methods of expediting the process: A plastic Kroger bag from under the kitchen sink, a shoelace to hold it in place. Ajax mashed up in raw hamburger. Shovel to the head.

I do own an acetylene torch.

Scratch that. I can't hide the truth of Dean's death from Jill, but perhaps I can disguise it. Another car, I could say. This car came flying around the corner, ripped the leash right out of my hand. I never caught the license plate, too intent on tending to Dean. Used the fireman's carry to bring the body home and everything.

In the end, Jill makes the decision for me. I look up, and she's running down the driveway, her worn, red bathrobe held together by a manicured hand. Even without makeup, with sleep caught under one eye and dried drool flaking from the corner of her mouth, as Jill crouches beside me and takes Dean's head into her hands, I think: *You, my love, are beautiful.*

◆   ◆   ◆

Jill won't talk to me. James Dean lies in her lap, legs at odd angles, head loose, jumping with every bump of the Jeep. At each jostle, Jill shoots a look my way that says, *Be careful,* and, as I slow down, bats eyes that plead, *Hurry up.*

It's no short trip. This is rural Kentucky, an hour from anywhere you've heard of. The nearest animal hospital is twenty miles of old roads away.

I reach for the radio, decide it's inappropriate, then change my mind and turn the dial. A fiery host argues back and forth with a listener. I was hoping for music. Before I can change it, Jill stretches over Dean, turns the radio off, and we're back to the hum of the Jeep and Dean's panting, the metronome of his quick, shallow breaths. It's the moment where one of us is meant to speak, and I'm still wondering who goes first when Jill interrupts the silence.

"You didn't have to do it," she says. "I would've stopped seeing Roger."

"But," I say, and my tongue catches on my teeth. So it's true. I knew this, sure, but it's different now, the admission making it more real.

Outside, apples bob in the morning light. We thread the orchard, then up a hill, and suddenly we're facing clear sky. From a field, a man on a stick waves a hand of hay, a crow for a hat, and I remember what it was like to be a boy, before life got so damned complicated.

Jill is crying. "How could you do this?" she says.

"Jill," I say, "it was an accident. I would never—"

I look at her. She looks back, searching my face for clues.

"Come on," I say. "Don't you know me at all?"

It's so much to explain, but I tell Jill about the deal and the walks. How, for years, this is how we did it. That I messed up. That I wasn't leaving for work. That I went to find Dean and didn't look both ways before I backed over him.

We continue down the road, the landscape mutating into a town. A drugstore here, post office there, and suddenly we're in Rosemont and the small animal hospital comes into view. It's an old house—green shutters, plank siding, and peeling white paint—that's been converted into a business. Out front, a sign features a caricature of a cat with a thermometer in its mouth. I pull into the parking lot. I'm afraid of what comes next.

"I'm sorry," Jill says.

"I'm sorry too," I say.

"Do you think . . ." Jill begins to cry again.

"I don't know," I say. "Let's take him inside and see."

◆   ◆   ◆

How I caught Jill and Roger last year: I came home from the firm early. Isn't that the way it always happens? I'd had a bad lunch with a client, awful conversation over lukewarm tortellini, and I'd been throwing up about once every hour since. There was no car in the driveway, no trail of clothes down the hall, no noise, even, to give me pause before I pushed open my bedroom door.

What I found was not fucking, just two topless people sitting beside each other, reading from the same book. It was strangely intimate, maybe the most intimate moment I've ever seen. Nobody knew what to do. Then I threw up all over the floor. Times, I wish I *had* opened the door to mindless, unbridled fucking.

◆   ◆   ◆

The vet's office is beige walls and wax plants, track lighting and tinny music piped through cheap speakers concealed behind flowerpots.

I'm filling out forms when Jill returns from a back room. She sits beside me on the long, narrow bench that takes up one wall. She looks terrible, face red and blotchy, hair like Medusa's.

"How is he?" I ask.

"I don't know," she says. "They won't tell me anything. They're doing X-rays. They asked me to leave."

Jill raises a hand to her face and traces the outline of one eye with a single knuckle. She mumbles something I can't make out.

"What's that?" I ask.

"I think I'm pregnant," she says.

When you hear something shocking, I mean something that just lays you out, you have a choice. You can accept it immediately, react to it, or not. I tend to stall.

"I'm sorry?" I say.

"Pregnant," she says.

"But, when? How long have you known?"

"I don't know. Maybe a month?"

"But we've hardly . . ."

"I know."

"Hold on. Do you mean—"

"I don't know," she says. "I'm just not sure. I'll have to go to the doctor, do the math."

I stand. I sit. I stand, walk once around the room, sit again.

"Sweetie," she says, and it's her turn to be the levelheaded one. "Calm down."

"Are you going to leave me?"

"What?"

"If it's Roger's, are you going to leave?"

"Of course not," she says. She takes my hand and squeezes. "I mean it. It's over now."

"So, what would we do with it?"

"Things can be done," she says.

I consider this, and a shiver runs down my spine. I try to picture it, try not to. And what would we call this, in our case? Extermination?

I won't raise another man's child, and yet, I don't think I could kill it either.

"What if I told you it wasn't an accident?" I say. "That I ran over James Dean on purpose?"

"What?"

"If I meant to hit the dog," I say. "Would you still want me around?"

Jill watches me, openmouthed. She lets go of my hand.

"Did you?"

"No."

I want a song to soar through the waiting room, suddenly meaningful and ironic. "Your Cheatin' Heart" or something. Something to make Jill cry. Of course, this doesn't happen. The same soft, classical music comes out of the speakers, some concerto or other. The thing swells, peaks, then falls away in a shimmy of violins.

"You," Jill says, "are an asshole."

◆   ◆   ◆

The first time I met Dean, I was drunk. Jill's parents had just died. We'd been to the viewing, then gone straight to a bar a few blocks from Jill's place. We were bracing ourselves for the funeral the next afternoon.

We were still in school at NKU, had only known each other a few weeks, but, standing by the caskets, Jill introduced me to one relative as her boyfriend. When I look back, it's as if there were never a choice in the matter. Neither of us had the chance to turn the other down, as though, in death, something had been decided for us.

Jill and I stumbled into her apartment and groped on the couch.

I was horizontal, Jill on top of me, taking off her shirt.

I looked to my right, and there was this animal, brown and white, broad-shouldered and squatty. His tail stood in the air like a middle finger. He was about six inches from my face.

"Jill," I said. "Jill."

Jill pulled her shirt from her face and looked down.

"Oh," she said, "that's James Dean. Say hi, Dean."

Dean growled. His teeth were white, but his gum line was black. He didn't bite, but he let me know he'd like to.

"Dean," Jill said, "you be nice." Then, to me: "Don't worry, he's really friendly once you get to know him."

We made love like that, Jill on top of me, the beagle beside me. Dean did not take his eyes off me the whole time.

. ◆ ◆

The veterinarian, tall and thin, forty or fifty, is not a bad man, but he's the bearer of bad news, and I think we both hate him for it. He frowns, but his handlebar mustache curls upward in a smile. He's probably given this speech so many times that it no longer holds meaning for him. They're just words, what he was taught to recite before he got his diploma.

"I'm sorry," he says in conclusion, "but there's nothing else we can do. It would be cruel to draw this out any longer. I think that the best thing we can do for"—he pauses, glances at his clipboard, looks back at us, and reassumes an expression of sorrow—"James Dean, at this point, is to let him go. We can help him do that. It won't hurt. It will be like falling into a peaceful sleep."

I look at Jill for confirmation, but she's gone, beyond words.

"Would you like to say goodbye?" the man says.

I turn to Jill. Nothing. I look back at the man and nod.

◆ ◆ ◆

The euthanization room is dim with weird halogen lights that cast an unsettling yellow-green glow over everything. James Dean is on his side on a steel table. He's been muzzled, and an IV tube extends from one paw to a bag hanging from a hook on the wall. The table looks cold. I touch it, and it is. There's something alien about the scene, like he's not even our dog. I expect Jill to burst into tears, but she displays no emotion.

"Here," I say. I unclip the muzzle and pull it away from Dean's snout. Suddenly, he looks more like the dog we both know. I pet his head, and he sniffs at my hand. He tries to shuffle forward, but his lower half doesn't follow his front legs' lead, and his nails scrape futilely against the table.

"Would you like to step outside?" I ask.

"Yes," Jill says. She moves toward the door.

"Wait," I say. "Jill, I'm really, really sorry about this. All of it." She stands at the door, her hand on the knob.

"Whatever you want to do," I say, "I'm your man. We're in this thing together."

Maybe it's the classical music coming through the thin walls of the next room, or that our dog is dying on a table in front of us. Perhaps it's something else entirely. But before Jill walks out the door, she smiles. She gives me a look that says, *At least we have each other*. That seems to say, *We can still make this work*. A look that says, *Don't worry. Love won't let go*.

◆   ◆   ◆

Now, it's just me and Dean. It's hard to look at him, so I look around the room. It's small, not like the offices where you take your pet for a checkup. No posters of breeds on the walls or tins of doggy treats on the countertop. This room is reserved for death. There are two chairs, a big padded one for the vet and a white, plastic chair, an old piece of patio furniture. I pick the plastic chair, which seems to open its arms to accept me as I sit, then grips my hips so tightly I wonder if I'll ever escape.

I force myself to look at Dean. Dean looks back. He's got his head balanced on his front paws. If you took away the IV tube, he'd look like one of those dogs you see on calendars with titles like *Beautiful Beagles* or *Purebred Hounds*.

"We had a deal," I say. Dean doesn't say anything, just watches me with his big, sad dog eyes. "We had a deal, you fucker."

Dean winces, and I know that he must be in terrible pain, that it's time to get this over with. As if on cue, the veterinarian walks in. He carries a small tray with a stiff, blue cloth draped over the top, like I won't guess what's underneath.

"If you're finished," he says, "I'd like to go ahead with the procedure." *Procedure.* He says it the way you'd say *spatula*. There's no inflection, no hint of what's in the syringe and what it will do to the dog.

"I'll need you to step out," he says. His face is kind, but his voice is firm.

"No," I say. "I think I'll stay."

"We generally don't recommend that."

"I want to watch you kill my dog," I say.

"Sir," he says, but there is nothing else to say.

"If you want me to sign a waiver or something, I will."

The man frowns. He pulls the blue cloth from the tray, revealing two shots.

"I'm afraid I'll need to put the muzzle back on," he says. "He tried to bite one of my technicians."

"Sorry about that," I say.

The vet steps forward with the muzzle, and something churns inside me. It seems undignified, like Dean deserves better. I may not like this dog, but all living things deserve to die decently. I believe that.

I jump up, the chair clinging to me for a second before clattering to the floor. "Wait," I say. "Don't put that on him. I'll take care of it."

The vet looks at me skeptically, then puts the muzzle away. I step up to the table and crouch so that me and Dean are eye and eye.

"Well," I say, "this is it, buddy." I make a fist around his snout and nod at the vet. The first needle goes in and Dean whines, struggles under my grip.

Quickly, the vet retrieves the second syringe. When the needle hits Dean's hide, though, he thrashes, pulls his mouth from my hand, and bites down hard on my thumb. The vet injects the last of the toxin, pulls the needle out, and, still, Dean doesn't let go. I try to pry my hand from his jaws, but he holds on tight.

He dies like that, my bloody thumb caught between his teeth. And, for the first time since we met, he looks happy.

Nudists

Outside, Mark's brother lit a second cigarette. Above him, tacked to a stone column, a sign directed smokers to other stretches of sidewalk. Joshua seemed not to notice the sign or, beyond the wide glass doors and across the crowded baggage claim, his brother.

Mark was in no hurry to have his brother's attention. The flight had been long, the movie unwatchable, his seatmate more than a little on the smelly side. And now he had Joshua to endure, Joshua, who, even as a boy, refused to let anyone shorten his name. Call him Josh, and he'd punch you in the arm, hard.

He watched Joshua smoke the cigarette to the filter, watched him drop, then grind, the butt into the sidewalk with the bright toe of a brown leather boot. When the doors opened and the boots shuffled through, Mark turned away. He tried to arrange his expression into something approaching happy surprise, and, when he turned back, Joshua was on him.

The hug lasted too long, past uncomfortable, then past that, until, gently, he pushed Joshua away, and they stood, studying each other.

Last he'd seen him, Joshua had looked weary, old for his age. Now, he was the kind of thirty that got carded at bars. He was lean, muscled, like someone who played sports, though Mark couldn't imagine it—Joshua kicking a field goal or working a basketball down the court. His skin was bronzed, hair black, curls tangled thick as sheep's wool. His hair had the appearance that comes from one's working very hard to make hair look messy. It glistened under the airport lights as though lacquered. Mark had expected a gut, an invasion of gray hairs, those plagues of age he'd endured himself. Had he hoped them for his brother? But Joshua looked better than ever, healthy, fit—*young*—and Mark told him so.

"You look good too," Joshua said.

"I got fat," he said. "You don't have to pretend I didn't."

Joshua shrugged. He ran a hand over his hair, which didn't move.

An employee of the federal park service, Joshua had pinballed from park to park before landing a permanent position at the San Francisco Maritime Museum. For two years, he'd held Mark to the promise to visit, a promise Mark had felt no real obligation to keep. He was always the one emptying his wallet for flights to Jackson Hole or Salt Lake or Tucson, wherever Joshua landed seasonal work. Joshua had never returned the favor, had never come to Vermont, never, in ten years, seen their home or Lorrie's garden in full bloom. And now it was too late. The house was no longer his. The flowers, which he'd let wilt, then die, had been pulled up. Where there'd been flowerbeds, the new owners had laid sod. It shone in the sun, neon, indisputable as Astroturf.

The baggage carousel snaked past them, silver, a river of ladders, rungs spinning. The other passengers from his flight had left, bags in hand, all but a woman in a yellow dress. Three times, a white duffel circled. A red ribbon fluttered from its handle. On the fourth pass, the woman cried, "Oh!" She got a hand on the bag and fought to pull it from the conveyor. Joshua stepped forward and, with an *Allow me*, lifted the bag and lowered it onto a cart stacked high with matching luggage.

"Thank you!" she said.

"My pleasure," Joshua said. He raised a hand, touched the brim of a hat that wasn't there. He turned to Mark, crossed his arms.

"Marisa's thrilled you came," he said.

Marisa was Joshua's girlfriend. She was smart, smarter than Joshua. Kinder, too, so that Mark often wondered what she saw in his brother.

But the bond was undeniable, and their relationship, whatever else it may have been, was not an unhappy one. It wasn't that Joshua and Marisa never fought. It was that they fought without raising their voices. Each laughed at the other's jokes. Each smiled when the other talked. Mark had stood in the doorway, once, and watched them wash dishes. They'd moved side by side at the sink with a shared tempo, Marisa humming something, hands working fast with a rag. They were good for each other, in dishwashing and in life, and, following a visit, Lorrie had never failed to point this out to Mark, illustratively, letting the fact stand for that which she couldn't—wouldn't—say.

"I think you'll like the place we picked out for Thursday," Joshua said.

Mark nodded. He wished suddenly and like hell that he hadn't come.

The carousel circled, bagless. A new group of passengers flooded the lobby.

"This right here is why I carry on," Joshua said.

He wanted to tell Joshua that he *had* carried on, that he'd been stopped at boarding by a flight attendant who insisted his bag was *oversized*. He'd argued, then pleaded. The bag would fit, had fit many times before. But it was no use. The suitcase had been ticketed and whisked away.

A siren squawked and the carousel shuddered to a stop.

"Fuck," he said.

"Easy," Joshua said. "It's just luggage."

But it wasn't just luggage. This, this very moment, was the culmination of everything that had conspired, that year, to wreck him. Everything resurfacing, the way it did daily, this day in the guise of lost luggage. He thought he might cry. Thinking it, he was ashamed, and then he was sure he *would* cry.

"Hey, they'll find it," Joshua said. "Till then, mi ropa es su ropa, you know?"

Mark nodded. Back in Burlington, he taught Spanish to dead-eyed adolescents, a fact he'd quit advertising on airplanes or anywhere people asked, *What do you do?* He hated being the dartboard for people's bad Spanish, their mismatched participles and mangled pronunciations. He loved language, loved it too much to hear it roll ugly off others' tongues, which was to say that, as a middle school teacher halfway to retirement, he had long ago committed himself to the wrong profession.

"I have a toothbrush you can use," Joshua said. "I always keep an extra on hand."

Who the *fuck* kept spare toothbrushes? It was too much. Mark wanted to turn and walk back onto the plane.

"Boy Scout motto," Joshua said, and, when Mark couldn't fill in the blank, he held up a hand in the trademark three-finger salute and said, "Be prepared."

◆   ◆   ◆

But what could have prepared Mark for that year? What prepares one for a life left under a bridge in blue water?

Three cars spinning was how one witness described what he'd seen. Lorrie's car was the one to go through the guardrail, to eat the sky and fall. The river was frozen, and the car cracked it open.

When Mark reached the river, he pushed past paramedics and reporters and saw what everyone saw: two circles projected onto the underside of the ice. They glowed like ghosts, like river moons. He vomited, staggered forward, was caught before he fell through.

As he watched, a shadow crossed one beam, then the other. The shadow grew in the light. He prayed that it was Lorrie even as he knew that it couldn't be Lorrie. The shadow was like a great fish rising, then an angel, and then the shadow was a man. The man appeared through a hole in the ice. He elbowed his way onto the ice and moved toward shore. He was pulled onto the bank by police officers in black coats with thick collars. The swimmer's feet were fins, his face a bubble of glass. A blue skin covered him, head to toe, and a tank hung from his back. A regulator's bulb fell from his mouth, and, shivering, the man pulled the mask from his face. He said nothing, only shook his head.

The next day, on the phone, Joshua had said over and over how sorry he was. He asked how he could help. When Mark suggested he board the first flight to Burlington, Joshua had said that sort of thing could be difficult, that he'd have to discuss it with Marisa, that it was a *tough time,* which meant that he didn't want to spend the money.

Two words, and Mark might have changed his brother's mind. *I'll pay.* Or, if his brother were a better man, simply: *Please, come.* Though, if his brother were a better man, Mark wouldn't have needed the words, and so he would not say them. He would not beg.

Silence stood between them like the quiet that follows the click of a pin pulled from a grenade. Then Joshua said he had to go. He'd talk to Marisa. He'd see what he could do.

But he had not come. And so they had not spoken, not until the year unraveled into autumn and a surprise showed up in the mail. It was Marisa's name at the bottom of the card in blue ink. The invitation to Thanksgiving dinner was hers. Mark had accepted. He'd been ready, then, to face his brother. Now, he was no longer sure that he was.

◆   ◆   ◆

Joshua drove fast, an arm out the window. He pointed and smoked. He had a park ranger's trademark memory and could, when called upon to do so, expound at length on his surroundings. Each San Francisco block brought another restaurant, storefront, or statue and, with each, an anecdote, a history, the confirmation or rejection of local lore.

Mark sat low in his seat, half-listening. He felt his pockets for his wallet, his keys, his phone. His suitcase held everything else. The bag would be delivered by morning. He had the airline's assurances.

Bad music shook the speakers of Joshua's car, something about *mammals . . . something, something . . . the Discovery Channel.*

"Here's the Haight," Joshua said. "Haight-Ashbury. Hippie shit. Late sixties, heart of the free love movement. Now it's a place you don't walk at night."

They stopped at a light. A man in a floppy stovepipe hat, red and white like the Cat in the Hat's, shuffled down the sidewalk. Ahead of him, a Mohawked woman jogged, tracksuit billowing.

"Freak show," Joshua said. "A lot of that here. Not just here, but *here*." He nodded, as if to indict the city, all of it, or maybe the whole West Coast. The song changed, and Joshua's arm returned to the cab and drummed the dash. Every few taps, his other hand left the wheel to stick an invisible cymbal.

The Mohawked woman was getting farther and farther away. She was tall and thin and moved with a bouncy, assured gait. Mark would have liked to run a hand over her head, to feel the smooth scalp turn to hair, then back to skin. He thought of highways, of the grassy medians that divide them. He thought—he couldn't help himself—of Lorrie.

They drove on until he was sure they'd left the city, and then the car approached a bend. Joshua took the turn hard, and Mark flinched. When they straightened out, he relaxed his grip on the door handle. It had been like this since the accident. His new apartment he'd picked by its proximity to school. Except during rainstorms, he walked to work.

They followed the road down a hill and joined a line of cars on the shoulder. The sight had been picked to astonish: the Golden Gate Bridge, many-spindled, majestic, and fat behind fog. They left the car, climbed a bluff, and looked down on the bridge, which seemed to Mark more red than gold. Trying to take in the bridge, the enormity of it in the fog, was like picturing a puzzle with gaps at the center and the sides. Below, ships navigated the channel. A sailboat cut through the mist and emerged from beneath the bridge.

"I stop here sometimes on my way to work," Joshua said. "Just to see it. An absolute feat of engineering. Took four thousand workers and four years to complete. 1.2 million rivets, each one solid steel." He sighed, shook his head. "Men died to make this bridge."

Far back as Mark could remember, Joshua had been like this. He was the kind of guy who took his truth where he could find it, and because, given his line of work, factoids were the morsels that made up his communion, he was prone to flights of trivial import, his life a kind of *Jeopardy!* He might note, with urgency, that the blind were known for their acute sense of hearing or that elephants sometimes ran trunks over the tusks of the dead. Invariably, he would follow these nuggets up with *It just goes to show you,* or *It really makes you think,* though he could never be depended upon to say just what something went to show or was meant to make one think. His metaphors went forever unfinished, as though to turn them toward relevance might diminish their vague power. The right listener might smile, amused or awed, but Mark was not the right listener. The treatises generally left him resisting the urge to roll his eyes.

As a child, Joshua had been drawn to nature documentaries. He'd harried the family at mealtimes with the sleeping habits of lions, the diets of zebras, the migration patterns of various African birds. Traits were occasionally attributed to family members.

"You," he told Mark over a dinner of hot dogs, "are a rhino." He didn't say why. Instead, he took a big bite of hot dog, mustard dropping onto his shirtfront. He set the hot dog down, and—Mark couldn't say why he remembered this so vividly—he pulled the shirt to his mouth and, nimbly as a cat, tongued the fabric clean.

Each evening brought new animals to the table, and what Joshua didn't know, Mark suspected he made up. He suspected this still.

On the bluff, Mark watched him. They shared the same hawk's nose, the same narrow forehead and cleft chin. Hard features. *Presidential,* Lorrie had said.

They shared the same blood. This was unmistakable, right up to the moment Joshua opened his mouth, at which point Mark always wondered how they could be brothers.

"This bridge," Joshua said. "It really makes you think."

"It does," Mark said, thinking how a moment can mean two things to two people.

He thought this and did not speak it. Neither did he remind the man at his side that a bridge in winter was what had killed his wife.

◆ ◆ ◆

They drove on, following the coastline, until they came to a kind of compound. Identical concrete units rose between trees from green hills, the buildings dark-roofed and many-antennaed. They had reached the Presidio.

"Former military base," Joshua said. "And now—"

"Housing for hippies?"

"You got it."

The units were small, three-storied, drab but for plants in window boxes and flags hung from ledges.

"Batteries line the beach," Joshua said. "The government was all set for the Japanese."

They took the streets through the compound too fast, up steep hills and down steeper ones. They nosedived down one slope until Joshua jerked the wheel and ground the car's tires into the curb.

"While you're here, it's important to angle your tires on inclines," Joshua said. He appeared unconcerned that Mark had no car and, therefore, no tires to angle. It was just another fact, a thing to know. "The city's notorious for runaway cars. This way, your brakes give out, you stay put. It's the law."

Mark reached into the backseat for his bag, then remembered he didn't have one. He was still in the passenger seat, still facing the back, when Joshua said something, his voice muffled, a near whisper.

"I'm sorry?" Mark said.

"This funeral business," Joshua repeated. "That's behind us, right?" He put a hand on Mark's shoulder and squeezed.

And what could he say? The funeral wasn't behind them. The very subject was a river to be crossed, a river rising fast and one that might never be crossed with Joshua so quick to dismiss it. If he'd come for an apology, Mark saw now he'd never get it.

"Marisa feels bad," Joshua said. "I tell her you're fine, but she won't believe me. She misses Lorrie. I made her promise not to bring it up." He undid his seatbelt and stepped from the car. He knelt, face framed by the open door. Beyond him, the sky sank into the ocean. "Just know, you say anything, she'll cry."

The door swung shut, and Joshua was across the parking lot before Mark could bring himself to follow.

◆   ◆   ◆

There had been a letter.

This wasn't long after the funeral, when the weight of what *was* pressed so hard upon Mark that he woke once, twice a night and sobbed. His dreams were ice, tires smoking, vehicles catapulted through guardrails.

Other dreams, he stood before an enormous arcade game, a pinball machine. Instead of balls, the bumpers rebounded cars. The cars spun and ricocheted, and Mark jammed like mad on the buttons. But the flippers were locked, always locked, and, one by one, the cars tumbled, fell, slipped past the flippers and into the mouth of the machine, swallowed, *gone*.

There were dreams of the river, the car bubbling, a hole in the windshield, and Lorrie's hair trailing, current-caught and swaying like kelp.

Another dream, the dream that gave voice to the letter, found him in the river. Water filled the car. Heels dug in the riverbed, he pulled at the handle, but the door wouldn't give. Lorrie's words were gurgles. The water would not stop coming. And then there was a hand on his back. And then there was Joshua. The car was lifted, heaved from the river to shore. Lorrie tumbled out in a rush of water and into Joshua's arms.

That morning, trembling, Mark had picked up a pen. The dreams were horrors, but they were his horrors, and Joshua had no place invading them. He didn't organize his thoughts. He wrote. Letters leaned angry into words. Words tangled into hateful sentences. There was no proofreading, no revision. His students, even the laziest, would have been appalled.

Furious, dazed, and half-asleep, he'd folded the paper, folded it again, addressed an envelope, and mailed the letter before he could change his mind.

He couldn't say, now, what the letter had said. Certainly there had been some *fuck*s in there, some *fuck*s and some *motherfuckers* that must have stood out no matter how sloppy the penmanship. There'd been a list of grievances: a model airplane stolen and broken in boyhood, a borrowed shirt torn at the sleeve, a seatbelt slung and the faint scar it had left on Mark's temple. The list had likely culminated with the missed funeral, but he couldn't be sure.

What blue rage had he been in, what boiling soup, to write such things?

His fury had since cooled. Now, it was an ache—persistent, arthritic—but nothing like the fire from before. No, the real fire was his own.

Joshua, after all, had not cursed her. Joshua had not heard the unspeakable pass between his teeth. Joshua had not flung Lorrie from the bridge.

No, that had been him.

◆   ◆   ◆

The clothes did not fit. Mark's stomach hung over the waistline of jeans he'd barely managed to button. Even the largest of Joshua's T-shirts clung to his chest, exposing his navel and the taut skin of his gut.

"It's a good look for you," Joshua said, and Marisa laughed through the hand at her face.

Like Joshua, Marisa looked healthy, fit, young. She credited the weather, the water, and her decision to move to a diet of all-natural and organic foods.

"We tried vegetarianism," she said, "but your brother missed meat."

Joshua lowed like cattle.

Marisa's hair was long and straight, still blond, and Mark wondered whether Joshua knew that Marisa was—as she'd once confided in Lorrie—going gray under all that gold.

Marisa had met them at the door, and, like Joshua, she'd held him for too long.

The past nine months, he'd become a connoisseur of hugs. There were the pity hugs, the obligatory hugs, even the few that meant sympathy, genuine and unforced. Marisa's was one of those, and it was only once she'd let go, his chest warm, that he missed how it felt, having a body in his arms, and he thought of the Mohawked woman, and he was afraid. Whatever was surfacing, pushing through, he wasn't ready.

Joshua and Marisa left the room, and he changed back into his clothes. His socks clung, sweaty, to his feet. His shirt smelled like the plane he'd flown in on.

He'd been given the spare room, which turned out to be a kind of oversized storage closet. Boxes and piles of papers had been pushed into corners. An inflated air mattress filled the floor, and an unzipped sleeping bag covered the mattress. A pair of towels and a washcloth sat stacked on a pillow. The room's walls were white, the ceiling low and mottled with what he'd once heard a Realtor call popcorn, the bubbly sealant that hid the seams of poorly hung drywall. The ceiling dropped from the doorframe's apex to the floor like the hypotenuse of a triangle. Already, he saw he'd have to sleep with his head at the door to keep from rising and cracking his skull in the night. He ran a hand over the ceiling, and it snowed, the sleeping bag, pillow, towels—all of it—mottled with a pebbly, white dust.

Joshua and Marisa were waiting for him in the main room. The room was sparsely decorated, furniture an assemblage of pieces salvaged from sidewalks and yard sales. Here and there, cups stuffed with cigarette butts dotted the landscape.

The room's focal point was a wide-screen TV perched on a coffee table. The TV was huge, the table too small for it. Beneath the table, three gaming systems sat piled beside jewel cases. Discs scattered the hardwood floor, a perimeter of silver puddles. Mark tallied the expense in his head. He wondered how many games a plane ticket would buy.

"We thought we'd lay low tonight," Marisa said. "We figured you'd be tired."

He wasn't tired. Already, he felt trapped by the small apartment and its quiet ashtray stink. How did Marisa, a nonsmoker, stand it? He couldn't imagine the three of them sitting there breathing the same stale air while evening turned over. But he said nothing.

He fell into the lap of a white, wide-armed chair. Across the room, Marisa and Joshua shared a couch. Above them, and through a window, the apartments of the Presidio were overtaken by trees and, beyond these, a blue, Pacific strip.

The silence in the room was approaching insurmountable.

"You have a nice home," he said.

"We like it," Marisa said.

"We were just happy to find a clean, safe place," Joshua said. "You wouldn't believe what it costs to live—" He stopped short, as though he'd said too much.

And then they were all thinking money, funerals and flights.

Mark turned to Marisa. "How's the world of physical therapy?" he asked.

She laughed. "You make it sound so *noble*. It's nothing like that. I massage the rich and the tense."

Marisa was famous for her back rubs. During visits, Lorrie

would remove her top and lie on the floor. Marisa would squat over her, working her hands between Lorrie's shoulder blades and down her spine. Afterward, Lorrie would always slip into his arms, limp and lithe. "Nothing sexual about massages," Lorrie would say. "They're relaxing, that's all," but Mark didn't believe her. Always, he could count on those nights to get some. Which was why, when Marisa offered, hands oiled, legs crossed on the floor, and his wife watching, Mark always said thanks, but no.

A bird flew past the window, then another.

"She's good," Joshua said. "Really good. Number one requested masseuse at Salon Six. Does all the San Francisco celebs. Robin Williams—"

"Okay, love," Marisa said. She raised a hand to Joshua's cheek. She had large, clean hands with trimmed nails. Mark could still see them kneading Lorrie's skin like floured dough.

"Sorry, Mark," she said. "Our client list is supposed to be confidential. We get stars, sure, but more has-beens than anything else. Reality hacks, old soap divas."

"Alex Trebek." Joshua laughed. "Hundred-dollar tip." He put his arm around Marisa.

"That was one time."

"Asked her to rub his mustache."

"He did no such thing," Marisa said.

But she must have gotten them on occasion, given her line of work, Mark thought—the inappropriate proposals, the special requests. He was curious but not curious enough to ask.

"You should let her give you one," Joshua said. "I mean it. When she's done, you won't have a care in the world." He turned to Marisa. "You have time tomorrow, right?"

"I have an hour," Marisa said.

But the suggestion had rattled her. Mark could see the surprise, see her register his seeing.

"That's all right," Mark said. "But I appreciate the offer."

"I insist," Joshua said. "I'll pay."

After that, what could anyone say? Marisa coughed. Mark watched the window.

Later, from his bed on the floor, through the thin walls, he heard them fucking. They were trying to be quiet about it, you could tell, but there it was, the rhythm of the bed, his brother's grunt, and, at the climax, not a moan from Marisa, but a breathy exhalation, like what comes just before the whistle—a teakettle's exquisite, satisfied sigh.

•   •   •

And who could say for sure that he hadn't killed his wife?

"Go to hell," he'd said, and what if she had? He wasn't a believer. Before that night, he hadn't given much thought to heaven or to hell, to an afterlife of any kind. He'd never believed—not really—that he or anyone he loved would die. At the river, though, the cold cutting through his socks and into his shoes, he'd watched the man in the wetsuit emerge from the water and he'd known for sure that some place followed this, that Lorrie was there, and that he had been her dispatcher.

Go to hell.

Fifteen years, they'd been fighting this fight. School let out at three, which left him alone for hours, bored, while Lorrie, a lawyer, worked late. He wanted her home. Was she on her way? And where had she been all evening?

But, that night, he did something he'd never done: He asked her, outright. He hadn't believed it, not really, only wanted the slap to sting. The truth was, she was very good at what she did. She got lots of work, and she refused to half-ass a case. This meant long hours, and if he wanted to talk fidelity, they could start with the smut she'd found under the bath mat. He'd suggested he wouldn't need magazines were she fulfilling her wifely duties, and she'd observed that such duties might be a little more palatable if he stopped calling work every ten minutes to make her feel bad. Furthermore, should he question her faithfulness again, *ever,* they were through—she'd file the paperwork herself.

"Go to hell," he'd said, then hung up. His cell phone had buzzed, then dinged with the message she'd left. He'd made no move to check it.

When, hours later, the house phone rang, it wasn't Lorrie. It was no voice he knew. He listened to the voice, heard something blossom, taloned and black, and then his understanding of the world came loose from his place in it.

That her death had saved them a divorce was no comfort, was worse than no comfort. And so what if the thing he wanted back wasn't *her,* but *them* or, if not them, an idea of them, of what they'd been, once, long ago?

He wanted her back, if only to tell her he was sorry, that he hadn't meant it, hadn't meant a word.

◆   ◆   ◆

Sunup, and Mark had to hustle to keep up. He and Joshua crossed the grounds of Victorian Park. They walked fast under the shadows of factories and canneries turned, this century, to shops and hotels. The windows of the buildings glowed, awnings striped and stretched to toothy grins.

They passed a beach. Offshore, swimmers moved in a line between buoys, all flutter kicks and swim caps, arms scissoring the bay.

The plan was for Mark to spend the morning at the Maritime Museum. He would see the ships, watch Joshua give his tourist talks, and then it was off to Salon Six for Marisa's massage.

"You're not *naked,* if that's what you're worried about," Joshua said. "There's a towel."

Mark pulled on his shirt collar. The suitcase had not arrived. Over the phone, an attendant had reminded him that today was the day before Thanksgiving, *a very busy day,* and that, in the future, Mark might *consider carrying on*. He'd wanted to scream. Instead, he'd returned the phone to his pocket and cut the tape on a cardboard box that Joshua had pulled from storage. The box was labeled FAT CLOTHES and was full of fashions maybe five years old. He settled on jeans and a white T-shirt with the black outline of a lion faded on the front. The clothes fit, but the odor of cigarettes was all over them, as though they'd gone into the box unwashed, which, for all Mark knew, they had.

Joshua wore his uniform, the trademark green slacks and tan, button-down shirt of the park service. His hat—perched high and unfriendly-looking on his hillock of hair—sported a brim stiff as the blade of a shovel. It was a forest uniform, one that made more sense on Smokey the Bear than it did on the beach.

They passed a trash barrel, and Joshua flicked a spent cigarette into it.

They continued up a paved embankment, across a street, and through an open gate to a small, weather-beaten building.

"Here we are," Joshua said.

Mark had expected a museum, something grand with a winding staircase, portraits of dead sea captains on the walls. But the building looked more like a public restroom. The front was brown wood, unsanded, and the roof was tin. The real attraction was just ahead, a dozen docked ships and a pier that caterpillared into the bay.

They walked the pier. The ships varied in size and age. There were naval vessels, holes cut from their sides for the mouths of cannons, and schooners whose sails hung like pirate ships'. The ships stood in various stages of disrepair, some bright, hulls gleaming, others rusted, in need of real work.

The crown jewel, Joshua said, was the *Thayer*, a tall ship with wide, white sails and a prominent black bow. A red stripe marked its middle. Its anchor chain disappeared into the bay, links big as refrigerators.

"A million bucks," Joshua said. "New hull, new deck, new mast."

The ship towered over them, sails flapping.

"These old ships, you can't just spit and scrub off the barnacles," he said. "Restoration takes time, craftsmanship. A lot of love."

A gangplank stuck out like a tongue from the ship and touched the pier. A traffic barrel, orange and white, blocked the plank.

"Closed to the public," Joshua said. "Belowdecks is a mess. But, next year, it'll be something to see."

He talked more about the ships, about plans for the park and the Facebook page they were designing that week. He talked, and they strolled until they'd reached the end of the pier. Joshua lit a cigarette and leaned against the railing. He stared out at the bay, where an island broke the water's surface like a turtle shell. At the center of the island stood Alcatraz, the notorious condemned prison turned notorious tourist trap. At the airport, Mark had come across posters, signs, and colorful brochures all advertising the not-to-be-missed San Francisco destination.

"Only five men ever got off that island," Joshua said. "Their bodies were never found."

"Sharks?" Mark asked, and Joshua shook his head. It wasn't sharks or the distance to dry land, he told him. It was the cold, the heart giving out before the body clawed its way to shore.

"It's all about conditioning," Joshua said. "You take an athlete whose muscles can keep up, he'll produce the heat to make the swim. Drop anyone else in this water, and in half an hour you've got yourself a Popsicle. They pulled a guy from the bay last week, your typical Joe Desk Job. Went hypothermic in ten minutes."

The wind changed direction, and Joshua's smoke was in his face. He coughed.

"Are you sorry you came?"

Mark said nothing. If Joshua was looking for comfort, assurances, he wouldn't get them from him.

Joshua put his cigarette out on the railing, exhaled, and, with a nod, as though something had been settled, let the butt drop into the bay.

"I think you'll like dinner tomorrow," Joshua said. "The place, it's no home cooking, but they do a good job. We went last year. Pumpkin pie's out of this world."

He ran a finger and thumb along the brim of his hat, then glanced at his fingertips as though checking for dust.

"Anyhow," he continued, "dinner's on me."

If regret was a malleable, shape-shifting thing, then his brother's was taking multiple forms—the massage, the meal—and why couldn't Joshua just say the words?

"You don't have to do that," Mark said.

"My treat," Joshua said. "I insist."

•　　•　　•

The foyer of Salon Six was spacious and high-ceilinged. The furniture was sleek, modern-looking. Contoured chairs littered the lobby, and Mark lowered himself into something resembling the tortured body of a compressed letter *S*.

He didn't want to be here, but neither did he want to insult Marisa. She and Lorrie had been, if not close, at least closer than he and Joshua had ever been. Lorrie wouldn't have wanted him mad at Marisa, and so he'd tried hard not to be.

Tables rose low from the floor like collapsed TV trays, and Mark reached toward the nearest for a *USA Today*. The paper informed him that the president, as per tradition, had pardoned a pair of Thanksgiving turkeys. The birds would live out their remaining days at a game ranch in Virginia. He put the paper down and shut his eyes.

A long morning had given way to an interminable afternoon. All day, he'd watched Joshua do his thing. The talks were collages of history and statistical tidbits: how many trees had gone into the construction of this ship; how many tons of steel had gone into that one; the precise dates during which a particular vessel had been seaworthy and why it no longer was. Men and women with sunglasses and shopping bags nodded, smiled, and held their squirming children's hands. Occasionally, someone posed a challenging question. Joshua had the answer, always, and, each time, an awed murmur rose from the park visitors like the call-and-response of a crowd watching fireworks.

Mark understood quickly why Joshua had stuck with this job. Here was work that allowed—no, *encouraged*—his brother's love of trivia, his brother's very nature: that relentless, uncompromising know-it-allness.

Was he jealous of the attention his brother got, the applause at the end, the admiration over facts probably forgotten before the shopping bags were unpacked, before the sunglasses left these people's heads? Jealous when, back home, he was lucky to keep the attention of two, three kids a class while he filled the marker board with conjugations or spoke at length about the subjunctive mood? Maybe he was. He didn't want to be.

A door opened to the waiting room, and Mark heard his name. He stood and followed a woman in white down a white hall to a small, white room. The room smelled like mint and incense. At the center of the room stood a long table. An O, like a spare tire, hung from the table's end. A few cabinets and a counter hung from one wall. One might have mistaken the room for a doctor's office if not for the lighting—dim—and the flicker of a candle on the countertop.

"You may disrobe and lie down," the woman said. She handed him a white towel, then she left the room.

He didn't move. A minute later, there was a knock at the door and Marisa walked in.

"Oh," she said. "You're dressed."

He hoped, right then, she'd let him off the hook. Together, they could tell Joshua whatever she wanted, whatever it took to keep him from lying down on that table.

But, no, she was giving him instructions, smiling, stepping out of the room.

When she returned, he lay naked on his stomach, face tucked into the table's spongy O. The towel covered his middle. The position wasn't a particularly comfortable one. It hurt his shoulders to lie flat with his hands at his sides, but it seemed wrong to let his arms hang from the table in air.

Marisa asked how his morning had been, how he liked the ships and whether he was enjoying the city. There was an opening and closing of cabinet doors, the scrape of a lid coming loose.

He said it was fine, all of it fine. That the day had been good.

"Your brother is so smart," she said. "I watch his presentations, and I'm amazed."

Something cold splashed his back, and then Marisa was rubbing vigorously. The oil warmed where she rubbed. He felt the towel fold down from his lower back, felt it tuck in around his waist. Through the O, he could see only the octagonal pattern and white grout of a tile floor.

"You have great skin," Marisa said. "Some backs, you should see them. They're so bad, I have to glove-up. And then the clients get mad because it doesn't feel the same, the latex. And how do you point out politely that they have too many zits or a rash or open sores?"

She rubbed hard, but her hands were soft, uncallused. Gradually, he relaxed. He felt warm all over.

"I get it now," he said. "I get why people like this."

He meant it. He closed his eyes. The room swayed. Light burrowed up his back and burst into his shoulders, then radiated, hot and bright, through his whole body.

"You're very good," he said.

"I've been at it a long time," she said. Then, lowering her voice, she said, "But not much longer. I'm in school."

She was studying sign language, she said. As a translator, she'd help people communicate with one another. The idea captivated her, how a gesture became words, how words became the movement of hands.

"I want to be that conduit," she said.

In Burlington, he'd had a pair of deaf neighbors. Summer

evenings, he and Lorrie would sit on their porch and talk while, across the street, the deaf couple sat on their porch and spoke with their hands. Always, he'd have to be reminded not to stare. But how could he not stare? The movements, the transmissions—they were beautiful. And Marisa's hands . . . the choice was perfect. The language had been made for hands like hers.

She worked his back, pressing, kneading. Her body's shadow glided through the candlelight and over his small patch of tile. Her fingers navigated his shoulders. She moved to the end of the table, and her shirt's hem grazed his hair.

He lifted his head, and there was her arm at his face. Veins pulsed, delicate and blue, the image suddenly lovely, this wrist, pale and soft-seeming, and these veins, tattooed in the shape of a tuning fork to her skin. Her wrist brushed his chin, and he kissed it.

It lasted a second, maybe less, a kiss so close to a breath, he let himself believe she wouldn't notice. But already Marisa was backing away. Her hands left his shoulders. He sat up, careful to keep himself covered. She was as far from him as the room allowed, backed into a corner beside the cabinetry and counter. The candle's flame danced by her wrist.

"Watch yourself," he said.

She brought her hands to her chest, but her eyes didn't leave his.

"I'm sorry," he said.

"Why did you do that?"

He didn't answer. He didn't know. He couldn't say why he'd done it, couldn't fathom the impulse or the compulsion to follow it. Or, he could fathom the impulse. Impulses came and went: the stove that said *Touch,* the red light that said *Run,* the ledge that whispered *Jump*. They came unbidden and, like the wishes of children, went ungranted. Far as Mark knew, it was this way for everyone.

Why this one, though? Why a kiss? Why now?

"Joshua would be so hurt if he knew."

"I wish you wouldn't tell him," he said.

Marisa's cheeks puffed and her bottom lip lengthened. She

exhaled, and Mark felt the wind across the room. She lifted his brother's clothes from the counter and set them on the table beside him. She moved to the door, opened it, but stopped short of the hall. She turned and stood in the open doorway.

"He's sorry," Marisa said. "I can promise you that. He's embarrassed. He's ashamed. We both are. We should have come, and we didn't. I can't explain it. There's no explanation good enough even if I could. All I can say is that we're sorry. But you know that. You have to know that."

The towel was bunched at his waist, and he smoothed it to his knees.

"Is that why you came?" she said. "To make us say it? To tell you how sorry we are?"

"Not you," he said. "I want to hear it from him."

Marisa looked away. Her hands clenched at her sides, and the material of her pants ballooned from her fists.

"You won't," she said. "You won't, and, what's more, you know you won't. Joshua doesn't work that way. Which is why *I'm* saying he's sorry, so you'll know. Because he can't say it. And because that should be enough. For a brother. It should be enough to know."

Knowing it, it should have been enough. And wasn't. He didn't know what would be.

"He cried, you know?" she said. "That letter? He wouldn't let me read it, but I found it, and I read it. It was . . . awful."

"I was angry."

"You're still angry. And none of us knows what to do. We can't go on until you give the word, and you're not giving it."

Her hands relaxed, fell open at her sides. She turned and pulled the door shut.

He dressed quickly. The towel he left on the table folded in a tight, white square.

◆　　◆　　◆

At the apartment, he showered. He wanted the smell off of him, the oil and the candle smoke. He stood beneath the showerhead until the door rattled.

"Hey, save some water for the rest of the planet," Joshua called. "Okay?"

His brother, the park ranger who would save the Earth except for the million cigarette butts he'd add to it.

He cut the water off, dried, and dressed. The room was steam-filled, condensation collecting on the mirror, the faucet, the backs of toothbrushes. Everything glistened in the wet. Beside the toilet, a bin overflowed with the wavy pages of old *National Geographics*. He left the bathroom damp, his brother's shirt bunched at the armpits and plastered to his back.

He found Joshua on the couch. He was still in uniform, shirt tucked but unbuttoned to the belt, a white T-shirt beneath. Mercifully, the hat had been removed. It perched, wide-brimmed, beside him on the couch. Joshua held a controller and, on screen, a man in silver armor lunged and leapt. Joshua's body bobbed in time with the little man.

"You want in on this?" he said. "I can make it two-player."

"I'd rather go for a walk," Mark said. "Clear my head."

"Marisa will be back soon," Joshua said. "If you wait, we can all go."

But Mark didn't want to wait. He didn't want to be there when Marisa got home.

"I'm just going to go now, if that's okay," he said.

Joshua didn't look up. There was a scream as the knight plunged his sword into a short, hobbity-looking thing. The creature collapsed, blood jetting from its chest, then it flickered and disappeared, a pool of blood left in its wake.

"Take the road down to Lincoln," Joshua said. "The first side street will bring you to Baker Beach. It's less than a mile. And be sure to check out the boulder end of the beach. Great view."

Mark felt in his pocket. He was missing his phone.

"Really, though, Marisa should be home any minute."

Mark moved to the spare room. He pulled the covers from the air mattress, one layer at a time, shook them, then lifted the mattress.

"Joshua?" he said.

He dropped the mattress. He patted his pockets, then pulled them inside out.

"Joshua," he called.

He retraced his steps down the hallway to the living room. He shook each of his shoes over the doormat. He opened the front door and glanced outside. He shut the door. His hands shook.

"Goddamn it, Joshua." He moved to the center of the room. He stood between his brother and the TV. Joshua craned his neck to see around him.

"Move," he said.

"Help me."

"In a minute. Move."

A cord, gray and umbilical, uncoiled from a box on the floor and into the controller in Joshua's hands. Mark grabbed and pulled.

Joshua stood. "Hey."

Then his hand was on Joshua's wrist and squeezing. The controller dropped, and he kicked it across the floor. He swung, but it was Joshua's fist that found his face.

He fell, arms windmilling. There was a crash, and he was on his back, the TV beneath him.

"What the fuck?" Joshua said. He stood over him.

"I can't find my phone." He brought a hand to his eye, rubbed it, then blinked the world back into focus. "You hit me."

"You took a swing," Joshua said. "I swung back. It's reflex."

Joshua offered a hand, pulled him up, and, together, they turned to take in the damage. The TV was shot, its screen a spiderweb. The coffee table's legs were gone, the gaming consoles crushed. Cords snaked out of the mess like intestines.

Joshua cradled his right hand in his left. The human hand had a bunch of bones—Joshua probably knew how many—and Mark wondered whether one or two had snapped.

He left Joshua standing over the TV. In the bathroom, he touched a fingertip to each of his teeth. He felt the bridge of his nose. Nothing bled. No, the fist had caught him in the eye socket. Even now, blood surged to the surface. By morning, there'd be a perfect ring.

Something else in the mirror caught his eye. Past his reflection, on the windowsill, beside the toothbrush his brother had given him: his phone.

◆   ◆   ◆

Dark water, blue sky, and already the sun was setting, just enough light to whiten the sand. A few beachgoers lingered, umbrellas bent to block the wind. One couple sat side by side reading books. Another dipped hands into a shared bag of potato chips. Another walked the shore. A dog, white and brown, raced seagulls up and down the beach.

Mark stood at the water's edge. To his left, the land curled into a point. To the right, a rocky outcropping, the boulders he guessed his brother had been talking about. Beyond the rocks rose the giant legs of the Golden Gate Bridge. He counted cars. There were hundreds, so many traveling at high speeds, neat and safe in single-file lines. He wondered how many cars crossed the bridge each minute, then thought how that was exactly the sort of thing that Joshua would know.

He'd made it out before Marisa made it home. But what came next? Maybe Marisa would say nothing. Maybe she'd take one look at the television and tell Joshua everything. Either way, Mark would be asked to leave. This would give him two days to kill. He pictured himself cross-legged on a motel bed, Chinese takeout in his lap. Or else a Thanksgiving dinner of Heinekens and mixed nuts in a hotel bar. Whatever came next, he knew he'd brought it upon himself.

He pulled off his shoes and socks and rolled the cuffs of his pants to his knees. The sand underfoot was cold. He stirred the surf with a toe, and the water was colder. He couldn't tell whether the tide was going out or coming in. He walked up the beach. The sand was scooped out in places, hollowed by wind, and he tucked his shoes into one of these hollows before returning to the shore. He picked the rocks and the bridge as his destination and walked toward them.

The beach was a confusion of seaweed and cracked shells, twigs and clear, bulbous sacs, like jellyfish minus the tentacles. He knelt, picked up one of these, and weighed it in his hand. The thing was cool and rubbery. He squeezed, and a stream of water shot from the sac's middle. He tossed it into the water and walked on.

By now, the sun had set, but he could see people gathered at the rocks. A tent glowed yellow, and a couple moved in rhythm to music that emerged, choked and reedy, from a radio. A small fire in a rock-lined pit shot orange sparks into the air.

He was cold and growing colder. He sat and felt the sand wet through his pants. He pulled the phone from his pocket. He lived with the fear that if he didn't listen, saving and resaving it daily, the message might be lost.

He pressed a button, and there it was, her voice on the phone, her last words: *Mark, this is silly. When you've calmed down, call me. Please. I may be a while. The roads are ice.* There was a long pause before she said: *For what it's worth, I'm sorry.*

How long had it been? How long between the message left and the bridge? Seconds? Minutes? Had the first car struck her hanging up?

Quickly, is how it would have happened, over before she had time to be afraid. Everyone said so, and he wanted to believe them. Wanted to, and didn't. What had she thought, seeing the guardrail, then going through it, ice rising to meet her, then opening to let her in?

Had he been the last thing on her mind? Had she blamed him or forgiven him?

He saved the message and flipped the phone shut. He stood. He could whip the phone into the ocean and be free, but that was just another impulse. He'd long since memorized the message, heard it with or without the phone pressed to his ear. He'd never be free.

And say he did it, say he managed somehow to forget her words, there were still home movies, photo albums—her picture to stare at and how, accusingly, she stared right back at him—still the old house to drive past. He'd wept to see Lorrie's flowers dug up, her gardens turned to grass.

He moved down the beach. At his approach, the campers stirred. The two dancers separated. The woman moved to a sleeping bag on the sand beside the fire, and the man joined another man at the water's edge.

When he was close enough to see, Mark stopped. The men were naked.

One, the man who'd been dancing, was maybe twenty. He had a potbelly and the jowls of a bulldog. He kept his gaze steady on the horizon. The second man was older, tall and thin. His hands were on his hips. His elbows stuck out like trowels. His hair, brown shot through with gray, was long and tied back in a ponytail. The tail touched the small of the man's back. A beard, tied in a matching tail, hung from his chin. The wind pressed the man's beard to his waist, a waist not indicated by tan line or pants.

The older man turned only his head in Mark's direction. The beard was bunched in places, banded by silver coils.

"It's not polite to stare," he said.

Mark hadn't meant to, but it had surprised him, the sight. He'd heard of nude beaches but thought they were a myth, like those highways out west said to have no speed limits. If those highways existed, he'd never seen them.

"I'm sorry," he said. "It's the beard. It's impressive." This was true. The rest of the man was unimpressive, shriveled, pinkie-sized in a pocket of dense, gray hair. He'd imagined nudists were nudists because they had something to show off, but he guessed not.

The man nodded. "I have a deal with God," he said. "I won't cut my hair until the war ends."

"Which war?" Mark asked.

The man smiled. "All of them." He brought a hand to his chin, scratched, then ran his fingers down the rope of hair. With its bunched bits, it reminded Mark of sheets knotted together, the kind children in movies tied to bedposts and hung from open windows to run away.

"If it's world peace you're after," Mark said, "I'm thinking you'll have that beard awhile."

The naked man frowned. "You're one of those."

"One of what?"

"A man who believes the way things are is exactly the way they'll always be."

The younger man at his side laughed. His belly trembled. But the bearded man turned and shook his head, and, wordlessly, the young man about-faced and made his way up the beach.

The sky was black, the bridge above brown. There was the rush of cars overhead and the whine of night insects turning on. The nudists, maybe ten of them and in various states of undress, watched him from chairs and sleeping bags around the fire. A topless woman dropped a log onto the flames, and there was an eruption of sparks. Embers feathered, then settled on the sand.

"That's quite a shiner," the man said.

Mark felt his eye. The skin hurt to touch, and he realized that he was shivering. He was used to cold but hadn't expected it in San Francisco, hadn't realized California wasn't always hot. And here stood this other man, still, at peace. He wondered how, without clothes, the man kept warm. He asked.

The man smiled. "Cold is a state of mind," he said. He bowed his head and closed his eyes. A gust of wind grabbed his beard and twirled it about his stomach. The man lifted one leg, drawing his knee almost to his chest. His penis poked forward, a cocktail shrimp from a Brillo pad. His arms stretched behind him until the hands met and his fingers interlocked. The man resembled a heron or else some prehistoric shorebird, long extinct.

Mark watched the water. The tide was definitely going out. The sand was stained where the water had been, and the surf no longer swallowed the stain.

After a time, the bearded man opened his eyes. His leg dropped, and he turned to face Mark.

"My state of mind has changed," the man said.

"I'm sorry?"

"I'm freezing my ass off." He winked. His beard swung. "There's a place for you by the fire, if you'd like."

The man joined the others by the fire, then looked back. He waved. A second hand beckoned, and then it seemed that all of them were waving.

His pants were the first thing to come off, and then his shirt. His boxers dropped, and the men and women around the fire cheered.

He wanted to go to them, to warm himself by the fire. But there was a better place for him. He felt the tug and turned to face the bay.

The water on his legs telegraphed the terrible mistake, but he didn't stop. He fell forward, and the cold took him. He went under. He pushed against the bottom. His face broke the surface, he breathed, and, soon, the water was warm.

◆   ◆   ◆

The four of them had shared a Thanksgiving, once, years before. Joshua and Marisa were a new couple when he and Lorrie had traveled to Tucson to see them. Joshua had given them all a tour of the Sonoran Desert, with its fierce, chalky landscape, its cactuses that stood, arms out, like tellers in a bank heist movie.

On Thanksgiving Day, Lorrie set the table. Marisa made a turkey, and Joshua carved. He cut into the bird, then proceeded to mutilate one of the breasts. Mark tried to help, encouraging Joshua to draw the blade gently over the meat and not to chop. "It's not a machete," he said.

They argued until Joshua plunged the blade into the turkey and sat down. Mark stood, unsunk the blade, and peeled smooth, even slices from the second breast.

None of which mattered, in the end, as, halfway through, the blade caught and the meat wouldn't give. The turkey, at its center, was ice. Marisa, it turned out, didn't do much cooking and hadn't known to thaw the Butterball before baking.

The bird was returned to the oven, but, by the time it was done, the meat was dry and crumbed beneath the blade. They ate, the four of them, not speaking, and though Joshua and Marisa would, over the years, invite them often for visits, there would never be another invitation to Thanksgiving, not before the one that came for Mark alone.

That night, on the foldout couch, Mark and Lorrie argued.

"You should be nicer to your brother," she said.

"I'm nice enough," he said.

"You're *not*," she said, and, the way she'd said it, it stuck with him.

"He'll kill himself with those cigarettes," Mark said.

At this, Lorrie pulled the pillow from beneath her head, held it to her face, and fake-smothered herself.

"What do you want from me?" he asked.

"I want you to try," she said.

"I'm trying," he said, but he wasn't, and he knew it, and he knew she was right when she said, "You could try so much harder."

She'd meant more than with his brother, of course. She'd meant with her, with their marriage, which had, just that year, taken an unexpected turn. Mark couldn't say what had happened. It was as though they'd been piloting a makeshift bicycle built for two. Approaching a tree, they'd veered, each in a different direction, and both been left on the pavement, bloodied, half a bike apiece.

They weren't the people they'd married. Their lives, their time and how they spent it, what they wanted and what came next—they'd changed, and Mark had been afraid.

"You're so *hard* on people," she said. "One day he'll be gone, and you're going to regret every word."

But Joshua wasn't gone, and it seemed a cruel joke now that Lorrie was.

That night, she watched him a long time. She did the thing he liked, tracing his face, a fingertip over his forehead, across his cheeks and chin, and down his nose.

She said, "I predict for you a long, unhappy life."

And then she fell asleep.

And then she'd stayed, stayed with him for years, trying to make it work, trying harder than him, trying right up to the second her car went off the road.

◆   ◆   ◆

It wasn't the old man or the young man who pulled him from the water. It was none of the nudists.

Though it was dark and he was too far out to be sure, he thought he recognized the figure moving down the beach, was sure he knew the gait, the frame lit up by firelight. The figure paused by the fire, turned seaward, and Mark knew who it must be, for who else would tear off his shirt like that, who else kick off his shoes and charge and dive?

And, then, he was there, waving and hollering, and Mark couldn't say how long it had taken. Things had slowed—the water's slosh, his brother biting the waves—everything a syrupy, bubbling churn. Joshua's teeth flashed. His words were roars. Then his hands were on him and Mark was in a headlock, his body trailing while Joshua reached one-armed toward shore. The water surged, and the arm at his neck loosened and tightened with every wave.

He'd been unprepared for that, for the force of the waves, the current and the cold. Onshore, the water had seemed a gelatin with a rippling skin. But, once you were in it, well, it was everything his brother had warned him it would be. How many bodies, he wondered, had this bay claimed, not only those who leapt from the bridge made famous for all the leapings but those, like him, who let the current carry them out and out?

But he couldn't take his brother with him. Joshua would go under before he let go, and so Mark would have to swim.

He yelled. He struggled and was not released. He swung and the fist met Joshua's jaw. Then he was free, and he swam. Joshua cut a path through the water, and Mark followed, followed until sand squeaked underfoot. He gave in at the end, gave himself to the cold and let Joshua pull him ashore, over sand and up the beach to the waiting fire.

But the fire wasn't enough. Stretched on a blanket by the flames, he felt nothing, his body an unmoving blue. The fire was a tangle around which bodies bobbed and spun. Joshua's voice was there, then a heaviness. Arms wrapped his chest, and he knew that the body was his brother's.

"Come on, people," Joshua called, and then there were bodies on all sides, bodies and hair, bodies and fat, bodies on bodies, until the numb turned to itch, the itch to pain—the worst pain of his life. Pins, trillions of them, needled his flesh. He shook, convulsed. The spasms, he couldn't hold them back. His teeth chattered until he could taste, and, when he could, he tasted blood.

In time, the chattering stopped. The shaking turned to shivering. The bodies pulled away, and then there was only Joshua at his back, Joshua shivering too. There was presence of mind now, enough to know that he was naked, he and his brother with him, enough to know and not to care. The heat came, and his body took all it could.

◆   ◆   ◆

A light glowed in the apartment stairwell, and Mark watched a moth crash into it.

On the stoop beneath the light, without letter or explanation, sat his suitcase. A yellow ticket was bungeed to the handle. The black piping that hugged the zipper's track had been coming loose, and now it hung, a rubbery cord that curled like a pig's tail along the ground.

"I told you they'd find it," Joshua said before saying, "I didn't mean that. I didn't mean 'I told you so.'"

Mark felt himself swaying. His feet throbbed and his arms ached. The cold had emptied him of sentiment, of longing of any kind. He wanted nothing more than to lie down, to be warm, and to sleep a good long while.

He owed Joshua an explanation. He couldn't say why he'd jumped in or what he'd been after, only that he'd never meant to get so far out. Except that, in the end, when he'd come that close to it, when he'd held up his hands, seen the shore and calculated the space between—when he'd known for sure he would sink before making it back—he hadn't been afraid.

"I'm sorry about the eye," Joshua said.

He nodded. "Sorry about the jaw." Joshua's face, where he'd hit him, was purpling, the jawline swollen, puffy fruit. "And the television."

"Don't worry about it."

"I'll buy you another one."

"Don't *worry* about it," Joshua said. He lit a cigarette.

Mark held out two fingers. He hadn't had a cigarette since college, had never really been a smoker. Joshua looked surprised, then looked as though he were trying to appear unsurprised, then passed the cigarette. Mark took a drag and coughed. His throat burned, lungs too, but he felt buoyant, untethered in just the right way.

Joshua lit another cigarette, and together they filled the stairwell up with smoke.

Overhead, more moths rattled the bulb.

Joshua dropped his cigarette and ground it out, and Mark did the same.

He wondered what waited inside. Marisa—he wouldn't know what to say when he saw her. But already Joshua had his bag in his hands and was moving through the open door.

They found Marisa on the floor, legs crossed, a screwdriver in her hand, a table leg in her lap. She stood at the sight of them, and Mark could only imagine how they looked to her, their busted faces, their salt-slicked hair. She might have demanded an explanation, and Joshua might have given it, but she didn't ask and Joshua didn't offer. Another something better left unsaid.

If she'd spoken of the kiss, his brother had dismissed it. But, seeing her, Mark knew she hadn't, knew too, right then, there'd be no motel room, no Chinese takeout. They'd pass through this, all of them.

From his neighbors, he knew the sign for *thank you*, a hand brought to the mouth and the arm tipping, unfolding from the body like a wing. His fingers found his lips, and Marisa smiled. He was absolved, forgiven before his hand left his face.

The Baby Glows

There is nothing else about the baby that one might call unusual, nothing uncharacteristic of other babies. The baby does not skip rope. The baby does not levitate. The baby cannot line up dominos across the kitchen counter with his mind. The baby just glows.

The baby is not bright like a fire or a star. His light is soft as a glow stick's, the kind you buy at a carnival and snap to make shine.

LUMINESCENT BABY SHOCKS WORLD! one headline reads. Another: FIRE BABY HOT TO MOTHER'S TOUCH!

The baby's body temperature is 98.6 degrees.

It startles the mother to open the nursery door to a radiant cloud over the crib. Then, she remembers, takes him in her arms, and holds him the way any mother would hold any baby.

The baby does not glow *sometimes*. The baby is *always* glowing.

It's only unusual because it hasn't happened before. Stranger things have happened: Babies born with tails. Babies with extra arms or eyes. Pairs of babies born sharing a stomach. This baby has no extra parts.

The baby is not magic.

A glowing baby comes in handy. Cradling the child, the father will travel downstairs in the night, finish laundry, search the pantry for snacks without flipping a switch. The mother doesn't like when the father does this. "The baby," she says, "is not a lightbulb."

Nothing else about the baby glows. The baby cries normal tears, drools normal drool, and—it must be said—poops normal poop.

And what becomes of a glowing baby? Will he grow into a glowing boy? Will he become a man who glows on his way to work, who confuses pedestrians at traffic lights? Will he marry, and, if he does, will his husband or wife wear a blindfold to bed?

He will require exclusive showings at movie theaters. He will cause headaches at airport security. Common sense says he'll never be eligible for the draft.

Some think that the older he gets, the brighter the baby will be. Some say his luminosity will fade with age, like childhood allergies. Others wager he'll beam at this relative wattage until, until—

One doesn't like to consider it, but the baby will die. One day, the baby, whether baby or man or boy, will be laid into a casket, the casket lowered into the ground. By then, one imagines, the light will have gone out. But one never knows. Perhaps he'll glow past his last breath, the way hair is said to grow for days from the dead. Perhaps.

Do you see him there, glowing belowground?

See the grass that grows from the baby's grave. See it sparkle. And a new species of incandescent worm to be discovered not far from the cemetery. And the moles that feed on these worms, their noses stars already.

There they go, tunneling, rocketing through earth, chasing those tender, smoldering fingers of snout, clawing their way up and up, and out, and into light.

The Disappearing Boy

The summer before sixth grade, we both hoped we'd turn into superheroes. When it was just the two of us, we went by our code names. I was Quicksilver, after the Marvel hero, a poor man's Flash. I was a born runner. Since the first grade, I'd always been the fastest kid on the playground, a fact undisputed at River Run Elementary, though, soon enough, middle school would find me in competition with older boys whose legs, dark with hair, would carry them at speeds I'd never match. Jason's moniker was more original. He dreamed of being invisible, but the only invisible hero we knew of was the Fantastic Four's Invisible Woman. I said he could be the Invisible Boy, but Jason said that was gay and dubbed himself the Disappearing Boy. We had our own gang too. Jason was the leader and I was his sidekick. We called ourselves the Silver Surfers, after another one of our favorite comic book characters. There was no one else in the gang.

It was a strange time in our lives, a difficult time. It was the summer we competed with one another for no good reason, seeing who could swim the most laps holding his breath underwater. By mid-June, Jason could do one lap and I could do two, the length of the public pool, down and back. I clawed at the water, kicked like a frog until my lungs screamed and fireworks went off in my head.

This was the long, hot summer of war games and tree forts, ice cream sandwiches and backyard tents, ghost stories and PG-13 movies, which Jason's mom rented whenever we asked, though we were two years too young. It was the summer of the new neighborhood and our secret hideout, the place where it all happened, where we first became acquainted with the flesh.

◆ ◆ ◆

We discovered the magazines in the basement of an unfinished house, a place older kids went at night to smoke and make out. Days, though, we had the place to ourselves.

The magazines: Neither of us had seen anything like them before. Here were women, just like our mothers, but with no clothes on.

The first time was only a glance. We knew we shouldn't have seen what we'd seen. Otherwise, we'd have been shown this before. What we'd seen was wrong, we just weren't sure how.

We spoke of the pictures to no one. The next day, we returned—to make sure someone had come back for them, we told ourselves—but the magazines were still there, a small, mildewed stack in one dusty corner of the basement. After some deliberation, we decided it wouldn't hurt to examine a few.

Jason opened one to a red, satin backdrop and a picture that spanned two pages. On hands and knees, a woman arched her back like a cat stretching after a nap. She wore nothing but a lacy, black scarf.

"Holy bastard!" Jason said. (This was also the summer we learned to swear.) Jason was better at it than I was. He modeled his obscenities, best he could, after R-rated movies, the ones he watched on HBO when his mom was out, which was pretty much always. There were the movies, and then there were the men his mom brought home. My mother wouldn't spring for cable, let alone HBO, and a man hadn't set foot in our house in years. This put me at a disadvantage when it came to cursing and was one more reason I envied the life Jason led.

Once we'd found the magazines, we spent most mornings in the basement thumbing through glossy pages. By July, we'd divided the magazines into two piles. Jason had his favorites, and I had mine. I liked the thin girls with smaller breasts. They reminded me of girls I knew. Now, seeing girls around town, I considered their clothes and what bloomed beneath. I'd notice a girl and think of my other girls, the ones from the magazines, and I'd wonder which one *this* girl, undressed, looked most like.

Jason, on the other hand, loved boobs. *Sweater cows,* he called them, as in: *Gimme them sweater cows!* His favorite pictures were of women with heaving bosoms and nipples the size of silver dollars, boobs so big they scared me.

Sometimes, a magazine in his lap, I'd catch Jason with his eyes closed, hands outstretched and fondling air.

"If you concentrate really hard, Kevin," he said, "I swear you can feel them."

Soon, the summer was all about bodies—women's bodies, my body, Jason's body. We'd pull our shorts down to see who had more hair, who was bigger. Then we'd look at the magazines and pull our shorts down again to see who was bigger *now*. Sometimes, after looking, Jason went upstairs to use the bathroom. Sometimes he was gone a long time.

◆   ◆   ◆

My mom asked about Jason's mom a lot.

"How *is* Tanya doing?" she'd ask.

"Fine," I'd say.

"Still smoking?"

"Yes."

"House a mess?"

Jason's mom and my mom weren't like Jason and me. They barely spoke to each other. Jason had no brothers or sisters, no father, and neither did I. Jason's dad was in prison in Salt Lake City. I never found out what for. I asked Jason once. I didn't ask again.

I have no memory of the father who left before I learned to crawl. He and my mother had been happy once, or so she said.

I don't know what drives people apart, or how a good man goes bad. I have two things from my father. One is the medal he gave my mother when he got back from Vietnam. The other's a love letter he wrote while he was over there, before he and Mom married.

I didn't find these until much later, as a young man helping his mother move in with her new husband. I liked that she'd kept them, liked the idea that there'd been love there once, that whatever force had brought me into the world had not been fueled by lust alone.

Except, rereading the letter, I saw why she'd kept it. A confession of love, the letter was also a confession of the documents my father falsified to get a medal he'd never earned. The letter, the medal—she hadn't kept them to remind herself of what she'd had. She'd kept them to remind herself of what she'd escaped.

◆   ◆   ◆

The day it happened, the thing in the house that changed everything, was a Wednesday. Wednesdays were War Days because they both started with W. That was the rule Jason had made, and it made a kind of alphabetical sense, so I obeyed. There were no other gangs to fight, so we'd declared war on the construction workers in orange vests building River Run Heights, the fancy, new development rising from the tree-cleaved swath of mud down the street.

Suburban sprawl, my mom called it.

"A fucking amusement park," Jason's mom said.

Bastard Heights was Jason's name for the neighborhood. A week earlier, Jason's mom had bent to pick up a newspaper from the driveway, and a man in a hardhat had whistled and hollered something unspeakable.

"Cocksucking roof jockeys," Jason said.

"Damnable asses," I said.

Our headquarters was the tree fort in Jason's backyard. The fort was a rope ladder and two boards nailed to a branch. We met there

Wednesdays and hatched our battle plans, plans yet to be carried out. That morning, though, would be different. That morning we were determined to get things done.

Since I was the fast one, I ran short reconnaissance missions, hiding behind the house nearest the neighborhood entrance, watching the workers, then reporting back to Jason whatever I'd seen. Jason waited in the fort and practiced being invisible.

"They're taking another break," I said, back from my last run.

"What are they doing?" Jason said.

"Eating donuts," I said. "And coffee. Some of them are drinking coffee."

"Excellent," Jason said.

We drew up what Jason called a *schematic*. The new neighborhood was not large, not yet. The woods had been cleared, the land divided into lots, but the subdivision's main road had only been paved for a few blocks. At one end, the road met our street. At the other, it turned to gravel and wound past houses in various stages of completion. That day, the workers were pouring sidewalks to run alongside the roads and circle the cul-de-sacs. Here, the children of parents far better off than ours would skateboard and ride their bikes without having to worry about cars.

Jason's plan was this: We would carve every vulgar word we knew into the soft concrete, ruining the men's work. They'd be forced to repave, or, better yet, they'd leave the sidewalk scarred by our handiwork. Already we imagined it, the shock of the rich kids who slowed their silver ten-speeds to read . . . could it be . . . PENIS?

Jason pulled a triangle of glass from his pocket, the curve of a broken beer bottle. Jason lifted the glass. It caught the sun like caramel.

"Vengeance," he said like a true superhero, "will be ours."

◆   ◆   ◆

By noon, the sun blazed and the workers had retreated to the shade of the bulldozers for lunch. One house at a time, we skirted our way down the road to the freshest sections of sidewalk, out of sight of the big men too busy eating and smoking to notice.

Jason knelt on the curb, pulled the glass from his pocket, and bowed his head. There was something ceremonial in this, though, at the time, I thought only of being caught, imagined those enormous arms holding us down, the men kicking us, battering us with their hardhats.

"Hurry," I said.

Jason was up to his knuckles in concrete. He slashed at the surface, and a trinity of genital slang took shape: COCK, CUNT, BALLS.

Jason moved to a new square, and, here, he carved words I'd never seen before, words I only knew must represent things terrible and profound and obscene: CLITORIS, LABIA, VULVA.

"Your turn," Jason said.

I took the shard from his hand and heard shouts, cries, cursing. The men were a long way off but coming fast.

"Fuckers!" one yelled. "You little fuckers!"

I dropped the glass. I turned to Jason.

"Go!" he said.

Oh, how we ran.

•   •   •

I'd never seen Jason move like that. Me, I'd always been the fast one, but Jason stayed with me the first thirty, forty yards. Then, he slowed.

"Secret hideout," he gasped.

"You little fuckers *better* run!"

I ran, looked back. A few of the men had stopped. They stood by the sidewalk reading Jason's scribbles. The rest kept on, closing in. I cut between two houses, and the house with the magazines came into view, the basement door open like an invitation. I'd lost Jason. Then he turned the corner, moving as though in slow motion.

He crossed the threshold in time for me to shut the door and pull him away from the windows. In the shadows, shaking, his hand on my arm, we watched the men run past.

"One more," Jason whispered. "There were five."

In a moment, a single worker stopped before us. He pressed his face to the window. His skin was dark, face unshaven, lips chapped. His bottom lip was divided by a vertical band of dried blood. But his eyes, when he smiled, were kind. He saw us. He winked. He would not tell.

Once the worker was out of sight, Jason dropped to the floor. He didn't say a word, didn't shout or moan. He simply lifted his foot, and I saw the nail protruding from the sole of his shoe.

◆   ◆   ◆

"I think I'm going to throw up," Jason said.

He sat cross-legged, his back to the wall. Every few minutes, he doubled over, forehead touching the basement floor.

"Kevin, this really hurts," he said.

"How deep?" I asked.

"Can't tell."

"Take off your shoe. Let's see."

"I can't, dumbass. The nail's *through* the shoe. I can't do anything until the nail comes out."

I thought back to health class, to my mother's warnings and a lone year of Cub Scouts, but I couldn't remember what to do for a puncture wound.

"I have to get this thing out of my foot," Jason said. "I can't walk home this way."

"Let me get your mom," I say.

"You step outside, they'll kill you."

"I'm Quicksilver, remember? I'll run the whole way."

"And leave me here to get my ass kicked?"

"You're the Disappearing Boy," I said. "Be invisible."

"Kevin!" Jason said. "What the fuck is wrong with you? This isn't a *game* anymore. There is a *nail* in my *foot*. There are *men* who want to kick our *asses*. Grow the fuck *up*!"

His voice rose, high-pitched and hysterical. His face was white, eyes wide. Watching him rock back and forth on the floor, foot cradled in his hands, I suddenly didn't like him very much.

"My mom can't find out," he said. "I'm not supposed to be here. I'm not allowed to play at the construction site. This is exactly what she said would happen, that I'd step on a nail."

"You can't just *not* tell anybody," I said.

"Oh, yes I can. I cut myself last year. I got the shot. I'll be all right once it's out."

It was crazy, not going for help. I knew that, but what choice did I have? A sidekick's never in charge, and boys don't tell on each other to their mothers, even when it's what ought to be done.

"Okay," I said.

"I have to pee," Jason said.

"Okay," I said again and helped him up the stairs.

◆   ◆

I'd never seen men kiss before. We came up the stairs, opened the door to the main floor, hobbled down a hall, and there they were in the living room, seated on the new carpet before the empty fireplace, faces pressed together, one's hands down the other's shorts.

They were high schoolers, maybe older, pale and thin. Their hair was dark, heads curdled with hairspray, spiky and horned. Their shirts were off, and I was surprised by their armpits, how hairy they were. The room smelled stale and sweet.

Seeing us, they pulled away, but they took their time about it. They faced us, and they might have been brothers, they looked so much alike. One wore sunglasses. The other had a tattoo on his stomach, blue stars around the belly button in a ring.

Jason, balancing on one foot, hopped back.

"Well," the one in the sunglasses said.

"Hello," said the other. A choked laugh shivered the abdominal stars.

Jason hopped and winced. "We won't tell!" he blurted. "Come on, Kevin. Let's go."

"Whoa," Sunglasses said. He stood, trailing a black T-shirt from the fireplace hearth. "What's the hurry?"

"My friend's got a nail in his foot," I said.

"Do what, now?" Sunglasses said. He pulled the shirt over his head.

"He stepped on a nail," I said. "Out there." I gestured toward the window, as though that explained everything.

"Jesus," Stars said. "Let's see!" He got to his feet and stumbled forward, leaving his own shirt on the floor.

Jason met my eyes. He was ready to run. But it felt like the wrong time, like we might not make it to the door.

"Show them," I said. I hoped they were harmless, that they'd see the foot, get their kicks, then let us go.

We made a circle on the floor, and Jason lifted his sneaker.

"No way!" Stars said. He looked away. "Sickness."

The nail stuck out an inch or two, bent in the middle. It was orange, the head caked with dirt.

"Bad place to keep your nails," Sunglasses said. He smacked Stars's arm, and Stars leaned too far to one side. He righted himself, then ran a hand through his hair.

"Give me your knife, retard," Sunglasses said. Stars's hand disappeared into his front pocket, for what seemed like forever, and emerged a claw with a black handle in it. His thumb stroked the handle's side, and a blade sprung from his fist. He stared at the blade a few seconds, as though confused by how it had gotten there, then handed the knife to Sunglasses.

Sunglasses turned to Jason. "First," he said, "the shoe must come off."

Jason didn't move as Sunglasses perched over his foot. I put my hand on Jason's shoulder. I'd seen people do this. It was supposed to bring comfort to a person in distress. Mostly, though, I was holding Jason down.

Sunglasses worked at the sole methodically, trimming away the rubber, carving a hole through which the head of the nail could slip when we pulled away the shoe. He hummed as he worked. Stars watched, entranced. Jason took lots of short breaths, not quite hyperventilating.

Sunglasses was careful, and the sneaker released. It was the sock that caught the nail and made Jason cry.

"Faggot," Sunglasses said. Stars laughed, falling all the way over this time and rolling onto his side. The sock off, Sunglasses retracted the knife. "Your turn," he said.

Jason shook his head. "I can't." He coughed and cried harder. "I have to pee. I'm gonna throw up." The brave boy from the morning was gone. The superhero with the battle plan and schematic was nowhere to be seen.

We sat a few minutes, waiting for Jason to settle down. Stars smoked a cigarette. Sunglasses twirled the switchblade. The house yawned around us.

"Well," Sunglasses said, "someone's gotta pull it out."

Stars put his cigarette out on the carpet, then flicked the butt into the fireplace. The spot was black, the fibers charred where he'd pressed the ash to the floor, and I thought it was a shame that he'd gone and ruined a perfectly good thing like that for no reason. Right then, I wanted to be out of the house, to get away as fast as I could. I couldn't leave Jason, but I could hurry things up.

"Let me," I said.

Jason nodded. He settled his bare foot on my lap. The nail flowered from his heel. There was no way to tell how far it went in. I grabbed the end like a syringe, my thumb against the head and two fingers beneath.

I pulled, up and out, fast. The foot rose, then crashed to the floor. Jason screamed. Sunglasses jumped. Stars cursed. A line on the nail revealed the inch that had nested in the flesh. It came out clean. The hole was not wide and there was no blood. Still, I stretched Jason's sock tight around the heel and tied it in a knot at the ankle like a tourniquet. I pulled the shoe on but left the laces loose.

Jason nodded and stood. He didn't make a face when his foot touched the floor. He was himself again. Instantly, I was demoted. He was in charge.

"I'm ready," he said.

I didn't see it coming, the hand that knocked Jason down. Stunned, Jason stood again, and again he was pushed to the floor. He stayed down. He drew his knees to his chest. Sunglasses drew the knife.

"That's it?" Sunglasses said. "After all we done for you? You're out the door without so much as *thank you*?"

"Thank you," Jason said.

"We did your ass a favor," Stars said.

"Thank you," Jason said, his voice grown shaky.

"Favors, favors," Stars said. He undid the button at his waist, pulled on the zipper, and let his shorts fall to the floor. He wore no underwear. The stars didn't end at his navel but followed a trail to a tangle of hair and something unfamiliar. What was between his legs was nothing like my own. It hung, swollen, distended, the end purple as a plum.

Jason began to cry softly.

One of the men laughed, and his laughter echoed in the open house. I'm not sure which of them it was, the man laughing, because I was already down the hall. I ran out the front door, down the steps, the driveway, the gravel road. Where were the workers? It was dark out, which didn't seem possible. It had just been noon. I ran, and I swear the moon rose overhead. The birds turned to crickets. Stars streaked overhead like confetti. The earth turned.

•   •   •

Jason didn't come to school in August, and by Labor Day he was gone. They packed up and deserted their house, which, I learned later, Jason's mother had never owned but had been renting for years. What they couldn't fit in the moving van, they left on the front lawn. All of it vanished overnight: chairs, lamps, a card table, my friend. I heard they went to Seattle, but that was just rumor. They might have gone back to Salt Lake, might have gone anywhere.

"I think Tanya wanted a fresh start," my mother said. "I tried to tell her, a new city isn't a new life, but whatever. Some people you can't protect from themselves."

Sometimes, when it was the two of us, over dinner or during a television commercial, my mother would ask, "What happened that summer, to you boys? You were so close, then it was like you weren't friends at all."

I'd shrug my shoulders.

"Was there a fight?" she'd ask. "A falling-out?"

"Not that I can remember," I'd say, and this would satisfy her, for a while anyway. She'd sigh and shake her head, saying, "Boys."

◆   ◆   ◆

I saw Jason once before he moved away. Summer vacation was almost over. A few weeks had passed since I'd run from the house. I'd spent the weeks worrying about what had happened, wondering whether I should tell my mother and whether Jason had told anybody. I wasn't sure what was done to Jason or what they'd made him do. That secret, I was afraid to keep it, and I was afraid to let it go.

In the end, I did nothing, save this: One morning, I went to his house. I rang the doorbell, but no one answered. I moved to the side of the house. Jason's bedroom was on the first floor, and, standing on tiptoes, I could see in through his window. He was lying in bed, propped up on a pillow. The TV had been moved to his room and balanced on a plastic milk crate in one corner.

I tapped the glass, and Jason came to the window. He was thinner than I remembered, eyes burrowed deep in his head. We stared at each other a minute. I didn't know what to say. It was Jason who spoke first.

"You left me," he said. His voice was different, muffled behind the windowpane, and I had to strain to hear him. "You ran away."

"I'm sorry," I said.

He moved closer to the window. His bangs licked the glass. "You haven't said anything?" he asked.

I shook my head.

"To anyone? Promise?"

"I promise," I said.

He didn't smile, but I could tell he was relieved. He returned to the bed. I tried to see what show he was watching, but an open closet door threw a shadow across the screen. I couldn't be sure the television was even on.

I never saw Jason again. After that day, he disappeared.

Later, much later, as a man, I would come across the definition of *quicksilver*, which means not only *fast*, but *fickle*, *mercurial*, *unpredictable*.

In this way, we both lived up to our namesakes.

The Heaven of Animals

Dan Lawson had made the trip before. After he discovered that his boy, Jack, was gay and threw him through a family-room window, after Dan's family left him, after he got sober and worked for years at redeeming himself in the eyes of his son—the language of regret transformed to checks that covered Jack's college tuition—he'd made the trip. Jack had taken a degree in marine biology, then a position researching ocean life on the Pacific coast. Dan had rented a moving van, and, towing Jack's car, they'd driven the three long days to California. Now, ten years later, he would make the trip alone.

That afternoon, Jack had called from La Jolla to say he'd be dead any day now. Someone was with him, but what he really wanted was Dan at his side, and could he maybe come, and soon?

The phone shook in Dan's hand like a live fish. His thoughts hurtled toward cancer, the scourge that had ravaged his parents, pushed friends into early graves, and, finally, taken the life of Lynn, his ex-wife and Jack's mother, a woman who, like her son, had been, if not too good for this world, then too good, certainly, for Dan.

But the problem wasn't cancer.

"I've got a pretty bad case of pneumonia," Jack said. His voice was raspy, unrecognizable. He paused between sentences to catch his breath.

"I don't understand," Dan said. He imagined the worst, and Jack raced to meet him there.

Jack said, "I've got a pretty bad case of AIDS." He told Dan about the hospitals. He told him about the drugs that had kept him alive for years and might have given him more, many more, had he not waited so long to seek treatment.

"I'm not the first to think if I ignored it, it would go away," he said. "I've killed men. I know I have. What I've done is unforgivable."

For years, Jack said, he'd suspected and been afraid to act until Marcus, a friend, had guessed and made him get tested. "The body's bad at keeping secrets," Jack said. "This disease, it tattoos its name on you in bruises."

He had traced the illness back to his high school history teacher. He'd been eighteen, impressionable, and the man had taught him everything but responsibility. Now, fifteen years later, the disease had run its course.

The line was quiet, and Dan fought to fill up the silence. "I'm sorry," he said.

Three days a week, Jack said, Marcus collapsed his wheelchair into the back of his car, drove him the half hour to San Diego, and wheeled him into a hospital where a technician waited to ease a needle between his ribs and pull pints of fluid from his lungs. But Jack had had enough of that. He would keep going only if Dan would come, after which he looked forward to drowning quietly in his sleep. He apologized for the morbidity of the confession, but not its directness.

Dan couldn't speak. He felt untethered. He held on to the phone, tight, as though to let go might cause him to float away.

Jack said, "I understand that I'm asking you to come to terms in minutes with something I've been coming to terms with for years."

That word, *years*. Dan winced to hear it. He brought a hand to his forehead, which was damp.

Not so long ago, he'd helped Jack set up his office and move into the house in La Jolla. Impossible that a decade could pass, *like that*, without visit or invitation.

Jack was silent for so long, Dan worried the line had gone dead. "I'm here," Jack said.

How extraordinary to think that—together, crossing the country—the virus had been with them even then, that already it had made a nest in Jack's guts without their knowing. How long, then, had Jack known? How long had he known and said nothing? And, if he had said, would Dan have moved to be near him? What did fathers *do*?

He would have tried harder, that at least.

"I have to go," Jack said, and, before Dan could protest, he was gone.

That night, Dan left his house and crossed the highway and walked down to the familiar shoreline. He watched the still, cold waters of the Gulf of Mexico. Two men sat on the beach. One chopped up a bonito for bait. The silver fish came apart in fat, red chunks, and the sand bloomed pink beneath it. The other man baited three-pronged, baseball-sized hooks with the flesh and cast the bait as far as he could into the surf. The men had rigged four poles in stands in the sand.

Jack was no fisherman. Dan had taken him once, but the boy had cried at the first catch. He worried over the fish's welfare, the silver hook caught in the jaw. Standing beside the livewell, looking in, he'd wept until Dan dipped a hand in, caught the fish by its middle, and returned it to the water.

Jack would grow up that way, sensitive, in love with the world above water and below. Later, those rare times they spoke on the phone, their conversations circled back, inevitably, to Jack's work, his study of an endangered species or his latest tide pool discovery. Jack's favorites were the seals that watched him work. He spoke of them often, their playfulness, their curiosity, how, on a hot day, they blanketed the rocks and basked. *Like marble,* he'd said once, *like stones curled over stones.* And, from his chair, elbows propped on a kitchen table twenty-five hundred miles away, Dan had seen them, the animals and the rocks, the sight startling him, like a drawer flung open to an intimacy of spoons.

On the beach, a fishing rod bowed. Dan moved closer. The man with the rod dug his heels in the sand. The line unraveled in a *whir*. The second man hurried across the beach, pulling in the other lines. "Black tip?" the man called.

"Bigger," the other said. The spinner screamed as the shark pulled more and more line. If it didn't tire, Dan knew, the line would run out and release, the shark swimming away, a mile of filament tracing its wake.

But the line did not run out. The hum subsided into the steady crank of the reel.

Dan imagined the men landing a ten-foot bull shark, the beast silvered by moonlight, thrashing the sand.

He didn't stay to see it. Instead, he walked down the beach to a bar and ordered a scotch, neat. He stared at the tumbler a long time. The drink would be his first in . . . forever, since the day he'd stood, drunk and disbelieving, in the glassy flowerbed over the body of his son, Lynn screaming for the other boy to call 911.

His deepest grief. His greatest shame. An act for which no conceivable penance existed. With the last tuition bill covered and Jack tucked away, far from his father as he could get, Dan had recognized that the thing he wanted most in the world was a thing he'd never have, and so he'd given up hope for forgiveness. A friend had suggested that perhaps Dan was already forgiven. That, by taking his money, begging his father's help, the boy had relented. Weren't these concessions of something like love? The idea was almost as believable as it was untrue. For Jack hadn't asked out of love. He'd asked out of necessity. The calls for help, when they came, were frantic. Jack had gotten into college but couldn't pay. He'd found work, but his ride had fallen through and he had to be in California by week's end. Dan was a last resort, always. He'd known this. He'd known and not cared, just as he knew that a decade of Christmas cards and the occasional phone call from California were born of nothing greater than a son's sense of obligation to his father.

Tonight, though. Tonight presented something new—a chance, final, but full with possibility. And just because forgiveness was a thing he didn't deserve, that didn't make it a thing not worth chasing. Only the entirety of a country lay between them. He couldn't get back the lost years, but he could cross the country.

From a payphone at the bar, he called his son. "Of course I'll come. I'll leave in the morning, first thing," he said, and Jack thanked him and hung up.

Dan returned to the counter, paid, and passed the tumbler, still full, to the man on the stool beside him before walking up the beach and back home.

Near sunup he fell, at last, to sleep.

♦   ♦   ♦

And woke late. He cursed himself, then cursed himself again when the car wouldn't start. The car was old and prone to breakdowns. It overheated. It stalled. It threw belts the way a dog shakes off water.

He checked the starter, then, relieved, moved to the shed. He pulled a battery down from its shelf. The battery was new, stolen from the garage. The job had never paid well, but the work was easy. He changed oil mostly, a simple service for which people handed over startling sums in the name of clean hands. The garage kept poor track of inventory, and, over the years, he'd lifted parts and merchandise to the tune of several thousand dollars.

He'd called Steve that morning to say he'd be gone awhile, maybe weeks. "Not if you want a job when you get back," Steve said, and Dan said that Steve could go fuck himself. He wouldn't sit around St. Pete's rotating tires while his boy lay dying on the other side of the country.

He wasn't really mad at Steve. Steve hadn't known he had a son. Few people did. Already, he felt the hand on his shoulder, Steve's apology upon his return. For days, the men would work in respectful silence, then, gradually, at break or in the pit, the jokes would sneak back in, the elbow nudges, talk of women and how best to get them into bed. Steve would be the last to forget. He might say, "If you ever want to talk about it," and both men would understand that those were just words.

Midmorning, the car cranked and Dan left town. In his trunk, he carried oil filters, belts, another battery, talismans against any force that might impede his progress. By noon, he'd traded I-75 for I-10, the interstate that would carry him west, a straight shot through six states, until, north of Tucson, he took I-8. He'd follow the signs to San Diego, then head north to La Jolla. He wouldn't need a map. He knew the drive as though he'd made it not a decade, but a day, before.

◆   ◆   ◆

The bridge was rust-colored and seemed to shudder beneath him. Beyond the bridge, a sign announced the state line, and the sun sank into the highway. He was suspended: Below him, the Pearl River churned, muddy as chocolate milk. Above, the sky squatted, pink and orange, the color pulled east across the blue, as though smudged by a thumb.

He crossed the water and pulled his car to the side of the road. He had not stopped in hours, and his sides ached with soda. He followed a path through tall grass and down a steep embankment to the water's edge. Cars flew overhead. Trucks roared. He unzipped and pissed into the Pearl. The current surprised him, the water rushing by, filmy, its surface like burnt plastic.

Downstream, a boy sat beneath the bridge, watching him. Embarrassed, Dan zipped up and walked over. The boy was young, seven or eight, his face black, his mouth drawn in a frown. He sat on an overturned plastic bucket and held a cane pole in his hands. A line ran from the tip of the pole to the water. A blue length of nylon ran from a loop at the boy's ankle and into the river. At the end of the blue line, the silver sides of a few small fish spun in the current. The boy wore dirty jeans, cuffed at the knee, and a torn white T-shirt. Across its front, in tall black letters, the shirt read: THE END IS NEAR.

"Sir," the boy said, "you just peed on my fish."

"I didn't see you," Dan said. "I'm sorry."

The boy watched him, then the water. Dan didn't know where they stood, whether the boy had accepted his apology. The river rolled by.

"Here," he said. He pulled his wallet from his pocket and a five-dollar bill from the wallet. The boy scrunched up his face.

"Man," he said, "what do I look like to you?"

Dan shook his head. He returned the money and the wallet to his pocket. The shoreline held a rind of foam. He nudged the foam with his tan work boot's toe. A chunk let go and floated away.

And then the boy was up. The pole's tip disappeared into the water. He turned the pole in his hands, winding the line around the cane. Something large splashed at the water's edge, a flash of gills.

The fish followed the cane up and out of the water and landed, flopping, on the bank. The boy straddled the fish, pulled the hook from its mouth, then stood and held it out. It was a bass, a largemouth, five or six pounds, big and gleaming. Its dorsal fin unfolded, webbed, against the sky, and its stomach hung, white and distended, between the boy's hands. It was a beautiful catch.

Dan reached forward. He meant only to trace the fish's side, to run a finger along the signature pinstripe, eye to tail—to feel the cool, smooth slime. But at his hand's approach, the boy pulled the fish back. Without a word, he dropped it into the river. The fish hit the surface with a terrific smack and was gone.

The boy waded into the water, and the river made wishbones around his ankles. His small catches darted, pulling futilely at their tether. He bent and let the current run over his hands, then dried his palms on the seat of his pants.

"Why?" Dan asked.

"Sow," he said. "Belly full of eggs."

Dan stared at the boy, his worn clothes, his gaunt face. Ribs hugged his stomach on either side.

Dan said, "But you're fishing for food."

"I throw her back now, next year there'll be more fish to catch."

The boy returned to the shore, knelt, and unfastened the stringer from his leg. He righted his bucket and dropped the line of fish into it. A few flapped their protest against the bucket's dry bottom. The boy stood and, with bucket and pole, made his way up the hill toward the highway. Dan followed. He wished suddenly that Jack could meet this kid. He would have admired the boy, his sense of—what was it—*ecology*? No, it was more than that, a kind of animal morality. He still couldn't believe it. The boy had thrown the fish back.

"What does it mean?" he asked. "Your shirt?"

The boy walked on but stopped at the top of the hill. Behind him, cars raced into Louisiana.

"The end is near," Dan said. "What does that mean?"

The boy looked confused. "It means what it says," he said.

"You mean, like biblically. Like the apocalypse?"

The boy shrugged. "I seen Him," he said. "Sometimes, when I'm under the bridge, I look up and He's coming over the water, walking just like you or me."

Dan waited for more. He watched the river, but he couldn't see it. He couldn't imagine a man, anybody, crossing the water, not the way he could when he closed his eyes and saw Jack's seals.

When he turned, the boy was already up the road. Dan watched until he was a speck against the sun. Then the sun dipped below the horizon, and the boy followed.

◆　◆　◆

Passing through Baton Rouge, Dan thought of the night when, miraculously, Jack was a voice on the phone. It had been five years, and Jack was finished at LSU. He had his degree and, now, a job. His voice was no longer a boy's, and Dan's heart broke to hear it.

They met at a restaurant near campus. Jack did not hug him, but stepped forward and shook his hand. Dan had braced himself for anything. He'd expected someone meek, effeminate, the teenage

Jack, who, for a time, Dan had forgotten how to love. But this Jack was tall and muscled, with a tanned face and copper-colored arms. He had a good, strong chin that reminded Dan of his own. He wore a sensible haircut.

Still, some things set Jack apart. Not the way he talked or dressed, not exactly, but a hiccup in his step, or the way his arms hung at his sides, or his habit of bringing one hand to his face when he spoke. He ordered a meal off the menu that would have been Dan's last choice, and, in conversation, used words at whose meanings Dan could only guess. He was changed—Dan couldn't say whether for the better—and their trip began like a foot, the truck's cramped cab a new boot, the men pressed like toes, close, each too close to the other.

The first day, they didn't speak. They listened to the radio and took turns at the wheel. At each stop, Dan checked the hitch that joined Jack's car to the back of the van. At a Texas motel, they took separate rooms. The second day, though, Jack told Dan about his studies and Dan discussed work at the garage, and that night they shared a room. By the third day's end, navigating the mountains of Southern California, the boot's leather had stretched, and they flexed, they laughed, breathed easy. Jack even asked Dan's advice on taxes and car repair.

They hit the ocean too soon. Dan didn't want the trip to be over. He didn't want to say goodbye. But he was not asked to stay. So, the next day, with Jack's belongings secured and the moving van returned, Dan stepped onto a plane. Had he been asked, right then, when he'd see his son again, he'd have said *soon*. But *soon* had turned to ten years, and Dan couldn't explain it.

He might, in those rarest, most honest of moments, have confessed that he'd been afraid, scared of what closeness required—an acknowledgment of boyfriends, of lovers, of a life he didn't want for his son. He'd wanted to appreciate Jack's *other* qualities, the kind heart, the elegant mind. But there were so many aspects of Jack to contend with, so many Jacks: the Jack who was gay and the Jacks who made up his son—the baby in the cradle; the toddler crouched, laughing, beneath the kitchen sink; the boy on the lawn—sunshine and the haze the sprinklers made, the water a mist, then steam, before it hit the ground—and Dan could not reconcile the one with the rest.

He'd hoped to learn, in time, to take Jack as he was, to not have to cut phone calls short, afraid of what he might hear, or who—a voice in the background or a man on the line, listening in.

He'd hoped to learn, in time, been certain there was time, always more time.

He drove on, past billboard-strewn Baton Rouge, across a wing of the Mississippi wide as memory, through Lafayette, past green fields and black swamps, and on, and on, toward Texas.

◆   ◆   ◆

Late in the day, he reached the rest stop outside Lake Charles. They'd taken their first break here. Jack stepped out of the van, stretched, and his spine marked his shirt like links in a chain. The hem lifted, and Jack's back was as dark as his arms. His was the skin of a man who spent his days not under cars, but on boats and knee-deep in waterways, bent to net specimens. Dan felt something at the sight of it, a pain, dull and deep, and another seeing the hairs—light, feathery—that traversed the hollow where back met waist. The fall from the window had broken Jack's arm, and the hairs had come out of the cast curly, elbow to wrist, a living nest.

Dan counted his cash. The first trip, business had been better, gas cheaper. He'd have to be careful. He had no savings to fall back on—nothing but the house and the car, both so far gone as to be of no real value. He bought two bags of chips from a vending machine, ate them leaning against the car, then found a phone booth, the old-fashioned kind with windows and a door that closed.

The man named Marcus answered the phone.

"How is he?" Dan asked.

"He's sleeping," Marcus said, and his voice was like hot gravel pressed to a fresh road. "Today wasn't terrible. But every day is different. Each day's a surprise."

Dan asked whether he was in a lot of pain, and Marcus said that he was.

"But he won't show it," he said. "He's being brave. He won't take the morphine."

Dan understood what Marcus meant, that Jack was waiting for him, that Jack needed him there faster, needed him now.

And how would Jack look when he saw him? He pictured a skeleton, bones draped in bedsheets, eyes swollen in their sockets, yellow as yolks.

"Make sure he eats," Dan said, and Marcus said, "You don't know what you're talking about. Food means nothing. We're way past food."

The man on the phone was not on Dan's side. He was dangerous, but he was all Dan had. He was the one keeping Jack alive, and so Dan would have to be careful.

"Just tell me when you'll be here and how I can reach you," Marcus said.

Dan promised to be there in two days. He would call along the way, whenever he stopped, wherever he found a payphone.

He thought Marcus was coughing before he knew he was laughing.

"Hello to the twenty-first century," Marcus said. "Cell phones and airplanes. These are not new things." And then Dan heard a screech, and then a recorded voice. The voice asked him to deposit more money. He patted his pockets for coins, then hung up.

Back behind the wheel, he considered pulling away, driving all night and the rest of the following day. He had come nine hundred miles. He still had far to go. He'd need caffeine, lots of it, or he could try to score a few turnarounds at a truck stop. He shut his eyes. The headrest was warm on his neck. He could almost see Jack beyond the windshield, stretching, stretching, his fingers tangled in sunlight, ready for takeoff.

•   •   •

Raindrops came through the open window and pelted his shoulder. It was early, still dark. Dan rolled up the window, then ran through the rain to the restrooms. He stood beneath an overhang, watching the water come down. He dreaded the day ahead, the monotony of the road, the tiny gas stations and blank faces of the men and women who worked the registers. And he was afraid. He feared that his tires, leather-smooth, would run off the road. He feared that the wipers, which rattled and slapped even in light rain, would seize and leave him blind in the downpour. And the one true fear, what all the other fears suggested: that he might not reach Jack in time.

Today, he would have to drive faster, go farther, and he did, until the silver smolder of the diner on the hill compelled him to exit. No cars filled the spaces in front of the diner, but a blue neon sign in the window glowed OPEN.

The diner was smaller than he remembered. They'd stopped here the first night, before finding a place to sleep. A gas station, long boarded up, stood in the adjacent lot. The vast absence of anything else extended as far as he could see.

Inside, Dan took a seat at the counter. Across the empty diner was the booth where they'd sat, Jack stacking sugar packets into towers until the food came. When they left, Jack said he'd forgotten something and ran back in. Then, through the window, Dan watched his son add a few bills to the tip he'd left, an embarrassment that made him feel cheap, accused. He wished Jack had just come out and said it. But Jack was not his father's son. Given discretion and confrontation, Jack would always choose discretion. Between these, Dan imagined a third way to be, but neither of them had ever been good at in-between, each already too much himself.

Through an opening in the wall, Dan could see into the kitchen. A man in a paper hat stood at the grill. He pressed bacon with a steel spatula. Before he'd learned cars, Dan had done this work. He came home nights stinking of lard and lemon-scented cleaner. Now, most days, he smelled of grease and gasoline, which was okay. Garage smells didn't bother him the way the restaurant had, how the food stink clung to your clothes, how it combed itself into your hair.

"Annie will be with you in a minute," the man said, without looking up.

Dan pulled a yellow menu from a greasy rack fastened to the laminate countertop. The menu was the kind with pictures in place of descriptions. Grainy photographs advertised the Hungry Man Breakfast, the Lumberjack Special, and the Ultimate Combo. The Ultimate Combo was pancakes, toast, potatoes, eggs, and a mess of meats. He was hungry enough to eat it all.

"It's a lot of food," she said.

Annie was short and wide around the middle. She wore a blue-and-white getup and an apron, as though she belonged not here, but in a diner from Dan's youth. Her hair, blond, then brown where the roots reached out, was brushed forward in a stiff wave over her forehead. The rest fell in curls that settled on her shoulders. The bridge of her nose was wide, but her skin was smooth and unblemished, her mouth small and red. Her eyes were blue pools, and her face narrowed from a high forehead to a point of chin, like an egg balanced on its tapered end. Jack had shown him that, how to balance an egg, how it wasn't something you could do only on the equinox the way people said.

She set a napkin in front of him, then weighted it with silverware. "Coffee?"

"Please," he said. He could order the enormous meal, but a meal took time. Jack would never know, but that thought, the not knowing, brought Dan no comfort.

"And toast," he said.

"Just toast?" Annie asked.

He nodded. Her features, in spite of them, or because of them, their strange assemblage, all of them added up to something he didn't want to admit.

Her eyes didn't leave his, and how much time had passed since he'd been with a woman? But she was no woman. She was no older than Jack the day Dan had found him in the other boy's arms. Children, all of them.

He looked away. He coughed. He pressed his longing into a ball, returned his menu to the rack with a slap, and, with this act, jettisoned his desire—that small, round ache—into the universe.

"Just toast," Annie called to the man in the paper hat.

The man grunted and shook his head.

Annie produced a mug from under the counter and filled it with coffee from a plastic-handled pot. She watched him with an intensity he missed from the years before he married. The way he looked now, his face, people gave him room in a crowd. Maybe it was the missing tooth. Maybe it was the scar that ran eyebrow to ear, or the sky that filled up an absence of earlobe. Souvenirs of his drinking days and of the fights and dares that accompanied those days. But, returning the coffeepot to its warmer, offering him a plate of toast, Annie didn't look afraid.

She smiled. "Anything else?"

"No," he said. "Thank you."

She tore a ticket from her pad and tucked it under his mug, then turned and busied herself with the coffeemaker. Her apron strings were tied in a bow at eye level. He tried not to stare. He ate quickly, guzzled his coffee, and left a five on the counter. He'd hit the bathroom, and then he'd be gone.

But, standing at the urinal, he wasn't alone long. He smelled her first, soda and maple syrup. The door opened behind him. It shut. A hand brushed his waist and took hold of him. He stiffened even as the last of the piss left him, and then she was pumping. The handle of her jaw found his shoulder, and he felt her heat, her apron-front warm against the back of his pants, all of it happening fast, familiar as bad TV, practiced as pornography.

"Wait," he said, but she did not stop. Her hand found his hair, his head pulled back, teeth like bee stings down his neck. He spun, and she fell away.

He found her on the floor, face hidden by hair, her apron a twisted, knotted thing. She was trembling.

He didn't have time for this. He knelt and put a hand on her shoulder.

"Are you all right?" he said.

The slap came hard. "Fuck you!" She screamed it. "Fucking pervert!"

Dan stood. He zipped up and buttoned the front of his pants.

"Molester!"

A crash echoed from the kitchen, and Dan knew what came next. Already he felt the policeman's hand on his head, the firm push into the back of the car. And how to explain this to Jack? His absence, it would be unforgivable as the window. It would be worse.

The screams kept coming. She kicked and squirmed.

"If I miss this," he said, but he didn't bother with the rest. He'd fought many men, knocked some unconscious, fucked up his fist with the snap of another man's nose. He'd never so much as pushed a woman. This girl, though—he could see himself doing things. Her foot caught his shin, and, right then, he wanted to take her head between his hands and lift her from the floor, wanted to squeeze until the screaming stopped.

"Heaven help you," he said. "Heaven help you if I don't make it out of here."

His words, and the thing that thickened his words, turned Annie's shouts to whimpers. Wide-eyed, she watched him.

Dan moved away from the door. He felt sorry for the guy, but he knew what this looked like, knew no explanation would suffice. He planted his feet. He'd get one chance at this.

The door flew open, and he threw the punch with everything he had in him. His arm was a rocket. It was a battering ram hammering the castle door. Splinters. His fist found face, something cracked, and the man was down. Annie didn't scream. She didn't move. The cook was out, his paper hat crumpled beneath him.

He stepped over the body. He didn't look back at Annie. He moved quickly from the restaurant and into the rain. In the rear-view mirror, though, pulling away, he could have sworn he caught a glimpse of the girl's face at the window, mouth open, and he couldn't tell which it was, whether she cursed him or called him back.

◆   ◆   ◆

Texas was a bastard, the road unraveling in a graphite blanket of forever. Blue sky had strangled the rain, and now steam rose in waves from the asphalt, the landscape blurred in a chemical spill of browns and reds. He passed derricks that bobbed like birds drilling the earth for food. He passed something dead and fly-covered on the side of the road, belly full of wings where buzzards crouched, heads burrowed in the carcass.

The afternoon brought with it the kind of heat that clogs your head and slows your thinking. He adjusted the air-conditioning to half-blast, afraid for the car and the overheating that could leave him thirty miles or more between gas stations. The radio was fuzz, and he drove long stretches without passing another car or truck. He was all over the road. He fought sleep. On this stretch, he and Jack had traded seats often and talked to keep each other awake.

He wondered whether Jack had made the fish up.

"I won't go back," Jack had said. "I mean, the project was funded, and I was in the Amazon, so I can't complain. But, Jesus, the number of things down there that can kill you. They have these eels, enough volts to knock down a grown man. They have stingrays, of course, and caimans, plus the catfish."

"How big?" Dan asked.

"Big enough that children go missing."

He pictured it, whiskers thick as garden hoses, the mouth pried open and the body inside.

"How about piranhas?"

"Well, sure." Jack smiled. He laced his fingers across his lap. "Really, though, their reputation overwhelms them. File them under 'Misunderstood.' They're like sharks. No open wound, you've probably got nothing to worry about."

"I'll keep that in mind," Dan said, "next time I visit the Amazon."

Jack nodded. He was waiting to talk. Dan knew Jack didn't hear half of what he said, and he didn't care. A week before, he wouldn't have believed he'd be crossing the country with his son at his side.

"What trumps them all," Jack said, "is this parasitic fish, an inch long. What it does is it slips between the gills of a bigger fish and eats its host from the inside out. Only, these fish, sometimes they swim into people—ears, anus, whatever orifice they find first. This guy I know, Toby, the thing wriggled up his dick and ate the urethra."

Later, Dan would blame the heat. But it was the fish, the idea, that forced him to the side of the road to dry-heave out the open door. In the van, Jack howled and slapped the dash.

All those years, and Dan couldn't shake it. At times, the thought snuck up on him, scaring him with its forcefulness, and he felt the fish inside him, not eating, but struggling to rip free.

Out his window, Dan watched distant mountains rise and fall. I-10 hugged the border with Mexico, and beyond this invisible line, the mountains scraped the sky for miles. The day was ending, and the land beneath him unflattened, road surrendering to dips and bends, channels of orange and red rock. Scarred cliffs marked the places dynamite had met the mountains and made way for the road. The rock rose in walls around him, earth—millions of years of it—etched in ribbons of sediment.

Another hundred miles, and he'd put Texas behind him. He drove on, fighting the fish the whole way. The sensation, when it came, rose, gut to throat, twisting, an ember in a fire, then lifting like ash.

◆   ◆   ◆

New Mexico welcomed Dan into exhaustion. Night had come. He drove until he could no longer keep awake for the next exit, then pulled the car onto the shoulder of the road. The desert lay beyond, a wide-open expanse of sand and sage, and he drove into it. He navigated past a boulder, past a clump of prickly pear, hands like paddles in the headlights, and brought the car to rest behind a tower of rocks where he hoped he wouldn't be bothered. He drained his last jug of water. He had a bag of beef jerky from an earlier stop, and he finished that too. At a BP, he'd meant to call Jack but found the payphone's receiver missing, the cord frayed as though chewed through by an animal. He would have to wait until morning.

He wanted sleep, but the heat and the car were suffocating, so he climbed onto the roof. He imagined the morning, snakes in his boots, and left them on. But his shirt he pulled off for a pillow. He lay back and let his legs hang over the windshield, heels on the hood. Above him, stars spilled out of a white rip in the night. A coyote called and was answered by another. A breeze swept his chest like the palm of a hand.

His eyes burned. He was going to make it. Against all odds— the car, the rain, the fight at the diner that might have left him in jail—he would reach his boy. Gulf coast to Pacific in three days.

Son, he thought, *stay. Stay and wait for me.*

◆   ◆   ◆

The morning was an orange, peeled and held fast in a fist, pulpy and hot. Dan cursed again and kicked a tire. The car should not have broken down. He'd tended to it the whole trip, monitoring fluid levels, topping off the gas tank, keeping the air low and the coolant full. It should not have broken down, but it had.

He'd woken at first light, freezing, and hit the road. At a gas station, he'd stocked up on food and water, changed his clothes in the bathroom, and driven on. The day warmed. The earth around him turned brown. The bushes were scorched, the landscape flat, calm like the surface of a sea. Ahead, the asphalt split the sea, an unbending avenue of black.

Half of New Mexico was behind him when the car first steamed and shook. An exit came into view. He took it and pulled into an Amoco station in time for the car to gasp and die with an unceremonious shudder. He waited an hour to add coolant and still the tank blew like a geyser when the cap came off. Antifreeze gushed green, bubbled and puddled on the ground where the thirsty air licked the pavement dry in seconds. An old man stood at the window inside the Amoco. He shook his head, and Dan hated him. He knew what the man was thinking, but Dan knew all about cars, knew this car better than any he'd owned. He just hadn't known what *heat* was, not really. His trip with Jack had been in May. But this was July, and one of the hottest summers on record, or so said the people on the radio. A few locals looked on from the shade of the awning that overhung the gas pumps.

"You let it cool down?" a boy called.

Dan shot him a look that could cleave meat. The boy looked away.

Hours passed, and the car would not cool down. Then, when the car did cool down, it wouldn't start, and Dan knew that his problem was that most delicate, most temperamental of instruments: the transmission. Only the smallest part needed to break off and cycle through to make a mess of your machine. At the garage, they called it *sudden catastrophic failure*. This was their way of saying: *Get ready to fork over thousands, you're fucked.*

In the distance, over vacancies of brown, an honest to God tumbleweed cruised by.

The car would not be repaired, not with the money he had or in time to reach Jack. He would have to find a new way. Whatever happened, his trip couldn't end like this, Dan stranded two states away. He'd come too far. He was too close.

He found the payphone beside the building, a steel box lashed to a cement pole that was planted between two restroom doors. Over the blue-and-white women's symbol, someone had carved CUNT. Over this, someone had scribbled the crude outline of a dick in black marker. It shot a thin, dark stream up the door.

To Dan's surprise, Jack picked up the phone.

"Marcus says you'll be here tonight," Jack said.

"That's the plan," Dan said. "How are you?"

"Dying," Jack said, "*still.*" Jack laughed, but the laugh was thin, almost a croak. Then Dan heard a voice in the background and the rustle of Jack resting the phone in his lap. They argued, and, when Jack returned, he sounded anxious.

"He wants to know when," Jack said.

"Soon," Dan said.

"Soon or *soon*?"

Dan said nothing. Jack wanted a promise he wasn't sure he could keep. A phonebook lay open on the ground. He nudged it with the toe of his boot. Its pages stood stiff, wavy in space, as though bronzed.

On the line, more argument, then Jack yelled, "He's coming, all right? Go away." A door slammed, and Jack apologized.

Across the parking lot, a tan Honda Civic pulled up to the pumps, a 2007, Dan guessed. A girl got out and walked into the station.

"Things okay there?" Dan said, but Jack didn't hear or didn't want to talk about it. What he said next surprised Dan, the past rushing at him like a wall of water over the desert floor.

"That winter," Jack said, "in the Florida house. All those sounds coming through the ceiling. You remember?"

"You couldn't sleep," Dan said. "You thought they were monsters."

"Remember what you told me?" Jack said. "To make me sleep?"

"I don't," Dan said. He did but wanted to hear his son say it.

"Angels," Jack said. "Angels in the attic."

He'd meant only to comfort the child. An invention, like the idea of a heaven for animals, a consolation to make easier the death of the family dog.

Jack's voice sharpened. "Ten years old, and I believed you. And I wanted to see them. I thought they'd be so beautiful. But I was afraid to go up. Until the noise stopped and the stink started. One night, I got brave. I pulled the cord and climbed the ladder, and you know what I found? *Squirrels*. Dead fucking *squirrels* all over the place."

Dan remembered it well. He'd poisoned them, then collected the dead into a garbage bag, tails stiff as handles, eyes glazed in a way that filled his dreams for weeks.

"I'm sorry," he said. "I didn't mean for you to—" But already Jack was speaking again.

"No," he said. "What I'm saying is, they're *here*, the angels. They weren't there, but they're here, now, in this house. I see them. Before I fall asleep, they fill up the ceiling."

Dan felt suddenly sick. He wondered whether Marcus had started the morphine, whether a fever had sunk its teeth into Jack's brain. Before his own father died, he'd claimed a troll crawled out each night from under the hospital bed to gnaw on his toes. The dying suffered delusions, Dan knew this. Still, he was sorry Jack saw things that weren't there. He wanted Jack still in the world when he arrived, awake and clearheaded. Maybe he was selfish to want it, but, when he knelt at Jack's side, he wanted his son to know who he was.

Jack was silent a long time before he said, "Dad?"

The word had not found his ear in fifteen years, and Dan trembled to hear it.

"Dad, am I going crazy?"

"No," Dan said. "No, you're just fine."

"Then, they're there, what I see?" Jack's voice, it had turned to a boy's.

"They're there," Dan said. His throat ached.

"And they won't leave?"

"They won't leave."

"Good," Jack said. "I don't want them to leave."

"They won't," Dan said, "I'll make sure of it." And he hoped he was not mistaken. Because the angels, if they went away, would be his fault. He'd brought them into the world, into his son's imagination, yet he couldn't control what became of them. And, should they vanish, what then? What chance then at Jack's forgiveness?

"Promise not to tell Marcus," Jack said.

Dan promised, and the promise warmed him with what the other man didn't know. Dan was trusted. Whatever the other man was to Jack, he wasn't his father, wasn't the one in whom the son placed his confidence at the end. He promised again, but Jack had already said goodbye, his words cut off with a click.

Time. The enemy had always been *time*. He walked past the Honda, dust-covered, waiting, and saw the thing he'd hoped for. He didn't want to do it, but he had no choice, could think of no other way. Buses, taxis, these took money. Hitchhiking wasn't new to him, but the travel was unpredictable, slow. He hurried to his car. He'd packed one bag. He pulled it from the backseat and walked, calm as he could, to the Honda. Beside the car, hoses hung from their pump, a trio of elephant trunks, wrinkled, their middles cinched by metal rings. And, through the open window, a rabbit's foot. It dangled like life from the chain, the chain from the key, the key snug in the ignition, a gift. Dan opened the door to California.

•　　•　　•

Except that he'd forgotten about the checkpoint.

He'd been sailing along, the car handling like a dream. He didn't have to fight the wheel to stay in his lane. He didn't have to squint past a bug-cluttered windshield. He'd driven the other so long, he'd forgotten what a car felt like less than ten years old, sixty thousand miles on the odometer.

And then the building was upon him, low on the horizon, its tower screaming several stories into the sky. It straddled the interstate, an upturned tuning fork. The station was there to weed out illegals, but Dan didn't doubt that stolen cars rode the Border Patrol bandwidth. And how quickly were tags called in? He'd had the car an hour. He could see no other roads, no way out. To turn here, make an about-face across the highway, guaranteed a cop on your ass in seconds. No choice but to kamikaze right into the thing.

The checkpoint was concrete, the roof blue, solar-paneled on either side of the watchtower. From the tower hung a huge and old-fashioned-looking searchlight. Along the building's front, red lights pulsed and signs ordered motorists to come to a complete stop. Ahead, orange cones funneled vehicles into two lanes. At the end of each lane, men in brown uniforms and black sunglasses either waved you on or directed you to the side of the road where more men in uniforms and sunglasses waited to interrogate you or peek into your trunk.

Cars took one lane, trucks another. He followed the car ahead of him, an eighties station wagon with whitewalls and wood paneling. His heart hammered in his chest. Then, without warning, everything went sideways. His last thought: *So this is what it's like, passing out.*

He woke to the rap at his window and rolled it down. He saw himself reflected in the sunglasses of the man. He tried not to appear frightened. The man was his age, his face like cracked leather. The hint of a mustache traced his upper lip, a few days' growth.

"Sir?" the man said. Beyond, cars pulled around them and rejoined the line ahead. Above, the sky shone, sun-bright and dizzying.

"Sir, are you all right?"

Dan felt hot all over. A bead of sweat rolled into one eye, but he didn't move to wipe it. The steering wheel, his hands fixed to it—he was sure if he let go he'd be out again.

"Please put your vehicle in park, step out of the car, and come with me."

Dan followed the patrolman to a door on the side of the building. The door read NO ENTRY / NO ENTRAR.

The room was small, crowded with shelves full of folders and books bound by black spirals. The uniformed man sat in the only chair. He reached into a large cooler on the floor and handed Dan a bottle of water. He gestured toward the cooler, and Dan sat. He drank. The water and the room were warm. He drained the bottle and was offered another. He wasn't thirsty, but the drinking bought him time. He tried to think up answers to the questions that would come next—his daughter's car, married, different last name, business trip—but the possibilities were endless, and he quickly lost track of the story he meant to tell. In one corner, an electric fan buzzed. The breeze didn't make a dent in the heat.

"We see this all the time," the man said. Dan nodded. He wondered whether the cuffs would be metal, or whether they'd use the restraints he'd seen on TV, plastic ones that sounded like zippers fastening the wrists. Prison wouldn't be new to him. He'd done two months after Jack. He had not asked the boy to lie for him, and Jack hadn't. In the emergency room, the nurse asked what happened. Jack only shook his head, and Dan was led to a small, well-lit room. An hour later, an officer escorted him from the hospital and into his cruiser. Dan in the backseat, a metal screen between them, the cop said, "It's fuckers like you give dads a bad name. If you're not knocking the kid around, you're hitting the wife."

Dan had never hit Lynn, or Jack before that. But he didn't argue. The whiskey was wearing off, and he could see the trouble he was in. He'd been on a bender, a week or two by then, and the sight of it, stepping into the room, Jack's face pressed to the face of the other boy, it had sent hot sparks up his spine. He'd regretted the reflex, regretted it before Jack went through the window, regretted it seeing his son still in air. He would have gone back, if he could, stopped time and stepped forward—the child suspended, aloft—would have cradled him, flown with him, dropped with him, broken the fall.

Dan sucked the water down.

"Everyday occurrence around here." The patrolman patted the cooler's side. "Reason we keep these around," he said, and Dan realized that the man didn't mean stolen cars but heatstroke, dehydration.

"One for the road," the patrolman said. He passed him another bottle. "You got A/C?"

"I do," Dan said.

"Use it."

Dan tried not to appear in a hurry. He cracked the new bottle and took a long pull. Air bubbled up in chugs. He lowered the bottle, balanced it on his knee. Finally, he held the bottle skyward, as though to offer a toast.

The gesture sent the patrolman to the door, and Dan followed the man into the heat. He nodded when he was told to *drive safe,* then pulled ahead to rejoin the line. At the checkpoint, they were no longer stopping cars. Everyone was waved through. He drove slow until the station disappeared from the rearview, then his foot hit the accelerator.

Sun sinking, the weight of what he'd done settled on him. Tracking him down would be easy. They had only to run the plates or the VIN from the car he'd left at the Amoco. Already, his name and face had likely joined a list of the wanted. His one chance: No way would they guess his direction. Back home, they'd have him, but that was all right. What he wanted, his investment in what was left of Jack's life, he'd have before heading home. Let them have him then. Locks, and throw away the key. So long as he saw his son, so long as he got a chance at goodbye, he'd allow it: the trip back, and whatever came after.

◆　　　　◆　　　　◆

Arizona loomed, a succession of boulder piles, of rocks that reached up and up, like arms, their shadows bent over the interstate, a playful, haunted geography. Catastrophe took only one rock to dislodge from its perch. Everywhere, signs warned of it, as though the driver could do anything in the face of bad luck.

He hit Benson past nightfall and recognized the exit he'd been looking for. He followed the signs to the parking lot and approached the motel. The building leaned, gingerbread-colored, one gust of wind away from falling over. A billboard boasted: BENSON INN: HOME OF TED, WORLD'S LARGEST GILA MONSTER!

A Gila monster really had been there, and it had been big. Black and pink in its beadwork, its face more toad than lizard, the animal had lain curled like a question mark on a slab of slate behind an aquarium's glass walls. Its tail was a tube, its jaw the curve of a soda can.

"Venomous," Jack said.

"I thought that was just snakes," Dan said, and Jack shook his head. Then, he surprised Dan. He moved to the desk and asked for a double. "To save money," Jack said. Dan nodded, but this was big, was about more than just money. They spent the night each in his own bed, each turned toward his wall, not a word past *goodnight*—but they were together, and Dan was awake a long time listening to the in-and-out of his boy's breath. Sometimes the breathing caught, followed by a thick, mucusy cough. Jack would stir, sigh, then fall back to sleep, and Dan would fight the urge to turn and look.

Inside, Dan found the lobby as he'd left it, as old and worn-out-looking as the woman who worked the front desk. The skin of her face hung in folds, and her chin begged plucking. Her hair, done up in gray waves, was wispy, thin as spider's silk. A tag fastened to her shirtfront read MARGARET in red, raised print.

He thought it was her, the woman who'd placed the key in his hand a decade before, but this seemed impossible, the kind of trick that comes when memory and hope collide. A row of incandescent bulbs flickered and hummed overhead. Paperback books crowded the counter. Dust coated the wide leaves of plastic plants in clay pots.

The woman named Margaret watched him a long time before she said, "Yes?"

"I'm here for Ted," he said. It was the wrong thing to say.

"We're no zoo," she said. "You want to see Ted, you have to stay the night."

He asked how much. Margaret sized him up, then looked past him to the car in the parking lot.

"Fifty," she said.

He opened his wallet. Five twenties lined the pocket. It was all the money he had left.

He offered forty. Margaret took the money and jerked her thumb at a cardboard box behind the counter. The box sat on a low table. Its corners had been reinforced with duct tape, and a pillowcase, sky blue with white stitching, lay draped where a lid should have been. He stepped past the counter and pulled the pillowcase away.

Inside, a lizard stretched from one corner of the box to the other. The creature was scaly and green, rib-thin. A ridge of black teeth traced its back like on a child's construction-paper cutout of a dragon. The sides of the box were crazy with claw marks, the bottom nothing but sand and a head of broccoli, wilted and gray.

This was not Ted. This was not even a Gila monster.

"This is an iguana," Dan said. He turned to face Margaret. She frowned, shrugged, scratched her side.

"What happened to Ted?"

"Park Service got him," she said. "I'm here thirty years and no one says a word. Next thing I know, this lady tells me I need a permit. Says Gila monsters are on the list. Not the endangered species list, but, get this, the list that comes *before* that list. *Threatened*, she called it. She called Ted threatened and took him away. Said she'd see me shut down, but it was all hot air."

He waited for more, but Margaret seemed to have reached the end of the story.

"Smoking or non?" she asked.

"I'm sorry?" He couldn't understand it. The Gila monster, it should have been there to tell Jack about. "I saw Ted," he would say, and Jack, remembering, would laugh. "Remember the fish you told me about?" he'd say. "Remember the diner, the sugar packets, how you covered the table with pink and blue towers? I stopped there, too. And this boy I met by the Pearl River, I've got to tell you about him." He needed this, needed Ted there at the bottom of the box. But Ted wasn't there.

Something had gotten fucked up. Something had gotten tremendously fucked up this time around, and here he stood, stolen car in the parking lot and the wrong fucking animal at the bottom of the box.

"Your room," Margaret said. "You want smoking?"

The aquarium was cardboard, and the cover, when it fell away, had revealed nothing, no monster, only this green pet-store reject.

"Sir?" She'd almost yelled it. Her fingers drummed the desk.

"I'm sorry," he said. "I never meant to stay."

The woman scowled. "Well, don't think you're getting your money back."

"Keep the money," he said. "Just let me use your phone."

She eyed him, suspicious, then shrugged. "Dial nine to get out," she said, gesturing toward a tan phone on a corner table.

The earpiece, when it touched his face, was sticky, warm as though it had just left someone's ear. A square blinked red beside the buttons. He dialed nine, then Jack's number.

Marcus answered, and Dan made no excuses.

"I'll be there by morning," he said. "Please put Jack on the phone."

"Just be patient with him," Marcus said. "It's been a bad day."

But he didn't know what Marcus meant. Jack sounded terrific, the best he'd been since the first call came.

"They drained the left today," he said. "It's great—I can *breathe*."

He waited for Jack to ask where he was. He was prepared to tell everything, to exaggerate or lie, whatever it took, only don't let Jack be mad at him. Except, Jack didn't ask. If he remembered Dan's promise to be there that night, he didn't mention it.

"I'm in Benson," he said. "Remember Ted?"

"Ted," Jack said.

"The Gila monster? The motel outside Tucson?"

Jack coughed.

"I'm making the trip," Dan said. "Just like we made it when you moved out there."

Jack said something, and Dan, sure he'd misheard, asked him to repeat it. Only, he'd heard right. Again, Jack said: "Mom?"

"I'm Dan," he said. "Your dad."

"Mom and me," Jack was saying, "we rented a truck this time and drove it cross-country and the lizard was there at this motel in a tank with a rock."

"Jack," he said, but how could he tell him? How did you tell someone politely that, at the time, his mother was already dead?

"And Mom asked if she could touch it!" Jack said. He laughed, choked, laughed again. "A venomous lizard! Can you believe it?"

"Son," he said. He needed Jack to remember because, if not this, what? What did they have? Nothing else, nothing shared, nothing from Jack's adulthood but the van, the stops, their words, three days.

"How *is* old Ted?" Jack said.

Across the room, Dan watched as the pillowcase was lowered over the box. The box rattled back. Margaret stepped away.

"Fine," Dan said. "Really just fine. He's got a new cage, a big one. Lots of room for him to run around."

"I'm glad," Jack said.

"You should see it," Dan said, and he had a wild thought. Maybe he could steal his son from the house, bring him here. Or, not here, because Ted was not here, but some right place, a place to make Jack happy. They could go to the beach, see Jack's seals. They'd have to lose Marcus, and he wasn't sure how that would go over. He'd have to see the man, size him up. On the phone, Marcus was someone not to be fucked with, but a man on the phone wasn't always the man in real life.

"I have to go now," Dan said. "I'll be there before you know it."

He heard static on the other end, a rustle, then Marcus, his voice a whisper.

"He's asleep," Marcus said.

"Just like that?"

"It's what happens."

Dan couldn't believe it. He imagined Jack muffled, the man's hand over his mouth. His son, thin, weak, flailed for the phone.

Marcus began to detail Jack's condition. He implored Dan to hurry.

Dan hung up.

His eyes burned. His stomach ached. Exhaustion foamed at the back of his brain, a bottle opened too soon after shaking. Already he'd bought the room. How easy it would be to check in, to fill up his ears with a shower's roar, then lie down.

But he couldn't do it. He had to move forward.

The highway unspooled under starlight. Dashes marked his lane. Bone-white, they sailed past his high beams with the regularity of a metronome. Sleep's tease was strong, but he felt a tug stronger than sleep, stronger than dread or regret, than death. An invisible thread ran over mountains, past rivers and roads, up his bumper and right through the windshield. The thread caught his throat and bound, at the other end, his boy's heart. A word, *the* word, for this—it wasn't Dan's, didn't belong to him.

And so he imagined the pull as the work of water. Blue, the

view from Jack's window, the Pacific a rectangle over the kitchen sink. It was water called him west—the waiting coast, the cold and silver crash of waves.

•   •   •

La Jolla was a city on a cliff, dips and hills, a trapeze flung above the bay. Trees were here, and wealth. Couples in matching sweaters walked well-groomed dogs through the crosswalks. Children in sunglasses and name-brand clothes talked into cell phones. Storefronts advertised merchandise that, on sale, cost a month of Dan's income.

He'd been a day and a night without sleep. All night he'd driven, stopping three times only. He'd gotten to where he could use the bathroom, buy food, and pump gas in five minutes. The whole way, he'd pushed the speed limit. He hadn't slowed down, not once, not even for the armadillo he'd sent spinning over the road like a top. Now, his head swam and his eyes, when he blinked, felt sand-filled and asymmetrical, his skull small.

He sat behind the wheel of the car on the street before a row of blue mailboxes. A box on one end held a quiet surprise: a maiden name—his wife's. He didn't know when Jack had changed his name or if it was official. He wondered which name the boy would be buried with, then shook this off. Some things were worth worrying about. His name wasn't one.

Beyond the sidewalk and up a hill, the building waited. Houses rose on either side, so close a man might stand between, reach out, and touch two walls. The buildings, a street's worth, stood white and red, stucco and brick, brightly shuttered, with Spanish tile on top. The sun, just up, painted the clay roofs pink.

For too long, he'd sat, trying to catch his breath. Now he stood and swung the car door shut. No matter what awaited him, no matter what looked back at him from the bed, he would smile. That was the first thing he would do. He would smile, and he would not cry. He would kneel, and, if Jack let him, he'd open his arms.

Jack's door hung orange inside the white frame. A brass ring marked its middle. It was only a staircase away.

Dispensation. Was that the word for what he wanted?

And how long would he wait before he begged?

He'd tried this once before. Long ago, after he'd served his time and sobered, he'd driven to Baton Rouge but been turned away at the door. He'd stood a long time at that door too, stood, then knocked, then waited, then knocked again, only for the door to open to Lynn's scowling face. He'd never learned whether Jack knew he'd come.

This door, though, when he moved to knock, stood ajar. Dan leaned and the door opened. Inside, a kettle's curve on the stove, dishes overflowing the kitchen sink, and, rolled at the wrist, a single latex glove. Thumb tucked under, fingers splayed, it hugged the floor like shed skin. Against the linoleum, two fingers gleamed red up to the knuckle.

Beyond the kitchen was the main room. Against one wall stood an enormous saltwater aquarium, and, circling inside, a pair of striped, spine-covered fish. Their bodies glimmered brown and white in the yellow glow of the tank light, their fins silk-webbed and see-through.

The first step, once he took it, set him moving fast. He moved through the kitchen and past the room with the fish, down a hallway and toward the two bedroom doors. One door stood open, the room a study. The walls were bookcases, the shelves spilling over into piles on the floor. Among the mounds was wedged a blue blow-up mattress, its black tail plugged into a pump the size of a cinder block. A duffel bag yawned at the foot of the bed, a red sock sprung like a tongue between unzipped teeth.

The other door was shut. He remembered to breathe. He pressed his palm to the wood, hesitant, as though to feel for fire inside. He waited.

And pushed the door open to an empty bed, the sheets strangled into a rope that stretched to the door. Beside the bed stood an IV stand and a cluster of gray-faced, many-buttoned machines. Wires and tubes hung disconnected along the floor. In one corner, a wheelchair lay on its side.

He felt a need, just then, to go to the chair, to right it, as though it lived, as though to lift the thing might save its life. The chair, once he had hold of it, was heavy. He tipped it up, tried to make it roll, but someone had set the brake. The floor's planks pushed back at the wheels with a sneaker's squeak.

He moved to the bed. He sat, ran his hand over the mattress. Stains the shapes of continents stared back through the scrim of the fitted sheet. His knees found his chin. His head found the pillow. It was soft, and he took one corner into his mouth. He tasted salt. He pulled the pillow over his head.

He wasn't sure how long he slept before a door's slam echoed down the hall. From beneath the pillow, he could see a sliver of floor, then shoes in the doorway. They were red with white laces, a white cap on each toe, the kind he'd worn as a kid, played basketball in. He didn't have to look up to know whose shoes.

"Don't say I almost made it," Dan said.

Marcus said nothing. The feet were planted far apart.

"Just, please don't tell me how close I was."

"He died last night," Marcus said. "You weren't even close."

◆   ◆   ◆

In the kitchen, Marcus boiled water. He was tall, thin and tan, his hair dark, cropped close along the sides of his head. His sideburns touched his jaw's hinges, and his face wore stubble's mossy mask. Black crescents cradled his sockets like the bottom halves of punched eyes.

At the kettle's whistle, Marcus tipped the water into a glass. The glass was beaker-shaped and tapered at the mouth like a vase. Coffee grounds waited at the bottom. The stream hit the grounds, swirled, and steamed. Together, they made mud, and the mud rose, bubbling. Marcus fastened a lid to the lip of the glass, and the two of them watched the brown water. In the other room, the fish tank bubbler hummed. Dan imagined the fishes' gill plates going in and out. Then Marcus pushed a kind of plunger into the mix, and a silver disc separated the grounds from what had been brewed.

It was a miracle, a horror—the world, and his son gone, blinked from existence. How a body, breathing, turned to lungs. He pictured them, sticky, deflated, gray balloons trampled into a wet sidewalk. And still the march of days, still sunrise and weather and water for coffee. Jack dead, and still beans would be dried and crushed, strained through water, and men and women would raise their mugs and read the day's news and make grocery lists and worry over coupons and wonder whether their tires were in need of rotation.

Marcus was talking oxygen, how everyone went by oxygen in the end. Oxygen or water, and, anyway, water *was* one part oxygen. Too little, too much, these were what killed you. You suffocated or swelled, dehydrated or drowned. Life was balance— imbalance, death.

Proportion. Equilibrium. A needle in the arm had kept water in Jack's body. A needle in the lung had kept it out. In this way, they'd kept Jack alive. In the end, his lungs had filled up faster than they could be emptied out.

Marcus poured coffee into cups and joined Dan at the kitchen table. He looked calm, and Dan couldn't stand it, how matter-of-fact he acted, as though every day your lover died and you sat and sipped coffee across the table from his father. Marcus watched the table, and Dan watched Marcus, wanting to throttle the calm from him.

"You have it too?" Dan asked.

Marcus started. Then, his face collapsed into something approaching amusement.

"Not all of us live with AIDS, Mr. Lawson," he said. "Some do. Some live with HIV. But most of us just . . . live."

"I only thought—the two of you."

"Friends," Marcus said. "It only seems like more because I was here at the end."

Dan thought of breaking the man in half. What held him back was *need*. Marcus alone knew Jack's final hours, his words, the last look on his face.

"Did Jack—"

"—say anything?" Marcus laughed. He seemed to Dan a man who, in this life, had enjoyed very little power, a man who now relished his dominion over the last half day and what had gone on in it. Marcus was smiling into his cup, but, when his eyes lifted, his expression was humorless.

"You want me to tell you he had some special shit saved up just for you, but no such luck." Marcus spun his mug in his hands. The steam rose in ribbons. "The magic words were supposed to be yours. *Your* words. Not his. This was your last chance, and, let's face it, you blew it."

Dan brought his mug to his mouth. The rim was chipped, the coffee strong.

"How much did my son tell you?"

"Enough for me to know what you were to him."

"And what was that?"

"A curiosity," Marcus said. "Last century's last holdout."

The mug was hot in his hands, but Dan would not put it down.

"I was trying to get used to the idea," he said.

"*Try harder*. The country's growing up. Before long, no one will be left, no one to accommodate what you call *love*."

Dan stood and launched his cup across the room. It hit and exploded. Coffee streaked the wall.

He moved to the door. One boot was on the stoop before Marcus's voice reached him.

"Squirrels," he said. "I don't know if that means anything to you, but, at the end, it's all he talked about. Squirrels in the bed. Squirrels running up the walls."

"Squirrels," Dan said. He gripped the doorframe to keep steady. His knees locked.

"The morphine," Marcus said. "That's probably all it was."

"Morphine," Dan said.

Marcus's shoulders heaved. His head dropped. His brow touched the table.

Dan winced. The fish was there again, set loose in his gut, writhing, careening to get out. He stepped inside.

Beneath the kitchen sink, he found a roll of paper towels. He wet one. He wiped clean the spot on the wall, then picked up the china fragments from the floor. He moved to the kitchen sink. He stacked the dishes, the trays, the pans caked with burnt food, all of it, onto the counter. He let the sink fill with soapy water and dropped the dishes in. And then—because what else could he do?—he began to scrub.

◆　　◆　　◆

The water, when his feet finally found it, was cold. His socks were balled up in his boots, his boots lassoed by their laces and slung over one shoulder. The cold climbed his legs, and he walked until the water reached his knees.

He had worked steadily for an hour. When the kitchen was clean, he'd stepped outside, his stomach still writhing. He could see the beach, and he walked to it.

He'd left without a word, Marcus collapsed at the table, a sentry over the dead.

Dan pushed through water, following the shoreline. The beach was not like the beach back home. The gulf ran to sand, but, here, the shore was crowded with stones, outcroppings of rock and reef. He walked until he hit a rock wall, the water too deep to go around. Steps were carved into stone, and he followed them to a ledge where he found megaphones and signs and people gathered.

"Save the seals," one woman shouted. And a man: "Let them live in peace."

Dan pressed through the people, past a brass plaque that announced his arrival at THE CHILDREN'S POOL, to an iron banister skirting the ledge. The towering rock on which he stood reached into the ocean where it met a concrete wall, the wall an arm, the arm beckoning water into bay. Below, a sandy cove lay carpeted with seals.

The seals numbered fifty. He counted them, then he counted them again. Half of the seals dozed. The others rubbed their sides and snouts with flippers or raised their heads to watch the waves. Their hides were white and black and brown, cloudy, the colors running together. Just like marble. Just like Jack had said. They were small, the seals, each no bigger than a sleeping child, and their bodies threw long shadows over the sand. A boy and girl, teenagers, sat, legs crossed, not far from the seals and holding hands.

A staircase traced the ledge and wound down to the cove, but, at the first step, a woman blocked his way. The woman wore a T-shirt, white with a blue seal silhouette across the chest.

"What's the cost?" he said.

The woman laughed, and he saw all of her fillings.

"Only your soul," she said.

"I'm sorry?"

"I'm not charging admission," she said. "I'm telling you why you need to leave the seals alone." Her hair was long, held back in a thick braid that swung when she spoke. "One foot on that beach, and you break nature's contract."

Dan looked down. Beyond the seals, following the wall, footprints crossed and recrossed the beach, the autograph of an impossible dance.

"We need to preserve nature's delicate balance," she said.

He hadn't meant to make her flinch, but now Dan found his hand on the woman's shoulder. He squeezed the shoulder gently, then brought the hand to his side.

"Sweetheart," he said. "Nature has no balance. You can stand here all day. You can keep as many people off that beach as you want, but, one way or another, those seals, all of them, are going to die. You and I are going to die. Because, you know what? You know what nature is?"

The shake of her head was so slight, the braid hung still.

"Nature is a fucking monster."

The woman hugged her chest. She stepped aside, and Dan made his way down the stairs and onto the beach. The couple holding hands looked up, then returned their attention to the seals. Twenty yards away, the animals yawned and turned in the sand. One of the largest watched the sky, its head bobbing, as though forcing something down its throat.

Jack had said how sometimes seals swallowed stones. "For ballast," he said. "The way a diver wears a belt to keep him down." Weight controlled a dive. Men weighted belts with lead. Seals ate stones. In this way, buoyed otherwise by fat or air, both animals sank.

Dan imagined filling up his gut. He'd start small, grains of sand, pebbles polished ocean-smooth, before he wore his teeth down chewing rocks. He'd obliterate the interloper, fill himself so full of stones the fish inside him would have no place to swim, then he'd swallow more—just watch, just wait and see—more and more, enough to grind the motherfucker out of existence. Then no more churn, no fiery, twisting thing.

He watched the seals, the couple on the beach. The girl stood, and the boy brushed sand from her pants. Then the boy stood, and, hand in hand, they climbed the stairs.

Dan watched the seals awhile longer, then looked past them to where the water met the sky. A line, pencil-thin, marked the place planes touched, so faint it almost wasn't a line at all. The end, the way he saw it, would be when that line lifted and the two halves crashed, a cosmic collapse. It would come, the end, when blue met blue.

Acknowledgments

Thank you:

My first teachers and earliest encouragers: Sandra Meek, Lawrence Baines, Marc Fitten, and Jack Riggs.

The MFA program at the University of Arizona, where I had the good fortune to work with Aurelie Sheehan, Buzz Poverman, Jonathan Penner, Elizabeth Evans, Bob Houston, Fenton Johnson, and Jason Brown. Thank you, Jason, for teaching me the meaning of the word *revise*. And thanks to my fellow students in the program, especially Rachel Yoder, Mark Polanzak, William Bert, Donald Dunbar, Joshua Foster, and Patrick Burns. It was a pleasure to write and learn with you.

Cara Blue Adams, for years of friendship. Yours was the best pen I've ever borrowed.

The PhD program at the University of Cincinnati: I could not have asked for better professors than Michael Griffith, Leah Stewart, Brock Clarke, and Jennifer Glaser, or better friends than Mica Darley-Emerson, Soren Palmer, Peter Grimes, and Christian Moody. Christian, you've always been there for me. *Gracias, mi amigo.*

For their support of my work along the way, I'd like to thank Lauren Groff, Ron Rash, Laura van den Berg, Holly Goddard Jones, Kevin Wilson, Claire Vaye Watkins, Clyde Edgerton, Matthew Pitt, Shannon Cain, Alissa Nutting, Erin Stalcup, David Scrivner, Lance Cleland, and Rachel Cantor.

Bret Anthony Johnston, patron saint of young writers, you're an inspiration.

Adam Stumacher, for the big assist.

Ashley Inguanta, for perfectionism behind the camera lens.

Justin Luzader, for your friendship, and for wisdom beyond your years.

Laurie Uttich, who read and commented on many of these stories in earlier incarnations.

Nicole Louise Reid, model citizen among writers, thank you for your friendship, endless encouragement, and good example.

All of my colleagues, students, and friends at the University of Central Florida. You keep work from feeling too much like work.

Ryan Rivas, Jared Silvia, Nathan Holic, John King, Pat Greene, Jocelyn Bartkevicius, Susan Lilley, and Phil Deaver, for making Orlando feel like home.

The Tin House, RopeWalk, Sewanee, and Bread Loaf Writers' Conferences, for the kind financial support. For their mentorship, thank you to Lee Martin, Joe Meno, Christine Schutt, Robert Boswell, Brad Watson, and Karen Russell.

Serenity Gerbman and everyone at the Southern Festival of Books.

Christopher Burawa and everyone with the Clarksville Writers Conference.

Joanne Brownstein and Jody Klein, for helping my stories find good homes.

My agent, Gail Hochman, for your patience, persistence, and the tireless advocacy you demonstrate on behalf of all of your writers. You continue to amaze.

My editor, Millicent Bennett, for believing in these stories and for never letting me settle for *good enough*. This collection could not have come together in the way that it has without your guiding hand. Working with you is a gift.

Everyone at Simon & Schuster, particularly Sarah Nalle, Maggie Higby, Mara Lurie, and Susan M. S. Brown.

The anthology editors who gave these stories legs: Kathy Pories and ZZ Packer; Jason Lee Brown, Shanie Latham, and John McNally; Murray Dunlap and Kevin Morgan Watson; Natalie Danford, John Kulka, Dani Shapiro, and Richard Bausch.

The magazine and journal editors who made these stories better, stronger versions of themselves: C. Michael Curtis; Alice K. Turner; Samuel Ligon; David Daley; Elizabeth Taylor; Steve Almond; Shara McCallum and Paula Closson Buck; Jeanne Leiby; Kathleen Canavan and William O'Rourke; Hannah Tinti and Karen Seligman; Matthew Salesses; Ann McCutchan, Miroslav Penkov, Barbara Rodman, and Hillary Stringer; Christine Larusso, Daniel Hamilton, and Ed Winstead; Linda B. Swanson-Davies and Susan Burmeister-Brown.

For their generous support of my work, I would like to thank the National Society of Arts & Letters, the Charles Phelps Taft Research Center, the UCF Office of Research and Commercialization, the UCF College of Arts & Humanities, the Arizona Commission on the Arts, and the Tucson Pima Arts Council.

Jeanne Leiby and Barry Hannah. You are missed.

Ken and Debbie, Chris and Jenny, Jon and Nicole: Thank you for your love and for welcoming me into your families.

My Grandfather George, Uncle Dave, and Aunt Sherrie. Every grandson and nephew should be so lucky as to have people like you in their lives.

Carrie Emmington, longtime reader and longtime friend, thank you.

Chad Swiggum, your friendship means the world to me.

Jonathan Jones, for reading these stories and never holding back. But, mostly, thank you for friendship beyond compare.

Chris and Naomi, for your warmth and loving-kindness.

My parents, for your unwavering love and affection. Without your support, this book would not be.

My sweet, hilarious, darling girls, Ellie and Izzy. Your lives are my pleasure.

Marla, my inspiration, first reader, best friend. You have my heart.

Earlier versions of stories from this collection previously appeared in:

"Me and James Dean" (as "Between the Teeth"), *Willow Springs,* 2006

"Venn Diagram" (as "The Geometry of Despair"), *The Chicago Tribune,* 2006

"Knockout," *Redivider,* 2007

"Lizard Man," *Playboy,* 2007

"What the Wolf Wants," *West Branch,* 2010

"The Baby Glows," *The Southern Review,* 2010

"The Heaven of Animals," *The Atlantic,* 2010

"100% Cotton," *The Southern Review,* 2011

"How to Help Your Husband Die," *Notre Dame Review,* 2011

"Refund," *One Story,* 2011

"The Disappearing Boy," *The Good Men Project,* 2011

"Wake the Baby," *American Literary Review,* 2012

"Nudists," *FiveChapters,* 2012

"Last of the Great Land Mammals," *Washington Square,* 2013

"Amputee," *Glimmer Train,* 2013

"The End of Aaron," *Printers Row,* 2013

Stories also appeared in the following anthologies:

"Venn Diagram," *Best New American Voices 2008*

"Lizard Man," *New Stories from the South 2008*

"Lizard Man," *Best New American Voices 2010*

"Me and James Dean" (as "Between the Teeth"), *What Doesn't Kill You,* 2010

"Me and James Dean" (as "Between the Teeth"), *Press 53 Open Awards Anthology 2010*

"The Baby Glows," *New Stories from the Midwest 2012*

About the Author

David James Poissant's stories have appeared in *The Atlantic, Playboy, One Story, The Southern Review, Ploughshares, Glimmer Train*, and in the *New Stories from the South* and *Best New American Voices* anthologies. His writing has been awarded the Matt Clark Prize, the George Garrett Fiction Award, the Rope-Walk Fiction Chapbook Prize, and the Alice White Reeves Memorial Award from the National Society of Arts & Letters, as well as awards from *The Chicago Tribune* and *The Atlantic* and *Playboy* magazines. He teaches in the MFA program at the University of Central Florida and lives in Orlando with his wife and daughters. Visit him online at: www.davidjamespoissant.com.

The Heaven
of Animals

David James Poissant

This reading group guide includes an introduction, discussion questions, ideas for enhancing your book club, and a Q&A with author David James Poissant. The suggested questions are intended to help your reading group find new and interesting topics for your discussion. We hope that these ideas will enrich your conversation and increase your enjoyment of the book.

Introduction

The Heaven of Animals, award-winning young writer David James Poissant's stunning debut, has been one of the most praised story collections of the year. Named one of Amazon's Best Short Story Collections of 2014; compared to the work of Richard Ford and Amy Hemple in the *Los Angeles Review of Books* and Anton Chekhov, Raymond Carver, and George Saunders in the *New York Post*; and the subject of a full-page rave by Clyde Edgerton in *Garden & Gun*, this "collection of vicious and heartbreaking vignettes" (*The Orlando Sentinel*) is a must-read for any fiction lover.

In each of the stories in this remarkable debut, Poissant explores the tenuous bonds of family—fathers and sons, husbands and wives—as they are tested by the sometimes brutal power of love. His strikingly true-to-life characters have reached a precipice, chased there by troubles of their own making. Standing at the brink, each must make a choice: Leap, or look away? Pulitzer Prize finalist Lee Martin writes that Poissant forces us "to face the people we are when we're alone in the dark."

From two friends racing to save the life of an alligator in "Lizard Man" to a girl helping her boyfriend face his greatest fears in "The End of Aaron," from a man who stalks death on an Atlanta street corner to a brother's surprise at the surreal, improbable beauty of a late night encounter with a wolf, Poissant creates worlds that shine with honesty and dark complexity, but also with a profound compassion. These are stories hell-bent on hope.

Fresh, smart, lively, and wickedly funny, *The Heaven of Animal* is startlingly original and compulsively readable. As bestselling author Kevin Wilson puts it, "Poissant is a writer who knows us with such clarity that we wonder how he found his way so easily into our hearts and souls."

Discussion Questions

1. Which story resonated with you the most? What do you think it is about that particular story that most appealed or felt most important to you?

2. After reading the final story in the collection, did your opinion and understanding of Dan Lawson change from your introduction to him in "Lizard Man"? If so, how? Was he able to redeem himself in your eyes?

3. How is Brig changed by his short but poignant night with Lily in the collection's second story, "Amputee"? Do you feel hopeful for his future after this night, or is he doomed to repeat his mistakes?

4. Precarious romances run rampant in this collection. Some couples make it through their obstacles, like the couple who fight to keep it together after the death of their daughter in "The Geometry of Despair." Other relationships are beyond repair. In your opinion, what qualities must a relationship have in the world of *The Heaven of Animals* in order to last?

5. In "100% Cotton," the narrator struggles with what it means to really communicate with another person: his deaf father, his dead mother, himself. How many different kinds of communication and miscommunication are there in the story? How does the mugger fit in? Notice how the unnamed narrator — who feels very alone — chooses to directly address the reader, as if the reader is present with him on that dark Atlanta street corner. Why do you think Poissant made that choice? Could the story have been told as effectively in a more traditional format? Why or why not?

6. The title of the story "Nudists" telegraphs the importance of the nudists Mark meets on the beach — yet, they are only a small part of the story. What makes them so important and title-worthy? What do you think their presence might mean or signal to Mark?

7. Consider the other stories in this collection that are written in the first person, or narrated by a character. How much did you trust the narrators' accounting of events, judgments of other people, and assessments of themselves? What qualities make for a trustworthy — or an untrustworthy — narrator?

8. "How to Help Your Husband Die" is the only story in *The Heaven of Animals* to be written as a directive, setting it apart in tone from the rest of the collection. What did you think of this instruction manual–like format?

9. Many of the characters in the collection are faced with death — their own imminent deaths or the deaths of loved ones. In what ways do the characters deal with loss or potential loss?

10. Which of the characters in this collection would you consider to be truly happy? What are the elements essential to happiness, in your opinion?

11. Love, guilt, forgiveness, atonement — these themes run throughout the collection. What other recurring themes did you spot? Overall, which theme do you feel is most important to the essence of the book, and why?

12. Bestselling author Ron Rash has praised Poissant for his "refusal to condescend to his characters." What do you think is meant by this? Do you agree with his assessment?

Enhance Your Reading Group

1. Choose a story or two from the collection to read at the start of your gathering. Then, as a group, discuss how the experience of hearing the story read aloud differed from the experience of reading it yourself. This is a good exercise for sparking further discussion.

2. Make a photocopy of the contents page for each member of your reading group. Ask them to consider how they felt after reading each story, and then to write one word describing that feeling next to each story's title. Once everyone has finished, share your word choices with one another. Did some word choices overlap?

3. Trace the inclusion of animals throughout the collection. Assign each member of your group a story and ask him or her to highlight or record every time an animal is involved. After discussing your findings as a group, consider what the animals bring to each story.

4. If *The Heaven of Animals* were an album, what songs would be on it? If it were a painting, what would it look like? Before meeting, ask the members of your reading group to create a piece of art, a poem, a playlist, or some other work of their choosing that relays their interpretations of the collection. These can be shared at the group discussion or kept private.

5. To learn more about David James Poissant and his work, visit www.davidjamespoissant.com.

A Conversation with David James Poissant

I have to ask: Why does the baby glow?

Maybe a better question would be, Why *wouldn't* the baby glow?

Truthfully, I don't remember how the image came to me. But, once it arrived, I couldn't shake it. The story then became a kind of thought experiment. If your baby really glowed, what kind of inconveniences would you face, and what might the upsides be? It's probably the most fun I've ever had writing a story, though I was surprised by the dark turn the story took at the end. I didn't really want to go there, but the end result of all life is death, so death felt like this particular thought experiment's inevitable conclusion.

On a more serious note, what first inspired you to write about, as author Claire Vaye Watkins put it in a review of *The Heaven of Animals*, "our weird, urgent attempts to understand each other"?

I think that we often hurt those we love most, often without meaning to, and I think that these hurts usually come about as a result of miscommunication. Like the narrator of "100% Cotton," I believe there's often something—pride, fear, shame, any number of things, really—that stands between people and keeps them from truly hearing one another. But we all want to be heard. We're desperate for love.

In life, I kind of wear my heart on my sleeve, but, for whatever reason, I'm interested in characters who don't. I seem to gravitate toward stories about people who can't quite say what they feel.

Some stories in this collection, such as "The Geometry of Despair," go on in multiple parts while others, like "Knockout" and "The Baby Glows," total only a page or two in length. When you are writing, how do you know when a story is finished? Or, how do

you know which stories can be told in only a few hundred words and which require a few thousand?

When I wrote "Venn Diagram," I didn't know there would be a "Wake the Baby," and when I wrote "Lizard Man," I didn't know there would be "The Heaven of Animals." Those sequels came later. The characters had more to say, and I wanted to explore later episodes in their lives (so much so in the case of Richard and Lisa that I'm currently at work on a novel about their family).

As for length, for me, the weirder stories, ones you might call fabulist or magic realist, stories like "The Baby Glows" and "What the Wolf Wants," tend to stay on the short side. I worry, with such stories, that I'll wear out my welcome or that maybe the story will collapse under the weight of its own conceit. Plenty of writers I admire, writers like Karen Russell and George Saunders, can cartwheel through the woods of weird for the lengths of long stories or novels. I haven't learned how to do that just yet, but I'm not ruling it out for myself for the future.

A majority of the stories in this collection deal with death in one way or another—some subtly, but most in a very overt way that the reader can't ignore. Do you find it hard to write about such a difficult subject? What encourages you to tackle the subject head-on?

Well, death is what we all fear most, right? I'm not sure that I believe people who say they're not afraid of death. Who wouldn't be? It's the great unknown. In some ways, it seems like the problem we're here to solve. We spend our lives preparing for our own extinction. We can ignore that fact or face it head-on. Maybe, by tackling death again and again, I'm hoping to take away a little of its power, its sting.

Though some animals throughout the collection are metaphorically personified, "What the Wolf Wants" is the only story to feature an animal that truly takes on human qualities—he talks, he drinks coffee, he wants moccasins. Is magical realism a category that you're interested in exploring further?

Absolutely. Writing, I'm equally as happy entering the woods of magic realism as I am sticking to the sidewalks of realism. This is probably less a product of any calculated choice than it is a by-product of my reading habits. I'll pick up a story collection by Kevin Brockmeier or Aimee Bender as quickly as I will one by Charles D'Ambrosio or Deborah Eisenberg. As a result, story ideas arrive both zany and grounded, and I do my best to write whatever comes to me. In a recent interview, Adam Levin, author of *The Instructions*, said, "I was taught that there's this division between realism and experimentalism, and I think that the other writers whose work I admire, as well as myself, we sort of don't care about that anymore. And it's not because it was ever irrelevant, it's just that now the point of experimentalism seems to be to still tell a good story and to move people." That sentiment strikes me as just about right. I'm wary of experimentation for experimentation's sake, but I think that the best experimental or magical stories, works like Donald Barthelme's *The Dead Father* or A. S. Byatt's "The Thing in the Forest," get at the truth of life and longing just as earnestly and honestly as work set in a realist mode.

Now, I'll be the first to admit that this is a seismic shift from where I stood in grad school. At the University of Arizona, I was entrenched in the realism camp, not because the program incentivized one ideology over another, but because, somewhere, I'd gotten the idea that one must pick a side and stick to it. Then, in 2007, a magazine called *Redivider* sponsored a contest for stories written on a postcard-size slip of paper. I wrote "Knockout" and won. Somehow, writing that story tripped a switch, and it wasn't long before I was writing about glowing babies and talking wolves alongside the realism that I still love.

Is there a particular character in this collection who you would deem your personal favorite, or to whom you can most relate? Conversely, which character did you find yourself fighting with the most?

That's a tough one. I admire the extravagant love that Grace showers upon Aaron in "The End of Aaron." In some ways, that love is selfish, but in most ways it feels absolutely selfless to me.

My heart is also very much with Brig at the end of "Amputee" and with the narrator of "100% Cotton." Their stories abandon them at moments of great internal struggle.

The character I fought with most would have to be Dan Lawson of "Lizard Man" and the title story. It was a struggle to climb into his head, and, once there, to try to see things from his point of view and to write from that point of view without condescending to him. I hope I've redeemed him by the end as well, but that's up to the reader to decide.

All of the stories in *The Heaven of Animals* were published previously in magazines, journals, newspapers, and anthologies. What was the process of putting them together in a single book like for you?

My genius agent, Gail Hochman, took a big chance on me, for which I'll always be grateful. When we put the collection together, we left out most of the shorter stories and anything that smacked of magic realism. The logic here was that it's hard enough selling a story collection these days. Why frustrate potential editors with a collection that can't seem to make up its mind what it is?

But after my genius editor, Millicent Bennett, acquired the collection for Simon & Schuster, she asked to see everything I had. I sent her another twenty stories, and, from those, we picked six to replace weaker stories from the original manuscript. In the end, we settled on sixteen stories that we both agreed were my best, regardless of length or style, the familiar rubbing elbows with the fantastical. "I didn't know this was allowed!" I said excitedly, to which Millicent just laughed, though, later, I'd realize that some of my favorite story collections do the very same thing. (Ron Carlson's *At the Jim Bridger* and Stuart Dybek's *The Coast of Chicago* come to mind.) Hopefully, if nothing else, the story selection represents my versatility.

The collection is bookended by Dan and Jack's story, beginning in "Lizard Man" and ending in the collection's title story, "The Heaven of Animals." Why did you make this choice?

I'd always conceived of the collection beginning and ending with those two stories. And, no matter which stories got put in or pulled out, and no matter how they were reordered as my editor and I sought to find harmony and balance in the collection, the one thing that never changed, one thing that Gail, Millicent, and I always agreed on, was that the collection should begin with "Lizard Man" and end with "The Heaven of Animals." There are at least two reasons for this.

First, for the rare reader who reads the stories in order, the last story will come as a surprise. Personally, I love when writers do this, when a collection, overall, is unlinked but then there's this gift of an unannounced story that features a character or story line in which the reader already has a vested interest.

Second, much of the collection is set in the South, but the final story leads the reader out of the South. Dan's journey takes him through parts of the country where stories like "Amputee" and "Nudists" are set. Rather than bring the collection full circle by starting in Florida and ending in Florida, I hope this choice gives the collection a different kind of cohesiveness.

Which short story authors would you say have most inspired your own writing?

Lorrie Moore and Ron Carlson for their ability to temper life's terrors with humor and wit. Charles D'Ambrosio for the pacing of his stories, that patient narrative unraveling. Amy Hempel for her gleaming prose and her ability, with a single sentence, to put an icepick in your heart. Rick Bass, for his breathtaking imagery and celebration of the natural world. Frederick Barthelme, who writes about the South I know more honestly than anyone I know, and whose novels *Tracer* and *Bob the Gambler* are two of the finest books I've ever read. And George Saunders for his humanity, the grace he extends to his characters, and the empathy he demands of his readers.

Those are the writers that I hope have, in some small way, rubbed off on me. If they haven't yet, I hope they will.

You are currently working on your first novel. How is the experience of writing a novel different from writing a short story or from creating a short story collection? Do you find one to be more difficult than the other?

On the one hand, writing a novel is difficult in that it's just *so* much book to write. On the other hand, writing and revising a story can take months, even years. It took me nine years to write and revise enough stories decent enough to fill a collection. The novel will have been written—knock on wood—in under four years. Something about sticking to the same characters and a single story line seems to make the process of finishing the novel go much faster than writing and assembling so many disparate stories.

That being said, the story form will always be my first love. I read far more stories than novels. A limitation of the novel form (and I'm not even close to the first person to say this) is that it can never be perfect, whereas a story can get there, or at least come pretty close. I think that Raymond Carver's "Cathedral" is a perfect story. I think that Melanie Rae Thon's "Xmas, Jamaica Plain" is a perfect story. I'm pretty sure I've never read a perfect novel.

If you could offer one piece of advice to aspiring short story writers, what would it be?

Read. Write every day, or as often as you can, yes. Seek likeminded peers to give you feedback on your work, yes. But, most of all, read. Read lots, and read widely. Find a writer you like, and read everything she's written. Read a story anthology, then get the books by the authors of every story you loved. The more you read, the more you'll begin reading like a writer. You'll read a sentence that makes your pulse race and you'll pause and ask, "How did the writer do that?" Once you start asking those questions, you're bound to go looking for answers and to bring those answers home to your own work. We call this "finding your voice." But finding your voice is just a matter of discovering the grab bag of stylistic tricks and tics from which you'll forever be borrowing—sometimes knowingly, sometimes unknowingly—from those who have come before you.

Ultimately, what do you hope readers will take away from *The Heaven of Animals*?

Honestly, I'm flattered at the thought of anyone reading my book, and readers are welcome to take whatever they like from it. But, if pressed, I'd say that, for me, *empathy* is the magic word. I want readers to empathize with these characters, to extend compassion to even the cruelest of them. Some of these stories are very dark, but I hope that, out of each, some hope shines through. To the extent that it does, I'll feel like I've done my job.